Praise for *The Next Ship Home*

"*The Next Ship Home* is a wonderfully immersive novel that kept me engrossed from the first page to the last. Through a seamless tale of immigrants, corruption, resilience, and hope, Webb illuminates a dark side of America too often lost to history. An important, timely read featuring a cast I loved to root for."

—Kristina McMorris, *New York Times* bestselling author of *Sold on a Monday*

"With meticulous research and deft prose, Heather Webb crafts an unflinching look at the immigrant experience, an unlikely and unique friendship, and a resonant story of female empowerment. *The Next Ship Home* is truly a beautiful and powerful book."

—Pam Jenoff, *New York Times* bestselling author of *The Woman with the Blue Star*

"Powerful and poignant, *The Next Ship Home* shines a literary light on Ellis Island's dark history, where the prejudices of the past often sit uncomfortably close to the present. Written with a clear passion for the subject matter, Webb captures the injustices, suffering, hope, and determination of a generation of immigrants. Francesca and Alma roar from the page and leave the reader caring for them deeply. A richly imagined novel and a must-read for fans of historical fiction. Brava!"

—Hazel Gaynor, *New York Times* bestselling author of *When We Were Young & Brave*

"A touching and intimate story of two very different young women who join forces in turn-of-the-century New York City to overcome the odds.

As a longtime fan of Heather Webb's novels, *The Next Ship Home* is her most accomplished and emotionally compelling book to date. The insightful historical details delving into the Ellis Island immigration process make this novel essential reading for anyone yearning to understand the roots of the American Experience. Highly recommended."

—Kris Waldherr, author of *The Lost History of Dreams*

"Centered around Ellis Island—symbol of America's greatest hopes and scene of some of her greatest travesties—*The Next Ship Home* is the heart-wrenching story of two young women fighting for freedom and independence. In this timely and utterly immersive story, Webb unflinchingly exposes the prejudice, sexism, and corruption rampant with the immigration system of the times while still weaving in hope that we can do and be better."

—Kerry Anne King, bestselling author of *Whisper Me This* and *Everything You Are*

"*The Next Ship Home* is one of the rare stories that will nestle itself in your soul and make a home there. Heather Webb creates two remarkable, endearing heroines that you will root for from beginning to end. Her depiction of Ellis Island and turn-of-the-century New York is lush with meticulously researched detail. But most striking, Webb tackles the thorny and complex issues of immigration and workers' rights with sensitivity and grace. Her message is compassionate and timely, and I was blown away by how deftly Webb weaves it through Alma and Francesca's stories. *The Next Ship Home* deserves a place as one of the great books of the American Experience."

—Aimie K. Runyan, international bestselling author of *Across the Winding River* and *Daughters of the Night Sky*

"Reading this story is like stepping back in time to the gut-churning experience of arriving at Ellis Island in 1902 and being willing to do anything for a shot at a fresh start in a new country. The vivid historical details, the fascinating setting, and the tenacity of this book's main characters kept me thoroughly engaged from start to finish. *The Next Ship Home* serves as a powerful and humbling reminder about the courage it takes to start over."

—Elise Hooper, author of *Fast Girls* and *Angels of the Pacific*

THE NEXT
SHIP HOME

A NOVEL OF ELLIS ISLAND

Heather Webb

sourcebooks
landmark

Published by Sourcebooks Landmark, an imprint of Sourcebooks
P.O. Box 4410, Naperville, Illinois 60567-4410
(630) 961-3900
sourcebooks.com

Library of Congress Cataloging-in-Publication Data

Names: Webb, Heather, author.
Title: The next ship home : a novel of Ellis Island / Heather Webb.
Description: Naperville, Illinois : Sourcebooks Landmark, [2022]
Identifiers: LCCN 2021003835 (print) | LCCN 2021003836 (ebook) | (trade paperback) | (hardcover) | (epub)
Subjects: LCSH: Ellis Island Immigration Station (N.Y. and N.J.)--Fiction. | Emigration and immigration--Fiction. | GSAFD: Historical fiction.
Classification: LCC PS3623.E3917 N49 2022 (print) | LCC PS3623.E3917 (ebook) | DDC 813/.6--dc23
LC record available at https://lccn.loc.gov/2021003835
LC ebook record available at https://lccn.loc.gov/2021003836

Printed and bound in the United States of America.
SB 10 9 8 7 6 5 4 3 2 1

For Kaia and Nicolas.
May you always know who you are and that you are loved.

"What, indeed, is a New Yorker? Is he Jew or Irish? Is he English or German? Is he Russian or Polish? He may be something of all these, and yet he is wholly none of them... The change he undergoes is unmistakable. New York, indeed, resembles a magic cauldron. Those who are cast into it are born again."

—Charles Whibley, *American Sketches*, 1908

Journalist urges government to intervene on behalf of Italians at condemned Ellis Island

James Mackle reports. *Manhattan Chronicle*.

March 1, 1902—After a recent trip to New York, journalist Roberto Giamatti returned to his native Rome outraged. Though his visit to the United States included time with his newly emigrated family, his main intent was to report on steamship conditions and their employees, as well as those conditions at Ellis Island.

Mr. Giamatti witnessed gross maltreatment of his countrymen, and especially of young Italian women passing through the halls of the infamous station.

After publishing a series of articles abroad detailing his findings, Mr. Giamatti urges the American government to intervene on behalf of those who will, one day, become citizens of the United States.

Commissioner Fitchie of Ellis Island was not available for comment.

1

*C*rossing the Atlantic in winter wasn't the best choice, but it was the only one. For days, the steamship had cowered beneath a glaring sky and tossed on rough seas as if the large vessel weighed little. Francesca gripped the railing to steady herself. Winds tore at her clothing and punished her bared cheeks, reminding her how small she was, how insignificant her life. It was worth it, to brave the elements for as long as she could stand them. Being out of doors meant clean, bright air to banish the disease from her lungs and scrub away the rank odors clinging to her clothes.

Too many of the six hundred passengers belowdecks had become sick. She tried not to focus on the desperate ones, clutching their meager belongings and praying Hail Marys in strained whispers. She wasn't like them, she told herself, even while her body betrayed her and she trembled more each day as they sailed farther from Napoli. Yet despite the unknown that lay ahead, she would rather die than turn back. As the ship slammed against wave after unruly wave, she thought she might die after all, drift to the bottom of a fathomless dark sea.

She couldn't believe she'd done it—left Sicilia, her home, and all she'd ever known. It had taken every ounce of her courage, but she and Maria had managed to break free. Dear, fragile Maria. Swallowing hard, Francesca looked out at the vast tumult of water and pushed a terrible thought far from her mind. Maria would recover. She had to. Francesca refused to imagine life without her sister.

She tucked her hands under her arms for warmth. Everywhere she looked, her gaze met gray, a slippery color that shimmered silver and foamed with whitecaps or gathered into charcoal clouds. Already she longed for the wide expanse of sea surrounding her island home in a perfect blue-green embrace, the rainbow of purples and oranges that streaked the sunset sky, the craggy landscape, the scent of citrus and sunshine. She wrapped her arms around her middle, holding herself as if she might break apart. Reminiscing about what she once cherished was foolish. Somehow, she had to find things to like about New York.

Freedom from him, if nothing else.

She would never again meet the fists of her drunken papa. At the memory of his bulging eyes and the way his face flowered purple, she rubbed the bruise on her arm that had not quite healed. She would no longer spend her days stealing so he might buy another bottle of Amaro Averna or some other liquor. Paolo Ricci could do it himself. He could tumble from his fishing boat into the sea for all she cared.

A shiver ran over her skin and rattled her teeth. Like it or not, it was time to go belowdecks. As she weaved through the brave souls who paid no heed to the wind despite the cost to warmth, she wondered briefly if any first or second class passengers had defied the cold on the upper-class decks overhead. The ship was tiered and divided into three platforms; the two above her were smaller and set back so a curious lady or gentleman might lean over the railing and peer down at steerage. As if they were a circus of exotic animals.

Francesca descended the ladder into the bowels of the ship. The air thickened into a haze of stink and rot, and the clamor of hundreds of voices floated through the cramped corridors until she arrived at the large room designated for women only. She passed row upon row of metal cots stacked atop each other, filled with strangers. Some women lounged on the floor in their threadbare dresses and boots with heels worn to the quick. Their eyes were haunted, their wan figures gaunt with hunger. One woman scratched at an open sore; another smelled of urine and sweat and squatted against the wall of the ship with a rosary in hand, pausing briefly in her prayer to swipe at a rat with greasy fur, driven by hunger, the same as her. The same as they all were.

Francesca tried not to linger on their faces and moved through the room to her sister, who lay prostrate on her cot, and reached for her hand.

"You're so cold," Maria said through cracked lips, clutching her sister's hand. "You'll catch your death, Cesca. Promise me you'll be careful."

Heart in her throat, Francesca swept her sister's matted curls from her face. Death was not a word she wanted to entertain. The terror they'd harbored since they'd sneaked away from their home in the middle of the night, that overwhelmed her each time she considered the unknown before them, was bad enough. Death had no place here.

"Nothing can catch me now. We're too close."

Maria smiled and a glimpse of her cheerful nature shone in her dark eyes. "That hard head serves you at last."

Francesca forced a smile, desperate to hide the concern from her face. Maria had always been frail, easily ill and quickly bruised, yet still she glowed with some internal light. Often, Francesca imagined her as a fairy, an angelic creature not of this earth. She laid a hand on Maria's brow. Her skin burned with fever, and sweat soaked through her gown. Maria had fallen ill on the first leg of their voyage from Palermo to Napoli and had worsened each day since. Francesca had worried the captain wouldn't allow them to board, but she and Maria had passed the inspection rapidly—after Francesca paid an unspoken price in a back room on a narrow cot. But they were on their way and that was what mattered now.

"Another few days, Maria," she whispered. After five days at sea, New York Harbor must be close. Once they arrived, they would need to find a doctor to tend to the fever immediately.

Maria moaned and turned on her side, her shoulder nearly scraping the underside of the woman's cot suspended above hers. "I'm so thirsty."

Francesca was thirsty, too. Their water rations had scarcely been sufficient, or their food for that matter. What did the crew care about a pack of hungry, dirty foreigners? They saw so many, week after week. Desperation was nothing new to them.

Francesca turned over her water canister in her hands. No one would part with their rations; she'd asked passengers in steerage all day yesterday and had finally given up. Poverty didn't move them, or the story of her very ill sister. Each had their own story of woe. And it was out of the question to approach second or third class passengers. A guard stood at each of the doors connected to the upper levels to keep the wanderers out.

Unless...? An idea sparked suddenly in the back of her mind.

"I'm going to find more water." She pulled the blanket around Maria's shoulders. "Don't try to get up again. You need to rest."

Francesca rummaged through their small travel case for the only nice things she owned. She pulled on her mother's finest dress, fastened on a pair of earbobs, slipped a set of combs into her hair, and kissed the medallion of the Virgin Mary around her neck. The medallion she had stolen two years ago.

For months, she had admired the shiny golden trinket as it winked from the hollow at the base of Sister Alberta's neck. It was the first time Francesca had felt the sharp edge of envy. A rush of shame soon followed. She loved the nun like family, and Francesca knew it was a sin to want what wasn't hers. One day when Sister sent her to fetch a book, Francesca found the necklace gleaming in a bright ray of sunlight that streaked across Sister's dressing table. She'd held it a moment, stroking the outline of the Virgin Mother with her thumb, wishing she'd had the medallion's protection. She'd been unable to resist it, and slipped it inside the folds of her dress. It wasn't until the following day that she wondered why Sister had sent her to look for a book that wasn't there. Perhaps it had been a test—a test Francesca had failed.

Francesca's chest tightened as she thought of the nun. Sister Alberta was a Catholic in exile, though she'd never explained why, and had lived two lanes away from Francesca and Maria in their little village. The nun had befriended them when their mother disappeared, taught Francesca to cook and both sisters to read and even speak a little English. Sister had loved them.

"You putting on airs for someone?" said Adriana, an Italian woman from Roma. She wore thick rouge, and though she was traveling in steerage, her dress looked finer than those of the other women with its lace trim and shiny beading. It was also vivid purple. All the better to attract male attention.

"I need more water." Francesca's gaze flicked to her sister and back to the woman she was certain traded lire for sex. Not that Francesca minded. She wasn't bothered by other people's choices, especially when it came to survival. God must understand need when he saw it, if he was truly a benevolent God.

Adriana crossed her arms beneath her bosom. "Plan on flirting with the captain for it?"

Francesca snapped the compact closed. "I'm going to the upper decks, see if someone will spare some."

Or perhaps she would just take their water. She was good at that, taking things.

"Better work it harder, *amore*, if you want to fit in with that lot." A woman with no front teeth rose from her bed and dug through a handbag tucked beneath her pillow. "Here. Have some of this." She held out an elegant bottle of perfume.

Francesca felt a rush of gratitude. She reached for the bottle and dabbed her neck and wrists.

"I've got some rouge, too." Adriana produced a small tub. "You'll have better luck with the guards this way."

Another cabin mate watched them quietly, pushed up from her bunk, and took something out of a bag she'd been using as a pillow. "It was my *nonna's*." She clutched a cashmere shawl to her chest. It didn't look new, but it had been well cared for and could still pass for acceptable among the upper class, at least Francesca hoped. "The gray will be pretty with your eyes," the woman continued. "Please, be careful with it."

Francesca hardly knew them, yet they lent their most precious belongings to help her. An unspoken sense of unity hung in the air. Tired of suffering, they'd all left their homes behind and hoped for better times ahead.

"I...I don't know how to thank you all," she stammered as a swell of emotion clogged her throat.

"Show those *puttanas* they aren't better than us," Adriana said, winking.

At that, Francesca smiled.

She blew her cabin mates a kiss to whistles and cheers. Holding her head high, she threaded through the narrow hallway, wound through a room filled with barrels and clusters of steamer trunks, and passed a huddled group of passengers playing card games. She approached the ladder leading to the second-class deck quickly, before she could change her mind, and ascended it.

And there, at the end of the next passageway, a crewman stood guard.

When he spotted her, he stepped to the right and crossed his arms, blocking the entrance.

She clasped her hands together like a lady should, stretched her five-foot, three-inch frame to full height, and, ignoring the thundering in her ears, marched toward the guard.

He stood stiffly in a navy uniform, the name "Forrester" stitched across his breast pocket in yellow thread. "I can't let you through, miss. There's no steerage allowed here."

Her stomach tightened, but she forced a smile. "Excuse me, Mr. Forrester, I am second class. I have friend in steerage. I visit her but now I return."

The wiry seaman peered at her, his gaze traveling over her worn shoes and dress.

Nervously, she dug her thumbnail into the flesh of her index finger, willing herself to remain calm.

"Second class, you say?" His eyes rested on her rouged lips.

"Yes. Excuse me," she said, her tone clipped as if she were insulted.

He stared at her for a long, uncomfortable minute. At last, he angled his body away from her, leaving just enough room so her body would brush against his in an intimate way.

She pushed past him, ignoring his groping hands, his breath on her cheek. Too relieved to be annoyed by his behavior, Francesca darted quickly down the narrow corridor. At the first door, she peered through a small oval window. The room was crowded with luggage. She continued forward, pausing at each window, becoming more anxious as she went. When she came upon the dining saloon, she found the door locked and the room empty. Though the evening meal wouldn't be served for another couple of hours, she'd hoped the room might be open for late-afternoon tea or libations. It must be the first class who were offered such luxuries. She huffed out an irritated breath and continued down the narrow corridor.

Ahead, she saw a young woman wearing a pale-blue frock with a fashionable bustle and a wide-brimmed hat trimmed with ribbons. She was prettily dressed, her frock likely one of a series that she rotated every other week, something Francesca aspired to have one day soon. As she neared the woman, the scent of roses drifted around them and filled the cramped space. Francesca met the woman's eye briefly and nodded, even as she stared back at Francesca like she were diseased.

Ignoring the uncomfortable exchange, Francesca continued to the end of the corridor to the last room before the cabins began. It was a storage room filled with barrels and shelves of foodstuffs. It, too, was locked.

She leaned against the door. Of course it was locked. They wanted to prevent thieves from pilfering goods—thieves like her. Sister Alberta's lectures about letting God provide rang in her ears. Yet had Francesca let God provide, she would have starved to death on more than one occasion. Had she let Him provide shelter and comfort, she would have suffered broken bones at her father's hand for many more years. God gave her plenty of free will, and with it, she chose to provide for herself. Only she wasn't doing that so well either.

She fought back tears. Maria needed water desperately. Could Francesca risk it, try first class? It would probably turn out the same, but she had to try. Fists clenched, she pushed back from the door. She weaved around several male passengers and a woman in a striped dress, pausing to ask them for water, but they first looked annoyed and then ignored her. When she reached the first-class deck, another steward stood watch at the top of the landing.

"You there!" He pointed at her. "You aren't allowed here."

Concentrating, she searched for the words Sister Alberta had taught her.

I need, You need, He needs, We need…

"I need…" she began tentatively. "You need Forrester." She shook her head. "Forrester needs you. The captain is angry."

The guard squinted. "What for?"

"The captain is angry," she repeated, willing her pulse to slow. "You go now."

"Nice try, miss, but I ain't leaving my post. Now be on your way."

"I—"

The door behind him swung open and a shrill voice cut the air. "Boy! I need your help at once!" A middle-aged woman draped in furs glared at him with expectation.

The guard's scowl gave way to one of feigned interest. "How can I help you, madam?"

"The linens on my table are filthy, and I want them changed immediately. That poor excuse for a waitstaff is ignoring me entirely, and I won't have it."

"I'm sure they'll be with you soon, madam."

"You would have me stand in the middle of the room while others are being tended to until someone *decides* to help me?" she shrieked.

"Of course not, madam," he said quickly, realizing his mistake.

As he darted after her, Francesca's knees went weak with relief. With haste, she followed them at a short distance to the dining saloon, but as the wealthy came into view in their elegant silks and jewels, her footsteps faltered. If the fashionable women she'd seen in second class had been intimidating, these women felt otherworldly as they sparkled in diamonds and bright red and blue stones, smiling and floating around the room with unimaginable grace.

What was she doing here? In that instant, she realized how completely ridiculous she appeared in her borrowed shawl and rouge, her modest earbobs and combs. She could never pass for first class. Not ever.

But as Maria's dear face flashed in her mind's eye and Sister Alberta's voice echoed in her ears, Francesca remembered what she must do. How far she'd already come.

"*Time to be brave, Cesca.*" She whispered Sister Alberta's words the day they had departed Sicilia.

Ignoring the bold stare of a lady dressed in cornflower-blue silk, Francesca followed the others inside the dining saloon.

Rows of tables dressed in elegant linens fanned around a center point in the room where a grove of potted trees made the space more welcoming with their lush greens. Above, the ceiling formed a dome of glass panels edged with shiny bronze. Francesca imagined sunrays streaming through the milky glass on nicer days, spilling over the crystal goblets and water carafes, and making them sparkle like diamonds. The dining room couldn't be more different from the dark hole crammed with unwashed bodies where she spent her days.

The startling contrast between what her life was, and what it could be had she been born in a different world, held her there, transfixed.

A waiter brushed past her, breaking the spell.

Francesca clutched her canteen tightly. There wasn't time for dreaming. Now was her chance. Pulse racing, she crossed the room, focusing on the full water carafes in the center of each table.

Several heads bobbed in her direction.

She picked up her pace. If someone stopped her, would they lock her in the holding cabin for criminals? When she reached the outer ring of tables at the back wall, she willed her hand to remain steady and reached for a carafe atop an empty table.

"What do you think you're doing?" A woman's voice came from behind her.

Francesca whirled around, slopping water onto the front of her dress. She hardly noticed the woman's scowl; she was too taken with her stunning black crepe dress lined with glittering beads, her thick fur stole, and long silk gloves tapered to her elbows. A feather adorned a jewel-studded band in her hair. The woman wasn't beautiful, but she possessed a learned grace evident in her posture and dress.

And she clearly didn't take kindly to steerage.

"Please," Francesca continued in broken English. "Maria is *malata*. My sister...she's very ill."

Pressing her lips together, the woman took in Francesca's worn cream-colored dress with dull buttons fastened to her chin, the cashmere shawl, her thin frame.

Francesca held her head high beneath the woman's scrutiny. "We need water. Please, my sister—"

"What a sad tale." The feather at the signora's crown bobbed as she spoke; the diamonds at her neck twinkled. She waved her hand in dismissal. "Be on your way, young lady."

"Mother, she just needs a little water." A gentleman joined the woman at the table, smiling kindly at Francesca. "And we have plenty."

"Thank you," Francesca said in English, and then in Italian, "I have my canteen."

The woman's expression turned sour. "She's speaking that filthy language. Really, Marshall, why must you pick up strays?"

A waiter approached the table, nostrils flaring and cheeks flushed. "I beg your pardon, sir. Madam." He tilted his head in a conciliatory bow. He said several things more that Francesca couldn't understand, then gripped her arm.

She cried out as his hand closed over the last painful bruise her father had gifted to her. It was a deep bruise, slow to heal—and the final push she'd needed to leave.

"Unhand her at once," the gentleman called Marshall said, tone firm. "She's done nothing to offend us."

Distress crossed the waiter's face. "Sir, she shouldn't be here—"

"I said, unhand her." Marshall's jaw set into a hard line.

The waiter dropped Francesca's arm and scurried away, red-faced.

Marshall motioned to her canteen. "Please, madam. Allow me." He unscrewed the lid, reached for the pitcher.

Eager to return to Maria, and to escape his mother's obvious disgust, Francesca willed him to move faster. *Mustn't snatch it from his hands,* she reminded herself. He was kind, in spite of his wealth, and that seemed a rarity.

He smiled at Francesca as he held out the full canteen. "There we are."

"Thank you."

"Would you care to join us?" he asked, motioning to the table. As he sat, something slipped from his jacket and fluttered to the floor. A card of some sort.

Stunned by the invitation, Francesca stood awkwardly without replying, her eye on the card he'd dropped. In her experience, men were never generous without wanting—or taking—something in return. She didn't need his fancy food that badly, even as her stomach protested wildly.

"Please don't take offense"—he paused as a flash of embarrassment crossed his features—"but you look rather hungry."

She reddened. She'd eaten porridge, stale bread, and bowls of watery stew for days, and little of it. Her mouth watered at the thought of clams and a little pasta, or lemon and olive oil on bread. Even salted fava bean stew sounded like a king's feast.

He cleared his throat. "What I meant to say is, we will have plenty as soon as we're served. Please, do join us."

She touched the buttons of her dress at her throat. The gentleman might be kind, but his mother wasn't, and the other women being seated at the table looked just as terrifying in their shimmering dresses and jewels. And there was Maria. Her sister needed her.

"No, sir," she said, regretting the plate of elegant foods she'd never have a chance to taste. "I go. My sister needs me."

He nodded, sending a lock of graying hair over his brow. "Very well then. I hope your sister recovers quickly."

She nodded. "*Grazie mille.*" Before leaving, she pointed to the card beneath his chair. "You lose it."

"Ah, my visiting card." He scooped it up and, after a moment's hesitation, gave it to her. "I hope you will consider me your first friend in America."

Blushing from her neck to her hairline, she glanced at the card. Marshall Lancaster, Park Avenue. Did he think she was that sort of woman?

"I am not prostitute," she said, sticking out her chin.

Mrs. Lancaster barked out a laugh before exchanging meaningful looks with her friends at the table.

This time Marshall blushed to the tips of his ears. "Oh, my! No, that is... I didn't mean to..." When he saw her confused expression, he said once more with emphasis, "*Friend in America.*" He held out his hand to shake hers, his face deepening to the shade of a ripe tomato.

"I am sorry," she said, her accent thick over the rolling r.

"Never mind." He smiled warmly. "Good evening, Miss... What is your name?"

"Francesca Ricci."

"Good evening, Miss Ricci."

Mrs. Lancaster glared at them both. "Yes, *good evening*."

Cheeks flaming, Francesca curtsied for the signora's benefit and headed for the exit.

One day soon, in America, she'd make sure she never had to beg for charity again.

2

Alma always obeyed.

She followed a clockwork schedule of chores each day, ticking them off the list one by one. Without complaint, she strung wet clothes on the laundry line stretching across the front room of their tenement apartment and swept the back step overlooking the outhouse. A rickety fence divided the yard from the street, but soon it would need to be replaced to keep out the vagabonds in their neighborhood who seemed to multiply by the day. The influx of "those people" made her parents anxious about her comings and goings, in spite of her twenty-one years. One never knew what an immigrant might do to a young American lady of superior standing. As the stink of the outhouse hit her nose, Alma coughed and her eyes watered. The sooner they left the neighborhood, the better.

Indoors, she made sure no one was watching and opened the cupboard, fishing behind the baking soda for her journal. A place where her stepfather would never find it. She hugged it to her chest, cradling its treasured contents: lists of foreign words and rules and slang, and page after page of Italian. She slipped outdoors again to steal a few minutes practicing the words the kindly priest, Father Rodolfo, had taught her when she managed to get away from the *bierhaus* for an hour or two on Sunday afternoons. Perhaps she could sneak away for a little while later today, since her stepfather was out on business.

Alma obeyed, most of the time.

After a few precious minutes of study, she'd need to help her mother in the kitchen for the bulk of the day's work. They prepared food for their family of seven and for the German customers who might happen upon their bierhaus beneath the apartment on the basement level. Their tenement sat on Orchard Street, crammed into a row of similar four-story buildings made of red sandstone and brick in the heart of Kleindeutschland. Little Germany. Two blocks north sat a neighborhood of Russians and Poles, many Jewish; four blocks to the west was the Bowery, a flourishing Irish neighborhood; and six blocks north, the Italians. The communities were together but separate and understood their roles. The Jewish and Italian populations floundered at the bottom as the newest to arrive on American shores, the Irish fought their way from the middle, and the Germans, Dutch, and English perched at the top. Alma's family and friends steered clear of the other groups when they could, knowing they didn't belong among the thieving Irish or amid the squalor the newly arrived immigrants brought to the city.

Alma had never questioned her parents' views. In fact, they'd instilled their own unease within her, so she turned to the one thing that helped quell it: she learned their languages, those who infiltrated the neighborhood and took their jobs. Those who turned familiar streets foreign and made the citizens of Kleindeutschland uncomfortable in their homes. In the process, she'd discovered that language was a tool—and a weapon. A means to disarm adversaries, or perhaps something she had yet to admit, even to herself. It was a means to understand them.

"Where do you live?" She recited the Italian phrase. "I would like some pasta. I need a pound of cheese." She skimmed through the easy phrases, her finger slipping down the page as she read, and stopped to review a few of the more difficult verb structures.

The lessons had begun when her older brother, Fritz, came home from work one day, lamenting how he couldn't communicate with the other workers, who were nearly all immigrants, and very many Italians. The Interborough Rapid Transit Company was developing the new subway system, and if he couldn't talk to them and be understood, he couldn't very well be promoted to the position of foreman. Alma had suggested he learn the language, promising to help him practice, and soon after, they'd met Father Rodolfo, a priest on Mulberry Street in the Italian section of the Lower East Side. Delighted by their request, the priest spent several hours every week teaching them after mass. Alma's mind preyed on the fascinating new sounds and rhythms, enlivening her dull days, and she quickly surpassed her brother's skills. She hadn't had any schooling since she was a young girl, and learning again felt like a kind of freedom.

She turned the page in her journal to a dialogue she'd written a few days ago, changing her voice when the speaker changed. She chuckled softly to herself as she attempted to sound male. Several minutes later, she tucked the journal in the cupboard. Her stepfather had looked on with disdain during those months she and Fritz had begun to learn Italian, and eventually he'd forbidden it. There was no use for learning the language of vagrants, he'd said. Alma's parents' feet were planted firmly in German tradition and the ways of the past, and they expected the same of her. The expectation weighed on her—their eldest daughter—pressing against her own desires until they all but disappeared somewhere inside her. Rather than argue with her parents and bring everyone distress, she remained silent, as was expected of her.

She joined her mother, and in quiet contemplation, Alma

pounded pork fillets and stirred the silky batter in which they would be dipped before frying. As she churned the thick liquid, it splattered on her apron and dribbled down the pot. She grunted in frustration. Why did she always spill everything? She cleaned up her mess, peeled a mountain of potatoes for boiling, and steamed a vat of sauerkraut steeped in beer, onion, and pork grease. Next, she threw together a mixture of vinegar and herbs, added water and black pepper, and ladled it over a beef roast to marinate for three days. In three days, there would be sauerbraten, oxtail salad to make, and piles of carrots and turnips to serve.

In three days, she would drag herself from the bed she shared with her sisters, the same as each and every day, and work through the monotony of another week.

Monotony and mundanity. *Insanity.*

The last few months, the walls of the bierhaus seemed to close in around her a little more each day until something buzzed inside her. A need. The need knocked against her ribs like an animal against a cage, desperate to be set free. And as she chopped another carrot, another turnip, another onion, her thoughts turned to the one thing she knew she wanted above all else: the escape into her studies, where she didn't have to be ashamed of being plain and timid, curious and studious. A place where her mind could roam freely, where she could dream of a different life. A grander one.

"It does you no good to have dreams," Mama always said with a kiss on the forehead. "They leave you dissatisfied with your lot." Alma didn't understand how her mother could accept her life without question, without looking to the future with some hope of change, even if a small one. Tradition was more important, Mama would say. It was a known aspect of their lives, comforting in its predictability.

And dull as dirt, Alma had thought more times than she could count.

She dropped the ladle on her foot, startling herself from her thoughts. She bit her lip to keep from cursing.

"Maybe you should wear gloves with grips on them," said Fritz, who swept through the room and grabbed the last apple. The fruit made a satisfying snap as his teeth sank into its flesh.

She tossed a carrot at her older brother, but he swiftly dodged the projectile and it crashed against the wall.

"Looks like you need to work on your arm, too," he said with a wink.

Alma adored him, even if he was stubborn as a mule and quick to anger at times. At least he never took it out on her. "Oh, shut up!" she shouted as he ducked outside, taking their youngest brother, Klaus, with him.

"*Gehe zum markt,*" Mama called from the larder. "I need sugar, eggs, and three pounds of bacon. Take Greta with you."

Alma perked up. She might have time to slip away to Mulberry Street afterward to meet the priest. "Can Else help with the potatoes? After the market, I'd like to visit Emma."

A little white lie never hurt anyone. She hadn't spent time with her friend in ages.

"For one hour, before Robert returns," Mama called. "We have a lot to do today still."

Alma's stepfather had traveled uptown to look at property, a place they might move to that was larger and in a better neighborhood. One that was primarily German. Should Robert return to find her gone before her work was finished, she'd be in for it. He looked for any reason to chastise her, remind her of her age, and complain she was not yet married. She was lucky, he'd say, that she could continue to rely on his hospitality. Robert Brauer couldn't be more unlike Wilhelm Klein, her beloved—and deceased—Papa.

"Else!" Mama called to Alma's youngest sibling. "Help with the peeling."

"Do I have to?" The seven-year-old whined and stuck her nose deeper into her book. Her list of chores had increased lately, as her arms grew stronger and her legs longer. In time, she'd be as tall and as capable as her sisters.

"You know what whining will get you. A switch to the backside! Now put that book down and get on with it." Johanna Brauer wiped her forehead with her apron and continued washing the beer mugs. She threatened a switch, but in truth Alma knew Mama had a soft spot for her children. She expected them to work hard, but she indulged their wishes when she could.

Alma smiled as she saw the book Else was reading, and whispered, "We can read together tonight before bed."

Else brightened, always happy to read with her big sister. Alma winked and slung her bag, filled with her precious journal, lead pencils, and a dictionary, over her shoulder.

"Let's go, Greta!" she called as she entered the main room of the bierhaus.

Her fourteen-year-old sister knelt on the floor, scrubbing a particularly grimy spot. "What is it?"

"We need some things at the market."

"Thank God. I'm bored." Her younger sister chucked the scrub brush in a bucket of suds. It splashed, spraying soap across the floor. Ignoring the mess, she slipped on a shawl and hat and assessed her reflection in the mirror on the wall behind the counter. Greta enjoyed any excuse to venture out, especially if she might meet new boys. Her delicate features and flirtatious smile captured their hearts all too easily.

Alma, by contrast, had a willowy frame and a face as plain as a boiled potato. Her best features were her bright blue eyes, the color of a summer sky, and her mind. She glanced at her reflection. She liked to think she looked intelligent, and that was good enough for her. She didn't place much value in beauty. It had done nothing for her mother but burden her with many children and seven people she must care for. Though Alma knew she must walk a similar path one day, she could scarcely imagine it. At least not anymore.

Not without Jacob.

She quickly shuttered the thoughts of him before the pain could rush in and turned to her sister. "You look fine, Greta. Let's go."

They pushed outside through a bustling crowd and walked beneath a row of awnings, some tattered and faded, others jutting proudly from their storefronts with crisp new cloth. Jewish bakeries, Italian coffeehouses, and German delicatessens nestled against each other in a colorful parade of nationalities. Shoemakers, taverns, tailors. Cart after cart jammed the thoroughfare while vendors and their customers swarmed in disorderly queues. Alma ducked beneath a sagging sign and around a heap of garbage, narrowly missing a fruit peddler.

"*Guten morgen, fräulein,*" Mr. Schuller said, tipping his hat at them. "Care for an apple?" He plucked one from the heap, rubbed it with his hands until shiny, and proffered the fruit to Greta. "And for your sister, too?" He smiled at Alma, though she knew he was only being polite to include her.

"Thank you." Greta rewarded him with a bright smile and took the fruit.

Alma declined and tugged her sister's arm, eager to get their chore finished. "He wants you to marry his son, you know."

Greta scrunched her pert little nose. "His son's a dog."

"And he makes his living from a fruit and vegetable cart. You'd be pregnant and poor"—she snapped her fingers—"like that."

"I'm not going to marry him." Greta rolled her eyes. "Really, do you have to be so dreary?"

Alma shrugged. "If you don't want to marry Joseph Schuller, then you shouldn't encourage his father."

"I guess you're going to live with Mama and Father forever." Her sister sniffed and wrapped her arms around her middle to ward off the cold. "You don't even talk to men who like you."

Greta romanticized marriage. Alma, on the other hand, was awkward around men, and she found polite conversation fatiguing, especially from possible suitors who wanted nothing more than a respectable wife and mother for their children. None were like Jacob. No one challenged her or asked about her opinions or thoughts. She and Jacob had loved each other since they were small children. When his family had moved to Minnesota a year ago, she'd been devastated. They'd exchanged letters feverishly for weeks, but as the months wore on, they became less frequent until she scarcely heard from him at all. One day, the news arrived that Jacob was engaged to be married, and the final threads of hope she'd nurtured of joining him in Minnesota were snipped.

They turned at the end of the block onto Delancey Street and headed toward the Schaller Market. Alma's gaze traveled over a row of building facades masking the crumbling decay inside them: dingy walls, poor lighting and ventilation, no running water. They teemed with as much vermin as they did people, all packed tightly inside, using every inch of space. She imagined the frames of the tenement building bulging like a large belly straining against suspenders, the windows cracking from the weight of too many bodies inside. In spite of the gloom and overcrowding, those who lived in this part of town had nowhere else to go. The Brauers were fortunate, though their apartment still consisted of a mere three rooms inhabited by seven people. At least they had the bierhaus below the apartment, too, and the promise of steady income.

Alma purchased the items on the list and tucked the sack into the basket. She'd walk Greta home quickly, and if Father Rodolfo wasn't available today, perhaps she'd walk to Motta's Bakery to practice listening to Italian.

"Let's go around the block?" Greta asked. "I don't feel like scrubbing the floor."

"Not today. I'm going to visit Emma. In fact, I'd like to get moving, or I won't have time."

Greta cast her a sidelong glance. Her bottom lip protruded slightly in a pout. "Why do you get to go out alone?"

"Father isn't home until later, and I'm twenty-one. I should say I'm old enough to walk a few blocks alone." She didn't dare tell Greta her real plan. Her younger sister couldn't keep her mouth shut. Alma had already learned that lesson the hard way.

Picking up their pace, they turned onto Orchard Street, slowing behind a group of women engrossed in conversation. Brightly colored scarves covered their heads and they chattered like a bevy of birds, their voices carrying over the din of the busy street. Alma strained to make out their conversation. They spoke in a guttural yet rhythmic language, from Eastern Europe, perhaps. She frowned, frustrated she didn't understand a single word.

A pack of children pushed around them, running wild without shoes and coats. Ahead, a horse-drawn wagon turned onto the street and came to a near standstill in the crowded lane. No one seemed to notice, or care, that the man in the wagon was trying to get through. In this part of the city, it was always faster to travel on foot.

A loud bang echoed along the street, followed by another.

The horses attached to the wagon reared back, and the cart took off like a shot. People scurried out of the way. Alarmed, Alma grabbed her sister's arm instinctively.

"What are you doing?" Greta asked, allowing herself to be led away.

"Look!" Alma pointed.

The driver pulled on the reins, and the crack of a leather whip rent the air. But nothing seemed to slow the spooked horses.

Pedestrians lunged out of the way.

The clot of women that had been in front of Alma and Greta continued their conversation, oblivious to the oncoming danger.

The cart picked up speed, swaying violently as the man tried to regain control.

Alma watched in horror as it veered on two wheels, narrowly missing a row of pushcarts selling roasted nuts and hot corn.

Several onlookers shouted at the women.

They didn't understand English, Alma thought, her eyes growing round. Not only didn't they understand, but they weren't paying attention. If they didn't move at once, someone could be badly hurt.

The cart thundered toward them.

"Look out!" a man shouted, waving to the group fanned across the street.

At last, the women scattered and they all made it to safety—except one, who hadn't moved quite fast enough.

Alma cried out, covering her mouth with her hand.

In seconds, the horses were upon the woman. The edge of the cart knocked her clear across the street, her body landing in a heap.

People gaped at the spectacle but continued on their way without offering a hand. Those who lived in this neighborhood had seen far worse. Vandals and gangs and whores.

Alma rushed to the woman without thinking. She could have

broken bones—she could have been killed. Panting, Alma crouched beside her. "Are you all right?"

The woman replied in a string of sentences that might as well have been gibberish. A small gash streaked her forehead with blood. Many of her teeth were missing, and the skin around her eyes and mouth creased like she'd spent her days exposed to the elements. When she finally stopped talking, she stared at Alma as if waiting for a reply. When none came, she clutched her ankle.

"Is it broken? Do you need a doctor?" Alma gestured to the woman's foot.

"Alma, stop this!" Greta hissed, running to her side. "They should have watched where they were going! You're embarrassing us."

She ignored her sister and helped the stranger to her feet. The woman's face crumpled in pain, and she launched into another unintelligible stream of conversation.

"What the hell are you doing, Alma?" Her stepfather's angry voice reached her before she saw him. Robert Brauer rushed to her side, out of breath. He scowled with disgust. "Leave her," he said. "She's not your concern."

Alma's heart sank. So he had returned from his business uptown. There would be no language practice, no hour of blissful freedom today. She looked back at the woman and tried speaking to her again, this time in Italian to see if she understood—to no avail.

Robert stared at Alma in surprise. "I thought I told you not to speak that foul language. I said, leave her! What has gotten into you, girl?"

Alarmed by Robert's tone, Alma glanced at him, noting the vein bulging in his forehead, and wondered the same. What had gotten into her? The woman was just another immigrant who had made living in the tenements more and more unbearable for their family. Suddenly feeling foolish, Alma stood.

At that moment, the woman's friends encircled her, everyone talking at once and fawning over her injury.

Robert placed one hand on Alma and the other on Greta and steered them away from the scene.

"Are you trying to ruin my reputation, Alma?" Greta demanded, stepping over a black puddle littered with garbage. "Paul Vanderveen is across the street. He could have seen us! Those women were disgusting."

Alma bit back a sarcastic comment. It was just like Greta to think only of herself and some boy, when the woman could have been killed. And that's why Alma had helped, she suddenly realized. She couldn't leave an injured woman in the street alone, no matter how uncomfortable it made her to help an immigrant.

"Greta is right," Robert agreed, moving swiftly along the street as they neared their tenement building. "This is the last thing we need. It's the last thing *you* need." He pointed a finger in Alma's face. "No wonder no man wants you for his wife."

She held her tongue, knowing anything she could say would make his temper worse.

"This is the priest's fault," he continued. "He's put ideas into your head."

Alma cringed at the memory of her stepfather's belt on her arm when he'd caught her returning from a meeting with Father Rodolfo, long after he'd told her not to go back there. Whether she liked it or not, Robert had every right to forbid her to see the priest while she lived under his roof.

An image of Papa arose in her mind, the way he'd take her on his knee in front of the fire with a book while Fritz practiced his mathematics at the table. A lump formed in the back of her throat. It had been fourteen years since Papa's passing, yet the pain never seemed to go, not completely. Her stepfather's open disdain for her didn't help matters. Her very presence and that of her older brother, Fritz, seemed to make him feel threatened. Robert Brauer couldn't abide the thought of his beloved wife having another man's children.

"Well, your concern for those people will make my news easier for you," Robert said, eyes stormy.

"What do you mean?" Alma asked. "What news?"

He didn't reply, and they bounded down the steps to their bierhaus below the street.

"Johanna!" He slammed the door behind them. "Johanna!"

Mama rushed into the room. "Christ, Robert, why the shouting? What is it?"

He filled a stein with fresh brew until it frothed at the rim. "I have good news. No one is interested in the property but us. We need more cash, but they say they'll hold it for us, if we can scrape the money together by autumn. They really want another German family to move in." He drank deeply from his mug. Wiping his mouth with his arm, he said, "This is where you come in, Alma."

"I don't understand," she said, hanging up her overcoat.

"You're going to help pay the bills. I've just gotten you a job. Given how you carried on in the street just now, I think you're the perfect person for it."

Alma froze. He would send her away from home to work? Sweatshops and harassment, low pay and long hours—she'd read all about it in the newspapers. Her monotonous day would be made worse, and she'd never have a chance to study.

Swallowing hard, she said, "Where, Father? Where am I to work?"

He grinned smugly. "Ellis Island. You begin Monday."

Alma gasped. *Ellis Island?* She looked at her mother, who said nothing and appeared overly busy stacking clean beer mugs. Had Mama agreed to send Alma off to work among a horde of unruly, dirty immigrants? It would ruin her reputation for possible suitors, surely—something her mother worried about a great deal, even if Alma didn't. Ellis Island must be out of the question!

"Mama?" she pleaded. "Am I really to work among the...the immigrants?"

"Your father made a very good case for it last night, *liebling*," Mama said.

A good case for it? She couldn't imagine what that could possibly be. Wouldn't her work there reflect poorly on the family? "But Father," she began. "I—"

"You're a burden, Alma," he said. "Another mouth to feed. And since no man will have you, and you've managed to scare off the few we've tried to set up for you, it's time you earned your keep."

They thought so little of her as to banish her to the immigration station? Knees weak, she dropped into a chair. What would she be doing? Corralling the immigrants they all despised? She looked at Greta who, for the first time ever, had a piteous look on her face. And in that moment, Alma was forced to believe it. This was really happening.

As shame burned through her, one thought played over and over in her mind. The infamous name for Ellis Island:

Tränen Insel, Island of Tears.

3

Cheers erupted somewhere on the steamship. Francesca bolted upright in her bunk and smacked her head on the low ceiling. She grumbled and rubbed the spot on her forehead. Had they arrived, or was it another drunken brawl in the smoking room?

She leaned over the edge into Maria's bunk. "Are you awake? We must be close."

"Yes." Maria's voice was small. "Go and see if we've arrived."

Francesca scrambled down the ladder at the foot of her bunk, fully clothed, boots laced. She didn't dare wear a nightdress to sleep, to put herself in a more vulnerable position than she already was. Most of the other passengers did the same—guarded their belongings, slept in their day dresses, prepared, even in slumber, to fight for what was theirs.

The corridors were crowded and dank, but everyone was abuzz with excitement. They'd arrived, or nearly! America was in sight!

When she finally made it on deck, she peered out across the ocean. In the distance, a dark strip of land rose from the sea. *America.* She'd soon be in her new home! She smiled as she turned her face to the sky. For only the second time during the voyage, the sun parted the curtain of clouds and burned off the misty gloom. Placid argent waters lapped against the hull of the ship. She watched the horizon grow nearer, inured to the garlicky scent of body odor around her and the push and pull of those seeking the ship's railing. Soon, they would be ashore amid the bustle of New York City, and the first order of business, after the doctor, would be to find a job.

She'd heard America had more jobs than people. She couldn't imagine such a thing as she looked out over the sea of faces on deck, but she hoped it was true. Perhaps she and Maria could clean houses or work for a tailor or, if they had to, take a position in a factory. She cursed her poor English and her terrible attitude those years Sister Alberta had pushed her to practice. Her mind didn't bend to her studies the way she wanted it to, or perhaps it was a lack of patience. Instead, she had memorized the soft skin of a ripe tomato, the weight of a knife in her hand as she chopped bright herbs from Alberta's garden or peeled the bumpy skin of a lemon. She felt most like herself in the kitchen.

Francesca scanned the passengers crammed on deck. The few women aboard wore embroidered aprons and headscarves, or jackets and gored skirts. The men's dress ranged from morning coats and derby hats or skullcaps to native dress of black pants, wide cloth belts, and colorful tunics. She couldn't imagine how such a vast variety of people could live in harmony. This America must be as great as everyone claimed it to be.

Another cheer erupted as a crew member snaked through the crowd. He stepped atop a crate and put a speaking trumpet to his lips. "Attention! Everyone! Attention!"

He continued his announcement, and though Francesca could scarcely make out a word, she listened intently. At last, she understood "third class and below" and something about pushing and being tossed overboard. As a few laughs rippled through the crowd, she bit her lip in frustration. She *had* to practice her English.

The crew member did a short wave and stepped down from his perch. Passengers cheered again, a few launching their hats into the air. The noise drew the attention of a second-class passenger, who appeared at the tiered railing above, and with a shout of "Tallyho!" the man dropped an orange and a few coppers. As the coins and fruit tumbled through the air, several people shoved each other, crying out, and leaped after the prize. Two more gentlemen joined the man at the railing and they, too, released coins. More passengers dove into the melee. Soon, much of steerage pushed and laughed and lunged for the prizes. The energy was infectious; all were happy the journey was coming to an end.

Francesca backed away from the tangle of bodies until she felt the cool steel railing at her back. Hand on her plain straw hat, she peered up at the men dressed in fine wool suits who had started the wrestling pit in the first place. They laughed and pointed at those making fools of themselves. One man's waste was another man's luxury, she thought, but none of it was worth a black eye.

Yearning for her first view of New York, she clutched the railing as the steamship chugged ahead at full speed. When at last the boat nosed into New York Harbor, she searched the horizon, seeking the beacon of welcome she'd longed to see since first setting sail. And there she was. Lady Liberty perched on her pedestal in a majestic pose, hailing newcomers to her shores. An American flag writhed in the icy wind beside her. Beyond, an eternal sweep of buildings crowded the shore. Barges, tugboats, and steamers cruised into the harbor from every direction, the sheer number boggling Francesca's mind. She wondered where they had come from, if they transported people or goods, or if they had traveled as far as she had. She smiled for the second time that day. New York appeared impossibly grand and modern, so unlike her tiny, sea-scrubbed home, and she could hardly wait to explore it.

The noise onboard grew deafening as passengers cheered and sang, tears flowing down their cheeks. All hoped for more than the life they had left behind, and why shouldn't they want more? Hope swept through her. She'd left the pain behind, too, and now she had nothing but a grand adventure before her, a new life. It would all work out, somehow. She knew it would.

She pushed through the thick crowd, stepping on toes and dodging elbows in her side, and headed to her cabin to prepare for arrival. Maria lay in bed still, but her eyes were open.

"Are we there?"

Francesca nodded. "We'll be docking soon. I know you're weak, but we'll have to pretend you're healthy. We don't want them to turn us away."

Saying the words aloud set a school of minnows loose in her stomach. If they were denied entry into the country… She couldn't go back to her father's house, no matter what happened.

Maria rubbed her dark eyes and rolled into a sitting position. "Help me with my hair?"

Francesca combed through the snarls in her sister's dark hair, fluffed it into a Gibson Girl style with a knot on the top of her head, and pinned on a straw shepherdess hat that had seen its better days. She studied her work. While Maria's hair was neat, her eyes shined with fever, and rather than having her normal olive tone, her skin had a sickly gray pallor. It was the best Francesca could do.

"You'll have to put on the show of your life," she said softly. "For us."

Her sister shrugged, her frail shoulders rising and falling. "I'll do what I can."

Sweat beaded on Maria's brow as she focused on standing upright. The determination in her clenched jaw, the quiet sadness in her eyes reminded Francesca of another time, another world in their bedroom in Capo Mulini. Their father had returned home from the docks one night, reeking of alcohol. He'd raised one fist to Maria and knocked her across the room. She'd smacked her head against a cabinet, and it had taken all of her strength to get up, but she'd risen, managed to stand on wobbly legs, and walked to their bedroom before collapsing on the bed. Tears had streamed down her face, and blood, too, but she hadn't uttered a word to him. Not even a whimper of complaint. Within moments, she had passed out, blood pooling on her pillow.

Francesca had felt a fury she didn't know she was capable of that day. She'd wanted to hurt her father savagely, hear him cry out for mercy, but she knew what he would do should she act out her revenge. He would go at Maria again instead of her—out of spite. He knew Francesca loved her younger sister almost more than she loved herself. Instead, Francesca had locked them both in their bedroom and pulled their bed in front of the door to keep her father from barging in again. They'd listened to him crash around the house for a short while, knocking things over and swearing until, at last, all went silent.

Francesca had longed for her mother that night with a kind of desperation that left her hollow. She would always wonder what had happened to Mamma. Perhaps she had simply grown tired of the abuse and poverty and had left them all behind, or maybe something more sinister had happened. The town had been rife with gossip for nearly a year after she disappeared. Maria had been inconsolable with grief. Panicked as she'd watched her sister grow thin as a whisper, disappearing into a dark corner of her mind, Francesca had distracted her with a gift of a stray kitten, instructing her to give the animal a home in the outbuilding of Sister Alberta's yard. Maria had loved the little gray animal with all her might. Francesca knew their father would have killed the kitten, had they brought it home. It was as if he hadn't wanted them to love anything, the way he hadn't and couldn't.

Francesca led Maria to the deck, her limbs tingling as she took in the commotion of hundreds of immigrants stepping from the ship onto dry land, Manhattan Island at last. The rumble of boat engines and voices mixed with the sharp whistle of a winter wind. Seagulls swooped above the docks in search of scraps, and a fine mist hung around the building tops like a lacy shawl. Buildings that touched the sky. Francesca gaped at their enormity—and their number—and at the city noise that roared like ocean waves in the distance.

As the masses disembarked, the first and second class passengers, who had the luxury of being accounted for and verified on the ship, rushed away, their forms slowly fading from view until they were swallowed by the city. Third-class passengers weren't so lucky and were funneled into a line to board a ferry that would take them a short ride across the bay to Ellis Island. Francesca lugged their single travel case with one hand and slipped the other hand into Maria's. She was glad they'd had so few things to bring with them—one spare dress each, a sleeping gown, hair combs, a rosary, a few odd personal trinkets, and, of course, her precious medallion. Less to carry meant less to lose, should something happen. And things always had a way of happening.

She squeezed Maria's hand gently. "How are you feeling?"

Maria tilted her chin. "Like a shiny new coin."

Francesca smiled, grateful her sister still possessed her sense of humor. "Soon, we'll look back on all of this and barely remember the journey. We'll begin our new lives together. That's all that matters. *Sempre famiglia, sempre sorelle.*"

Maria managed a wan smile. "You mean always sisters, always in trouble."

Francesca giggled and kissed Maria on the cheek. "Not this time. Our luck is about to change."

Face as gray as the sky, her sister looked like she might faint. "I hope so."

An icy gale sliced through Francesca's too-thin coat and dress, and she flinched at the intensity of a cold she hadn't known existed. It didn't help Maria one bit to be exposed to the elements. Francesca glanced overhead at an ambivalent sky; the sun played coy as it slipped behind a dark curtain of clouds before sharing its golden face again.

She breathed deeply, trying to calm her fear and put worrisome scenarios out of her mind. Determined not to let her nerves show, she focused her gaze on the front of the line.

A man in a dark uniform with shiny brass buttons and hat shouted, "Next!"

The line moved forward little by little; immigrants met the inspector, answered a question, and boarded the ferry. After a half an hour of waiting, the sound of loud voices came from the back of the line. Many passengers turned to locate the source of the disturbance.

Curious, Francesca followed suit. Her eyes widened.

A guard directed an immigrant man to the front of the queue. "Herold, we've got a live one!" he called.

The immigrant yanked his arm away, and his dark eyes shifted back and forth like a trapped rabbit's.

Francesca pulled Maria closer as they passed.

"Let's get you accounted for, fella." The inspector at the front of the line extended his hand to attach a tag to the man's coat inscribed with a large X.

The immigrant blocked the inspector's hand. He shouted something in a foreign language and wrapped his arms tightly around his travel bag.

"Sir, everyone has to wear a tag." The inspector planted his feet several inches apart, as if he was bracing himself for impact. "Do you understand?"

The man shouted again, his eyes darting from the inspector to the other guards gathering around him. Sweat ran down the man's temples in spite of the frigid air. His clothes hung in rags from his gaunt frame, and an unwieldy black beard covered much of his face. He didn't seem stable, or perhaps he was simply afraid, starving, and exhausted. Like the rest of them.

"What's he doing?" Maria asked, exasperation filling her voice. "I need to lie down."

"*Lui è pazzo,*" Francesca whispered.

Maria nodded. "You're right. He does look crazy."

Cautiously, the inspector attempted to affix the tag one more time.

This time the immigrant threw a punch.

The inspector was faster. He grabbed the man's hand midswing and twisted it behind his back.

As a cry tore from the passenger's lips, the three guards standing by pounced on him. He kicked and screeched, at last biting someone, and nearly got away. Swiftly, the largest inspector caught the immigrant around his waist with one muscular arm and dragged him toward the ferry.

"I'll keep an eye on him," the inspector shouted as he held fast to the man. "But I'll need another guard to stand by."

A guard joined him, and the two forced the immigrant aboard.

A titter went through the crowd, and the fear in the air grew denser, more palpable. The message was clear: should the passenger receive an X on their tag, they were finished. Not everyone would be admitted to America, even if the ship captains had given them passage. They'd be detained at Ellis Island until they were to take the next ship home.

Francesca flinched as the man howled one last time before he disappeared from view. She wondered how he'd managed to get as far as he had. Now he would be sent back to Napoli at the ship captain's expense. One would think the captain might be more discerning, but as she glanced at her very pale, very ill sister, she was glad he wasn't.

The line inched closer, and at last, they reached the front.

"Name, nationality, and number," the inspector barked at her.

Before Francesca could answer, Maria began to cough, a deep rattling inside her lungs that went on for what felt like an eternity. When she caught her breath, she wiped her mouth, and the moisture streaming from her eyes, with her sleeve.

Not daring to meet the inspector's eye, Francesca patted her sister's back softly and offered her the water canteen.

Virgin Mother, per favore, don't let them send Maria home, she chanted in her head. If Maria was sent away, she'd have to go, too. She would never abandon Maria, not for all the world.

After a deep drink, her sister caught her breath and forced a limp smile. Francesca rested her hand lightly on her sister's back for support.

"Someone needs a doctor, I see." The inspector's meaty face scrunched into a scowl, but his eyes were kind.

"Yes." Francesca forced a playful grin. "She has small cold. She be better soon."

His eyes roamed over Francesca's face, full lips, and the swathe of dark curls swept atop her head. As he looked her over, she sensed, as she often did with men, that he found her attractive and it melted his defenses, even if only slightly.

"Name, nationality, and number," he repeated.

"Francesca and Maria Ricci, Sicily. 472 and 473."

The guard cross-checked the numbers with the ship registry and wrote their information on tags before attaching one to each of their coats.

"Go on." He waved them forward.

"Thank you." Francesca fluttered her eyelashes at him.

"You handled him nicely," Maria said as they stepped aboard.

Francesca laughed softly, and it felt good for a change. They had passed the next gateway between them and their new home, but it was not yet time to feel relief. She knew the hardest part was yet to come.

After a short ferry ride across the bay, they docked at the small island, and Francesca helped her sister disembark.

"Brave face, *cara mia*," she said.

Maria produced a small smile and squeezed her hand.

The building's dozens of windows, red brick, and large spires topped with copper domes gave it a formidable appearance, like an imperious guard standing watch over the bay and the city beyond, ever prepared to defend its shores. The rumors Francesca had heard about Ellis Island had frightened her and Maria so much that they'd almost abandoned their travel plans. But these were just rumors, she had convinced her sister, and people enjoyed nothing more than telling a good story. Yet as they joined a line that snaked toward the immigration center, the island's nickname flashed through her mind.

L'Isola delle Lacrime. Island of Tears.

A gust of wind tore over them, and Francesca wrapped her shawl more tightly around herself. As if the building weren't inhospitable enough, the weather did its best to rattle them, too.

As they made their way toward the entrance, throngs of men and women clogged the walkway and fanned across the lawn, waving signs and thrusting pamphlets into their faces in a swirl of confusion.

Peddlers on boats cruised the shore selling all sorts of foodstuffs. One offered a strange yellow food that curved like a letter *c*. Francesca had never seen it before, and judging by the short line to purchase it, she wasn't the only one. She took in the clusters of people spread out across the front walk and the lawn near the entrance, the signs, the unsmiling faces in the crowd. The chaotic flurry of activity and noise. Exhaustion settled over her like a fog.

"It feels like we're on exhibition," Maria said softly.

"I know," she said, stroking her sister's hand.

As they inched nearer to the door, a group of nuns spotted them and swooped upon them like a flock of seagulls. The tallest sister held a sign that read MISSIONE DI DAMA DI MOUNT CARMEL.

"*Miei amici*, have you come to America alone?" a round nun with cherry cheeks asked in Italian.

"I… Yes, we have," Francesca replied, grateful to hear her native tongue. "We're sisters."

"Is a relative going to greet you on the island?" Concern flickered in the nun's eyes.

Francesca paused, uncertain she should share their plans so openly with a stranger, nun or no. She glanced at Maria. Her sister seemed to read her thoughts and shrugged—and promptly fell into another coughing fit.

Registering their hesitation, the nun pressed a pamphlet into Francesca's hand. "We are here to help you. If you need anything, I visit each Tuesday. My name is Sister Elena."

"*Grazie, Sorella Elena.* But I'm hopeful all will be well."

The tallest nun looked at her then, a hawkish expression in her close-set eyes. "Hope can be a foolish sentiment, *signorina*. Be smart instead." She tapped her temple with her fingertip. "See us immediately if you have any trouble. Don't give your money to anyone for any reason, and ignore any untoward advances. Immigrants—especially women—make good targets."

Francesca swallowed hard and looked at Sister Elena again, hoping to find something soothing in her expression or some reason to discount the harsher nun's words.

Sister Elena smiled warmly as her wimple flapped in the wind. "Don't be afraid, be smart, as Sister Claretta so kindly said." She flicked a chastising look at her companion. "And remember, we're here on Tuesdays."

Francesca nodded, though the tall nun's advice sounded like a warning bell in her head.

"The line is finally moving." Maria's voice was thick with fatigue.

Francesca led them up the crowded walk and entered the ominous building.

Missionary accused of intimidating women at Ellis Island, acting as boardinghouse runner

James Mackle reports. *Manhattan Chronicle*.

March 10, 1902—Lutheran pastor J. R. Wagner of the Lutheran Immigrant Home was denied access to Ellis Island Friday morning. Mr. Wagner was called in on charges of forcing young women into places of employment against their will. In a detailed report, the minister was accused of accepting funds to funnel ignorant foreign women into "good Christian homes" as servants, as well as running an unsanitary boardinghouse.

Rumors are surfacing that other staff at the Ellis Island station may be involved in similar rings pushing immigrant women into brothels run by gangs in the city or in Philadelphia.

The National Women's Christian Temperance Union demands female inspectors be hired at the immigration station to promote the welfare of female immigrants. No progress has been made to that end.

"Something must be done to protect the young women who accept directives on good faith, but who are taken advantage of in a variety of ways," says Margaret Ellis. "A call for reform is absolutely necessary."

4

On Monday morning Alma dressed and pinned her hair to her head. Today it began—the daily trip to Ellis Island—and she felt wretched. She'd hardly slept the last two days; her mind had churned with every horrible scenario she could imagine. She headed downstairs for breakfast in the bierhaus, where her parents and Fritz were already gathered at the table. After pouring herself coffee, she reached for a slice of bread and *käse*, her favorite cheese spread. Both tasted like sawdust, but she forced them down anyway. She'd need the energy for a long day.

Her stepfather glanced over the rim of his coffee cup. "I know you aren't happy now, but you'll see this is best in time. You're a grown woman, Alma. If you won't marry, then you need to help the family. Besides, John Lambert will look out for you."

She gulped down the rest of her coffee, not trusting herself to deliver the polite agreement her stepfather wanted to hear. She *was* alone. She was an interloper in her own home, an unwanted nuisance Robert couldn't rid himself of fast enough. Though John Lambert was a regular customer at their bierhaus, the thought of seeing the inspector at Ellis Island didn't calm Alma's nerves in the least. The gentleman had hardly spoken to her in the past. She paused, midbite, suddenly realizing John Lambert was likely the person who had helped Robert secure the position for her. She sighed. She didn't even know what she'd be doing at the immigration station, and neither had her step-father. He didn't care as long as she was gone. She set down her bread, her stomach too uneasy to eat anything else.

Mama spread jam liberally on her bread. "It will be good for you. You'll learn service and gratitude."

Alma felt the sting of injustice and stood quickly to bring her dishes to the sink. She'd waited on her siblings and customers—and helped her parents—all her life. She knew nothing but service for others. But it would do her no good to argue. She knew it wouldn't change anything.

Her brother joined her at the sink, clapped her on the back. "It's six o'clock. Time to go, working girl."

She glared at Fritz while pulling on her overcoat, scarf, and gloves and followed him outdoors. Though the sun hadn't yet risen, lights flickered in bakery windows, and the scent of hot bread and cinnamon wafted on the air. Peddlers rolled their carts into position, eyes bleary and shoulders hunched beneath their coats. She didn't envy them. Working outside all winter meant facing few customers, bitter winds, and damp feet from piles of slush. She burrowed into her coat a bit deeper, tucking in her chin to protect it from the frosty air. She would be facing those bitter winds daily now, too, on her ferry-bound commute to Ellis Island. The thought blackened her already dark mood.

The sleepy neighborhoods melted away as they neared Bowery Street and Chatham Square. One could hardly call the tenements quiet, regardless of the time of day, but Chatham Square was a differ-ent affair entirely. The red-light district roared with trains suspended on tracks overhead, and colored lights flashed in the windows of gentlemen's clubs where scantily clad women traded their virtue for their wages. Flophouses and taverns, and some of the cheapest merchants in the city, populated the busy intersection. Alma did her best not to stare and attempted to put on the air of an experienced woman of the world.

As they passed Finnegan's, a man stumbled through the pub's door and landed face-first in a pile of garbage. Several prostitutes gathered outside the brothel next door and pointed and laughed at the drunk, who was now out cold.

Fritz chuckled. "That will hurt tomorrow, the moron."

Alma walked around the man's prostrate body, trying not to laugh.

Fritz crossed the street, and as she followed him, she eyed his wide shoulders, made larger from months of digging trenches for the soon-to-open subway trains. She was glad he'd insisted on escorting her all the way to the ferry her first week of work. Fritz was her favorite person in the world, her best friend. She had missed spending time with him lately, his new position as foreman keeping him busier than ever before. He was a natural leader and the hardest worker she knew, always had been. She couldn't help but beam with pride when she thought of all he'd accomplished, and the way his bosses had already noticed how capable he was. And in a small sense, she was proud to have helped him get there with their Italian lessons.

She tucked her hand in the crook of his arm and felt her churning stomach calm a little. "I'm glad you're here."

"It's a rough neighborhood. I couldn't let my little sister go it alone." He winked. They walked beneath a series of large pipes that hung overhead and ran the length of the street as far as the eye could see.

"What are all of those pipes?" she asked. "They weren't there the last time we walked through here."

"They're protecting bundles of wires." Fritz bounded up the steps to the train platform. "Electric cables had to be moved aboveground while we dig the trenches for the trains. You wouldn't believe the mess underground. That's why so much of the digging has to be done by hand. It's been a giant headache. One wrong move and half of the city loses power, or something catches fire."

"That's why you've had longer hours?"

"That's a big part of it, yes."

She didn't have the opportunity to venture out of their neighborhood very often beyond visiting the park or attending church, but it was impossible to miss the massive trenches where streets used to be. The construction clogged the flow of carriage traffic and even disrupted the steam-driven cable-car tracks in the Bowery. The whole city moaned about it constantly, and the disruption made headlines in the *New York Times*.

"Don't be afraid of the job, Al," her brother said as they settled into a seat. "We both know you need to feed that brilliant mind of yours. This will keep you busy. You're not happy at home."

She knew he was right; the last year had become unbearable, the confines of her life suffocating. Still, Ellis Island wasn't what she'd had in mind—at all. "But why did they have to send me there, of all places?" She wrinkled her nose.

He smiled and his light-blue eyes looked almost gray. "You'll get used to it, and maybe save a little of your own money. Wait until you see how great it feels. You'll be able to buy a new book or two."

That was Fritz, always seeing the brighter side, God love him.

Finally, the train pulled into the station, exhaling a great breath speckled with soot as it sputtered to a stop. She fell into step beside her brother, and after a few minutes' walk, they arrived at Battery Park, an expanse of greenery dotted with trees that sat on the rim of the bay. Only now, the ground had just begun to thaw, and the lawn was covered by patches of melting snow.

Fritz cupped her shoulders with his large hands. "I'll meet you here at seven thirty. If I'm not here right away, wait for me. I don't want you traveling through the Bowery alone."

She nodded glumly. The evening seemed an age away.

"Good luck." Fritz strode off at a clip, anxious to get to work on time.

With a feeble wave, Alma made her way carefully along the winding walk, slick with ice, toward Castle Garden. The legendary, circular sandstone fort perched on the very tip of Manhattan Island next to the water's edge, overlooking the agitated band of water where the Hudson met the East River. For all the horrible stories she'd heard about the former immigration center, it looked fairly innocuous, perhaps because in recent years it had become an aquarium. Next to it sat the barge office and the docks for the ferry, *Ellis Island*, where she had been told to board. She walked to the farthest point of the land and peered out at the bay. The water churned as barges and smaller boats ferried against the tide. In the not-so-distant horizon, the Statue of Liberty raised her beacon to the sky. And yet, Lady Liberty gave her back to Ellis Island. Squinting, Alma made out the immigration center's four domes in the haze of early morning light. Soon, the center would be like a second home to her.

Alma turned and walked to the docking house where people were beginning to cluster to board the ferry.

A young woman noticed Alma standing alone and within minutes had filled her in on how and where to board through the ferry house. Her name was Helene Bach, and she seemed kind and eager to talk so Alma listened politely, though she couldn't help but wish for a little peace and quiet before the trying day ahead.

Helene paused to put on another coat of lipstick, though she already had a perfect pink sheen on her lips. "The immigrants have to dock here first as well, be sorted, and ferried out to the immigration station. The waters are too shallow there at Ellis Island. All of the oyster beds and sandbars make the steamers run aground."

"Is that so?" Alma said, though she didn't care one way or the other how the immigrants arrived. Helene went on and on about a hundred other things Alma didn't need to know or care about, but nonetheless she continued to interject appropriate comments as if she were fascinated.

"The guards and inspectors do the sorting," Helene said. "Speaking of the staff, I'd say there are almost a thousand of us, but we're still sorely in need of help..."

Alma's eyes glazed over, and when the woman finally stopped talking, Alma thanked her and moved swiftly away to join the crowd gathering by the dock. She tried to put on a brave face, but everyone looked so important. Nurses in their white hats and dresses, and men in dark suits dotted with brass buttons and a gold badge above the left pocket. A handful of women wore light-gray skirts and aprons that looked exactly like Helene's. Alma wondered what their job was at the station.

Soon, the ferry pulled away from port and steamed across the inky waters of the bay. Alma watched the city awaken and change shape as she drifted farther from it. Buildings came to life, the lights flickering on, one by one, and she imagined the machinery within them growling as it roared to life. The sprawling skyline grew distant, smaller, and for the first time, Alma felt as if New York City, her thriving, crowded, awe-inspiring home, wasn't the center of the universe after all. It wasn't even the center of her world. Not anymore. Her life was about to change in immeasurable ways; she could feel it.

They docked a short time later. Heart in her throat, Alma

disembarked and made her way up the walk, pausing briefly to take in the elegant yet daunting building. She knew from the newspapers a fire had ravaged most of the wooden buildings on the island five years before, leaving a burnt shell of what had once been the immigrant processing center. Having learned from the catastrophe, the government had commissioned a new building made of red brick and limestone. She tilted her head back to gaze at the four large towers crowned with copper domes. The windows glowed weakly in the morning light as if awakening from a long slumber. The island had been infamous for centuries, a place to hang pirates and criminals, or runaway slaves. Perhaps spirits haunted the island still. She shivered at the thought. The last thing she needed right now was to ruminate on ghostly stories about the place that already frightened her.

Reluctantly, she entered the building to find one large room. Massive windows ran along the outer walls and threw light into the center of the room, where trunks and travel cases were stacked high. There were signs indicating train tickets and foodstuffs for sale, and many people milled about already. Employees scattered immediately upon entering to their respective offices and positions.

No one noticed her. No one directed her here or there. And she hadn't yet caught sight of John Lambert even from a distance. Instead, she watched everyone busy themselves, not having the faintest idea what to do.

Inhaling a deep breath, she mounted the staircase to the second floor. She paused to look up at the towering ceilings and massive chandeliers. Long benches ran through the center of the hall, stretching from east to west, and at the end of each row, a desk flanked the lines.

She turned abruptly to find a member of the staff and nearly stepped on a janitor toting a mop and bucket.

"I am so sorry, sir," she said. "It's my first day and I'm not sure where to go." The words tumbled from her lips.

The irritation drained from his face, leaving in its place disinterested brown eyes and a bored mouth that drooped down at the corners. "Do you know which department?"

"I'm looking for Mr. John Lambert," she replied.

"Come with me." He motioned her forward and strode briskly across the room.

Relieved, Alma clutched her skirt and dashed after him.

"There he is, the tall fellow." The janitor pointed to a row of desks. "Good luck, miss."

Relieved to see a familiar face, she headed to Lambert's desk. He seemed to be sorting through a stack of papers.

As she approached, she slowed and caught her breath. "Mr. Lambert, hello."

"Ah, yes, Robert's daughter," he replied in German. "It's nice to see you again, Alma." He eyed her closely, taking in her form and face, curiosity in his eyes. She squirmed beneath his gaze, knowing her plain appearance didn't add up to much.

Noticing her discomfort, he smiled, transforming his features to something vaguely attractive. "You'll be joining the matrons. Mrs. Keller will be your direct supervisor, then me of course, and Commissioner Fitchie."

"Thank you, for the opportunity, sir. My family is grateful." Even if she wasn't.

"Not at all. We need the help. The crowds are large and many of them are needy, as you will soon see. You'll barely have a moment to think, but the pay is reasonable, especially for a young woman."

Large crowds and barely a moment to think? It was all she could do not to groan audibly.

When John noticed her expression, he laid a hand on her shoulder. "Don't worry, Alma. It'll be fine. Just remember one thing. The immigrants aren't the brightest of human beings. Keep them in their place. You work for the U.S. government now, so you are their superior."

Her mouth went dry. Good God, he made them sound like ruffians.

"Now let's get you to where you need to be before the steamer arrives. Follow me."

As they walked rapidly to a room in the eastern wing, Alma clutched her handbag at her side, her stomach as tumultuous as ever.

When they reached the matron's office, he nodded. "Here we are. If you need anything at all, don't hesitate to ask. Good luck."

She felt a wave of gratitude at his kind offer of help and thanked him. With a last glance at the only familiar person in the building, she joined the stalwart woman with rigid posture standing in the middle of the room.

"Stand with the others." The matron gestured to a group of women in a line facing forward, awaiting instruction.

Alma looked quickly from one face to the next, taking inventory of who was there, what they wore, the way they stood erect, shoulders back. All ignored her but a pretty blond with dark eyes whose lips twitched into a trace of a smile. It was Helene, from earlier! Grateful there was at least one friendly face in the bunch, Alma felt her shoulders relax a fraction. She wished she'd been more open with the young woman on the ferry ride.

"Smith, O'Malley, Schmidt." The supervisor scanned her list. "You'll take the baggage room this week. Jansen, De Vries, and Baker, you'll take the medical inspections rooms. The rest of you will rotate between the registry office and the detainees' quarters."

Mrs. Keller reminded Alma a bit of her mother, both in stature and manner. She wore an apron tied securely over her full figure, not a single dark hair appeared out of place, and her bearing matched that of a militiaman. A well-worn track of worry lines furrowed the skin on her forehead, and a cross dangled from a chain around her neck. She looked just the sort who would spend hours praying to atone for sins—real and imagined.

"I'll take the registry office this week with our new hire," she barked. "And you are?"

"Alma Brauer, ma'am," she said. "Mr. Lambert sent me."

Her head jerked up sharply. "Mr. Lambert, you say? It wasn't the Immigration Bureau?"

"He knows my father, ma'am."

"I see." The lines on her supervisor's forehead deepened. "And do you know him well?"

Alma glanced at the girls in line. Every face presented a careful mask of disinterest, except a young woman with mousy-brown hair and a petite frame who glared openly at her. Alma flinched at the unexpected hostility.

"I don't know him well," she replied.

"Very good." Mrs. Keller clapped her hands sharply. "Ladies, hop to it. I'll see you at lunch." She motioned to Alma. "Let's find a uniform for you."

Alma struggled to keep pace with her supervisor as they darted down the hall.

"You're to report to me each morning at precisely seven forty-five for your day shifts," the woman called over her shoulder. "You'll work night shifts as well, once I put together a schedule. We work in rotation to make it fair for my girls. For the evening shifts, you're to report to me promptly at six thirty."

Alma's steps faltered. Night shifts? She would be spending nights on this godforsaken island? She swallowed a rush of panic and tried to focus on Mrs. Keller's instructions.

They turned the corner and stopped abruptly. Mrs. Keller unlocked a storage closet and rummaged around inside, producing a simple gray dress, apron, and cap. "This looks like it should fit. If not, I hope you know how to sew. It's the best we can do." She thrust the clothing into Alma's hands.

"Should I change now?" she asked.

"Of course, but let me give you a few quick instructions first. The rest you will have to learn as you go. Are you American born?"

Alma nodded, bewildered by the question. "I have lived here all my life."

The woman nodded curtly. "Good. Do you speak languages other than English? It isn't required, but it's one of the most helpful tools here, as you'll soon see."

Alma brightened. "Yes!"

The matron flinched at her enthusiasm. "There's no reason to shout."

"I'm sorry." She smiled for the first time all morning. "I speak German and English, as well as some Italian, and I understand a few Russian words and phrases."

The matron's brow lifted in surprise. "You'll use plenty of Italian and learn Russian quickly. They're sailing in by the thousands."

"I'll practice as often as I can," Alma said, breathless. "I love speaking in another language. It's like speaking in code. Like I get to be someone else. Languages fascinate me and—"

Her supervisor crossed her arms. "Are you quite through?"

Heat swept across Alma's cheeks. Why had she gone on like that?

"I'm sorry."

"As I was saying, your knowledge of foreign languages will come in handy." She took Alma's hand roughly and dropped three flag pins—German, Italian, and Russian—into her palm. "Pin these to your uniform. Matrons have many duties and they vary widely, depending on the day. We are explicitly responsible for helping female immigrants and their children and, at times, their entire families. Do not try to play the hero. You're not to take any chances, do you understand?"

She wondered what the woman meant by "taking chances," but instead of irritating her further, Alma nodded. "Yes, ma'am."

"We take lunch in the dining hall on the ground level between noon and one o'clock, if you have time, that is. There isn't much time to take breaks. We work very hard here. This is not a job for the weak-minded, or for silly girls, do you understand? Oh, and you may address me as Mrs. Keller."

"Yes, Mrs. Keller."

The more Alma learned, the more she wanted to leave. But complaining, or dwelling on the negative, wouldn't help the work go any faster, and it certainly wouldn't make her any friends—not that she expected to have many. She'd never been very good at it. She'd let her duties at home and her studies fill her time; it was far easier than the risk of being called too dull, not pretty enough, or too strange for being disinterested in the local gossip or who was courting whom. Emma had been one of her few friends, and even then, they'd drifted apart in recent months.

"Today you'll work with me in the registry office," Mrs. Keller continued. "We'll give out snacks to the children, help with inspections, and assist immigrants who need to be detained. The inspectors ask questions, review papers. They're trying to find reasons to deport the immigrants, you see. It's often a tense situation and very emotional for the passengers, so you need to follow instructions. We aren't here to make friends. We are here to keep our country safe from the worst kinds of people. We detain those who do not meet our standards for further questioning or until the next steamer is ready, and send them home immediately. Am I making myself clear?"

"Yes, Mrs. Keller."

"Commissioner Fitchie runs the show here. And Alma"—Mrs. Keller leaned in—"stay out of Fitchie's way. In fact, avoid him if you can. There are a few others you should avoid, but you'll learn that, in time, on your own." Her blue eyes clouded in warning.

Alma blinked. What did that mean? "I... Yes, Mrs. Keller."

"Get dressed in the toilets and meet me in the registry office in fifteen minutes." The matron didn't wait for a reply and shot off down the hallway.

Alma exhaled a breath. It was time to get to work.

5

Alma shifted from one foot to the other, trying to decide where to stand. She watched the inspectors diverge and go in all directions, shuffle papers, and verify their fountain pens and stamps had ink. Mrs. Keller had hurled a list of responsibilities at her, led her to the registry office, and promptly abandoned her to tend to some emergency. Alma glanced at the clock. At any moment, the immigrants would arrive, and what should she do then? Her gaze traveled the room once more and rested on John Lambert. He'd seemed a pleasant sort of man at the bierhaus, always had a kind word for her mother, and he'd been friendly with Alma that morning. Well, she would work hard to gain his favor, and perhaps he'd have something nice to report to her parents.

The sudden clamor of people entering the building arose from the baggage room on the floor below. She took in a steadying breath. She wished fervently Mrs. Keller's stout form would appear on the staircase, and a matron did appear—the woman with mousy-brown hair who had glared at her during the morning lineup. She spotted Alma and headed in her direction.

"What are you doing here?" the woman asked sharply.

Alma frowned. For some reason, this matron had taken an

instant dislike to her and she didn't know why. Or perhaps she was the unhappy sort who took out her life's frustrations on anyone standing in her path.

"I'm sorry… I'm not sure what to do, or where to stand."

"You'll float through this room much of the day and take orders from the inspectors or Mrs. Keller. I'll be working in here today, too. Oh, and don't flirt with the inspectors."

"I would never—"

"Some can be very charming," she cut in.

Alma frowned. Flirting with another employee couldn't be further from her mind.

"I'm Amy Terrine, by the way."

"Alma Brauer."

"Yes, I know." Without another word, Amy headed to the other side of the room and loitered near one of the inspector's desks.

Speaking of flirting. If Alma didn't know any better, she'd say Amy was flirting with the tall inspector near the doorway.

The sound of voices grew louder until it boomed against the vast ceiling, and in a matter of minutes, hundreds of immigrants flooded the hall. Europeans from various countries packed inside, wearing ornate garb with vivid colors made of hemp and dyed wool, headscarves, suspenders, and all manner of native dress. They wore hats with furry earflaps and leather vests and tall boots, or threadbare dresses covered by shawls and tattered cloaks. Face after face, nationality after nationality. Yet it wasn't the sight of the human faces in every shape, size, and color, or even their bizarre clothing, that struck Alma first—she was used to seeing such things in her own neighborhood—it was the stench. She choked on the smell of greasy hair and the ripe tang a body could acquire only after many days without bathing. But there was another scent, too, so strong and pungent it could only be attributed to one thing: the heady odor of garlic. It permeated the air as if it oozed from their pores.

She coughed into her sleeve, a fresh wave of irritation rippling through her. How could her parents send her to work in such a place? Among these people! She peered at the foreigners who queued in front of the inspectors' desks. Though the vast majority of the immigrants were men, there was also a line of women and children. A handful of women traveled alone. She remembered the brothels she'd passed that morning at Chatham Square, the way the prostitutes showed their breasts for coin. She wondered if some of these women would find themselves in the same situation. That's what she'd always heard about female immigrants from her gossiping neighbors—and her parents.

Noise echoed from the rafters and against the tiled floors. Every sound, every movement, and the hundreds of voices and crying children became deafening with nothing to absorb them. The benches in the registry office filled quickly, and the remaining immigrants waited in a long queue. Unsure of what she should be doing, Alma walked slowly along the line to see if anyone needed her. Many of the men stared back at her boldly, but she forced herself to hold her head high, never making eye contact. She heard Lambert's words echo in her mind. She was the one in a position of authority working for the government, even if her heart skipped wildly in her chest.

At the front of the line, a dark-haired woman gripped her son's hand and trained her eyes on the inspector's desk ahead. The little boy's pants stopped a few inches below his knees and several buttons had gone missing from his jacket, leaving gaping holes between his undershirt and vest. The child must be freezing, and the mother looked cold as well, without a woolen overcoat or proper gloves. Her eyes darted from the row of inspectors to Alma's face and back again, determined, focused.

Alma waved at the little boy, who smiled shyly and tucked his face into the fold of his mother's skirt. His mother didn't notice and yanked him forward as the line moved.

Alma circled back along the male line again, studying the passengers silently and trying to guess from which country they hailed. A man with long curls on either side of his ears clasped his hands and unclasped them several times. Shuffled his feet. For a brief instant, he met Alma's curious eye. Something flickered across his face and then his gaze darted back to the inspectors' desks, a muscle flexing along his jaw.

Alma paused, a realization dawning. *They were afraid.* The immigrants clutched their children and belongings like someone might snatch them from them. Fear painted lines across their foreheads, deepened the grooves around their mouths, and their nervous sweat permeated the air. She considered their predicament: abandoning their homes, their loved ones and friends, and perhaps fleeing some unmentionable atrocity. God knew what they had been through before they had decided to sail for America. Here, at Ellis Island, all of their fright, courage, and—most of all—hope funneled into this one moment: passing through the registry office to the stairwell, the exit to their freedom, and to possibilities of which they could only dream before now.

An unexpected wave of sympathy washed over her. She'd been so nervous all morning, she hadn't considered what the immigrants must feel, or even considered them at all. Why should she? She wound back toward the female line. One woman wept openly against another's shoulder. Alma chewed her lip, wondering what she could possibly do about it. But her job was to help, wasn't it?

"Can I help you with something, miss?" she asked.

The elder of the two women wrapped her arm around the other.

"My sister left 'er gentl'man behind in London." Her British accent was so thick it could have almost been another language. "She's gutt-ed. But there'll be other blokes. American ones." The woman grinned, revealing a mouth crowded with crooked teeth.

"Not like my Peter." The weeping woman blew her nose into a handkerchief.

"Will you stay in the city?" Alma asked.

The older sister shook her head. "Soon as we meet our bro-ver at the train, we're off to Boston. Away from the barmy man who—" She stopped short as if she realized she might be saying something she shouldn't. "We're happy to be here is all, miss. Free to do as we please."

"Well, good luck." Alma moved along the line, her mind churning. *Free to do as they pleased. Freedom.*

She hadn't given the word much thought before. What freedom was there in working in a factory—or a brothel—living with too many people cramped inside a very small apartment, scraping by on meager wages? There might be opportunities in America, but there were no guarantees. Alma wondered if she would risk so much, give up her home, possibly even her family, for the chance at a dream. It was an intriguing thought.

"Alma! Come here!" Mrs. Keller screeched, motioning her to a line where the doctors were conducting their initial exams.

Relieved to see her supervisor at last, she maneuvered swiftly through the crowd. "Yes, Mrs. Keller?"

"Show these women to the holding room. They've been flagged and need a thorough medical exam before inspection."

"Yes, Mrs. Keller," she said, regarding the two young women, both with dark eyes and curls and olive skin. Pretty if poor, and too thin. One of the sisters looked as if she was about to lose the contents of her stomach. Alma touched the woman's arm gently. "I'm Alma Brauer. Follow me."

The sister who seemed well nodded and slipped an arm around the other's waist.

Things didn't look good for them. Alma hoped she wouldn't have to be the one to tell them the bad news.

6

*I*nside the immigration center, a blast of warm air enveloped Francesca. She breathed a sigh of relief. Maria's hands had turned icy, and she looked weaker by the minute. Francesca slipped her free arm around her sister and watched the crowd amassing inside a large open room. Some joined a line that wound up the staircase while others filed to a podium where watchmen collected trunks and larger baggage. Still others loitered near food stalls on the back wall.

A burly guard pushed his way through the throngs and waved his arms overhead.

"Everyone must have a medical exam!" he shouted, shepherding them forward. "Leave any large baggage on the first floor, and follow the line upstairs to the registry room. Women and children, join the line on the left, men on the right."

Francesca put together enough of what he'd said to get the gist and joined her sister in the queue leading upstairs. "*Ave Maria*, look at all of the people."

Her sister grimaced and brought a hand to her forehead. "I'll never make it, Cesca. I need to sit down."

She squeezed Maria's hand. "Just a little further and I'll see about a doctor, I promise. You can do this."

Francesca didn't voice her fear: bringing too much attention to Maria's illness might give others cause to deem them unfit to enter the country. Her thoughts and worries twisted and turned over until she felt as if she'd go mad. If only the line would move faster.

When they reached the second floor two hours later, she heaved a sigh of exasperated relief. At last they could see the inspection stations. She stared at the enormous arched ceiling and the rows of benches, every last seat filled by someone waiting for their turn. A great cacophony of excitement and fatigue, and a palpable tension flowed around her. They all wondered if they'd be able to enter the country or instead, be packed up and shipped off. She turned her focus to Maria's grip to keep her grounded.

Ahead, a group of doctors skirted along each line, stopping to inspect every immigrant who entered the hall. When it was their turn, Francesca held her breath.

"Hello, I'm Doctor Smith. Your name?"

"Francesca Ricci, and this is my sister, Maria."

The doctor did a quick examination of Francesca's scalp, hands, and skin. "Stand very still." He leaned in, extending a metal rod with a hook on the end toward her. "I'm going to look into your eyes."

He touched her cheek with cold fingers.

She flinched.

"Do not move." In a swift movement, he pinched her eyelid between his thumb and forefinger, tucked the edge of his tool beneath the lip of her eye, and flipped up the flap of flesh to look inside.

"Oh!" She pulled away, shocked by both the pinch and the nearness of the doctor.

He conducted the same tests with Maria's scalp and skin, her eyes, studying Maria's movements closely. "Now, turn to your left." He used his finger to indicate the motion.

Maria turned—and swooned, crashing backward into Francesca.

Francesca caught her and cradled her sister's head against her shoulder. "She has a cold. She needs bed for some days, but she—"

"I can see that," he interrupted.

His steely tone sent her stomach plummeting. He rattled off some instructions, all the while frowning and motioning to a woman who stood in the wings.

The woman moved toward them swiftly. "Yes, sir, can I help?"

The doctor fired off more instructions to the young woman, who nodded and replied.

Francesca's heart thumped wildly. What was happening? When Maria began to cough again, this time the doctor covered his face with a handkerchief.

"Sir, I do not understand," Francesca said.

The woman beside him touched Maria's arm lightly. Her milky-white skin was sprayed with freckles, and she wore a set of flag pins attached to her blouse. "Hello, I'm Alma Brauer." Her gaze flicked to Francesca. "You are her sister?"

Francesca nodded, relieved by the woman's gentle nature.

"Follow me."

"Alma!" A stout, older woman in the same uniform shouted several things across the room. She waved her arm about and looked furious.

As confusion swirled around her, Francesca tried desperately to remain calm and met her sister's frightened eyes. She encircled Maria's waist with her arm. "It's all right, cara," she whispered.

The screeching older woman joined them, her blue eyes locked on Francesca like a hawk on its prey. "Are you both ill?"

Francesca shook her head. "My sister is ill."

The woman assessed Francesca quickly, and she spoke in rapid

English, not bothering to try to make herself understood. She said something to Alma Brauer who stood awkwardly beside her.

"Do you know what she's saying?" Francesca whispered in her sister's ear.

Maria frowned. "All I caught was the word 'problem.'"

Francesca forced a smile for the older woman's benefit, hoping to soften her, but when her steely gaze didn't waver, Francesca's stomach tumbled like a rock over a cliff.

"Follow Miss Brauer," the woman barked. "She will show you what to do."

"Where we go?" Francesca asked.

"This way," Alma said, leading them swiftly down the hall, farther and farther away from the registry office.

Francesca blinked away the tears stinging her eyes. She had to be strong for Maria, no matter what. She couldn't show her fear.

They joined a crowd of female immigrants corralled into a room at the end of the hall where they waited until the older woman from before joined them. She shouted instructions to the others dressed in identical aprons and gray skirts. Francesca stared at their tidy hair and dress, their folded hands. There was no room for error here, no mercy for those waiting to be released. Her stomach churned as she glanced at Alma Brauer on the supervisor's right. She seemed as afraid of the head matron as the immigrants were, judging by the expression on her face.

"I am Mrs. Keller, supervisor here," the woman barked. "Take a seat." She motioned to the immigrants to be seated on the benches along the back wall.

They moved sluggishly to the benches, pulling their children or mothers or sisters with them. One by one, Mrs. Keller asked them questions, scratched something on her notebook, and directed them to a woman on her staff.

"Your names?"

Francesca replied and the woman marked her paper.

When Mrs. Keller said something else, Maria replied weakly. "We no understand. *Siamo Italianas.*"

"Alma," the supervisor said, motioning to the freckled matron with the flag pins. "Help me with this."

"*Parli italiano?*" Alma asked.

"You speak Italian," Francesca replied, a flood of relief washing over her. "What's happening? My sister has a little cold, but I'm not sick."

"I'm going to take you to the medical examination room. It's required when an immigrant is ill. Follow me, please."

Her Italian was stilted and her tone unnatural, but all that mattered was Francesca understood—they were going to examine Maria further, and there was no denying how sick she was. Heart in her throat, Francesca tugged Maria along, stumbling after Alma as they walked through the hall. They joined another smaller group of women who waited in a line along the wall outside what must be the examination room.

One at a time, the immigrants were called inside.

An inspector passing in the hallway stopped to assess the mass of women and made his way over to Alma. They spoke, but Francesca noticed the way he looked past her at the women in line and then at Francesca, far longer than she liked. She met his eye with a hard stare and grabbed Maria's hand in solidarity.

The examination room door opened and a man called, "Next!"

"You'll enter together since you're family, and don't worry, I'll translate for you," Alma said, ushering them inside.

The inspector in the hall slipped in behind them and stood at the back of the room, where two other men clutched a pen and pad of paper.

The room was cold and nondescript with bare walls. Several large cabinets with glass doors and shelving ran along the wall and were filled with metal instruments of some kind. A long, flat table sat in the middle of the room, and two desks flanked it. Heart pounding against her rib cage, Francesca stood beside her sister awkwardly, awaiting instruction.

She squeezed Maria's hand, and as she did, her sister's terrible cough reemerged.

One of the doctors strode toward them and touched Maria's forehead. He frowned, pulled an instrument Francesca had never seen before from around his neck, put it in his ears, and placed a metal disk to her sister's back. "Breathe deeply, please."

Alma translated and Maria tried to do as she was told, but she couldn't inhale without coughing.

The doctor tried listening to her chest again. "There's fluid in your lungs." After feeling along her throat and looking in Maria's ears, he conferred with the other men at the desk, who scribbled furiously, taking down all he said.

"Miss Ricci, I'll need you to open your blouse."

When Alma explained, Maria's eyes widened in surprise. "Cesca?" she rasped. "They want me to undress, in a room full of men?" Another terrible cough followed.

"This is indecent!" Francesca protested in Italian. "My sister has never been exposed."

Alma placed a hand on Maria's shoulder. "Don't worry, they're all doctors." Though her actions were mollifying, her expression was not. The matron's skin had paled even more, if that were possible, and she seemed as shocked as they were.

Francesca shook her head. "No, I'm not going to ask my sister to do something she doesn't want to do."

Miss Brauer translated for the doctors.

"If they won't do what we tell them to do, they'll be deported," the inspector chimed in without waiting for Francesca to reply.

Francesca flinched at the word she understood too well: *deported*. The rumors she'd heard about this wretched place raced through her mind, and her hands began to shake. They must do what was asked of them or be deported, indecent or not.

"What's it to be?" the doctor pressed. "We're very busy, as you can see."

Francesca nodded at Maria. "We don't have a choice, *cara*."

With effort, Maria unbuttoned her blouse, revealing a worn corset barely able to do its job. With her breasts exposed, the doctor placed his instrument on her heart. She startled at his touch and looked as if she might swoon again. The doctor held her arm to steady her.

"It's all right," Francesca said. "I'm here." She glanced at Alma, whose cheeks blushed as red as cherries.

The doctors spoke rapidly, wrote a few things down, and at last, Maria was given the order to get dressed.

"We'll have a look at you next, miss," the doctor said to Francesca, pulling out a fresh sheet of paper from his notebook.

When Alma translated, Francesca stepped backward. This was absurd. She wasn't even sick! She glanced at each of the men and met the eye of the inspector, who bared the smallest hint of a smile. He wanted to send her back to Italy, the bastard. Furious that she had no choice, she hastily unbuttoned her blouse. It wasn't the first time she'd been naked in front of a man, but she had chosen when to trade her body for something she wanted. It had happened only twice before and she had no regrets. She'd learned a few things in the process, and knowledge was something she was beginning to respect.

As the doctor went through the same series of tests, she willed her face to go blank. To trade a horrible life for a new one was worth it. This moment was inconsequential in the end. She looked from one doctor at the table to the other, and finally the inspector. He was the only person who would meet her eye. He studied her so intently he seemed to be considering her character. Perhaps that was something inspectors must do: decide if the immigrant was worthy of entering their country, based on the shape and size of their breasts. Based upon their reactions to indecent probing. She felt like a zoo animal on display.

Before being given permission, she swatted the doctor away and buttoned her blouse. "I am well."

He regarded her sternly but didn't protest. After writing a few more things, he gave the paper to Alma.

The matron visibly relaxed and led them out of the room. "We'll need to check in with Mrs. Keller again, now that the examination is finished. This way."

The muscles in Francesca's shoulders eased a fraction even as Maria leaned heavily on her. They took slow, measured steps back to the holding room. As they entered, the supervisor took the sheet from Alma, glancing briefly from Francesca to her sister, and wrote something down on her list.

"I just have a few more questions for you," Mrs. Keller said. "Why did you come to America?"

"We must leave Capo Mulini," Francesca replied. "Leave Sicilia."

The matron nodded. "And why is it you had to leave?"

"My father... I... Family problems. We go to America, far from Sicilia."

"Are you waiting for a male relative to meet you? A brother or uncle, a fiancé perhaps?"

"No."

The woman asked something else.

Francesca frowned. "I don't understand."

Another immigrant waiting for inspection snickered, and in Italian she said, "She wants to know if you're a whore."

Francesca blushed hotly. "No!"

Mrs. Keller nodded. "Very good." As she continued too quickly in English, Francesca looked to Alma to translate.

When the questions were finished, the woman nodded. "Well then, I'm afraid we'll have to send you home, Miss Ricci. You can't enter the country without either a male family member to greet you or an employment letter."

Francesca felt her insides sliding like jars on an uneven shelf. She glanced at Maria, eyes wide, no longer trying to cover her panic. Her sister's graceful features crumpled and she began to weep.

Francesca couldn't bear Maria's anguish. She bit her lip, holding back her own tears. There had to be another way.

"We have uncle in Chicago." Francesca spit out the lie before it fully formed in her mind. She hadn't the slightest idea how far away the city was and how much time it would buy her. The only thing she knew about Chicago was that other than New York, many Sicilians had emigrated there. "Nico Ricci is my uncle," she continued. "I send letter so he meet us."

"You should contact him immediately," Alma replied.

"Send a telegram today," the supervisor demanded.

In Italian, Alma added, "Better be quick about it. It may take some time for your uncle to travel here to meet you."

"Thank you." Francesca swallowed her panic. It would buy her time to think of something else, some other means to stay in the country.

Mrs. Keller said something to Alma, who glanced from Maria

to Francesca, uncertain. The reply to Alma's hesitation was sharp, and the young matron's face drained of color. She scurried quickly to Maria's side, joining another matron, each taking one of Maria's elbows.

In an instant, they shepherded her sister toward the door.

"Where you take her?" Francesca shrieked and raced to catch up with them.

"Cesca!" Maria called over her shoulder. "What are they doing?"

"Where my sister go?" Francesca demanded, fear seizing her chest. "Where she go, I go!"

Hands gripped Francesca's shoulders. When she shook them off, a second matron joined in, dragging Francesca backward.

"Maria!" she cried, attempting to wrestle away. "I'm coming! I'll find you!" They wouldn't send her sister home to Italy without telling her, would they? The thought was all the impetus she needed. With all her strength, Francesca shoved the women off and dashed after her.

Maria's sobs echoed in the corridor. "Cesca!"

Pain tore at Francesca's heart. "I'm here. I'm coming!"

When only an arm's length between them remained, hands closed over Francesca's arms on either side once again.

"Calm yourself!" a matron said in Italian, wrenching Francesca toward the holding room. "Your sister is going to the infirmary, where she'll get proper care. You'll have a chance to visit. We need to limit contagion. This is for your safety, too."

Tears gathered in Francesca's throat. "But I can't leave her. She needs me."

She didn't voice aloud a terrible thought worming its way into her head—that she didn't know how they would treat Maria once out of her sight.

"We'll take good care of her," the woman replied. "Now, follow Mrs. Edgars. She'll get you set up in the detainees' quarters, where you can rest."

Francesca cast a look over her shoulder at Maria's retreating form and imagined her sister's forlorn pleas, the fear in her eyes. She couldn't bear it. She stumbled blindly as she was led away, trying to get a hold of herself, but it was no use.

Not knowing when she'd see Maria again, or how long they had before they'd be thrown out of the country like garbage, Francesca felt her tears, at last, broke free.

7

*A*lma watched the exchange between the sisters, a stone in her throat. She hated this job. Watching sisters be separated, sending people home as their hopes were destroyed. How was she to stomach it day after day? This was her new life, and her stepfather's doing. He'd banished her here, and there was absolutely nothing she could do to change it.

Per Mrs. Keller's instructions, she led the sickly Maria Ricci to the new hospital, though she didn't know what to do from there. She'd have to make things up as she went.

They exited the main building, wrapping their overcoats tightly around their shoulders against the cold, and walked the distance to the narrow land bridge that connected newly constructed Island Two to the main island. Much of the area was still under construction, and Alma had heard plans were already in place to build a third island. When she'd learned the original hospital was a ferry permanently docked at the entrance to the main building, she'd been horrified. The ship must have rocked on the waves, day in and day out, making the terribly ill passengers worse. At least now there was a proper facility where the sick could recover.

As they walked around a mound of dirt, Maria stumbled on a

loose rock. Alma caught her arm and steadied her, supporting the bulk of her weight. "Are you all right?"

Maria grunted and paused to catch her breath. "My sister. Where are they taking her?"

"It's all right, Miss Ricci. Your sister is being shown to her sleeping quarters. There's no need to worry about her."

Maria's hollow gaze met hers. "They won't send her away, will they? Back to Italy?"

"I think it's best you focus on getting well," Alma replied, not willing to commit one way or the other. In truth, she didn't know if Francesca would be sent home.

"Please, help my sister," Maria implored her. "Without me, she has no one."

"But she has you," Alma replied lightly. And how was she supposed to help this woman anyway? Francesca Ricci was one of hundreds Alma had met only that morning, never mind the thousands she would meet flowing through the door each week. It was an impossible request, and she was not prepared to bend the rules, especially as a new employee. Especially for an immigrant.

When Maria said nothing, Alma added, "She has your uncle in Chicago, too."

"Yes, my uncle," Maria said, voice flat.

Alma's brow raised at her tone. She wondered if there really was an uncle. She cast a sidelong glance at Maria, taking in her pallid skin and withering frame, and wondered how this young woman on the edge of death still worried more for her sister's welfare than her own.

When they reached the hospital, a nurse met them at the door and shifted Maria into her arms. Relieved, Alma gave the nurse what limited information she had from the inspection.

"Miss Brauer"—Maria lay a bony hand on Alma's shoulder—"do

you have a sister or brother? What would you do for them, if they needed you? If you were all they had in the world. I'm begging you, please help Cesca get to New York."

Alma thought of Fritz and petite Else, of teaching Klaus how to play cards, and even Greta and their constant bickering. Should something happen to any of them—should Fritz be hurt on the job site—pain tore through her at the very idea. She nodded grimly. She would try to help, if she could. But only if it didn't interfere with her work.

Relief passed over Maria's face, and she allowed the nurse to take her inside.

Despite the wind blowing off the water and the damp cold of a winter afternoon on the verge of spring, Alma walked slowly back to the registry office, Maria Ricci's skeletal face lodged firmly in her mind.

Alma survived her first few days of work and tried to adapt to the frenetic rhythm of her new routine. She learned quickly that the immigration center was nothing more than a long rectangle. The two largest rooms and the majority of the building spanned the middle of the rectangle, and the remaining rooms were tucked into pockets at either end of the building and along its sides. The first floor was primarily the baggage room and a train ticket counter, a currency exchange booth for those who needed American dollars and coins, and a handful of food vendors selling sandwiches and other smaller, easy-to-carry items. The second floor housed the registry room where immigrants were accounted for; the detainees' quarters, where they bathed and slept; and also many offices for clerks, interpreters, and medical examinations.

As she'd learned while escorting Maria, the hospital and laundry buildings sat apart on Island Two. Alma had been assigned to the hospital wing only once so far, and she was glad of it. She'd watched the sick struggle for breath or battle aches in their limbs and felt, for the first time in her life, completely helpless, smaller even than the quiet, plain barmaid she'd been raised to be. The sight of the ill and dying had followed her home that night and crept into her dreams, and she'd awoken with one thing on her mind—the Ricci sisters.

Alma rubbed her tired eyes and peered across the bay through the ferry window. After her conversation with Maria, Alma knew Francesca was lying when she'd said she had an uncle in Chicago. The sisters were alone. Alma decided she had nothing to gain by trying to help these women, no matter what she'd agreed to. Maria's health had not improved—Alma had seen it for herself in the infirmary yesterday—and if she were to...not make it, Francesca would be deported immediately after her sister's passing.

As the ferry pulled into port, Alma overheard a nurse say that not only had a steamship already docked in Manhattan in the evening after the center had closed and was forced to hold all passengers aboard until morning, but they were expecting a second ship later that day. Alma sighed. One day, she hoped she would acclimate to the fatigue and the noise, to the endless stream of starving, desperate people, but today wasn't that day. She ached for silence and the peace of home. She'd never considered her home quiet—far from it, in fact—but now it felt like a haven. Wearily, she headed inside, climbed a flight of stairs, and walked past the registry room to the matron's office. She lined up with the other matrons for their morning check-in and, after, headed to her post. Alma had learned not to become too comfortable in one position. Mrs. Keller rarely let her remain in a post for long.

As the passengers flooded inside, Alma stared at the sea of humanity, overwhelmed. Their voices and coughs, the shuffling of feet and the scrape of their baggage on the floor—it all combined into one great roar against the rafters. The crush of bodies warmed the drafty building until a light haze of hot breath and body odor enveloped them. And this was only one shipload of people. Day after day they came, an endless stream like a faucet left on by accident. She imagined where they might travel to after they left Ellis Island. Another city, or to the country? Philadelphia or Boston? New Jersey? The West? Ruminating on these thoughts, Alma prepared a tray of milk cups and crackers for the children and carried the precarious contents up the stairs to the registry room.

"Excuse me!" She projected her voice, but her words dissipated instantly in the din of hundreds of people moving through the building. Balancing the tray with care, she angled her body away from the crowd. If someone bumped her, she'd make a terrific mess. She was already a bumbler; the last thing she needed was a little help in that direction.

She made a turn through the room, distributing the snacks. As she neared a poor mother with five children, she realized the two older boys were shouting at each other and their mother hissed threats in what sounded like Russian. The older boy ignored her and shoved his younger brother, both crashing into a man behind them. Frustrated, their mother jerked one boy away from the other, but the older son wrenched out of her grasp. The sudden movement knocked the mother off-kilter and she stumbled sideways, hitting Alma's arm.

Alma lurched forward. Milk sloshed over the rims of each cup and pooled in the bottom of her tray, but she managed not to dump the entire load on the floor or herself. She breathed a sigh of relief.

The mother scolded her sons and boxed them on the ears.

Alma concentrated on the woman's speech, listening intently to its cadence and trying to pick out some word or phrase in Russian she recognized. She noticed the way the syllables clawed at the back of the throat and rolled into a sensual growl. When she heard the word for children, she smiled broadly. She'd understood something! Proud of herself and excited by the prospect of tuning her ear to a new language, she vowed to add an hour of Russian to her Italian studies in the evenings.

The mother looked at Alma, her eyes contrite, and said something unintelligible.

"Do not worry," Alma said in Russian. It was a phrase she'd learned from Mr. Chernov, who ran the deli on Delancey Street.

Something like relief crossed the woman's face. She'd been embarrassed by her children's behavior. As she unleashed another stream of Russian, Alma stared at her blankly, not understanding a word. Instead, she shrugged and held up a cup of milk.

The mother smiled weakly and nodded in thanks as Alma gave each child milk and crackers. She'd scarcely finished when the nasal shriek she was coming to recognize sliced across the room.

"Alma!" Mrs. Keller staggered toward her, arms loaded with ledgers and a stack of paper. "I need a hand here. Helene can pass out the crackers and milk."

Helene, the friendly blond matron, made a face behind Mrs. Keller's back as she took the tray.

Alma bit her tongue to keep from laughing. Perhaps she'd made a new friend.

"Here, run these to the clerk and see them filed." Mrs. Keller dumped the stack of ledgers and papers in Alma's arms. "When you're finished, I'll need your help with an Austrian family in the game room."

"Yes, Mrs. Keller." Alma huffed under the weight of the bundle. Would her supervisor interrupt every task today? Alma had been running all morning, leaving a half-finished trail behind her.

"Don't dawdle," Mrs. Keller barked, rushing off in another direction.

Helene smiled. "Would you like to have lunch later?"

"Yes," Alma said, relieved to have someone to show her around who didn't feel the need to shout orders or sneer at her. "That would be nice."

"Great. But you'd better get going or the dragon lady will come after you." Helene nodded in Mrs. Keller's direction.

Alma smiled. "I guess I'd better. See you at lunch."

Helene winked and melted into the crowd.

Alma hurried in the direction of the clerk's office, weaving around people playing marbles in the halls, a man staring listlessly at a photo in his hand, and a pack of children gathered around a spinning top. Other staff rushed to their destinations as if their feet were on fire. "No time to waste, too much to do" was the silent mantra that seemed to fuel them all.

She turned the corner leading to the clerk's office—and promptly crashed into someone. The papers took flight and fluttered to the floor.

"No!" she cried, imagining Mrs. Keller's face. She would have to realphabetize them all. She groaned as she set upon the pages, hating her constant clumsiness.

"I'm so sorry." A man in a neat dark suit bent to the floor to help.

Noting instantly he was Irish by his accent, Alma glanced at him. A pair of bright-blue eyes looked back at her.

"I can manage, thank you," she said, sighing.

He ignored her cool dismissal and bent to help her anyway. "It's all right, miss. I never mind helping a lady in trouble."

She couldn't help but laugh. She wouldn't exactly call herself a lady in trouble.

His ears burned bright red at her laughter. "Please, let me help." He shuffled the papers into an even stack and began to sort through them. "You look too young to be working here. You must be new."

"I am, yes." She made a stack of the letter A's. "Though I am not quite as young as you think." She gave him the ghost of a smile. "I'll be twenty-two soon."

"You need a cane, do you? Why, you're practically an old maid."

Alma giggled. It had been ages since she'd had anything to laugh about. She'd forgotten how good it felt, the warmth bubbling up inside her and the lightness of spirit that followed. She was grateful for it today, even if it was with an Irishman.

"I'm Jeremy Kerrigan," he offered. "An interpreter in the office behind you, just there."

An interpreter? But he was Irish. The Irish didn't care about school and learning as far as she knew. They were tough more than intelligent. Bawdy more than refined. She studied his face more closely. His eyes shone with good humor, his ivory skin was dotted with freckles, and dark waves framed his face. He looked older than her, perhaps around thirty years old or so.

"What languages do you speak?" she asked, trying to keep the surprise from her voice.

"Russian, Croatian, and Bulgarian. English, o' course. Also a little Chinese."

He spoke five languages! She should be so lucky. Forgetting her assumptions about him, she felt the first inklings of excitement. "Do you work with the clerks as well?"

"I do," he said, handing her the letters G through M.

"That's where I was headed," she replied.

"Why don't I deliver them for you? I caused the mess, after all."

He was kind *and* friendly. And he clearly had a keen mind if he knew all of those languages. She studied his face an instant and then continued sorting through the letter *F*. "Are you sure?"

"I insist. But only if you tell me your name."

She couldn't help but return his smile. "I'm Alma Brauer."

"Good then, Alma Brauer. Glad to meet you."

As they sifted through the last of the papers, she wanted to tell him she enjoyed linguistics, too. That she spent all of her free time studying, even on Sundays after church and at the family picnic, and longed to learn more. But they hardly knew each other, and she felt her familiar timidity creep over her.

"That's the last of it." Alma gave Jeremy *Q* through *Z*. "I should be going. My supervisor is probably wondering what's keeping me." In fact, Mrs. Keller was probably purple in the face by now.

He smiled. "Well then, have a fine day. Perhaps I will see you again soon, Alma Brauer."

She stood and in Russian said, "Good day, Jeremy Kerrigan."

When his eyebrows arched in surprise, she suppressed a smile, turned on her heel, and walked away.

8

Though the day dawned bright and cold, the days were growing longer and soon spring would arrive, thawing the ground and painting the landscape with color. Alma wondered if she'd make it through spring at Ellis Island. She'd spent the last two weeks learning the various positions, but she didn't feel less overwhelmed. She'd worked hard all day, helped her mother and sisters in the evenings, and after, stayed up late into the night to study. Working in a shoe factory where she didn't have to deal with people all day was beginning to look more appealing. Her head throbbed and a light nausea swept over her from lack of sleep. Someday soon, she'd have to negotiate with Mama about giving her time to herself, the way Fritz had when he'd started work on the subway. It was only fair. Alma was exhausted and deserved a break.

That morning, everyone moved about deliberately and methodically at the immigration center as always, like the well-oiled gears of a clock. Alma had been running around, trying to keep up with Mrs. Keller's demands. As she walked back to the matron's office in search of her supervisor, she stopped outside the library. A small boy lay on the floor beside the door, kicking and wailing and doing his best to coerce his mother into giving him what he wanted. The woman bent over him, cajoling and pleading, and likely promising him treats she might never be able to deliver, judging by the looks of her ragged dress and dingy hat. The child cried louder, rolled into a ball, and gave his mother his back. Several people had now gathered, waiting for them to move so they could use the library.

"You need to control your child, ma'am," Alma blurted out, clinging to her last threads of patience. "If he doesn't stop this behavior, you'll have to go to the detainees' quarters, or outside, until he calms down. A library is meant to be quiet."

"Why don't you try to control him?" the woman replied, scowling at Alma. She scooped up her son and led him away while he screamed over his mother's shoulder.

Those waiting entered the library without so much as a look of gratitude thrown Alma's way.

She exhaled slowly to control her temper. She was tired of Mrs. Keller ordering her about like a child and interrupting her every task. Tired of the starving and needy who filled the center day after day. Tired of people in general. Alma rubbed her face with her hands. She craved silence. Outside the matron's office, she rested her head against the wall and closed her eyes. She just needed a minute to herself.

"Alma, you're just the person I was looking for." Mrs. Keller breezed through the door. "I need you in the hospital. There's a larger load than usual today, and they could use our help. Hop to it. I'll be right behind you with a group who are allowed to visit their relatives today." She shooed Alma with her hands.

The day wasn't off to a good start and now this—working in the hospital, her least favorite post. She groaned inwardly, remembering the stench of the sick and the medicines, the way the patients turned restlessly in their beds. She felt so helpless among the ill and dying that it made her anxious.

She headed outdoors, across the land bridge to the hospital, pausing briefly to peer at the bay and at Lady Liberty, framed by a blue sky. At least it was a sunny day. As she entered the building, the odor she'd remembered hit her nose and the brilliant blue sky faded from her mind.

Nurses zipped about from patient to patient, at times trailing a doctor. Alma imagined all the work they must do on the doctor's behalf—likely most of it. She thought she had it bad as a matron. At least her duties didn't entail changing bedpans and swabbing wounds or pustules. Shuddering, she continued through the room, nearly bumping into Amy Terrine, the rude matron she'd been avoiding since the day she'd met her.

Alma did her best to ignore Amy and checked in with each of the doctors to see if they needed help with translations or anything else. She assisted a Prussian woman and also a nurse distributing a pile of clean bandages to each of the stations. When she reached the station nearest Maria Ricci, Alma looked down at the young woman, who lay very still in her bed. Her skin was waxen, her eyes ringed deeply with purple and blue, and though her chest rose and fell, Alma could hear the rattling in her lungs with each breath.

She definitely wasn't better. Alma felt a tinge of regret for Francesca.

"Shouldn't you be doing something?" Amy called over Alma's shoulder. "We aren't supposed to fraternize with the patients."

Alma wanted to tell Amy to stick it in her ear. Instead, she smiled at her and in a sarcastic tone said, "Thanks, Amy. I didn't know that."

Amy returned an equally sweet smile. "Nurse Rose asked if we'd help clean the medicine trays." She pointed to a series of carts laden with a variety of bottles and medical utensils.

Alma began at the front of the room with a rag and a bucket of soapy water. When the trays were clean, she dried them and replaced the bottles. Those that were empty she set aside so the nurses knew which needed to be refilled.

"What do you think you're doing?" Amy demanded. "I told you to clean the trays! Now you've gone and mixed up which bottles belonged at which station."

"I thought they'd like to know which needed filling—"

Amy placed her hands on her hips. "So you thought you'd take it upon yourself to make a decision that isn't yours to make? What if they used the wrong bottle on the wrong patient? You think you're better than the rest of us, don't you. I knew that the minute I laid eyes on you. You're so aloof. Speak all of those languages like you're some kind prodigy or something. You talk down to the rest of us."

Alma frowned. She talked as if she read a lot of books, with proper vocabulary, was all. She couldn't help it if this woman felt insecure about that. Alma thought of the suitors her parents had brought around the house. They'd always been threatened by a woman who knew too many things, who could speak to a wide variety of topics. Frustrated, she crossed her arms over her chest. "What are you talking about? I've never spoken to you outside of the most basic communication for our duties."

"It's the way you look at us. You never talk to any of us."

Alma's stomach clenched. Did the others feel this way, too? Did Helene? Alma didn't think so; Helene had always approached her first. Regardless, Alma had never intentionally given anyone the cold shoulder. She was just a little timid and quiet-natured, and completely inundated by the sheer number of people with whom she came into contact each day. Perhaps she needed to put in more of an effort to be friendly. The thought only exhausted her more. "That wasn't my intention. I—"

"I really don't care," Amy said. "Just return the bottles to their rightful place or you'll be in for it."

Flustered, Alma gathered the bottles she'd set aside and began putting them back on what she hoped were the right tray. She reddened as she realized Amy was right. She couldn't remember which bottles went where.

Amy, meanwhile, stood with her arms crossed, glaring at Alma.

When Alma reached for the last bottle, she stared at it a moment, trying to remember where it had come from, and at last set it down on the tray stationed beside bed number three. That was it then. She blew out a breath and reached for the bucket of soapy water.

"Now, empty the bucket and clean it out." Amy gave her a light shove toward the sink.

Water slopped over the edge onto the front of Alma's dress and ran down her legs, soaking her hosiery.

Something inside her snapped. She dropped the bucket, whirled around, and shoved Amy back.

The matron's eyes widened as she stumbled backward, knocking into a large bottle of iodine behind her.

Alma watched in horror as the bottle tipped and crashed to the floor, shattering to pieces. The brown liquid that had once been inside it oozed over the tiles.

"Good going!" Amy hissed.

"You pushed me first," Alma protested—and cringed. She sounded like her brother Klaus after he'd just whopped Else on the arm. She looked past Amy and saw that Mrs. Keller had arrived, escorting a group of immigrants from the detainees' quarters for visitation. Worse still, Francesca Ricci had slipped in sometime before them without permission and had gone unnoticed, but now, she stared at Alma. She'd seen Alma's terrible behavior.

Alma ducked her head, her anger draining away. Where had that come from? She should have ignored Amy, who seemed generally grumpy all the time. Quarreling with that woman wasn't worth getting into trouble.

As Amy clambered to her feet, she started in on a barrage of insults but not before Mrs. Keller and a nurse made a beeline toward them.

"What is going on here!" Mrs. Keller said, crossing her arms. "Amy, go to the registry office at once."

Amy tossed a scathing look at Alma and headed straight for the door.

When the matron had disappeared from view, Mrs. Keller took Alma by the arm. "You'll only get a couple of warnings, and this is one of them. Do you hear me? I can't have my girls destroying property and wasting the medical staff's time. And the very last thing I need is to have my girls bickering amongst themselves. We have work to do! Is that clear?"

Alma blinked rapidly against the tears pricking her eyes. She wanted to hide in her bedroom, under the covers, away from this infernal place.

"Pardon me, *signora*—madam." Francesca stood at Alma's elbow. "Miss Brauer did not break medicine. I did, and they shout at each other. I'm very sorry."

Alma's mouth fell open and she started to protest, but Francesca shook her head slightly, silencing her.

"Well then," Mrs. Keller snapped. "You'd better watch yourself in the hospital, or you won't be permitted to return. The medicine is very expensive."

"Yes, I am sorry." Francesca's tone was contrite, but her eyes were steely. She didn't like Mrs. Keller much, that was clear.

Alma didn't understand. Why would Francesca help her? She had nothing to gain by it but scorn.

A doctor motioned for Mrs. Keller to join him, and she skated quickly to his side, the incident of the iodine bottle forgotten, at least for the time being.

Francesca looked at Alma, her dark eyes turning soft, but said nothing.

"Thank you," Alma whispered. "I'm so tired, and I—I don't know what came over me. I... Why did you lie for me?"

In Italian, Francesca replied, "Sometimes we need a little help, sì? And you were kind to my sister."

Alma hadn't been kind, she'd been matter-of-fact, efficient like always, and as she looked upon this immigrant woman who had sailed so far from home with so little, and who still put herself at risk for another person she hardly knew, Alma felt ashamed of her own behavior from the morning and over the last weeks. At her lack of compassion for what the immigrants must endure, both in their own countries and here, at the center and beyond. The tears she'd managed to hold back all morning filled her eyes.

"I'd like some time with Maria," Francesca said softly.

"Of course." She swallowed hard. "Thank you."

While Alma cleaned up the mess she'd made, she watched Francesca Ricci dab her sister's brow with a cloth and pray beside her bed, from a distance.

9

Francesca slept poorly in the detainees' quarters, just as she had on the ship. Women packed into row after row of metal bunks suspended over each other that squeaked with every movement. But she didn't complain. At least she had a warm, dry place to sleep, even if she was being held against her will, trapped at the border in some in-between existence while Maria recovered. Only, her sister's health didn't appear to be improving. In fact, the last time Francesca saw her, it had taken all of her self-control not to weep. She scrubbed her face in the communal sink and pulled on her cloak. She'd have another chance to visit Maria that morning, but she dreaded what she would find.

She trudged through the center and made her way outdoors to the hospital, a matron at her side. She weaved through the hospital beds, her legs filled with lead. When she reached Maria's bedside, she sat and stared bleakly at her sister's ravaged frame. How could everything have gone so wrong? The voyage across the ocean was perilous for Maria's health, the medical exam humiliating, and now Francesca wasn't sure the inspectors would allow them to enter the country after Maria's recovery. Francesca rested her forehead against her sister's arm. But Maria's health came first, above all else. If Francesca lost her—

She couldn't face what lay ahead without her sister.

She kissed her medallion, offering up a Hail Mary. She had to be strong, for both of them. She'd always had to be. She looked across the room at the rows of beds, filled with the sick. Nurses flitted around the infirmary, clearing bedpans, adjusting pillows, and administering medicines. One nurse pushed a trolley cart with covered dishes from the cafeteria. Coughing and moaning mixed with the rumble of lowered voices. Francesca would give anything to leave this place. Anything at all.

A doctor who had been tending another patient headed in her direction, Alma Brauer at his side. Their paths kept crossing. The young matron was reserved, but Francesca was grateful to her both for translating when she needed it and for showing concern when she'd realized how sick Maria was. She could see Alma was new to her job and didn't like it much. Francesca hoped she might take advantage of that fact somehow, if she needed to.

"*Buongiorno*, Francesca," Alma said.

She nodded.

"Good morning," the doctor said, sitting beside the bed. "Let's see how our patient is doing."

As he checked Maria's pulse and temperature, and listened to her heart and lungs, Francesca watched his expression change from concern to certainty to pity. She crossed her arms to brace herself and moved quickly away to the window. The Statue of Liberty was the only dot of color in a scene washed entirely gray. She felt as if she were sinking into it, as if she might disappear inside of the gloom. She watched a flock of gulls as they alighted on the narrow lawn. Some pecked at the cold ground while others waddled across the walk in search of scraps of food left behind. Her gaze wandered to the harbor waters swishing insistently against a shore she had longed for more than anything in her entire life, until now.

Cara Maria. Santa Maria, she whispered. *Per favore, save her. Save my sister.*

The doctor murmured something behind her about no improvements and the high fever, and she receded into her mind to escape, falling back in time to three years ago. At home, the summer days stretched out before her like a languorous cat in a shaft of sunlight. Papa was out at sea for long hours during the summer season, and she and Maria had all the time in the world to do as they pleased. A particular afternoon arose in her memory, one full of laughter and a sun hotter than a frying pan. They'd stolen blood oranges from an orchard down the lane and run barefoot all the way to the rocky beach near the boat docks. They hadn't eaten much more than fish in days, so the sweet fruit tasted like heaven.

Maria combed the beach, searching for crabs and sea creatures unfortunate enough to wash ashore. Francesca trailed behind, staring out to sea. Somewhere amid the waves, their father cast his nets and smoked cigarettes, cursing his wretched life. She closed her eyes and tilted her face to the sun, willing it to burn away every thought of him. One day, she would find a way to leave, and she would bring Maria with her. They'd say goodbye to the fearful nights they spent locked in their bedroom once and for all.

"There's a fish!" Maria cried, her dark head bent over a bowl of rock with a tidal pool inside it. "We need to move him or he'll die. Come see!"

She looked at the fish to humor Maria. "There's seaweed in there, too," she pointed out. "He won't die." She sat down on the edge of the rock and swirled her feet in the pool, using her toe to nudge the trapped creature.

"A gull will swallow him up by morning. I'm going to find something to scoop him out." Maria scrambled to her feet and headed toward the docks.

Francesca gathered her skirt and bunched it into her arms, walked across the sand, then waded out into the surf. The salt water stung the cuts on her feet from running barefoot, but she didn't care. She felt alive in the water. One day, the water would be her escape, take her far from this island that held nothing for her but a small life of poverty and pain. She deserved more—they both did—after all they'd endured.

Moments later, Maria raced past her into the sea, carrying an old piece of netting, the rescued fish flapping inside it in agony. She splashed as she ran, her skirts twisting between her legs, and stumbled, falling face-first into the surf. The fish flew from her hands and disappeared into the water. Maria surfaced a moment later, sputtering in the waves.

Francesca laughed at the spectacle. "That's *some* rescuing."

"He's free now, isn't he?" Her sister giggled, water streaming down her face in rivulets.

Francesca waded over to help her to her feet.

"Why can't we stay like this forever?" Maria slung her arm around Francesca's shoulder as they fought the surf.

She had stared into her sister's laughing dark eyes, the identical shade of their mother's. "Happy, you mean?"

"Happy," Maria had replied, smiling.

When they'd reached the shore, she'd shouted, "I'll race you to Sister Alberta's!"

Maria had squealed as Francesca bolted, running as fast as she could across the mounds of sand that burned the soles of their feet.

The memory faded, and Francesca blinked rapidly, focusing on a blurred view of New York Harbor. Pain battered her insides until she felt bruised. She didn't know how she would do this without her sister.

How she would survive the pain. Without Maria, every promise of the new life before her felt hollow. Francesca's knees buckled, and she reached for the back of the chair to steady herself.

"*Sono qui.* I'm here," Alma said softly. "If you need anything."

She glanced at the young woman, whose blue eyes were contrite. "*Grazie.* I..." She choked on her emotion.

"Miss Ricci?" The doctor cleared his throat.

"Yes," she rasped, forcing herself to meet his eye.

"You should make your goodbyes as soon as possible. I'm afraid there's not much time left. I'm sorry."

"No." Francesca shook her head vehemently. "I can't. There must be something we can do. No, no, no." She sank to her knees beside the bed, buried her face in the blanket. Maria stirred and slipped her hand onto Francesca's head, sparking a flood of tears. Francesca didn't bother to hide them this time. Her beloved sister was dying and very soon would be gone.

Though the doctor gave the nurse a paper from his notebook, as if it was just another transaction to write up and dismiss, his eyes were apologetic, his tone soft. "I'm sorry, miss. There's nothing else we can do." Without delay, he crossed the room to tend to another patient.

Francesca stared at Alma, looking for a sign that this wasn't real, that it was all some horrible mistake.

But the young woman paled at the spectacle of Francesca's grief. "If there's any way I can help you..."

Francesca stared at the matron, unable to speak. She had no words, couldn't conjure a coherent thought. Make her lips form sentences. Maria. Her Maria. *Ave Maria.*

Francesca took her sister's hand in hers and brought it to her lips. "*Dio mio,* Maria, how on earth am I to do any of this without you?"

At the sound of her sister's voice, Maria's eyes fluttered open. Slowly, she turned her head. Through waxy lips she pushed out the words, "You're brave, Cesca. And strong. You don't need anyone."

"How can you say that? I've never done a single thing without you." The pain welled from deep within and shook Francesca violently. Her dearest, most precious sister would slip from this world to become a memory, just as her mother had. If there was a God, he wouldn't do this. He wouldn't take everyone from her. He wouldn't leave her so completely bereft.

"*Ti amo*," Maria gasped. "Tell Alberta... Send my love."

A sob tore from Francesca's lips. "Please, Maria. Please don't go. I need you here with me." She wept so hard she felt she'd be sick. "I love you."

She looked at her sister's face, swept the damp hair from her forehead, and for a moment saw her five-year-old sister racing after her down the street at home, golden sunlight pouring over her, and the two of them collapsing together into a heap, giggling. She saw little Maria chasing gulls on the beach and collecting shells. The two of them snuggled deeply under the covers of their little bed to keep warm. Together—always. *Sempre sorelle.* Soon, there would only be one.

Maria placed her skeletal hand, light as a butterfly, on Francesca's arm. "Promise me." She paused a long moment to catch her breath. "Promise me, Cesca."

"Anything," she rasped, tears streaming down her cheeks.

"Promise me you will thrive in America, for us both."

10

Alma left the hospital anguished and unsettled. She'd never witnessed anyone dying before, or seen a person so utterly bereft. And for better or worse, she'd begun to care for the Ricci sisters' welfare. She went back to her work in the registry office and spent scarcely an hour there when she felt a hand on her shoulder.

"The boss wants you in the hospital again," said a matron whom Alma had yet to meet. "There's an Italian, gone off the rails. She's screaming and no one knows what she's saying. A young woman."

Alma's stomach dropped. Maria must have passed.

"I'll go now," she said and hurried outdoors to the hospital and through the sick ward.

As she neared Maria's bed, several nurses stood by on alert and one reached for Francesca. She had thrown herself across her sister's body and slapped away the hands that reached to detain her. She pawed at the shroud covering Maria's face.

Alma's heart squeezed as she raced to the young woman's side. "Miss Ricci—Francesca, please, they must prepare her for...for burial." She stumbled over the Italian.

"She hasn't seen a priest," Francesca's voice rasped. Her nose ran, and deep purple circles ringed her eyes. "She didn't have her last rites. Please, she needs a priest to pray over her. She deserves to go to heaven!" Her voice became shrill. "They've put this tag on her like she's…like she's…"

"Don't remove it," Alma said calmly, glancing at the tag around Maria's wrist. "It's an identity tag." She reached for Francesca and, in an uncharacteristic display of affection, laid a hand on her back. Francesca didn't pull away, and Alma exhaled a small breath. "I will see about a priest now. I'm so sorry, Francesca."

"Where will they bury her?" she asked, the frenzied look in her eyes beginning to ebb.

"I'm not sure…" Alma stammered. "I'll ask."

Francesca nodded and relaxed her hold on her sister a fraction.

Alma quickly relayed Francesca's requests in English to the nurses.

"Why didn't she request a priest for last rites before now?" the chief nurse said, closing her eyes and pinching the bridge of her nose with her thumb and forefinger. "We have one here today. Leslie," she called to another nurse, "fetch the priest."

"Yes, Nurse Rose." The woman hurried away.

"Do you know where she'll be buried?" Alma asked.

"She's Catholic, so probably at St. Mark's in Brooklyn."

"What are they saying?" Francesca demanded, not daring to move away from her position beside her sister.

"It's all right," Alma said. "A priest is on his way. He'll pray with you and then you must say goodbye, Francesca. Maria will be buried properly, in a Catholic cemetery."

Francesca's tears began anew. "Thank you."

Though Francesca seemed relieved, Alma felt vaguely nauseous. After her sister was buried, Francesca would be deported—Alma knew the uncle from Chicago was a fabrication—but perhaps that was best, now that she was alone. Surely she had some family other than her father in Sicily? Alma glanced at the still feet poking out from beneath the edge of the blanket. Maybe Francesca didn't have anyone else. Wasn't that what Maria had intimated? Alma didn't know what to say, what to do to console Francesca, so she looked on quietly, hoping against hope that she had guessed incorrectly and this Nico Ricci from Chicago would appear. Perhaps then Francesca could begin again.

Francesca stared at the empty bed where her sister had taken her final breath. No sign of Maria remained—no indentation in the pillow, no wisps of dark hair strewn across the blanket. The odors of cough syrups, cinnamon, and quinine tablets were replaced by vinegar so strong it burned her nostrils. She knew she would be escorted from the hospital momentarily, but she couldn't seem to find the strength to leave on her own.

They'd taken Maria away to a cemetery filled with lost souls who didn't belong in America, or in their homelands. Francesca closed her eyes against her imaginings of her sister in a coffin, deep underground, forgotten and unknown by everyone but her. Pain surged through her, and yet she couldn't seem to shed another tear. It was as if her heart had been buried, too. The only comfort had come from the priest who had prayed for Maria's soul. Though Francesca wasn't certain prayers helped, she knew Maria believed in their power, and this simple act would have made her happy.

"I'd like to help you with your paperwork." Alma Brauer interrupted her thoughts.

Had she been there all along? Francesca squinted as if peering through a haze. Yes, Alma had remained by her side through the prayer and while Maria had been taken away. Though Francesca didn't really know the young woman, she was grateful for her calming presence. Everyone else had gone.

"You've had no luck contacting your uncle in Chicago, sì?" Alma asked.

Francesca stared at the matron without replying; her grief paralyzed her, echoed inside her as if she were an empty vessel. But Alma waited patiently for her, hands folded.

At last, Francesca managed to shake her head.

Alma replied in slow but steady Italian, "I know this is difficult for you, but I'll do everything I can to help. The Catholic missions will be here tomorrow and can make inquiries on your behalf."

Francesca noted the softness in the young woman's blue eyes. Alma Brauer was the first person in America who didn't treat Francesca like she was beneath her.

"*Grazie*. I—" Francesca bit her lip, trying to decide if she should reveal the truth. Soon, the inspectors would discover there was no uncle, but Alma might help her. What did she have to lose now? Everything in the world that mattered to her was gone.

"I lied."

"I'm sorry?" Alma's fair brow puckered.

"I don't have an uncle in Chicago. But I can't go back to Sicilia. I have to try to find a way to stay..." Her throat closed again.

"Signorina Ricci—"

She wiped her eyes on her sleeve. "Francesca, *per favore*."

Alma's face twisted into a pained expression. She sat on the edge of the bed, resting her hands on her lap. "But you don't have a choice. Without a male relative—"

"I'll show you why I can't go back," Francesca said. She glanced around the room and decided it didn't matter if a few sick female patients and a handful of nurses saw her bared shoulders and back. She unbuttoned the collar of her dress and the front panel. Slipping the dress over her shoulders, she turned, giving Alma a view of her back.

Alma gasped.

"My father burned my skin with the rod he used to stir the fire. He set his sights on Maria one evening, so I shoved him as hard as I could. He hit his head on the counter, and blood dripped into his eyes. He didn't like that." Her hands began to tremble at the memory, how he'd hurt Maria so often. Francesca wondered if he would be glad her sister was gone, or if he'd regret not having such an easy target. He'd despised Maria's gentle nature, the way she'd give in to anything seemed to make him all the more furious.

But no one could ever hurt her again, said a voice in her head.

"How could a father be so vicious?" Alma whispered as she looked at the scar twisting over the plane of Francesca's back. "You were brave. To leave, I mean. I admire your courage."

Francesca averted her eyes, buttoning her dress quickly. She couldn't stand to see pity painted so plainly on the young woman's face. It would be Francesca's undoing, break her into pieces, steal the last of her bravado and then fling it out to sea. Sister Alberta had been so good at caring for her and Maria, swiftly and tenderly without a word about the wounds at their father's hand. Within minutes, Sister would tend to the cuts and bruises—the blood—dry their tears, and have them stuffed with sugared lemon peels. Somehow, the nun sensed she shouldn't discuss the horrible acts. To say them aloud made their father's behavior more real and gave the sisters' pain too much power.

"If I return, one day he will kill me." Francesca's tone was flat, matter-of-fact.

Alma fiddled with the sash on her apron, chewed her nail, and began to pace. She paused a moment and began to pace again. "I shouldn't do this. I could lose... Well, never mind that." She met Francesca's eye and said, "I'll try to find a way to get you through inspections somehow. If you will trust me. Can you do that?"

Francesca studied the matron's face, her skin as white as milk except the freckles dotting her nose. Alma Brauer couldn't be any more different from her, and perhaps the young woman didn't even like her, but none of that mattered. Not when Francesca had so few options, so little hope.

She fastened the buttons on her dress, stood, and slowly nodded her consent. "I can do that."

She had no choice but to take this stranger at her word.

11

The following morning, Alma stalked across the lawn of the immigration center with purpose. She was eager to speak with the Catholic missionaries on Francesca's behalf but had little time before reporting to Mrs. Keller. Alma didn't know what she was thinking, offering to help an immigrant break the law. *Break the law!* She was an employee of the government, yet she was helping a woman enter the country illegally! An Italian, no less. She could be fired—or worse. But Francesca Ricci had put herself in harm's way, lying for Alma that day in the hospital when she'd pushed Amy, and Francesca had had nothing to gain but more grief. Never mind that the poor woman deserved a little good fortune. Alma had thought of nothing but the terrible scar all evening. She'd awoken convinced she must help Francesca in whatever way she could; Alma couldn't condemn her to that life.

On the lawn, many groups waved signs to offer the immigrants their services, forming an impenetrable wall of people. She recognized Margaret Ellis of the WCTU and knew a little about the YMCA, the Salvation Army, the Hebrew Immigrant Aid Society, and the Daughters of the American Revolution, but she didn't know anything about the other groups who helped direct the immigrants upon arrival. Though *help* was a dubious word. Some truly did wish to help the immigrants, while others were there merely to champion their own causes or prey on the immigrants' desperation and ignorance. Alma pushed past them, imagining how the immigrants must feel at seeing the hordes rushing around them, speaking in a language they didn't understand.

At last she spotted a shivering mass of black-and-white-clad women, the tallest nun waving a large sign with uneven block lettering: MISSIONE DI DAMA DI MOUNT CARMEL. She started in their direction as another gust of wind rushed over the crowd. The sign's too-large face caught the wind, knocking the nun who held it off her feet. The sisters gathered around her, their black habits fluttering in the breeze. They looked like a flock of crows around a fallen bird. Alma watched as they promptly hoisted the nun to her feet and plucked at her clothing, her limbs, and readjusted her head covering. When they decided all was well, they turned their attention to a ferry pulling into the dock. A new load of immigrants had arrived.

She ran the rest of the way, eager to complete her errand before they were all too busy.

"Good morning," she said, rubbing her hands together for warmth.

"I wouldn't call it good," the tall nun who held the sign grumbled. "Spring should be here already."

"Sister Claretta!" A rounder nun with cherry cheeks glared at the other. "I'll give you the weather isn't agreeable, but remember your gratitude. And your manners."

Sister Claretta huffed, a cloud of warm breath forming instantly in the air. "I'll remember my gratitude when I've had some hot coffee."

The round nun proffered a smile. "I'm Sister Elena. What can we do for you, dear?"

"I've come on behalf of a young woman named Francesca Ricci," Alma said. "She's from Sicily, speaks some English. Her sister has just died."

Sister Claretta's scowl softened. "Here on the island?"

Alma nodded, remembering Francesca's hollow eyes.

"God rest her soul," Sister Elena said, making the sign of the cross. "Does she need us to say prayers over the body?"

"A priest was called and the body will be buried soon. Truthfully, I'm here to ask about how I might help Francesca enter the country."

"There's no one to account for her?" Sister Claretta asked. "No family?"

Alma moved aside to make way for a group of bedraggled immigrants making their way to the front door. Several were so thin, their cheekbones protruded grotesquely, sending a ripple of pity through her. She couldn't get used to the sight of misery and starvation. Day after day, they came from afar where it appeared no one was content or well fed. The longer she worked at Ellis Island, the more she understood why her neighborhood was filled to bursting—who could blame these people for not wanting something more, a better life here in America?

"Miss Ricci has no one. No family," Alma said, dragging her gaze away from the crowd entering the building. Soon, Mrs. Keller would be looking for her.

Sister Claretta's dark eyes hardened. "Then there's nothing we can do."

"Please," Alma said. "There must be something. She was abused horribly at home. I can't bear to see her sent back to Italy."

Sister Elena's eyes filled with sympathy. "Our housing is full for at least six to eight weeks or more, but we can try to help her find a space at a boardinghouse. First you'll have to find a way to get her through inspections."

"How will I do that?"

"You'll have to be inventive," Sister Claretta said, looking past Alma at a group of men working their way toward the nuns.

Alma's shoulders slumped. Short of talking Francesca into marrying a stranger, Alma had no ideas. The only other option was an employment waiver, and Francesca should have had it secured before she set sail. Alma would have to tell her the truth about her very limited options—tomorrow. For now, Alma couldn't bear to see the despair on the young woman's face again.

She thanked the nuns and dashed indoors. She tried to hurry, winding through the people flooding inside the building, but she was forced to slow. Her height offered her an advantage, and she peered over the heads of many in the crowd, looking for a place she might squeeze through more easily. She was going to be late to morning lineup, and Mrs. Keller wouldn't hesitate to let her have it. Sighing, she decided to take a different hallway, though it was in the wrong direction from the matron's office. She could circle back around outside through the side door to avoid the cramped corridors.

She'd made a good choice. This section of the building was empty. As she reached the end of the corridor, she saw two gentlemen in a corner outside of the commissioner's office, deep in conversation. She recognized Commissioner Fitchie's squat frame leaning against the door, but she didn't know the other gentleman, who was tall and wore a nice suit. He clearly wasn't a part of the staff at Ellis Island. She tried not to eavesdrop as she approached, but their voices carried and it was impossible not to hear.

"He's on my back, Tom," the unknown man said. "I don't know what to tell you."

Fitchie frowned, and his whole demeanor changed. "They don't need to know, is all I'm saying," he said, tone clipped. "There's a whole lot of meddling in Washington right now, and it's none of their damned business. Roosevelt doesn't know the first thing about what goes on here, and he couldn't possibly understand what we're dealing with."

Alma's ears perked up at the mention of their new president. She'd heard rumors President Roosevelt was displeased with how immigration operations were running, in particular at Ellis Island.

"I know, but you can't carry on as you have, or it will be your neck," the man said, just as Alma passed them in the hall.

"Good morning," she said brightly, pretending not to have heard anything.

"Young lady, good morning," the commissioner said. "Wait a minute."

"Yes, sir?" She paused, trying to keep her face neutral. She could feel the other man's eyes on her.

"I need you to run an errand for me." Commissioner Fitchie disappeared into his office and returned with a sealed envelope. "See to it that Inspector Lambert receives this, would you? And don't open it."

"Of course. Yes, sir."

She hurried away, envelope in hand, wondering what she was delivering to John Lambert. And what in the world did the mystery man mean by "you can't carry on as you have, or it will be your neck"?

Mind whirring, she set out to find John Lambert.

Missing paper trail points to undocumented immigrants, fraud

James Mackle reports. *Manhattan Chronicle*.

March 25, 1902—Many counts of fraud have been uncovered at Ellis Island, according to a report by special investigator Inspector Peter Thompson. The inspector discovered last week the ledger used to track citizenship is missing large numbers of certificates, believed to have been sold to passengers that were unlikely to be admitted into the country. The ledger works on a two-part system in which the certificate is torn from a stub where details about the newly arrived immigrant are documented. Months' worth of stubs appear blank.

Though supervising staff allegedly monitors the daily inspection of immigrants, it is now believed there is collusion at the highest level. Commissioner Thomas Fitchie, upon returning from his vacation, demanded his employees not share information with Inspector Thompson or his staff.

12

*A*lma hardly acknowledged Fritz beside her on the train ride home. She thought of Francesca's dark eyes, the hunger there, and an air of courage about her that Alma had never seen in anyone before, much less felt herself. She had always dreamed of another life, beyond the walls of the bierhaus, beyond the banality of becoming a wife to a man who found her merely acceptable. She dreamed of something that felt less like being dutiful and more like *living*: visiting Germany one day to see her parents' homeland and meet her cousins and aunts they'd left behind, studying to her heart's content, and perhaps working away from the home doing something she chose that excited her. But she had so few choices of her own, so little control over her own life, even now.

And if she had dreams in her small life, she couldn't deny others had dreams, too. Francesca's struggle had made that clear. The young woman deserved a chance at truly living, not just surviving.

The train whistle sounded, and a great whoosh of steam filled the air. Alma followed Fritz to the platform and down the steps to Chatham Square.

"What's got you so preoccupied?" he asked, breaking the silence.

"I don't know." She hiked her skirts and stepped over a pile of gray snow.

"Sure you do," he said. "Come on, Al, tell me."

"You seemed lost in your thoughts, too." She dodged his question, unsure she wanted to tell him about Francesca. She knew her brother would caution her to mind her own business, to put her head down and work hard to gain her boss's favor rather than help a stranger who might very well cause trouble for her. That was the only way Fritz knew how to be—work more efficiently and harder than everyone else. He took great pride in the way he gained the trust of the men who worked below him as well as those ranked above him, and he deserved it. His promotion last year had felt like the obvious next step. Alma firmly believed he would be running the IRT one day in the not-too-distant future. She took pride in working hard as well, but it didn't define who she was, not the way it did him.

"We're talking about going on strike." A cloud gathered in his light-blue eyes. "We deserve a pay raise, and we want a few hours knocked off the workday. Conditions are dangerous." He sighed. "They have to give us something, or people will walk."

"When?"

He shrugged. "I'm not sure yet, but it looks like it's a certainty if negotiations don't go well. I've worked my tail off. We all deserve a raise, damn them." He ran a hand over his tired eyes. "My boss is already talking about moving me into the offices at some point, away from the job site, which is great for me, but I can't leave my men to fend for themselves."

"They're lucky to have you."

Fritz grabbed her hand to lead her around a puddle. "I hope so. They know the conditions are dangerous at the very least. We don't need another fire underground." He exhaled tiredly. "I still can't believe we lost those men."

Alma had been horrified to hear the news of the fire underground in one of the new subway trenches. Two months ago, a worker had lit a candle to warm his freezing hands, igniting five hundred pounds of dynamite. Five people died instantly, and another one hundred were severely injured before the blaze had been put out. Fritz had come home covered in ash. His eyes were still haunted when he spoke of it.

"You're doing good work, Fritz. Surely the bosses will come around," she said, squeezing his hand. "I'm so proud of you."

He smiled gratefully. "Always my biggest fan, aren't you?"

She returned his smile.

They walked another street block, the sounds of the city filling the silence between them in an orchestra of bicycle bells, horses' hooves, and the patter of boots on sidewalk.

"Now your turn," Fritz said. "What happened at work?"

She hesitated, parsing out what she wanted to share, and decided on the truth. If she was his biggest fan, he was hers, and she trusted him implicitly. "There's a young woman from Sicily who needs a male relative to sign for her so she can enter the country, but she doesn't have any. She's a sad case, Fritz. I feel for her. Her other option is to have an employer sign work papers for her." Alma's pace faltered. "What if..." But why hadn't she thought of it before? She threw a side-long glance at her brother.

"What?" he asked.

"Do you think Mama would sign an employment waiver?"

His sandy eyebrows knitted together. "For this woman? Do you even know what kind of person you're dealing with? She might have connections to a gang. You know how the Italians get mixed up in that Mafia business."

"I believe she's trustworthy, if that's what you mean. And not every Italian joins street gangs, Fritz." If he met Francesca, he would see just how absurd his assumption was.

"I'm just trying to make a point. You don't know anything about this woman."

"She's alone. Her sister just died in the hospital on the island. Her father is a terrible man, beat her at times, which is why she left home in the first place. Her life depended on it."

His jaw clenched. "Sounds like a real bastard. I don't know how a man can knock a woman about and look himself in the eye."

"She has braved all sorts of things and came all this way to start over," she continued.

"I don't know, Al." He moved around a stack of empty crates left on the street outside a fruit market. "Would we be responsible for her?"

She shrugged. "I don't think so. People lose work all the time, and they aren't shipped out of the country when that happens. They just get another job. I think it's only a matter of getting her here, into the city. After that, she's free to do as she pleases."

Even if Mama didn't want to hire Francesca legitimately, the employment waiver could at least get the young woman off the island. And if anyone cared to question Francesca's "employer," Mama could say Francesca worked there a short time before Mama realized she didn't need her after all and let her go.

They turned onto their street as a brisk wind blasted between a row of apartment buildings and rushed down the street. A few hats flew into the air, and several forgotten pamphlets caught the current and rode the wind far above their heads. Alma braced herself and picked up her pace.

"Good luck talking *Robert* into it." Fritz enunciated their stepfather's name with exaggerated respect. "You know how he hates Italians."

"Well, Francesca is beautiful."

He laughed. "What does that have to do with anything?"

She shoved him playfully. "I don't know, but it can't hurt, right? Maybe *Herr* Robert will be more open to her because she has a pretty face."

Fritz ran a hand through his shaggy brown waves. "Maybe, though her looks might also invite trouble. Not with Robert, of course, but others."

The unspoken words hung in the air between them. The fate of many immigrant women, in particular those from the Italian provinces or from Eastern Europe, was to find work in the only way a woman could make money easily: in the brothels in Chatham Square or in the Bowery, run by either the notorious Jewish gang, the Eastmans, or their Italian rivals, the Five Points Gang.

"Speaking of Italians, have you heard about what's happening on Mulberry and Mott Street lately?" he continued. "There were some arrests made a few days ago."

"What is it with the gangs lately?"

"It isn't the gangs. It's the anarchists." His voice dropped an octave on the last word.

Alma felt a familiar prickle of worry. Fritz held regular anarchist meetings at the bierhaus and showed no signs of stopping them, even with the riots that had taken place in the Midwest, New Orleans, and right here in the city. The anarchists were pushing for unions to glean more control from their employers and lawmakers, for better hours and working conditions. Employers were pushing back by firing "troublemakers," and Fritz led the way among his friends, truly believing he could effect change, something Alma admired in him. And yet, it was dangerous. Police were cracking down on their meetings, and many had been arrested.

"Be careful. If your boss finds out about your meetings, you could lose your job."

He glared at her. "I'm not just another worker. I'm one of their foremen. They trust me."

"All the more reason to be cautious. Your friends are hotheaded." And sometimes they were idiotic, she wanted to say. Fritz's best friend, Paul, had a busted lip from one of the riots only a few weeks ago.

Though the anarchists believed in maintaining order through small communities and volunteerism rather than a larger government that abused power in the name of their own interests—a peaceful philosophy at its core—the movement often attracted the wrong kinds of people. And these exact people had been in the news lately: those who favored violence over reason. President McKinley had been shot and killed by an anarchist last year, fueling even more bad press. Alma couldn't believe Robert still let her brother hold meetings at their bierhaus. She supposed it was because her stepfather had grown up with anarchism in Germany and it felt like second nature to him. The movement abroad had come about in opposition to monarchies and dictatorships, corruption, and the unfair plight of the common man, and it had landed on America's shores with the immigrants. Now, it was tied to the laborers' plight. This is where Fritz had become a part of the movement, but none of those peaceful beliefs mattered if he was caught hosting meetings or arrested. The police could shut her parents' business down, and then where would they be?

When they reached their apartment, Fritz paused outside the door. "I'm not stupid, Al. I know how to handle myself, and I sure as hell won't be telling everyone what I think at work. There's no time for that, anyway." He pushed open the door.

"I know you're not stupid," she replied. "It's the others I'm worried about, bringing the trouble here." She unbuttoned her overcoat.

"Don't worry about it."

Catching the irritation in his voice, she let the topic drop. She wouldn't win an argument with him when he was tired. Not that she could sway her stubborn brother when he set his mind on something anyway. As he headed upstairs, she turned to the kitchen.

The smell of pork sausages wafted around her in a welcome cloud.

"*Guten abend*." She greeted Mama with a kiss on her cheek. And rather than wait and lose her nerve about the waiver, she dove right in. "I have something to ask you."

Johanna Brauer moved quickly to the vat of sauerkraut, scooping a large helping into a bowl before tossing a sausage link on top. "We'll talk after dinner, *liebling*. Take this to the gentleman in the green jacket."

Alma obeyed, despite her annoyance. If she had to wait until later, it would make her jittery all evening. Besides, her mother would be exhausted and in no mood to discuss it by night's end. Now was definitely better.

Alma served the plate to the gentleman, who didn't even nod in thanks before digging into his dish. She helped serve several other hungry customers and, during the quick break afterward, seized the opportunity.

"The question I want to ask… Well, it's more of a favor."

Mama refilled a stein with beer. "What is it?"

"I know a young woman who needs a work permit," Alma began. "Would you consider signing one?"

Mama turned to her, eyebrows raised. "What? Why would I do that? I don't want to pay anyone outside of the family. We've had a profitable season, and with your wages and Fritz's contributions, we'll be moving uptown by the fall for sure, with money to spare."

"You won't have to hire her," Alma persisted. "All you'd need to do is sign the employment waiver so she could be admitted, and then I'd help her find another—"

"What do you mean 'so she could be admitted'?"

Alma bit her lip. This was precisely what she'd been trying to avoid—bringing up the fact that Francesca was an immigrant—but it was too late now. Once Mama was on to a scent, she wouldn't let up until she had pried the truth from Alma.

"She's an immigrant from Sicily, and she's completely alone. I'd like to—"

The words died on her lips.

Her mother stared at her wide-eyed, as if Alma had just asked her to commit murder. "You're asking me to sign a paper stating that an *Italian immigrant* is going to work for us? And it's not even true! You want me to *lie*"—she spat out the word—"to the Bureau of Immigration. Put our business and home at risk for some, some—"

"I understand," Alma interrupted, her shoulders drooping. "I shouldn't have asked."

"Why do you feel like you need to help a perfect stranger? You have no idea what she might be like. We could risk our reputation if we took her on, or worse. What if she's mixed up with those gangs?"

Alma huffed out a frustrated breath. Her mother had said—practically verbatim—exactly what Fritz had predicted. "Mama, her sister just died and her father is a cruel man. I can't condemn her to that life. She's so deeply sad, and she's only about my age. I want to help."

She watched beer drip from the spout into the basin beneath it, used to catch any overflow. She couldn't imagine being in Francesca's predicament. Francesca made Alma feel ashamed of her small life and steadfast routines and inspired her to do *something—anything else.* For now, this act of kindness was her something: helping a woman who had helped her, and who had come too far and had suffered too much to be turned away, even with its risks. She deserved this chance.

Mama crossed her arms. "Can't she find a job elsewhere?"

She shrugged. "I don't know. Who would I ask?"

Her mother took Alma's hands in her own. "Why don't you ask that priest of yours, or the nuns? They're Catholics, and Italians besides. They might find something for her."

Alma nodded, though she knew that wasn't an option either. The nuns had already told her so, and a priest couldn't very well hire a young woman. It was out of the question.

"If you saw her, Mama, you'd know why I asked. If you spoke to these people, day after day..." To her surprise, she felt a rush of emotion flood her throat. Whether or not Mama spoke to them, Alma did, and it was wearing on her, thinking of the immigrants as the enemy every day when what they wanted was as basic as filling their bellies and being treated like human beings.

Her mother's eyes softened and she tucked a stray wisp of hair behind Alma's ear. "We can't afford to risk what your father and I have built for ourselves. Certainly not for a stranger. I'm sorry, but your friend will have to find her own way, just as we all do."

Alma didn't reply, but she wanted to say that some had an easier way than others, through no inherent superiority but simply by the luck of being born at the right place in the right time—or with the right nationality and ethnicity. She could see that now, understood what she had been taught all her life wasn't the only way of doing and being and believing. It was only one small and narrow view, and she wanted to make things right, at least for Francesca.

But sadly, it seemed that wasn't meant to be.

President Roosevelt dissatisfied with conditions at Ellis Island, change ahead

James Mackle reports. *Manhattan Chronicle.*

April 10, 1902—The president is said to be dissatisfied with operations at Ellis Island as news of inappropriate conduct has reached Washington. Speculation suggests Commissioner Thomas Fitchie will soon be replaced by a new head of operations. In fact, there may be a complete overhaul at the immigration station over the coming months.

President Roosevelt emphasizes no position is safe, including those held by senior staff, if the office holder does not act with integrity toward the immigrants.

Once again, Commissioner Thomas Fitchie was not available for comment.

13

All night and the following morning at work, Alma had racked her brain, trying to think of some way to connect Francesca with an employer, but as soon as she'd settled on a friend of the family's whom she might ask, Alma changed her mind. They'd have the same reaction as her mother. No one wanted another Italian in their neighborhood, and no one would take a risk for a stranger. Alma had managed to avoid the detainees' quarters all day but knew she'd have to make her way there eventually and tell Francesca that it was over.

Sighing, she shifted the stack of paperwork to her other arm and continued to the clerk's office. Perhaps she'd stop on her way to say hello to Jeremy. Though she knew he spent time at his desk working through forms and transcripts, she often passed him in the registry office where he helped inspectors with translations. She suspected he also spent a fair amount of time preparing for the hearings of more indeterminate cases, drafting records or translating where necessary. The hearings determined whether or not the immigrant should stay in the country or go; if they had enough income or earning potential, or if they would become a burden to the state. The hearings also determined if the immigrant was of upstanding moral character. Though not glamorous, at least Jeremy's job wasn't passing out snacks to families and shepherding the sick, the detained, or the frantic through the halls. And he didn't report to a strict supervisor who never seemed satisfied. Alma envied him.

She knocked before entering his office.

"Morning," he said, smoothing the front of his suit jacket. "What have you got for me there?"

"Oh, these are for the clerk," she said. "More forms to file. Something dreadful, I think."

His brow arched. "That sounds jolly."

She smiled. "I don't usually read what they give me, especially if I'm in a rush."

"Well, now, where are you rushing off to?"

"The usual. Fetching things for the children, racing after Mrs. Keller, helping the inspectors. Drying lots of tears."

"Is that all?" He winked.

She laughed. "I suppose I should be going, shouldn't I. I thought I'd say hello since your office is next door to the clerk."

"Wait." He moved around the desk. "I'm glad you came by. I have a few things that need translating, and I don't speak Italian. Care to help?"

She perked up. "Yes!"

He grinned. "I thought you might." He motioned her over to his desk. "These few sentences here, and also this piece of underlined text."

She scanned the shorter piece and then the next, translating what she could while he made notes. When she finished, she smiled. "All done. If there are others—"

"Actually, there are...er, there will be. Would you mind helping me out from time to time? I know you're busy, so don't put yourself out now." He reddened. "That is... I thought you would be interested in translation work, so if—"

"Yes! I am, yes." She laughed at her own enthusiasm. "I'd be happy to help!"

He chuckled. "All right. I'll send for you."

A broad smile split her face. "Terrific." She stood awkwardly at the edge of his desk, not quite ready to go, though she knew she should.

He raised a brow at her. "So." He cleared his throat. "Have you been practicing your Russian?"

She nodded. "I'm surrounded by it every day, so I'm forced to, though I wish I could spend more time working quietly in an office." It wasn't just the relative quiet of his office, but his work: the interpreting, the constant learning, the respect. Others admired his abilities—and paid him to use them. She couldn't imagine being so lucky. The very possibility of it made her giddy.

"You have the mind of an academic," he said, winking. "You prefer to stay locked up with books than to be among the living."

"When you put it that way, I sound positively horrid."

He chuckled and a dimple appeared in his left cheek. "It takes all kinds for the world to turn, don't you know. I admire your keen mind."

She blushed. "I've always found language fascinating. Since I was a child, I've seen it as a sort of code that unlocks secrets."

His expression turned thoughtful. "It is like a code, of sorts. When you know a person's language, you come to find out who they are. Their language goes hand in hand with their customs and their nationality, and the way they think about things, too."

She leaned toward him, her passion for the topic bubbling to the surface. "I feel like a different person when I speak another language. Like I have a secret identity. Have you ever felt that way?"

"Now that you mention it...yes, I have."

"I wonder if people look at me differently, too." She thought of the way Robert glared at her when he heard her speak Italian.

"I'm certain they do," he said.

At his change in tone, Alma met his eyes and blushed. The moment she'd heard his Irish lilt, she'd assumed Jeremy would be like everything she'd heard and read about the Irish. That they were crude and limited in intelligence, and that they liked a good fistfight more than just about anything. They dealt in dirty politics, and most of all, they were lousy drunks. This man was not only kind and well spoken, but highly educated and a gentleman. She was embarrassed by her foolish assumptions and glad he didn't know how she'd initially viewed him. Each day at Ellis Island, she realized how little she knew about anything.

As the silence grew between them, she shifted to the other foot. "I suppose I should get back to work."

"Aye. Me too. But if you'd like to stop by later in the week, I'll show you a few things about what an interpreter really does."

"Thank you. I'd like that."

As she dropped off the papers in the clerk's office, she imagined herself in his shoes. Her heart began to race. What if she became an interpreter? She'd need schooling first and probably some sort of testing. Perhaps a bit of help from Jeremy to show her the ropes. Maybe one day, he might even put in a good word for her.

As this rosy new picture began to form in her mind, she lost herself in daydreams until she felt a tap on her shoulder. Helene looked quite pretty, even in her uniform. Her iridescent blue earrings sparkled, and she wore a smile.

"Lunch today?" Helene asked. "I heard they're serving some sort of fish. I'm not sure if it's edible, but I'm starving."

Alma laughed. "I'll brave it today, too."

"Say, did you hear about that Italian girl? She died here! On the island. Can you imagine dying *here*?" Helene said, leaning in. "It's terribly sad."

Alma felt the smile slide from her face. "Yes, I was there. She was a nice woman."

"And her poor sister is probably going to be deported."

Alma nodded but didn't share anything else. She felt a loyalty to Francesca and didn't want to talk about her as if she were another downtrodden immigrant passing through the halls that had meant nothing to anyone there. She wasn't. Francesca's struggles had surprisingly touched Alma in her short time here.

Feeling the warm rush of emotion spread through her chest, she changed the subject. "Did your parents take you to the concert on Sunday?"

Helene perked up. "Yes! It was fantastic. We went to Carnegie Hall, saw a classic music performance." She detailed the pieces and the instruments—completely outside of Alma's realm of understanding or experience—and again, she wondered why Helene worked at Ellis Island if her parents could afford concert tickets.

"Helene, do you like working here?"

She shrugged. "It's better than having a governess beat your knuckles bloody for not doing your work. I can't...read the letters on a page. They change shape as I'm trying to read them." She frowned as if remembering her frustration and confusion.

Alma stared at her, bewildered. "Really? I've never heard of such a thing."

"Well, it happens, and I can't seem to learn anything. So I work and it keeps me out of my mother's hair." Her friend looked away, and Alma realized she was embarrassed. "We can't all be prodigies like you, Alma."

She wasn't a prodigy, was she? She learned quickly. Maybe faster than most, but sometimes that felt like a curse.

"You don't want to be like me, Helene." She smiled. "You make friends easily. I'm terrible at it."

Helene forgot her embarrassment and grinned. "Hey, do you smell that? Smells like pickled herring."

Alma groaned. "Not again."

As they entered the cafeteria, Alma's gaze fell upon a figure sitting alone hunched over a tray. Something tugged at her heart. It wasn't Francesca but it could have been, with the woman's dark hair and worn dress, the hollow cheeks.

It was time to tell Francesca the truth. After lunch, Alma would track her down and tell her what she'd been dreading all day. Francesca had to go home.

14

*F*rancesca tossed her pen on the tabletop. She'd taken to spending most of her time in the Ellis Island library while Maria was in the hospital, and now it was a place of refuge.

Maria.

Her sister came to mind as often as Francesca breathed. Maria, her beloved Maria. The pain came like a firebrand, searing and intense until her body trembled with it. They'd never build a home together, or visit the places in America they'd dreamed about; there would never be cousins and holidays filled with family. Francesca wept, wiping at her eyes with the heels of her hands, hoping no one in the library noticed her tears. She didn't want to explain her loss to a stranger, and though she'd seen her fair share of immigrants crumpled in sorrow during her journey, she didn't want to be like them, felled by despair and need. She wasn't like them. She refused to be.

She pulled herself together, forcing her attention on the English dictionary and a few loose sheets of paper. Even practicing her English was a welcome distraction. As she wrote row after row of the new words she'd learned, her thoughts turned to Sister Alberta. Her friend would be amazed by Francesca's sudden dedication. Learning

English was as difficult as she remembered, but if she wanted to be an American, she had to try. She was fortunate she knew how to read and write at all. So few in her village could.

She practiced for some time, and as each hour crawled by with no word from Alma, she thought she'd go mad. When would the matron return with news? She'd put all of her hope and trust in the matron's hands. It was Francesca's last chance. She had spoken to her only yesterday, but Francesca's time at the immigration center was rapidly coming to an end.

When it was time for the midday meal, everyone headed to the cafeteria. Francesca followed, though she wasn't the least bit hungry. Given how little she'd consumed since leaving home, she couldn't afford to skip many more meals and decided to try. She needed her strength to face the next chapter of her journey, wherever it might lead her.

The cafeteria was crowded, as she'd expected, and overly warm from the crush of bodies. Light spilled from a row of windows on the far wall. Tables stretched across the room. Francesca watched as women stationed behind one long counter served food from gigantic pots, sweat on their brows, to a long line of hungry immigrants that snaked all the way out of the door. The line moved quickly, though, and soon she'd made her way to the front. She gathered her utensils, plate, and tray.

"Hold out your plate, miss," a woman in the cafeteria instructed her, giving her a stern look. Francesca did as she was told and received a helping of peppered herring. "Enjoy."

She tried not to show her disgust for the preserved fish and moved down the cafeteria line to the next person, who piled on a scoop of sweetened beans. Next came stewed prunes and a chunk of white bread and, finally, a glass of milk. If this was what they called food in America, perhaps she didn't want to stay after all. Glumly, she found a seat and picked at her bread.

Soon, she felt eyes on her.

She looked up to see several people at the table staring at her. She glanced down and, conscious of their scrutiny, focused on chewing. When she looked up again, a stout blond man with a full beard said something to her in a language she didn't recognize. Another man across from him waved a hand at her.

Francesca shrugged to illustrate she didn't understand them and ate another bite of bread. The man's volume increased. What did he want? She was minding her own business, trying to eat her lunch. She shifted in her seat and tried to remain calm.

When she didn't respond, he frowned and pointed his finger at her, releasing another stream of unintelligible words.

Another man approached her, standing behind her with his tray. "Do you speak English?"

"A little," she said, glancing over her shoulder at a group of people who appeared to know one another. They spoke loudly and laughed, looking almost identical to these men in their strange dress.

He grunted and pointed at a table across the hall. "Italians there. Polish here."

Flushing, she swallowed a dry chunk of bread, wishing with all her heart that Maria were here. Somehow, this would all be less mortifying if her sister were at her side. Though she had as much a right to be here as the next person, Francesca stood, carried her tray to the other side of the cafeteria, and found an empty spot at an "Italian table." When the familiar strains of her native Sicilian dialect floated around her, she felt her mood sink further. She thought she'd come to America to start over, to be better somehow. To be different. Yet everyone urged her to stay with her own countrymen. How naive she'd been.

She finished her lunch and was walking to the door when the stern matron with the cross necklace headed her off.

"Miss Ricci..." The woman continued, but Francesca didn't understand much of her speech.

When she stared blankly back at the matron, the woman tried again.

"You haven't heard from your uncle? Do you have any other family?"

Francesca swallowed hard. "No, but I—"

"Fine. You'll be booked for the next steamer to Naples on Thursday," the matron said firmly.

"In two days?" she choked. In two days, she'd leave America. Depart for Napoli. *Two days.*

She'd failed Sister Alberta, failed Maria. She'd failed herself.

"Can I... Can I speak to Alma Brauer?" she asked, voice hoarse.

The matron's brow arched in surprise. "Miss Brauer can't do anything more for you." When she saw Francesca's expression, she added hastily, "However, she's in the registry office. She might have a quick minute to speak with you. Actually, you're in luck. There she is now."

Alma looked harried, as if she'd been running all day. A pretty blond woman was at her side.

Francesca crossed the room hurriedly to greet her.

"*Buongiorno,*" Alma said, her voice tight. "I haven't had a chance to find you yet today, but I had planned to after lunch." She looked down. "I'm afraid I have bad news."

Francesca looked down at her hands. More bad news then. She gazed across the room, unseeing. In a flat voice she said, "I leave in two days."

"Yes," Alma replied softly. "I'm sorry."

"The mean woman said my ticket is booked." Her eyes blurred, and she blinked rapidly to regain her composure. "There's so little work at home, I don't know what I'm going to do. And I can't go back to Papa."

Alma touched Francesca's shoulder lightly. "I asked my family to sign for you as an employee, but they declined. I'm so sorry, Francesca. I wish there was something else I could do."

She looked at Alma, her plain face and vivid blue eyes. Although unlike her in every way, Francesca liked this woman. She was earnest and thoughtful, and she had never spoken to Francesca like an inferior. She was sincere and trustworthy, something Francesca couldn't say about many.

She tried—and failed—to force a smile. "It was kind of you to ask. Thank you for trying. I am grateful."

Alma moved to let several people dump their used silverware and plates in the dirty dish tubs and walk past them to the door. "Francesca...if we could find someone to sign an employment waiver... Do you know any other Americans? Or even Italian friends. Anyone I could ask on your behalf? Anyone at all? It's a long shot, but we still have two more days."

Francesca started to say no—and then her eyes widened as an idea came to her. She knew another American! And he had been extremely kind to her. Hands shaking, she fished inside her handbag for the card she'd saved from the ship. "I know another American! Marshall Lancaster. He was kind to me on the ship." Though she tried to control it, she felt hope creep into her voice. "He said I could call his family once I was settled. To consider him my first friend in America."

"Does he live here in the city?" Alma took the calling card, her eyes bulging as she read the script. "He lives on Park Avenue!"

"He gave me water for Maria... His mother wore pearls and diamonds."

Alma laughed at her expression. "The Park Avenue types tend to wear jewels, or so I've heard. I haven't met anyone that wealthy before.

Maybe they'll need more staff? To clean the house or the garden, or something. Do you have any skills? Do you mind working as a maid?"

A tiny flame of hope flickered to life inside Francesca. "I'll do anything. I can cook, but if he asks me to scrub floors, or to be his laundress, I'll do it. It doesn't matter what the job is, I—" She laughed at her own enthusiasm, and grasping Alma's hands in hers, she said, "This will work. It has to."

"We'll certainly try!" Alma slipped the card into the pocket of her apron before glancing over her shoulder as if she was worried someone might see her. Biting her lip, she added, "I'll go to Mr. Lancaster's tonight. I can't promise anything—"

"Thank you! I... Thank you so much. This will work, Alma. Sì, this will work. I'll find a way to repay you. Some day."

Alma grinned and her eyes lit from within. "You already have."

Francesca threw her arms around the matron and embraced her tightly.

When Alma pulled away, Francesca saw the matron's mood shift rapidly. Fear flashed in her eyes. Francesca followed her gaze to the mean older matron from before, who circulated around the room. The one who had called her a *puttana* and told her she must leave in two days. Something about what Alma was doing wasn't a part of her duties, clearly, and it made her nervous. The last thing Francesca wanted was to cause trouble for Alma.

"Go," Francesca said. "I'll look for you at breakfast tomorrow."

In English, Alma replied, "And I'll let you know what Mr. Lancaster says."

"Thank you. And Alma?"

"Yes?"

"Your Italian is very good. Better than even two weeks ago."

The young woman grinned widely. "I've been practicing."

15

Alma waved at Fritz as she bounded up the steps to the train platform after work that night. His thick hair curled around the edge of his cap, and he almost looked like a boy again.

"I need to head uptown before I go home," she said, "and if you don't want to come with me, I understand. I'll go alone."

"Well, hello to you, too," he said, pulling his wool hat down to cover his ears. "What for?"

"I'm doing a favor for a friend."

He shot her a sidelong glance. "Someone I know?"

"No."

"Is this one of your new coworkers?"

"No."

He jabbed her in the ribs with his index finger. "Aren't you being mysterious. Do you want me to come with you or not?"

She shrugged. "Of course, but if you're going to give me an earful about why I shouldn't do this, I'll go on my own."

He grinned. "Working out there in the big world is toughening you up, little sister." He tugged a strand of her hair.

He was right. She could feel herself changing—her timidity falling away—and she was beginning to like this new version of herself.

"I'm going to help the Italian immigrant I told you about," she said, pulling her glove off to fish a coin out of her purse. "I need to convince this man to sign an employment waiver."

"Wait a minute. A man she doesn't know is going to hire her? What sort of work is this?" He stepped to the side to allow a couple of businessmen to rush past him.

She rolled her eyes. "Do you think I'd really send her to a gangster or a pimp? I'm hoping Mr. Lancaster will hire her as a maid or a washerwoman. Something like that."

"Where does this fellow live?"

"Park Avenue."

Fritz whistled. "Your little friend is already connected in high places. I'd definitely like to see this."

Alma smiled. He was too curious to resist coming with her, even as tired as he was.

They waited in a short line and purchased their train tickets. He looped his arm through hers as they boarded the train.

"To be honest, I'm relieved you're coming with me." She sank down next to him on a seat. "I was worried how it would look to have a strange woman, unescorted, on the Lancasters' doorstep at this time of night. That's just the sort of thing that matters to rich people."

As the train gained speed and they began their northbound journey, Alma read the employment waiver she'd brought with her for the third time. What if Mr. Lancaster turned her away? Or what if he wasn't at home? She bit her bottom lip, anxious to get there. Francesca had only two more days. Should Mr. Lancaster decide not to help, all would be lost for her.

But at least I will have tried, she told herself, *at the cost of my own neck.* Should Mrs. Keller find out Alma had become involved with an immigrant's welfare and hustled a job for her, Alma likely wouldn't be returning to Ellis Island. She might even face some questioning from the police.

Her stomach swarmed with bees the entire walk from the station to the Lancasters' home, yet she hesitated only a moment when they arrived. She couldn't let Francesca down now. And there was something more; something inside Alma had begun to uncoil and stretch—even Fritz had noticed it—and it urged her forward now.

She peered up at the intricate frieze along the front-facing edge of the house, the sweeping staircase that led to an oaken door and large ceramic pots already flourishing with early spring flowers.

"Would you look at this place," Fritz said, mouth agape as he took in the house's splendor.

"I know," she said, looking down at her matron's attire and at Fritz's muddy trousers. It was probably best to knock at the staff entrance. The Lancasters wouldn't take kindly to receiving a pair below their station at the main door, especially with one of them so unkempt.

"You do all the talking," Fritz said, a dubious expression on his face.

Gathering her nerve, she took the steps that led below the street level to what she assumed was the staff entrance and banged the knocker against the door.

A butler in a fine coat and tie greeted them, his chest puffed out like a peacock's. "Can I help you?"

"Hello, I'm Alma Brauer and this is my brother, Fritz. Is Mr. Marshall Lancaster at home?" She flashed his calling card.

"He isn't seeing visitors now, miss. Perhaps you can call again another day."

Alma bit her lip and advanced a step closer. "I must insist on seeing him. Please, it's urgent."

"Has he made your acquaintance, Miss Brauer?"

"No, but I'm here on behalf of Francesca Ricci, a young woman he met on the steamship several weeks ago."

"Is he expecting you?"

"No, I—"

The butler held up his hand to stop her. "Then you will have to come back another time. Good day."

He began to close the door, but Fritz caught its edge with his well-muscled hand. "Look, Mr. Lancaster will be angry to learn he missed us. And we wouldn't want to anger him, now, would we?"

The butler took in Fritz's scruffy appearance, lips pinched. "One moment, please." He closed the door in their faces.

"That cretin acts like he's better than us." Fritz glanced down at his slacks, at the mud caked around the bottom hem and on his work boots. He looked up, amusement in his eyes. "Well, I suppose I am a little dirty, aren't I?"

"Maybe a little." Alma laughed softly, grateful for his humor in the awkward situation.

The door swung open again. "Right this way, Miss Brauer, Mr. Brauer." The butler turned stiffly and led them inside a spacious kitchen filled with the aroma of roast beef and vanilla cake and something else buttery. A round woman worked fastidiously over the stove, singing as she went, and a second older woman sat in a chair at the staff dining table mending a pair of stockings.

Everyone paused in their duties to stare at them.

"You may wait here as the master requests," the butler said and reached for a pair of fine shoes he'd been in the midst of polishing when they'd called at the door.

Neither Alma nor Fritz sat at the table and instead watched the butler finish his task as if it were the most interesting thing in the world.

Within minutes, a round but elegant man in an impeccable suit, his hair slicked expertly with almond oil, bounded down a set of steps into the room. "Good evening. I'm Marshall Lancaster. My butler tells me you're here on behalf of Miss Ricci."

Alma was struck immediately by the gentleman's English accent. So he was an immigrant, too. She'd never met an immigrant from the upper class before, but then again, how would her path have crossed with his? First class wasn't expected to suffer the inconvenience of waiting in long lines or being questioned like the masses that passed through the halls of Ellis Island. And Mr. Lancaster certainly didn't seem the type to take a tour of her end of town to stare at the poor and the working classes like a spectator, unlike the many journalists in recent years.

Fritz held out his hand and shook Lancaster's hard enough to elicit a slight grimace on the older man's face. "Good evening, sir. I'm Fritz Brauer, and this is my sister Alma."

Alma nodded. "How do you do, sir."

Mr. Lancaster eyed his staff, who suddenly pretended to be thoroughly engaged in their duties. "Why don't we take tea in the parlor? We'll have more privacy there."

He led them up a staircase, through a marbled hall decorated with colorful panels of stained glass, and into a sitting room. They stood awkwardly a moment, taking in the silk-covered furniture, plush Turkish rug, and a chandelier that looked as if it was made of the finest crystal. There were three portraits in places of prominence on the walls: one of a woman dressed in a stunning white gown and feathered hat, a teardrop pearl necklace at her throat; another of a young girl who couldn't be more than ten; and one other of a gentleman in black smoking jacket and tie.

"Please, make yourself comfortable," Mr. Lancaster said. "Let me just call for tea." He reached for a bell.

"Don't get anything dirty," Fritz whispered in Alma's ear, gingerly sitting on a settee that didn't look sturdy enough to hold his weight.

Alma assumed it was a settee anyway. She'd never seen one before. Neither had she seen so many gleaming brass candelabras. She sat on the edge next to her brother, not allowing herself to sink into the cushions.

The maid scuttled across the room, rolling a silver tea tray into the parlor loaded with cakes, bread and jam, and cured meats.

Alma accepted a plate and steaming cup of tea. She tried not to fidget and to eat carefully, but as she took a bite of the sponge cake with raspberry jam, she forgot her nerves for an instant and sank into the cake's fluffy yet moist texture. With the tart raspberries, the cake was even better than Mama's strudel. She gulped it down more quickly than she should and reached for a wedge of bread and butter. As she brought it to her mouth, she fumbled it in her clumsy fingers, catching it just before it landed face-side down in her lap.

Fritz swallowed a laugh as she wiped away the slick of butter from her hands.

Mr. Lancaster noticed the near-miss but was too polite to acknowledge it. Instead, he broke the silence. "How do you know Miss Ricci?"

Alma dabbed at her mouth awkwardly with a napkin. "I met Miss Ricci and her sister at Ellis Island. I'm a matron there."

He nodded. "She was a lovely young woman, disadvantaged to be sure, but lovely just the same. How is her sister? I hope she has recovered."

Alma placed her teacup in its saucer. "I'm sorry to say her sister, Maria, has passed away in the hospital on the island."

His eyes filled with contrition. "Oh, how terribly sad for her. Please give Miss Ricci my condolences."

"I will, thank you." Trying to work up the courage to ask him the dreaded question, she glanced down at the tips of her boots where the leather had begun to wear thin. "You must be wondering why we've come."

Mr. Lancaster gripped the delicate porcelain cup with thick fingers and sipped the milky brew. "I'll admit, I am a little confused."

With a deep breath, she filled the gentleman in on the Riccis' humble beginnings. Lancaster remained silent, watching her closely through her explanation.

"She's been through quite a lot, you see," Alma continued.

"And where do I come in, Miss Brauer?"

"I was hoping you might consider... What I mean is, would you happen to have any work Francesca might be able to do for you? If you signed her employment waiver, she could complete the routine inspections at Ellis Island and be in the city by tomorrow evening."

"I see." He stood, walked to the bar, and poured himself a scotch. "Care for a scotch?"

"Please," Fritz said through a mouthful of jam cake.

Lancaster splashed a finger of scotch into a glass and handed the delicate crystal to Fritz. "It's Lagavulin."

Fritz grinned and accepted the scotch. "Thank you, sir. I can't say I'm all that familiar with scotch, but I'm open to suggestion." They clinked glasses. "Cheers." When he sipped the liquid, a range of expressions crossed his face.

Lancaster chuckled. "It takes some getting used to. It's smoky and earthy, but that's what I like about it."

"It puts hair on your chest for sure," Fritz said.

Lancaster laughed heartily. "I suppose it does."

"Sir," Fritz began. "My sister here is the smartest person I know. She's diligent, hard-working, and trustworthy. The best kind of person. She wouldn't risk embarrassment and possible unemployment unless this young woman was worth it. I'm not sure what you can do for this Miss Ricci, but I hope you will consider my sister's request."

Alma held her breath, watching Mr. Lancaster swirl the scotch in his glass. She leaned forward on the settee. Waiting, hoping, inwardly imploring Mr. Lancaster to agree. She had only one more move she could play to persuade him, but she didn't want to violate Francesca's privacy and the trust she'd placed in Alma.

Mr. Lancaster swallowed the rest of his scotch in one gulp. He glanced first at Fritz and then at Alma. "I know this isn't what you were hoping to hear, but I'm not certain I can make this work. Mother actively dislikes Italians, truth be told. I'm sorry Miss Ricci is in trouble, but she's lucky to have an advocate in you both."

Alma set down her cup on the mahogany table polished to a shine and met the man's eye. She'd have to do it, to share Francesca's secret. She hoped it would be enough. She took a deep breath and laid her last card on the table.

"Perhaps, sir, there's one more thing you should know."

16

Francesca sorted blindly through her small travel case, repacking her meager belongings inside it. Her mind had traveled over a well-worn path of fears: the journey home, where she might live, her father seeking answers from Sister Alberta and what that might mean for her beloved friend. And then she thought of Alma Brauer, and her heart flooded with a fierce hope that Alma had been successful last night. Francesca paused to finger the embroidered collar of Maria's dress. At least her sister couldn't see her suffer, though it was little consolation. Francesca would suffer a thousand times for only one more day with Maria—even a few more hours where they could talk or laugh or face what came next together, no matter how difficult it might be.

"*Sempre sorelle,*" she whispered, willing the swell of sadness to subside. Maria would want her to be brave.

She joined the line for the communal shower, and when her turn came, she accepted the cake of soap they offered and scrubbed herself clean. Detainees had to wash daily if they stayed on the premises as well as wash their clothing; it was a mandatory rule at Ellis Island. She was thankful she had more than one dress as she watched those without shiver in the temporary robe the matrons had provided for

THE NEXT SHIP HOME

them while they waited for their turn in the showers. After a quick wash, she cleaned her teeth.

Soon after, everyone began to file into the hallway to make their way to breakfast in the cafeteria.

As Francesca brushed her hair and pinned it in place, she noticed a woman at her cot, counting a roll of dollar bills and folding them into a pouch in her change purse. The woman looked over her shoulder to see if anyone was watching her. With most of the crowd gone, her eyes landed on Francesca. Francesca glanced quickly at the floor, pretending she hadn't seen what the woman was doing, and busied herself towel-drying her hair. Satisfied no one had seen her, the woman rolled her purse inside a piece of cloth and stuffed the bundle at the foot of her cot beneath a blanket. She glanced around quickly again and joined the others headed to the cafeteria.

Francesca felt the itch in her fingers to lift the blanket and seek out the bills. Spirit them away in her skirts. Exchanged to lira, the money would support her for weeks in Napoli, or at least until she found a more permanent situation. But it would be wrong to rob the woman. She'd likely saved for a long time to make her way in America.

Francesca stared at the woman's cot. If she took the money, could she live with herself? But could she survive in Napoli—or New York, for that matter—without it? Survival seemed more urgent than a nagging conscience.

She dashed to the cot. Glancing over her shoulder just as the woman had done, she confirmed she was the only person in the room. A matron stood at the door, waiting for the rest of the detainees to vacate so she could lock it, but her attention was diverted by someone else in the hallway. No one would ever know.

Hands trembling, Francesca lifted the blanket.

As she unrolled the fabric and pulled out the purse, she wrestled with her conscience. What if the woman reported the money missing and a search was initiated?

Many of the immigrants had American money on them, she reasoned, and the inspectors didn't know how much each person carried with them until final inspections. Besides, she would be gone by tomorrow. Stowed away in the bottom of an ocean liner before the money would be found missing. She hesitated an instant, touched la Madonna at her neck. Sister Alberta would be so disappointed in her if she could see Francesca, but she couldn't and Francesca needed the money as desperately as the other woman. Perhaps more.

Pulse thundering in her ears, she pulled out the bills, peeled off three, and stuffed them inside the sleeve of her dress. The rest she left in the purse. This way, they could both have what they needed. She shoved the remaining money back into the handbag and rolled it up exactly as she'd found it.

"Are you finished yet?" The matron at the door, by the name of Helene, poked her head inside the room. "You're going to miss breakfast."

"Yes. I am finished," Francesca said.

She left, stomach still clenched with nerves. At the end of the hallway, she veered left, went down the stairs, and rather than going to the cafeteria, stepped outside for a walk. She wasn't likely to see Alma until the midday meal anyway, and until then, she'd bide her time in the fresh air.

Once outdoors, she inhaled a deep breath and her pulse began to slow. The sun heated the brisk morning air, a whisper of warmer temperatures to come. It was a nice day at last—in time for her to leave, she thought bitterly. The weeks she'd been stranded on the island were the final days of winter, and she would miss the beauty of the spring. Sighing, she avoided the crowded front walk, where a ferry had just docked and the missionaries had begun to descend, and walked across the sprawling lawn on the western part of the island past a row of benches. A group of men kicked a ball; several clusters of children devised their own games, chasing each other, laughing. It seemed others had the same idea as her, to enjoy the fresh air while they waited. She continued to a relatively secluded spot where the lawn ended at the farthest edge of the island. From there, she could see clearly across the bay to the majestic city beyond it.

Her throat thickened as she looked at the vast expanse of buildings and a city she might never know. A dream just within her grasp.

"Francesca!"

She turned to see Alma bounding across the lawn. She must have news. Francesca's heart leaped into her throat, but she put on a brave face and waved at the matron.

"There you are!" Alma panted. "I've been looking for you everywhere. A matron spotted you leaving the building, or I would have never found you." She caught her breath, turning her face to the sun a moment. "It's turning out to be a lovely day, isn't it?" She smiled and laid a hand on Francesca's shoulder. "And nicer still when you hear my news."

Her lungs tightened, but she carefully kept her voice steady. "What is it?"

"I met Mr. Lancaster." A generous smile spread across the young woman's face. "He agreed to sign an employment waiver for you! And he didn't just sign it. He's offered you a job! You don't have to leave!"

Francesca cried out and threw her arms around the matron's neck and promptly burst into tears. She was free to begin another life! And she'd live it for herself, and for Maria. Her sister hadn't died in vain.

Alma patted her back awkwardly. "I know, it's surprising. I thought he'd turn me away because of his mother, but I convinced him otherwise. In the end, he said he would enjoy watching Mrs. Lancaster 'learn about the modern world,' I think was how he put it."

Francesca wiped her eyes and laughed at her sudden change of fortune. "I'm—*mi dispiace*—I am sorry. I'm just so happy!"

As relief crashed over her, her mind raced with what was next. Inspection, finding a place to live, warmer clothes. Unable to control her excitement, she embraced Alma again, the awkwardness of not knowing each other well falling away like autumn leaves.

"What did Mr. Lancaster say? What is the job?" she asked, wiping the tears from her cheeks.

"Their cook was fired recently for burning too many roast chickens, so he'd like to hire you to take her place."

A cook. Speechless with joy and gratitude, she wiped at another flood of relieved tears.

"I don't know how I'll ever thank you," Francesca said at last.

"Sometimes we need a little help. Someone very wise told me that." Alma smiled widely.

Francesca returned the smile.

"The other news," Alma continued, "is that I took the liberty of speaking to the nuns from the mission on your behalf, and also the Christian society, but their beds are full right now. There have been so many ships lately. So I thought…I thought you might stay with us, at my family's apartment? If you'd prefer to find a place on your own, I understand."

Francesca grinned, this time, as a wave of joy washed over her. The thought of facing the enormity of New York for the first time on her own had made her a little queasy, but now, she wouldn't be scrambling to find a place to sleep for the night. "Yes, *grazie mille*. Oh, Alma. *Grazie.*"

"Good, that's settled," Alma said. "If you like, you can go through inspections and then wait here at Ellis Island until the end of my workday and we'll travel together. Or you can take the next ferry and meet me later at Battery Park. I understand if you'd rather leave as soon as possible."

"I wait," Francesca replied in English. She couldn't believe her sudden change of fortune.

"All right," Alma said. "My brother will meet us at the dock to escort us home."

Francesca touched Alma's shoulder. "This means much to me."

"I'm sure you'd do the same for someone in need," Alma said warmly.

But Francesca didn't know if she would be so giving to a stranger. She thought again of the stolen bills she'd taken in the bunkhouse and shook her head. "Not everyone would do what you have done."

Alma smiled, her pleasure evident by the glint in her eyes. "I'm glad you'll get to meet my brother Fritz, too. He helped me convince Mr. Lancaster to hire you. He said he'd like to meet this woman who has managed to convince his dutiful sister to be so bold."

She smiled. "I meet your brother."

Alma glanced at the docks as a ferry pulled in with a new load of passengers. She sighed heavily. "I'd better get to my post. I'm about to be very busy. And we need to cancel your reservation for the ship!"

"*Andiamo!*" Francesca said, following her new friend inside, her spirits flying as high as the gulls wheeling across the sky.

Travel case in hand, Francesca joined the line in the registry room. Hundreds of people were waiting in various lines and on benches, waiting to be called for final inspections. She watched the inspectors from a distance, how they looked over their notes and asked the immigrants questions. The process lasted a matter of minutes, sometimes even seconds. At that point, they'd wave the immigrant through, or for the occasional few, the immigrants were asked to step aside to await further instruction. At last, she wouldn't be one of them.

Eyes fixed on the staircase leading to the exit, she couldn't help but daydream about what lay ahead. The Lancasters were so wealthy she could scarcely imagine what their home would be like. Their kitchen must be large, stocked with beautiful cookware and herbs and foods she'd never seen before. She'd work hard to learn new dishes and new techniques, do her best to please them. Her cooking skills were rudimentary, but she knew she had a knack for it. Sister Alberta had always told her so. In no time, she'd woo Mrs. Lancaster with bread rubbed with olive oil and rosemary, and her fresh pasta with lemon, herbs, and wine.

Two hours later, she, at last, advanced to the front of the queue. She instantly recognized the inspector behind the desk. He was the man who had entered the medical examination room when she and Maria had been forced to expose their breasts. He had also been the one to threaten her with deportation. Her palms grew clammy, and all of the joy she'd felt during the morning evaporated. This man would look for reasons to send her home.

He stared at her intently a moment before reading her name, assigned number, and date of birth. "Is this correct?"

She nodded.

"Why did you come to the United States?"

She had practiced this line many times and knew it well. "I wish to make new start with work."

The inspector's gaze traveled slowly over her face, lingered on her chest, and continued south and back again. If he aimed to make her feel uncomfortable, she wouldn't show him he'd accomplished his goal. Her eyes never left his face.

He pursed his lips, his eyes lingering on her chest again. "My, aren't you a pretty one. Women who look like you shouldn't travel alone."

She made sense of the words slowly. He wanted to intimidate her, or coerce her into admitting something that wasn't true. She'd seen it too many times from her father, and she knew what to do with a man like that. Though her hands shook, she stuck out her chin. "I come for job. Work and make money."

"Yes, indeed, you'll work for money." He leaned over his desk and winked.

She flinched and muttered a stream of Italian.

"We speak English here, miss." The inspector bared his teeth. "Now, is someone here to greet you?"

"I have job." She pushed the signed employment waiver across his desk.

His brows shot up. "Marshall Lancaster? He's the biggest tea merchant in the city."

She nodded. "I am his cook."

"I'll need to review your papers, Miss Ricci. Make some inquiries to see if it's an authentic signature."

She shook her head to show she didn't understand.

He said slowly, "I need to see if these are real."

That, she understood. Panic flared inside her. What if he decided the signature was a forgery?

His eyes roved over her frame again. "But. I'd be willing to let you go, if you paid a small fee, that is."

"Fee?" she asked.

"A...price." He winked.

She knew what the man wanted. They had all been the same, the men who needed to feel powerful, those who had been mocked and ridiculed as children. Those who were unloved. They were starved inside, and desperate to prove to themselves they were strong and worthy, to feel whole again. She knew the kind all too well. She'd seen it with the *polizia* in Sicilia at times, and with her father. Their need to wield power over others was weakness disguised, and this vile man was no different. Still, he was her way into the country, like it or not, and she must play his game.

"You sign, and I give something for to you." She tripped over the English words.

He leaned forward. "And what might that be, Miss Ricci?"

"Is there place we can go? I show you."

Hunger flickered in his eyes. "Meet me at twelve o'clock, sharp, outside the clerk's office. Do you understand?"

She peered at him with a hard stare, until he finally looked away. Now he knew she wasn't afraid, that she was in charge of herself, her body. "*Sì.* I see you at twelve."

17

*I*t had been a long morning, partly because Alma had been running from one end of the immigration center to the other all day, delivering paperwork, corralling children in the halls, and assisting Dr. Murphy during his medical inspections, and partly because she knew Francesca was waiting for her. Alma had hours left before she could leave, and the staff still had a few hundred immigrants left to process.

Francesca must be through inspections by now and was likely impatient to leave a building that must feel like a prison to her. Sometimes Ellis Island felt like a prison to Alma, too, as if she were locked up with the masses in some alternate hell she couldn't escape. Other days, she almost enjoyed her work. She'd begun to acclimate to the busy days and had made a friend in Helene. They rode the ferry together to and from work and sometimes ate lunch together.

Alma's stomach rumbled. Speaking of lunch, she'd missed it and her energy was starting to flag. Glancing at the clock, she made a quick decision to stop by one of the snack stands. She had enough time to make it there and back if she rushed and the line wasn't too long. She wound down the steps to the baggage room on the bottom floor, past a crowd purchasing train tickets. On the far eastern end of the building, vendors advertised a selection of sandwiches and snacks, small personal items forgotten or lost in the voyage, and the odd shoe shine. She scanned the signs and jumped into line to buy a pastrami sandwich. Suddenly ravenous, she tapped her foot impatiently as she waited for the customers in front of her to move along, until one person remained.

"No English," the man said to the vendor and pointed to a boxed lunch someone else had tucked under their arm.

"You want a boxed lunch?" the vendor said gruffly. "Pastrami, ham, or liverwurst? I've got beef tongue, too, and sardines." He pointed to a series of signs above his head in at least eight languages.

Instead of replying, the immigrant held out a five-dollar bill.

The vendor snapped it up, took a box from the stack on the table behind him, and handed it to the immigrant. He counted out two dollars in change and poured the coins into the immigrant's outstretched hand.

The man nodded his thanks and put the coins in his change purse.

Alma watched the exchange in surprise. The vendor had definitely miscounted the change. And clearly, the immigrant couldn't read.

"Excuse me," she said, "you've shortchanged that man. I saw you count the coins, and you didn't give him enough." She placed a hand on the immigrant's shoulder to stop him before he disappeared in the crowd.

The immigrant looked confused, so she tried several phrases in different languages to no avail. She pointed to her money and, enunciating slowly, said, "Money. More money."

"What are you, a nun?" the vendor grumbled, tossing the remaining change on the counter, all the while glaring at Alma.

The immigrant bowed his head at Alma to indicate his thanks and scooped the money into his palm.

"What do you want?" the vendor sneered at her.

Her cheeks flamed with indignation. She'd thought she was helping them both, but given the vendor's response, he'd clearly meant to shortchange the immigrant. The thief!

"Never mind," she said, furious, unwilling to give him her business. She started in the other direction. She couldn't believe the nerve of that man, stealing from someone, especially when that someone didn't understand English or know how to read. She'd assumed the rumors about swindling and extortion at Ellis Island had been just that—rumors. How wrong she'd been.

Flustered, she headed to the second floor. She'd never buy anything from that vendor again.

"Hiya, Miss Brauer."

Startled from her thoughts, she looked over her shoulder at a smiling Jeremy Kerrigan.

"Oh, Jeremy. Hello." His morning suit was a deep green today. She noticed the way the color accented his eyes.

"Have you turned twenty-two then?" he asked. "You look a wee bit older than the last time I saw you."

At the welcome and unexpected distraction, she laughed, recalling their first conversation about how terribly "old" she was. "I'm not twenty-two yet, but my back has been going out on me from time to time."

It was his turn to laugh. "Having a nice day, I hope?"

"Nice enough, thank you."

"I've saved something for you," he said. "It's in my office, if you can spare a quick minute."

"Just a quick minute. I'm coming back from lunch."

"Sure, sure."

Curious about what he wanted to show her, she followed him to his office.

He fished inside the top drawer of his desk and produced a small children's book. "One of the best ways to improve language skills is to translate books," he said. "Start with the basics. I've read this so many times I have it memorized." He placed it gently in her hands.

She turned it over. A drawing of a pear tree had been painted on the cover and, beneath the image, the title. "It's in Russian?" she asked.

He nodded. "I hope it isn't presumptuous. I—"

"No... I... It's wonderful, thank you. I'll work on translating it tonight."

He rewarded her with a crooked smile. "I'm not insulting you by giving you some kid's rubbish, then?"

She smiled warmly, so very pleased by the gift. "It's perfect, really. Thank you."

He flushed a little. "Right. I suppose we should get to work."

"We should." On her way to the door, her stomach rumbled again, a reminder of her abandoned meal and the dishonest vendor. She paused in the doorway. Though she hardly knew Jeremy, he seemed the trustworthy type.

"I saw something today," she said. "It was a vendor. He gave an immigrant the incorrect change, and I believe he did it on purpose because when I pointed it out to him, he swore at me. I wasn't sure if I should report him or who to tell, or... I don't know. I was so mad, I left without even buying the sandwich I'd gone there for in the first place."

The laugh lines around Jeremy's mouth smoothed and his eyes became guarded. "A lot happens around here that would surprise you. But I'd suggest you steer clear of the trouble."

"Shouldn't I tell someone?"

He looked pensive. "That depends on who you tell. Since you're still a relatively new employee, I'd say it's best not to meddle, if you know what I mean."

She nodded, but she didn't know what he meant.

When he saw her expression he added, "Listen, there have been some rumors about the commissioner going around. Just stay out of sight until things settle down. It's unclear who is on his side and who isn't. Best protect yourself for now."

She remembered what she'd overheard in the hallway between Commissioner Fitchie and the unknown gentleman. The reports of Roosevelt's displeasure over the immigration center's policies. If something was going on behind the scenes, she didn't want to unwittingly find herself in the middle of it.

She nodded. "Thanks for the warning. And for the book." She hugged it to her chest and ducked out of his office, mind racing. She wondered what Jeremy had meant by "steer clear of the trouble." What kind of trouble could there possibly be in reporting a thief? And what was happening with the commissioner?

Suddenly the end of the day couldn't come soon enough.

18

*A*t a quarter to twelve, Francesca stood outside the clerk's office watching members of the staff and immigrants wander past to the cafeteria. By ten past the hour, almost everyone had gone to lunch and she resorted to wringing her hands. Perhaps the inspector had decided the form from Mr. Lancaster wasn't enough, and he had changed his mind about their transaction. What would she do then? Francesca had a feeling Alma couldn't do much for her if an inspector had made a decision.

At that moment, the inspector appeared and without slowing his pace said, "Follow me."

Heart pounding in her ears, she followed him down the corridor and into another room. As she entered, she took in the nondescript desk and chairs, filing cabinets, and several empty coffee mugs in need of washing. When he closed the door and the lock clicked, they were completely out of sight of any passersby.

"I want my papers." Her voice sounded strong and steady in spite of the fear that rushed up her spine.

He replied, but she couldn't understand him, so when she didn't respond in kind, he slipped his arm lightly about her shoulders and guided her toward a filing cabinet in the corner of the room. He opened the cabinet and pulled out her papers. As he laid them on top of the cabinet, he said something else. Frustrated, she frowned and reached for them.

He caught her fingers in his.

She pulled away and averted her eyes, not wanting to remember the inspector's smooth skin and perfectly trimmed beard, his dark eyes. She wanted to erase the details of his face from her mind and forget the smell of witch hazel lingering on his skin from his aftershave.

"I take those." She pulled her hand from his and reached for the papers.

"Not so fast. I haven't decided if I should let you go." He slid his arm around her middle, ran his free hand across her cheek, and trailed his fingers down her neck and across her bosom.

She shifted her face to a careful blank expression. This was his price, and she'd all but offered it to him. It was a small sacrifice for gaining what she wanted, and she wanted it too badly to refuse. But she would not give without securing what she needed. "First"—she shoved the paper in his face—"you sign paper."

He grinned at her canniness, showing a row of perfect teeth, then reached for a pen and, with a flourish, signed the document and a certificate that allowed her admittance. After, he pulled her close and crushed his mouth against hers. His hands found the curve of her breasts and wandered lower until he'd lifted her skirts.

When his hands touched her bared skin, she focused on the ceiling and replayed the mantra in her head she knew to be true: her freedom was everything and she would have it. Her life would begin again, become all she wanted it to be, and this would be nothing but a distant memory, like those of her father. A dirty little stepping-stone to a better life. She had always done what she must, without looking back, and she would do it again. This moment didn't matter; it was a tiny dot on the long, moving timeline of her life.

She burrowed inside herself, evoking the fortress she'd created, born of pain so many years ago. She'd been good at hiding there, in a place of otherness where the world around her faded until it didn't exist and she was safe. Her body wasn't her own but a mere vessel of the earth, and she hovered somewhere above it, weightless.

As the inspector moved, he whispered something in her ear, and for once, she was glad she didn't know more English. He couldn't break her; he wouldn't live in her mind after the deed was finished. After he was finished, he could go to hell.

Some minutes later, she righted herself, smoothed her hair, and choked out a string of slurs she knew he wouldn't understand. Anger was better than grief—or fear—and she allowed herself to fill to the brim with it, to burn with the heat of a thousand Italian suns. This worm of a man was pathetic and now held nothing over her. She had the signature she needed.

"I go now." It wasn't a question.

As she turned toward the door, he grabbed her arm. "If I hear about you whoring in our fine country, I'll have you arrested. Is that clear? It's illegal, and deportation would be next."

She bit back the urge to spit in his face.

"Do you understand!"

"Sì."

"Well then"—he smiled—"welcome to America."

19

◦◦◦◦◦◦◦◦◦◦

Shoving away the image of the inspector's brown eyes, the curl of his lip as he leered at her, Francesca descended the staircase leading to freedom. *Freedom*. After the months of planning and the long weeks of travel and being marooned on this godforsaken island, she could at last move on to a life of her own.

The baggage room on the bottom floor was nearly as crowded as the registry room. People milled about, bought train tickets for the next leg of their journey, exchanged their foreign currency into American dollars. Between two large pillars, a crowd of American citizens waited for their loved ones to arrive, hope and excitement etched on their faces. Some held up signs with names scrawled across them. Paul Nowak. Isabella Ferrini. Edgar Stravinski. A woman rushed past Francesca squealing and fell into another woman's arms. They embraced and laughed and cried. A gentleman greeted a woman and children stoically with only a nod to welcome them to their new country. Near them, two lovers kissed as if the world might end at any moment. They were all a rainbow of emotions, colors, and sizes, and she found herself sorting through the crowd to find the faces that looked most like hers.

As another young Sicilian woman leapt into her brother's arms,

Francesca felt a rush of regret. She would never have this sort of reunion. Her thoughts turned to Maria's shriveled body, and then again to the smell of the inspector's breath that lingered in her memory. She squeezed her eyes closed. It had been worth it. Even with the inspector's greedy pawing and the mockery in his eyes, she'd never regret the deed, just as she would never regret what she'd given up to be here, no matter how precious. Dear Sister Alberta and her gentle ways, the craggy hills of home that smelled of limestone, the golden stretches of sand, and the well-worn path through the orange grove. It was all in the past now. She felt for the medallion at her neck and kissed it, giving thanks to the Madonna for her strength. She knew the Virgin Mother would forgive all Francesca had given away—and what she'd taken to survive—even if Sister Alberta's God wouldn't.

In spite of the cold, she headed outdoors to wait for Alma on a bench by the dock. She thought of Alma's and Mr. Lancaster's concern for her welfare, perfect strangers who were kind when they didn't have to be. It was a reminder of the good in the world, and one for which she was grateful in that moment. She might have sacrificed a lot, but she'd also gained a new friend—and an employer—without even setting foot in the city. That was more than she could have hoped for. She felt her mood lighten and began to daydream about what the Lancasters' house would be like. Marble fountains and rich draperies, fine music in the evenings, and a kitchen bigger than anything she'd ever seen.

As the sun slid toward the horizon, the air turned cold as a blade. Her breath formed a cloud that hovered a moment until a breeze carried it away. Shivering, she peered at the imposing building she'd grown to despise. *Good riddance.* If she never had to lay eyes on it again, it would be too soon.

When her hands felt like blocks of ice, Alma—at last—joined her at the dock.

"You're here!" Francesca leapt to her feet.

"Let's get out of here, shall we!" Alma said.

A burst of joy surged through Francesca's limbs. Dear Maria, Santa Maria, she was going to America!

As they boarded the ferry, her happiness faltered only an instant when Alma asked her about the inspections. She beat back a wave of nausea, unwilling to mar the happy moment with an ugly memory. After the short ferry ride to shore, they walked silently to a clutch of bushes where a tall figure lingered in the shadows beneath the rising moon. In the dark, the looming cityscape framed his silhouette.

"Fritz!" Alma called, reaching for Francesca's hand. "*È mio fratello.*"

Moonlight streamed across the young man's face, lighting a pair of high cheekbones, a prominent chin, and a pair of searing blue eyes that were a different shade of blue from Alma's. He wasn't exactly handsome but he was finely featured. An unspoken thought passed between brother and sister, and Alma nodded slightly.

Francesca wondered what it meant. She'd need to become very good at reading body language until her English improved.

"Francesca, meet my brother Fritz."

Fritz removed a dark-brown derby hat from his head. "Pleased to meet you."

"Hello," Francesca said. "Thank you for help with Mr. Lancaster."

"Happy to be of service." He revealed a nice smile as he placed his hat back on his head.

In a mixture of Italian and English, Alma said, "I'm starved. You may have to help us serve some customers at the brewery, but a little serving in exchange for a place to sleep will work for you, I hope?"

"Yes!" Francesca replied. She'd clean their house top to bottom if she had to. She was relieved to have a place to lay her head for the night and glad to put her idle hands to work. Perhaps it would help keep her thoughts at bay.

Fritz's eyebrow arched in surprise. "She'll be staying with us tonight?"

"If I can convince Robert and Mama, yes."

Francesca didn't miss the surprise in Fritz's voice. So Alma hadn't asked her parents yet? Francesca's stomach clenched. She hoped her parents were as kind as her new friend was.

Alma switched to German, and brother and sister went back and forth until Fritz rubbed his hands together. In English he said, "It's freezing. Let's get going."

Francesca fell into step beside them, taking two steps to their one. "Your father is tall?" she said, attempting humor with her limited English.

Fritz chuckled. "Yes, he was tall. Before he passed away, that is."

"Oh, I am sorry—"

"That was years ago," Alma added quickly. "Our stepfather's name is Robert Brauer. Mama is Johanna. You'll meet our siblings, too. There are five of us in all."

Francesca couldn't imagine having such a large family, though she had always wished for one.

"Do you have any brothers or sisters?" Fritz enunciated slowly for her benefit.

Alma nudged Fritz.

"What?" he asked irritably.

"Her sister—" Alma began.

"She died," Francesca added quickly. To say the words aloud cut her like a knife, and the finality of living the rest of her life without Maria hit her again, pain rolling through her strong enough to take her breath away. She swallowed and focused on the road ahead, waiting for the pain to subside.

"I'm sorry," Fritz said. She didn't—couldn't—reply, and after an awkward moment of silence, he pointed at her suitcase. "Can I carry that for you?"

When she felt she could speak without crying, she thanked him and gave him the few precious belongings she owned. She didn't know these Brauers well, and yet, she gave herself over to them willingly. Sheer exhaustion prevented her from acting otherwise, or perhaps it was relief there were good people in a world that had been so cruel. As another knot of emotion rose in her throat, she guided her thoughts back to the landscape.

They walked the rest of the way to the train station in silence. Alma helped her with her ticket, and within minutes, they glided over the city, lights and buildings hurtling past them. Francesca couldn't wrap her mind around the size of the city, the endless stream of lights twinkling in windows and from lampposts. There were as many lights in this city as there were stars in the vast skies over her island home. She wondered at the way life could change in an instant, until it was barely recognizable. How one could move through their days numbly, inured to their surroundings, days passing into years. She wished she had cherished what was good about her home, however little, while she had it, but she had been too wounded. Too desperate to flee.

When they arrived at their stop, they paced quickly through the city streets. Francesca nearly had to run to keep up, but she was glad to make haste. Exhaustion leaked from every pore.

"This is our street," Alma said as they turned onto a crowded block.

Some of the storefronts were closed, but a glow emanated from the windows in row after row of apartment buildings and taverns. The air smelled of melted snow and mud until the breeze shifted, bringing a thick cloud of factory smoke. People shuffled along the street, stepping around broken furniture, over piles of manure, around garbage. Ahead, a small crowd gathered. Shouting echoed against the building fronts. As they neared, Francesca realized several of the men were fist-fighting.

"Come on." Fritz tucked his free hand under Alma's elbow. "Let's cross the street. And whatever you do, don't make eye contact."

"Is it the Eastmans?" Alma asked, voice low.

"By the looks of it. And the Five Points."

"It's the Italians and the Jews. Turf wars," Alma whispered, translating for Francesca.

The Italians? She cringed as she thought of the gangs at home and the way the *capofamiglia* warred against each other. People often ended up dead. She felt a flash of embarrassment and disgust when she considered what Francesca and Fritz must think about these people who came from her island, especially when there were plenty of good, God-fearing people. She remembered the way Mrs. Lancaster had sneered at her, how the Polish men in the cafeteria at Ellis Island wouldn't let her sit at their table, and the many hateful comments and stares she'd endured since she'd arrived. No one liked Italians, it seemed, and the gangs made it that much worse, with their thieving and the way they brutalized those who opposed them. Her weariness deepened as she thought of the long road ahead to prove herself different from what was expected of her.

The noise grew as the men began to jeer and their scuffle became more violent.

Francesca could feel the change in both Fritz's and Alma's demeanor as they picked up their pace. When they were directly across the street from the group, something metallic caught the moonlight, and the brawling men paused.

"Ah, hell," Fritz said, his tone turning gruff. "He's got a gun. Do you understand, Francesca?"

"There is danger," she said, pulse pumping in her ears.

"Yes," he said. "But we're very near home."

They raced along the street, putting more distance between them and the gang. When they reached a large red building, Alma and Fritz bounded down a set of stairs abruptly, leading to a door below street level. Francesca ducked after them, trying to catch her breath.

Just as they opened the door, the prattle of gunshots rang out in the night.

Fritz shoved Francesca and Alma inside and locked the door behind them.

Alma gasped in a breath, and Francesca clasped her hands together to keep them from shaking.

"Well, that was lucky," Fritz said, "We got here just in time."

A stout woman as tall as Alma met them at the door and fired off something in German. Francesca was beginning to recognize the alternating guttural sounds and decisive finish, and the sharpness so unlike like the undulating music of her native tongue.

"They had a gun," Fritz said in English. He removed his hat and coat and hung them on an already-full coatrack by the door. "Can I take your coat?"

As Francesca removed her coat, Alma said, "Mama, this is Francesca Ricci."

Mrs. Brauer stared baldly at Francesca. "I'm Johanna Brauer."

"Mrs. Brauer, hello."

Alma switched to German, and Francesca tried not to stare at them as their voices escalated, but she could hear the anger in Signora Brauer's voice. She watched Alma hunch forward as if she were a child being scolded. After another exchange of heated words, Alma's mother rushed to the counter and filled a large mug with beer. She handed it to Fritz, who accepted it gratefully and disappeared into a back room.

Francesca had the distinct feeling she wasn't exactly welcome.

Alma noticed Francesca's expression and patted her on the shoulder. "It's all right. Let me show you our bierhaus."

Two long tables ran the length of the room. A dozen or more customers ate, talked, and sipped heartily from their mugs, and a warm glow emanated from the hearth. The rich scent of sausages made her stomach rumble. The bierhaus was clean but cozy, cheery even, and for the first time, she relaxed a little. Behind the counter, a young woman refilled empty beer steins. A much younger girl helped wash dishes.

"That's my sister Greta," Alma said. "She's the next oldest, and Else is our youngest. My brother Klaus is twelve. He's probably in the back with Fritz, my father, and the rest of Fritz's friends."

Francesca smiled at the children. Greta was beautiful, if a little aloof, with her golden hair and fine bone structure, and Else was a round-faced little sprite with missing front teeth and long brown plaits down her back.

"We brew most of the beer ourselves, but we also carry two of the popular brews from Germany," Alma explained in Italian. "I used to prepare the food every morning, but now that I work at Ellis Island, Greta helps with the cooking chores, and my other siblings help with the cleaning."

"A big family."

Alma smiled. "And we all pitch in to make things run smoothly."

"Please speak English," Francesca said. "I must learn."

"This is the main room, and in the back is a private room," Alma continued in English as Francesca had requested. "Fritz often hosts his friends here." She pushed the door open and several men peered back at them. Fritz sat at the head of the table, devouring his dinner as if he hadn't eaten in weeks.

"Are you hungry?" Alma turned to Francesca.

"A little," she replied, realizing she hadn't eaten all day. She'd been far too nervous, and with the inspector—she quickly shuttered the image of him. "Yes, very."

Alma dished up two plates of sausages, potatoes, and a thick slice of bread, and they joined Fritz. The others spoke German, and though Francesca didn't understand, she didn't care. She was far too hungry—and too relieved to be here, in the city, in America.

As she drank deeply from her glass, she met Fritz's eyes over the rim.

He chuckled.

Self-conscious, she put her napkin to her mouth, imagining a giant smear of meat fat across her cheek or a chunk of potato on her chin. She dug into her food again, happy to have such a flavorful meal that was also cooked well. She hesitated before she reached for more bread.

"Please help yourself, Miss Ricci," Fritz said, amusement etched into his features.

She pointed to his almost-empty plate. "I eat fast before you eat everything."

He looked at her an instant in surprise and then laughed heartily. "That's fair. I suppose I'm hungry, too."

She smiled, pleased he understood her humor.

Alma dug her elbow into her brother's side. "Can you blame her? She's been eating in that cafeteria every day."

"This is the best thing I've eaten in weeks," Francesca said in Italian and started in on a mound of potatoes.

"What did she say?" Fritz asked.

Alma switched to English. He replied to Francesca, and Alma slapped him on the arm. He said something else, and they dissolved into laughter.

Francesca frowned at her plate. Were they talking about her? She hated not understanding.

Alma flashed a smile. "My brother is embarrassed his joke didn't translate."

Francesca met Fritz's eye and said, "You are not funny."

He roared with laughter.

She warmed to the happy sound and smiled.

"This is true. I'm not funny." He replied slowly to ensure Francesca understood him.

They finished their meal all the while sharing a little about their family and their lives. Francesca talked about Maria, Sister Alberta, and the seaside village where she grew up, though she carefully avoided any mention of her father and her reasons for coming to America. Fritz might think less of her somehow, and for a reason she couldn't explain, that mattered to her. Alma translated only what was necessary.

Mrs. Brauer paused at their table with several empty plates leveraged expertly in her arms. "That's enough fun for now, you three. I need some help."

"We'll be right there." Alma stood, and Francesca followed.

"I'm going to talk to the men for a few minutes, but I'll help you clean the pots in a bit," Fritz said, sliding into a seat next to a friend already deep in conversation.

"Are you sick?" Alma glanced from Fritz to Francesca. "You've never offered to help me with the pots before."

He winked and joined the others in their conversation.

Francesca followed her friend around the main room of the bier-haus, collecting dirty plates from customers. After they had scrubbed most of the dishes, she broached the awkward subject on her mind. "Your mother didn't approve of me staying with you. I can go. Is there some place nearby I might stay?"

"You'll stay here," Alma said firmly. "Don't worry about Mama. But I must forewarn you, we have no space upstairs in the apartment. All of the beds are filled, and there is a pallet on the floor for two of my siblings. You would have to stay here, in the bierhaus. I have one extra blanket, and we can make a pillow out of towels for you. If you wear your overcoat over your nightgown, you should be warm enough."

Francesca squeezed Alma's sudsy hand with her own. "I don't know how to say thank you."

Alma beamed. "Having a new friend is thanks enough. Let's finish up here and find that blanket."

20

Alma was glad to see the customers in the bierhaus disperse. It was uncomfortable watching the men stare at Francesca as if she polluted the very air they breathed, and Alma didn't quite know what to do about it. She suddenly felt responsible for Francesca—protective even—and wanted to help her ease into her new life.

Mama went upstairs to go to bed, and Robert started behind her but paused, turning on the step.

"Girl, you looked a mess with that filthy apron and your unkempt hair. Don't forget you represent me and my establishment. I'll not have my daughter running off customers because she's ugly."

Alma's cheeks flushed hotly. He'd never come out and said she was ugly, not directly. What was worse, he'd scolded her in English instead of German, probably in the hopes Francesca would understand it. He had always done his best to embarrass her and to remind her of her place in the household—at the very bottom. He seemed to take satisfaction in exerting a sort of cruel power over her, demanding her obedience even if he directed her in a mean-spirited way. But what could she really do about it?

"Yes, Father," she managed to say.

When he'd gone, she met Francesca's eyes. The young woman

looked away quickly, pretending not to have understood the exchange, and Alma's flush deepened.

They didn't go to bed right away and talked well into the night, sharing more about their families, the story of how Alma came to work at Ellis Island, and speculating about Francesca's new employer.

The morning came too soon.

Alma prepared for work rapidly, and after a quick breakfast, she and Francesca walked with Fritz to the train. Alma, now accustomed to the ride to work, no longer needed her brother to walk with her and enjoyed the taste of freedom, the freedom of being on her own, but today, she wanted to make sure Francesca knew her way to the Lancasters' home on Park Avenue. They rode uptown and, after, walked the remaining blocks from the station to the Lancasters' address. As the sun rose, the city came alive. Forsythia had begun to bloom in clouds of bright yellow in the small garden plots throughout the neighborhoods, and the rare patch of grass was sprinkled with green. Alma was grateful for the color seeping back into the landscape. Winter had never felt so long.

Birds had begun to nest in the row of trees along the street, their song accompanying the sounds of the city, the hum of industry awakening to another day. Alma wondered what Francesca thought of New York and considered how different it must be from her home. Alma had never given thought to how an immigrant must feel making their way through a place like Manhattan, or beyond, into a country of which they knew little.

"I have a day off from work on Sunday," Alma said. "Perhaps I can show you more of the city, and maybe introduce you to Father Rodolfo. He's the priest who taught me how to speak Italian. Fritz is off work, too."

He shot her a warning look. "We have the family picnic. And I'm meeting friends at the park, too."

"She can join us," Alma said, voice light. Many of the German families in their neighborhood met at Tompkins Square Park every Sunday from early spring through late fall. They brought food to share, kicked a ball or played cards or chess, and watched the world go by as they enjoyed their day of rest. The ground had thawed, in spite of the enduring cool air. Happy daffodils had already sprouted and gone, and tulips flaunted their elegant petals. By noon, the lingering nighttime chill was mostly gone. It would be a perfect weekend to begin their picnicking season.

Francesca looked hesitantly at Fritz before replying. "I don't want to be any trouble."

"You won't be intruding," Alma and Fritz said simultaneously. Alma glanced at her brother, eyebrow raised. He'd sure had a quick change of heart.

Francesca smiled. "*Molto bene.* I go to your picnic."

"Good," Alma replied, returning her smile. Perhaps she'd introduce Francesca to Father Rodolfo another time.

As they arrived at the train station, Alma glanced at her new friend, who stood nervously, hands clasped tightly in front of her. Alma was suddenly glad she didn't have to work for such a wealthy family, in a new city, in a new country.

"It'll be great," Alma said with an encouraging smile.

"Mr. Lancaster is a real gentleman," Fritz said. "I think you'll like him as a boss."

Francesca nodded, but Alma could tell her friend didn't really grasp everything he'd said, so she translated. "Of course you can stay with us, too. We'd be happy to have you until you're able to go to the convent."

In German, Fritz said, "Mama is going to kill you."

"She's done nothing but be helpful and polite," Alma replied. "And she slept on the floor in the bierhaus! It's not as if she's inconveniencing anyone. Besides, you keep staring at her. She must not be all bad."

"I'm staring at her because she's a stranger living in our house, Al." He looked past her, pretending to watch a man on his bike who carted a too-large box atop his handlebars, but Alma knew better. Fritz was embarrassed she'd noticed his staring.

Alma rolled her eyes. "You're staring at her because she's beautiful. And friendly and spirited, too."

"You go to work," Francesca cut in, clearly sensing they were talking about her. "I find my way back to the bierhaus later."

"Are you sure you can find the way?" Alma asked.

"Sì. Yes, thank you. And thank you, Fritz." She kissed his cheek and descended the steps leading to the staff entrance of the Lancasters' home.

Fritz froze, stunned by the show of affection.

Alma poked him in the shoulder. "It's just an Italian goodbye. Now let's go, handsome, or we'll be late."

They headed back to the train and continued their separate ways to work.

By the time the ferry docked at Ellis Island, the sun had inched higher overhead, brightening the morning sky. Alma left the beautiful spring morning behind and went to the matron's office to put away her things.

She'd scarcely hung up her coat when Mrs. Keller clapped her hands to gain everyone's attention.

"Ladies, line up, please!"

The matrons scurried to their places, awaiting instruction. Alma stood next to Helene, who whispered something about lunch and quickly pushed her shoulders back, her eyes forward, as Mrs. Keller made her way down the line. Their supervisor looked more haggard than usual, the grooves around her mouth and on her forehead a map of her fatigue.

"Good morning, ladies," a man's voice came from the doorway.

Everyone turned to see a stout gentleman of medium height with a mustache and thinning hair. He wore a pristine dark morning suit and vest, and a burgundy necktie in the latest fashion. He was an attractive older gentleman, but judging by the way he held his shoulders, he was wound as tight as a bowstring.

"Commissioner Williams, do come in," Mrs. Keller called. "Ladies, I'd like to introduce you to your new commissioner of operations here at Ellis Island."

There was an audible gasp by a few of the women. So Fitchie had been fired after all!

Commissioner Williams nodded. "It's a pleasure to be here in the service of our president, and for the good of our country. I look forward to getting to know you all."

Helene glanced at Alma, her eyes widening a fraction.

"I intend to make some changes here at the immigration station," he continued. "There's a lot of work to be done if we're to ensure things are running smoothly. Our primary goal is to protect our country from indigents, but we must also treat the immigrants as every human being deserves. If you have any questions or concerns, about anything, please relay them to your supervisor or directly to me. Is that understood?"

"Yes, sir," they said in unison.

"Very well. Have a good day, ladies. Mrs. Keller." He nodded and promptly disappeared into the hall.

"Well then," Mrs. Keller said, grabbing her notebook. "Let's see about the duties today."

As Mrs. Keller called off their assignments, Helene shot Alma another look, one that relayed exactly what Alma was thinking: she wondered what kind of changes the commissioner had in mind.

The day flew by in a blur of activity. Alma had been assigned to the registry office again, and one thing after another had gone wrong, souring her good mood from the morning. A child had thrown a tantrum and spilled his milk on the floor, soaking her shoes. After a long wait in line, two men had shoved each other, igniting a shouting match. She'd had to call an inspector to help break up the argument. She'd translated for a hostile gentleman from Germany as well, who'd degraded and insulted her. Frazzled, she glanced at the clock. Two more hours and she could go home, take a break after a very long day.

An inspector waved at Alma from across the room to help with a translation. It was a simple one, and the German fellow thanked her before he continued on his way to the staircase leading to the exit. After, she roamed idly through the massive registry room and glanced up at the arched tiled ceiling, the enormous light fixtures overhead, and the endless windows brightening the space while waiting for her next errand. As she reached the far end of the room, she overheard a snippet of a conversation and paused.

"Like I said, I can make this a lot easier for you," the inspector said. "We can skip the investigation hearing and you can be on your way."

Her gaze skimmed over the immigrant's appearance. He had a smaller stature and light coppery skin, and he walked with a limp. Perhaps there was a medical issue with his leg?

In heavily accented English, a reply. "I give money?"

"That's right," the inspector said.

Alma's brow shot up, and she leaned a bit closer to them.

"I have silver locket?" the immigrant said.

"Cash will get you out of here in under an hour."

The man set down a small case on the floor and reached inside his jacket for a beat-up wallet. He picked off a few bills.

"That will do nicely," the inspector said. "Now, let's see about signing your papers."

Alma couldn't believe what she was seeing. Indignant, she approached the inspector's desk. "Excuse me, can I be of service?" She looked pointedly at the inspector, her eyes straying to the name badge pinned at his breast. *Inspector Miller.*

"No, we don't need your help," the inspector said. "I'm signing the citizenship ledger here, and this gentleman will be on his way."

The immigrant picked up his suitcase, nodded at Alma politely, and limped through the registry room to the exit.

She stared after him, not sure what to do. The inspector had bribed the man! She wondered if the immigrant would have been deemed unfit with that limp. Surely he had a higher likelihood of becoming a ward of the state. If so, the inspector must—by law—deny him entry. She paused a moment, trying to decide whether or not she should confront the inspector. There was nothing she hated more than confrontation, but she believed the staff at Ellis Island played an important role, one of honor and responsibility, even if the work was disagreeable or difficult at times. They were employees of the United States government! And this was all wrong.

"Excuse me, sir." She cut off the next immigrant in line and stood at the edge of Inspector Miller's desk.

"What do you want?" he demanded. Annoyance stamped his features. "As you can see, I'm very busy here." He gestured at the long line behind her.

"You took that man's money."

"Listen here," the inspector said, eyes narrowed in warning. "I did him a favor. He got a pass when we both know a hearing would see him deported. He was happy to pay a small fee, so mind your own business. Now. Run along, or I'll report you to the new commissioner for shirking your duties."

She reddened at his reprimand and continued on her way, doing another turn through the room, the echo of hundreds of voices reverberated through the halls. The inspector was right. What did she know about the situation? Perhaps the immigrant didn't care about the bribe. She thought of Francesca, how she would have paid any price to make it through inspections and off this island. But Alma was very glad the young woman hadn't had to do such a thing.

Alma should have known not to speak up; she'd learned from her stepfather it only brought punishment or ridicule. She'd even received a well-timed slap or two from Robert when he'd felt the need to exert his will over hers. Hadn't she learned to keep quiet and mind her own business?

Perhaps she should keep her mouth shut from now on, just as she'd been taught.

21

*F*rancesca stood on the step outside the Lancasters' home, trying to steady her racing heart. It would be all right, she reassured herself. Mr. Lancaster might change his mind about employing her, but he had already given her the thing she needed most—entry into the country, and that couldn't be taken away. She peered up at the gleaming building, one of a whole row that faced an equally elegant series of buildings across the street. A budding tree shaded a portion of the first-story window, and a curled iron railing ran along a set of steps leading to the front door. It was early still, so early as to be rude to knock on that magnificent carved door for first introductions, so she decided to go for a walk, see a little more of the neighborhood, and get her bearings.

As the sun climbed higher in the sky, she walked up Park Avenue, careful to count the number of city blocks so she could find her way back to the Lancasters' home. *Her new place of employment!* She smiled at her good fortune, and the fear and pain that had knotted in her chest for weeks began to ease a little. Sunlight spilled over pedestrians in the street and turned windows into mirrors that reflected the golden light. Newspaper boys bustled down the walk, shoving pages into anyone's hands who would take them. Hundreds of people streamed along the street on foot, on bicycles, or in fancy carriages that looked far superior to the hackney cabs she'd seen in Alma's neighborhood.

The streets were pitted from continuous wear so that rainwater collected in murky puddles. The air smelled of cool damp tinged with soot. As she passed city block after block of homes and storefronts, her head dizzying at the sight of them all, she felt the city's weight to her very bones. The immeasurable expanse of stone and brick and steel, of people. And, if one had money, the endless array of choices. She'd been overwhelmed by Napoli when she and Maria had arrived in the city for the first time, but it couldn't compare to the vast modern infinity of her new home.

Soon she made her way back to the Lancasters' home. Gathering her confidence, she took the steps to the entrance. As she reached for the knocker, the door swished open.

A butler assessed her with a cold stare, his brow wrinkling when he noted her dress, her clear lack of status. "This is the Lancaster residence. What can I do for you, miss?"

"I am Francesca Ricci. The new cook."

Mouth twitching, he opened the door wide. "We were expecting you, but next time, use the servants' entrance."

"Yes," she replied, blushing. It hadn't occurred to her there would be two entrances. She'd never been to a house like this one.

She followed the butler inside, gaping at the splendor of the ceiling in the front hall, rising at least fifteen feet. Overhead, sunlight bent through rectangles of beveled glass etched with flowering vines that threw patterns on the floor. In every nook, vases burst with flowers, and on the wall opposite the door there was a large oval mirror encased in a gilded frame. Francesca's gaze traveled over the marble staircase leading to the second floor with its shiny railing dipped in gold. Her head reeled at the grandeur before her.

A poor fisherman's daughter had traveled thousands of miles to find herself in a beautiful home fit for a queen. Her heart felt like it might burst. Fingering her medallion, she followed the butler through the foyer to a set of stairs hidden by a door. As they descended, the smell of yeast and baked fruit rushed her senses. The kitchen spanned the entire basement floor. An assortment of copper and cast iron pots hung in neat rows from hooks over a grand stove and along the wall. There were two ovens, two sinks, a large prep table, and one long table with chairs, presumably for staff dining. The rich aroma of brewed coffee wafted around her, and she felt her stomach rumble in spite of the breakfast she'd had with the Brauers a couple of hours earlier.

"I'm Charles Smith, valet to Mr. Marshall Lancaster," the man said. "Meet your direct supervisor, the housekeeper, Mrs. Maryanne Cheedle."

Mrs. Cheedle nodded curtly but said nothing. She was too busy assessing Francesca's frayed overcoat and dirty hem.

Charles waved his hand at a young woman beside Mrs. Cheedle. "This is Miss Janie Ward, lady's maid to Mrs. Lancaster."

The woman was pretty, with soft brown hair pulled into a chignon at the nape of her neck and clear brown eyes, but fatigue had settled in the lines around her eyes, and her mouth was drawn into a shrewd pout.

"Hello," Francesca said.

Janie didn't reply and promptly gave Francesca her back.

Francesca stiffened. Neither the maid nor the housekeeper seemed particularly overjoyed she'd joined the staff. In fact, they ignored her while she was introduced to two other maids and a footman whose names she instantly forgot.

A woman burst into the kitchen then, tray in hand, her cheeks aflame. As she set down her tray, she hastily wiped her eyes on her apron and hustled to the sink to wash her hands, and perhaps to hide the fact that she was crying.

"And this is Miss Claire Deveaux," Charles said. "She's the head cook."

As he kept talking, Francesca strained to understand, making out something about the Lancasters and also the word *utensils*.

"Miss Ricci," he went on, "the staff lives here, in house in the servants' quarters. In a couple of days we'll have your bed ready. Until then, I trust you will find your own accommodations."

Her eyes widened. She hadn't expected to live here! Trying to suppress her obvious delight, she said, "Thank you, sir. That is good."

Janie the maid joined Claire at the sink and patted her on the shoulder in a comforting gesture, whispering something in her ear.

Claire shrugged off Janie's hand. "I'm fine, really. I need to go to the market." She turned to face Francesca and introduced herself properly, after which she gathered a basket and pulled on her overcoat. When Francesca remained awkwardly in the middle of the room, Claire led her to the door. "Market, Francesca. Food. We need a new menu for supper tonight. Madame isn't happy."

Francesca wondered if that was the reason for Claire's tears. A trickle of dread wound through Francesca's limbs. Their mistress must be as difficult and unpleasant as she'd feared.

"Yes, the market," Francesca said, and they barged through the staff entrance door into the street.

As the cold air hit Francesca, she wondered what her sleeping arrangements would be like. She'd have to travel to the Brauers' again that night, and she suddenly wished she'd written down the directions. Her worries grew as another thought occurred to her. When would she be introduced to the Lancasters? It struck her then that

Mrs. Lancaster might not even know Francesca had been hired. But she could worry about that later. For now, she had a job to do. A faint smile touched her lips as she walked apace with Claire.

She had a job to do.

The first few days of work, Francesca watched the servants on the Lancaster staff closely to learn their way of addressing one another, their tasks, and the pace of the household. All the while, her stomach knotted with each disdainful look thrown her way, each measured comment said within earshot. She didn't belong here, they said, in every way but directly. She tried harder, worked longer, scrubbed the pots until they gleamed, and hoped one day soon they would welcome her as one of their own. For now, she had to begin in the only place they offered to her—at the very bottom.

As the other staff busied themselves with various tasks, Francesca followed Claire around, preparing for lunch. Sometime well into their chores, Mr. Lancaster—exactly as she remembered him, with a round cheery face and kind eyes—bounded down the stairs quickly, despite his thick middle.

The staff scurried to and fro to their posts a little faster than usual.

"Hallo, Miss Ricci." He smiled broadly and smoothed the front of his silk suit in a way that appeared to be a habit. "Welcome to my home.'"

"You are kind, sir. I am happy to be here."

"I'm rather looking forward to your dishes." A cloud passed over his features. "But I hear condolences are in order. I was sorry to hear about your sister."

She caught just enough to understand his meaning—her sister.

"Thank you, sir." She swallowed, her eyes roving from face to face as the others took in the exchange. They knew nothing about her and nothing about what she'd sacrificed trying to make her way to this very kitchen. No one had asked, and she hadn't wanted to share a precious memory of Maria with people who didn't care one way or the other what Francesca had suffered.

Your sister is gone. A voice echoed in her head and pain gathered in her chest, creeping up her throat. Not now, she told herself. This wasn't the time to let the sorrow engulf her, and she shoved it away, sealing it behind a door.

Mr. Lancaster kept talking, and Francesca struggled to keep up with her limited English. When he paused at last, she said, "Thank you."

A look of confusion crossed his features, and she felt herself go red.

"Well then, carry on, everyone," he said. "And Miss Ricci, it's lovely to have you. We're thrilled you're here."

This, she understood and smiled.

As he retreated upstairs, she turned to find several envious pairs of eyes on her.

Perhaps he hadn't welcomed everyone to his household in such a way. She didn't know why her circumstances moved him to treat her differently, but she was glad of it. At least she had one ally in the house, and it was best that it was the master.

Janie crossed her arms and openly glared at Francesca. "'We're thrilled you're here,'" she said, mimicking Mr. Lancaster. "Aren't you just a catch."

A catch? Francesca wondered what that meant. Whatever it was, the maid hated her for it. The last thing Francesca needed was an enemy, so she ignored Janie, trying not to let the woman intimidate her.

"Wipe that sour look off your face or it will get stuck that way, Janie," Claire said and sent Francesca into the larder for some flour.

As she ducked inside, she smothered a smile, until she heard the sound of heels clacking on the stairs and a voice she hadn't forgotten, even after hearing it only once before. She froze, hiding in the safety of the larder's shelves, out of sight.

"Claire," Mrs. Lancaster said, "the Armstrongs will be dining with us tonight. I'd like to change the menu to a lamb roast with mint jelly and dauphinoise potatoes. You may choose the vegetable and a first course. And perhaps a Victoria sponge? Unless you have time to make those cream puffs I so enjoy."

"Yes, of course, madame," Claire said. "Tout de suite."

Francesca saw Claire glance nervously at the clock. They'd already created a menu and been to market, so now they would be tight on time.

"And you'll tell Mrs. Cheedle when she returns from the post office?" Mrs. Lancaster said. "I want the house to be spotless."

"Yes, madame, of course." Claire smiled.

"Very good. Janie," Mrs. Lancaster snapped at the maid, "come with me. There are things to be done."

Janie cast a smug glance in Francesca's direction, happy to be relied upon by her mistress, and followed her upstairs.

When they'd gone, Francesca exhaled and stepped out into the kitchen. She'd have to face Mrs. Lancaster eventually, but today wasn't that day. Thankfully.

She joined Claire at the stove. "I can help?"

"Oh, you'll help all right. We don't have a moment to waste, chérie. Mrs. Lancaster won't stand for anything less than perfection, especially with guests."

Francesca had a feeling she wouldn't stand for less than perfection at any time.

22

*A*lma walked back from the cafeteria after lunch, debating whether or not she should report Inspector Miller. She'd watched him all day, and it was a good thing, too. He'd taken money from two other immigrants in as many hours. She'd seen the new commissioner flit in and out of the registry office all day and willed him to notice the inspector's activities, but his timing was off. Perhaps she should do as Inspector Miller had asked and mind her own business. She made another slow turn through the room, noticing the queues were longer than usual and every bench was filled. Two ships had arrived that morning, one with Greeks and the other with Russians. People congregated in every inch of space; the cafeteria was jammed, and the lines at the other food vendors wound through the baggage room. It was going to be a long afternoon.

An inspector waved Alma over to his desk. She elbowed her way through a large cluster of men whose weary expressions mirrored how she felt. In front of the inspector's desk stood a husband-and-wife couple and a daughter who couldn't be more than five. They all had dark hair and eyes, and ivory skin, except the little girl, whose honey-colored locks were in braids. She clung to her mother as if afraid she might slip away. Their clothing was colorful and neat, if frayed around the cuffs and collars.

"Do you speak Russian?" the inspector asked Alma as she approached.

"A little," Alma said.

Relief washed over his face. "Tell that man to shut his trap. No one understands a word he's saying, and he keeps going on and on."

She didn't state the obvious to the inspector: the immigrant didn't understand him either, and there was no need to be so rude about it. It accomplished nothing. She pulled a small notebook from her apron pocket. She'd translated most of the inspection questions into Russian a few days ago with Jeremy's help, followed by a list of replies, but she hadn't had time to memorize them yet.

When Alma greeted the family in Russian, the young wife looked as if she would weep with gratitude. Slowly, Alma explained they were to answer a series of questions, and once they were finished here, they could be on their way. Though she still found the language awkward on her tongue, she worked slowly through the list.

What is your occupation?

Who paid for your passage?

What's your final destination in America?

Are you deformed or crippled?

Who was the first president of the United States?

How many stripes are in our flag?

Are you a polygamist?

Are you involved in the labor movement?

On the last question, Alma had written *anarchist* in parentheses. The immigrants had learned quickly to deny they were anarchists, and though it wasn't illegal to enter the country as an anarchist— yet—there was talk President Roosevelt might soon institute new laws. Now that Commissioner Williams was here, it was only a matter of time.

The husband and wife exchanged looks, and Alma repeated the final question.

"Why aren't they answering you?" The inspector looked past the family at the long line behind them. "Let's get moving, or we'll be here until midnight."

"Give them a minute," Alma replied. "They may not understand, or I may have used the wrong word." She listened intently as the couple spoke to each other, catching a word or two she recognized but nothing more.

The inspector took off his spectacles, threw them on the desk, and massaged the bridge of his nose with his thumb and forefinger. "What are they saying?"

"I asked them about the labor movement, and that's when they started arguing."

The inspector's eyes narrowed. "If they can't answer the question, then they're out." To them, he said, "I'm sorry, but you are denied."

They looked at the inspector blankly.

"Shouldn't we let them answer the question?" Alma asked, exasperated. "Let me try again."

"I don't care what their answers are. They're denied. Next!" he yelled.

"Please, that seems absurd not to let them answer the question."

"I said, denied! Next!"

A man behind them moved around the family to the inspector's desk and held out a paper. The inspector snatched it from his hand and read it quickly, the Russian family forgotten.

With the help of her notes, Alma explained the situation as best she could to the family, who now appeared even more rattled than before by the inspector's behavior.

The young wife burst into tears. The husband's face went red with fury, and in a mixture of very poor English and Russian, he said, "I'm in the labor movement, but she isn't. Let her pass. My brother lives in Brooklyn and works on the railroad. He will take care of her."

"Sir," Alma called to the inspector after he'd waved the single man through. "Won't you let the wife and child enter?" She encouraged the husband to repeat his reply.

"No," the inspector said, after he'd heard the man's explanation. Ignoring their pleas and their tears, he wrote something in his ledger. "Miss Brauer, assist them with their steamship tickets and take them to the detainees' quarters. They're to go home on the next ship."

"Sir, the woman, and clearly the child, aren't a part of the labor movement," Alma protested. "It's only her husband. Her brother-in-law has employment and lives in the city. He'll come for them. And might I remind you, sir, that being an anarchist isn't illegal."

The inspector's voice went cold. "Miss Brauer, you know how dangerous the anarchists are. If there's even a chance..."

She knew full well that some were and many were not, but now wasn't the time for a political debate.

"The child will starve if you send them home," she interrupted him. "Look at her."

The inspector glanced at the little girl, whose dress swallowed her frame, and sighed heavily, marking an adjustment in his ledger. "Fine. But the husband will stay for more questioning."

The woman and child wailed, and even the husband looked as if he might shed a tear. They had a terrible decision to make: return to the wretched poverty where they might all starve to death, or separate and possibly never see each other again, should the man not be admitted. As the husband consoled his wife Alma felt a twinge in her chest. Since she'd started at Ellis Island, her usual logic and beliefs were flipped and spun and turned inside out until she couldn't understand who she was before she'd been there.

She couldn't believe the way she'd swallowed her parents' opinions and ideals whole, and adopted them as her own. Not anymore. Not ever again. Alma saw the same desires and needs as her own painted on the faces of those who swept through these halls. When she felt she could do nothing, tears threatened or melancholy settled over her, and she found herself lamenting a system—and a life—that was profoundly unfair. She wondered how her country could preach about justice and equality when even God had created no such thing.

Alma thought again of Inspector Miller. Perhaps he would have admitted this Russian family for a little money, and would that have been so terrible? She couldn't help but think there were more important things to consider than anarchism when denying someone entry. She watched the tearful couple hold each other fiercely. Turning away those who were willing to work hard as laborers, something the economy desperately needed according to Fritz, seemed shortsighted.

She contemplated her change of heart toward the immigrants as she tended to her duties. Though she felt some sympathy toward them, she had to admit, the issue was complex. The staff couldn't very well allow every immigrant who arrived on their shores into the country, so how did they decide who could stay? For the first time in her life, she realized things weren't black and white, not even the laws of the land. That nearly anything could be justified, given the right circumstances.

She mused over these thoughts for the rest of the afternoon. When at last the arduous day drew to a close, she trudged toward the matrons' room to collect her things. Mrs. Keller didn't bother to greet her as she pulled on her coat; she was too busy briefing those who were working the night shift. Alma watched the others flowing into the room, their eyes tired, while she waited for Helene.

"How was your day?" Alma followed Helene to the door.

Her friend sighed heavily and turned a weary pair of brown eyes on Alma. "I guess it was my turn to deal with crazy."

Alma made a sympathetic groan. "I had to split up a family today. It was horrible. I almost cried myself."

"Those are the worst," Helene grumbled, rubbing her neck. "And I have to go to my aunt's house for dinner tonight." Her family was German, too, though her relatives had immigrated several generations before. Most of the Bachs had moved uptown to Yorkville long ago, away from the tenements, just as Alma's family planned to do.

As they walked to the ferry, Alma fell into step beside her. "If you saw an inspector breaking a rule, would you turn him in?"

Helene cocked an inquisitive brow at her. "Who was it?"

Alma recounted the story. When she finished, she was surprised by Helene's sardonic smile.

"My advice is to ignore it," Helene said. "We have to do the best we can, pick the lesser of the evils. Have you seen Commissioner Williams cornering employees? He's on a manhunt because Roosevelt is on his back, but no one is talking. And if you want life to be easier for you, you won't either."

Alma considered Helene's warning as they boarded the ferry. That made two warnings—one from her and one from Jeremy.

A brisk wind blew off the water, and a bank of clouds drifted across a fiery sky. Soon, the sun would set, and one by one, the city lights would flicker to life.

"Are you going to tell me who it was?" Helene asked, voice low.

Alma leaned closer. "It's Inspector Miller."

"Oh." Helene waved her hand in dismissal. "Believe me, he's not the one to worry about."

She sat back in surprise. "Wait, who is?"

"If you haven't seen him at it yet, you will soon enough."

"Tell me, Helene," she urged, her curiosity piqued.

Helene shook her head and with a grim smile ended the conversation.

Alma wondered who Helene was referring to, and found herself more than a little disgusted at the thought of another inspector—a man who held the fate of the immigrants in his hands—taking advantage of his position.

She watched the strip of buildings grow larger, taller, as the ferry chugged toward the Manhattan port.

New York City, the land of opportunity, she thought bitterly, *for some.*

23

Alma and Fritz headed uptown to meet Francesca at the Lancasters'. They'd decided it best after all, assuming she might welcome the assistance after only a short time in the city. During the train ride, Alma mulled over Helene's warning. She wondered which inspector she should watch. She mentally ran through the list of inspectors, trying to place them all firmly in her mind, searching for some signal she had missed, some clue as to whom Helene might be referring to. Exhausted by her line of thinking, she glanced at her brother. He sagged with fatigue.

She tapped his shoe with her foot. "Tough day at work?"

He ran his hands over his face and yawned. "You could say that. We're moving uptown starting next week. Going deep underground instead of building from above. This will mean more dynamite."

"So a greater likelihood of accidents."

He nodded. "And when the fellas don't speak English, it makes it difficult to get the point across."

She watched him stretch in his seat. "There's more that you aren't saying, though, isn't there?"

He sighed heavily. "It's just the talk of another strike again. We managed to get a pay raise last time we went on strike, but a ten-hour work day?" He glanced at Alma and shrugged. "Sure, we'd all like to work less, but the commissioner is coming down hard on us to finish. They want to open the subway next year sometime."

"Next year?" she asked, incredulous. "That seems impossible."

"You're telling me. God, I need a beer."

She patted his knee, ignoring the filth on his trousers. She thought about digging and toiling in the damp underground for work every day and, for once, she felt for Fritz. In the past, she'd envied his freedom to come and go as he pleased and to collect his own wages, but his work no longer sounded appealing—even compared to the difficult days at Ellis Island. For the first time, she felt an inkling of gratitude for her stepfather's insistence on sending her out into the work force, and to John Lambert for getting her hired at the immigration station. As draining as it could be, and as emotional as it seemed to make her, she felt she was doing a true service for her country and for the people who passed through the station's halls. On some days, she even felt proud of her work. What's more, she'd finally discovered what she truly wanted. To go to school to become an interpreter. Now she needed to figure out a way to talk to her parents about it.

They walked quickly to the Lancasters', eager to gather Francesca and head home. Alma hoped Francesca had ideas as to what her sleeping arrangements would entail. Mama had made it abundantly clear Francesca wasn't welcome, and though Alma had ignored her the first night, and would again that evening, she didn't know how long she would truly get away with it.

When they knocked on the servants' entrance, the housekeeper welcomed them inside the cozy kitchen. A few household staff tended to their duties as the delicious aroma of garlic, onions, and tomatoes wafted around them. And some other scent. Fried fish, perhaps, and olive oil.

On cue, Fritz's stomach growled loudly. He laughed and placed his hand on his middle. "It smells delicious. I'm starving."

"Hello!" Francesca greeted them in English with an Italian kiss on each cheek. Her eyes sparked with light, sweat dampened her hairline, and the apples of her cheeks were stained pink.

A rush of warmth flooded Alma's chest at seeing the young woman so cheerful. Fritz, on the other hand, blushed like a schoolboy as Francesca kissed his cheek.

"We wanted to make sure you knew how to find the bierhaus, if you need to stay again tonight," Alma said.

Relief flickered briefly in Francesca's eyes. "You are so kind. Yes, I do, and I've just finished everything," Francesca said, switching to Italian. "The former cook will stay for two more days while she waits for her next place to be available. I can move in when she's gone, so I'll be a part of the live-in staff!" She was so happy, she appeared on the verge of kissing them both again.

"That's wonderful!" Alma squeezed Francesca's shoulder. "I'm so happy for you."

Alma glanced at Fritz, who was quiet through the exchange, but he watched Francesca closely.

"Give me five minutes!" Francesca said.

"No problem." Alma smiled. Having a new friend outside of the carefully controlled circle of traditional German families her parents had cultivated was more than welcome, it felt like a gift. Even if the other Brauers hadn't warmed to the idea yet.

When Francesca reappeared at the door, she gave Alma and Fritz each a hunk of bread rubbed with olive oil and sprinkled with salt, pepper, and herbs.

"For the stomach." She smiled and pointed to Fritz's middle.

"Thank you. I wasn't sure I could make it home." When he bit into the bread, he made an approving sound. "You're an excellent cook."

She smiled as she watched him devour the bread. "You are excellent eater."

They all laughed.

They made their way southbound to Orchard Street. When they arrived at the Brauers' bierhaus a little over a half an hour later, they ducked inside, relieved to call it a night.

"Well, don't stand in the doorway," Mama shouted over the bar top. "Come give us a—" She stopped when she saw Francesca.

Alma pretended not to see her mother's glare. Once she explained the situation, Mama would have to let Francesca stay. Wouldn't she? It was only a couple more days.

Alma looked over the room, noticing it was busier than usual. The first warm breezes of the season were probably to blame. She and Francesca went to work serving plates, filling steins, whisking away dirty dishes. Fritz, meanwhile, headed to the back to eat, and not for the first time, envy lodged in Alma's gut. While he relaxed after a busy day, she and Francesca worked a second shift.

Irritation flared, and she peeked in on her brother in the back room. "Fritz!" she called. It came out as more of a shout.

"Sis?" He turned, glancing at her and then at Francesca, who was bent over the end of the table with a clean cloth. When he took in Alma's expression, his own turned sheepish and his shoulders drooped. "You need a hand?"

She was surprised he knew what she wanted but relieved. "We could clear the room in lightning speed if we had one more pair of hands, and then Francesca and I could sit and eat, too."

"All right. Can't have my baby sister going hungry." He grinned and collected two fistfuls of glasses and brought them to Greta, who was busy washing. In seconds they had cleared all of the dirty things and set the empty places at the tables for the next round of customers.

God love him, Alma thought. If only more men could be like him—and unlike her stepfather. She peered toward the back of the room where Robert sat sprawled out at the table, his cheeks ruddy. He laughed at something another of the men said and slapped him on the back. Anger prickled through her, and she vowed not to talk to her stepfather tonight. She didn't have the patience to be polite after such a harried day.

As Mama and Greta topped off the last of the beer steins, the bell above the door jingled. Three new customers entered and flowed directly to the bar. Alma took care of their orders and, at last, filled three plates of food for her brother, Francesca, and herself. They could eat quickly, help clean up a bit, and escape upstairs. Mama could hardly expect them to do more.

"*Mangiare,*" Alma said as she handed Francesca a plate.

A few heads turned to stare at the person who had spoken.

"Well, I see you're harboring a dago, Brauer," one of the men said to Robert.

"They work for sausage," her stepfather replied with a shrug, and the men dissolved into boisterous laughter. His red-rimmed eyes betrayed how many hours he'd been drinking already.

Alma cringed and noted with relief that Francesca hadn't understood the slur or her stepfather's comment. She knew her friends and family preferred to "stick with their own," but such rudeness in their bierhaus with a guest was embarrassing. She led Francesca to a seat at the opposite end of the table.

Alma's stepfather swigged from his stein. "Our little Italian is here for a few days, I hear. Isn't that right? At least she'll give us something pretty to look at instead of your ugly mugs." They all laughed again.

Alma stabbed a piece of her pork schnitzel a little too hard, and her knife clattered on the tabletop. She wished he would shut his mouth.

"Father, she's a lady," Fritz said sternly. "I'd appreciate it if you would respect that."

"Did you hear that, Robert? She's a lady!" The men at the table teased her stepfather.

They dissolved into laughter again.

"I am good worker," Francesca blurted out. "Smart. I understand."

"She has a respectable job, working for a wealthy family," Alma chimed in, furious Robert had allowed the conversation to go in this direction and embarrassed Francesca had understood. The stupid drunkards needed to call it a night and be on their way.

"I work at Park Avenue," Francesca continued, laying down her frock.

"Well, well," one of the men said. "Straight from the boat to Park Avenue. A regular rags-to-riches story. She sure is pretty, though, isn't she, comrades? Real pretty. Hey, little dago, why don't you come sit by me?"

Robert guffawed until he began to choke.

"Don't talk to her that way." Fritz's voice came low, menacing. "I'm warning you."

The men glanced at Fritz, surprised, a damper falling over their good humor.

Even Robert's laughter stopped abruptly.

Francesca met Fritz's eye. He held her gaze an instant and nodded.

Alma ate hurriedly, suddenly desperate to take her new friend upstairs to hide until the men had all left. When they'd finished, she and Francesca helped Else and Greta briefly in the kitchen and afterward headed to the bedroom.

Some hours later, the noise in the hall had subsided, and they crept back downstairs to make Francesca's bed.

Fritz was sitting at a table alone, reading through a stack of papers. An anarchist pamphlet sat on top. Alma bristled. It wasn't like him to make a poor choice but entirely usual for him to be obstinate about it. She feared a terrible incident would befall him before he'd desert his cause.

Francesca touched Fritz's forearm lightly. "The men..." she said. "Thank you."

His bright eyes darkened. "Any friend of my sister's is a friend of mine, and I look out for my friends."

Francesca rewarded him with a blinding smile. "*Grazie.* I am a friend."

"Yes," he said, a smile at his lips. "I believe you are."

Alma had never seen Fritz be so protective of anyone but her. She smiled a secret smile. Francesca had already won over her brother.

Humming to herself, Alma left the two alone to talk and fetched the blankets for Francesca's bed.

24

*F*rancesca awakened for the last time in the Brauers' home and moved about the dark as if it were her own, turning on the gas lamps and setting the table with Käse cheese spread, jam, and brown bread, like she'd seen Mrs. Brauer do. She lit the stove to boil water for coffee and to heat some leftover sausages they'd set aside last night for the morning. Preparing the table for the family was a simple form of payment for letting her stay, and she knew Mrs. Brauer hadn't wanted her there, even for another few nights. Francesca only wished she could make them fresh Sicilian *brioche col tuppo*, a buttery and fragrant knot of bread she'd eaten many mornings in Sister Alberta's kitchen.

She rolled her head from side to side, trying to release the crick in her neck. Despite the uncomfortable pallet she'd used for a bed, she'd slept like the dead and had deeply strange dreams. She was searching for Maria, at home on the island, and when she finally found her sister, she was crying. A baby bird had broken its wing. *It's going to die, Cesça*, Maria had said, her cheeks stained with tears. *You can't give up. You have to try to save her.* But as Francesca reached for Maria, she was swept into a midnight sea. Francesca fought the current to reach the shore, but the moment she'd touch the safety of the sandy bottom, a wave would drag her out to the depths and the dream would replay again.

Francesca had awoken with an ache in her chest so profound, she felt as if she'd split in two. Maria was gone. She couldn't believe her sister was really gone. She would never see the incredible home where Francesca was to live. Never make friends. Never celebrate Christmas or the wonder of snow in the city. Francesca would, however, do them all. Guilt and despair—disbelief at life's reckless cruelty—ravaged her heart, and she'd soaked her makeshift pillow with her tears until the early morning hours. It was her will that forced her from bed to stand on her feet again. To face another day.

Fritz ambled down the stairs with a yawn but paused when he saw her bustling about the kitchen.

"*Buongiorno.* Good morning," she said, grateful for the interruption from her thoughts. "I make coffee."

"*Buongiorno*," he replied with a clumsy accent, making her smile.

It was kind of him to try, though she wasn't sure what she thought of this Fritz Brauer. She didn't trust men and their rough hands, the way they used women for their own needs, or their sharp words that cut beneath the skin. She studied Fritz from below lowered lashes, the line of his lean but muscular shoulders, his callused hands and his bright eyes. She wondered if he was as crude as the rest. He didn't seem hostile; no latent anger hid in the angle of his jaw, but one never knew. Sometimes the most benign face hid the darkest secrets.

They filled their plates, sitting in silence as the coffee began to work its magic through their bodies. Francesca spread thick butter on two pieces of bread. She'd need her strength, and though she'd eaten well the night before, her stomach felt cavernous again. She bit into the bread, wishing it were slathered in lemon curd or prune-plum jam, but she had no right to complain. The Brauers fed her well. She'd eaten roasted apples with cinnamon, potatoes and cabbage, different versions of pork steaks and sausages. With each bite, each new dish, she'd ruminated on the stark differences between German and Italian cuisine. All was simple but tasty, and the food was certainly better than anything she'd had on the ship or at Ellis Island.

As they ate, Francesca listened to the sounds of the tenement, and the city, awakening. It was never completely silent here, even in the dead of night, and she was grateful for it. The rumble of wagons and the chorus of voices inside the building and on the street distracted her from the silence that gnawed at her insides. The absence of a voice for which she longed.

"I can walk you to work again, if you like," Fritz said as he popped a wheel of sausage into his mouth. He explained something to her, but when he realized she was concentrating on his mouth, he stopped. "Oh, you don't understand. Well, it's not important. More coffee?" He jumped to his feet, slamming his knee into the tabletop. Rubbing the spot, he muttered under his breath.

"You have the grace," she said, her voice even.

He let out a surprised laugh. "You're funny, Francesca."

She smiled slightly. "I like to laugh. It has been a long time."

He refilled their coffee cups. "Why did you leave Italy?"

The mention of her home triggered a wave of images—the way she'd had to flee her own father, their constant poverty as he spent all their money on drink, the well-worn memories of her mother and the pain of her disappearance. There wasn't any reason she should share her secrets with this man, a virtual stranger, but something about his earnest face lent her courage to say the truth aloud.

"To escape many things. My father, memories of my mother." She drank deeply from her cup. "I came to start over, for a better life."

He reached into the larder for a small leftover tart. "You'd better eat this then. Apple tarts make everything better, especially life."

She laughed suddenly, and an unexpected warmth spread through her.

In the lamplight, his light-blue eyes glistened like ice. "I'm glad you're here."

She smiled hesitantly, unsure of what he could mean or how she should respond, but at last said, "I am happy, too."

A thumping came from the stairwell, and Alma bounded into the room, her hair pinned hastily on top of her head. "I can't believe I overslept! I never do that." She sighed as she stirred milk into her coffee. "It'll be a long day."

Francesca wanted to reassure her the day would pass quickly, but her own long day stretched out before her. She thought of the dazzling home that looked more like a mansion with chandeliers and velvet drapes and a staircase made of fine wood and marble. The silk-covered sofa and chairs, and the many rooms set aside for guests. But it was the kitchen that delighted her most. When no one was watching, she had run her fingertips over the long row of glass jars in the pantry that held so many fragrant herbs. She'd arranged the vegetables in a colorful array, like a work of art ready to be painted. But wasn't food art? She believed it was, even as she continued to learn more techniques from Claire. Briefly, Francesca wondered if she would see the Lancasters that afternoon. Worrying her napkin between her fingers, she imagined Mrs. Lancaster's reaction when she discovered Francesca under her roof.

"I'm afraid I won't have time to take you to work today, Francesca." Alma gulped down her breakfast and stood. "Do you think you can find your own way?"

"You go on," Fritz interjected. "I'll take her."

Francesca stiffened at the idea of being alone with Fritz, nice as he was. But they would be on the streets and on the train with plenty of other people around, she reminded herself. It wasn't as if they would be alone. She relaxed a little and nodded in agreement.

In a flurry of activity, they dressed for the weather and headed to the train station. Alma waved goodbye as she climbed the platform to a southbound train. On the northbound train, Francesca chose a seat next to a window, and after a moment's hesitation, Fritz slid into the seat beside her. She inched away from him, careful not to brush his leg. She toyed with the handles of her handbag, and after several minutes of uncomfortable silence, she attempted conversation.

"Do you like work?" she asked.

"Well enough," he said.

She frowned. Sometimes her mind sifted through the foreign words and she landed on some understanding, and others, their meaning flitted away, just out of her grasp.

Noticing her expression, he enunciated carefully. "Yes, I like my work. Most of the time."

She smiled. "It is good to have a job."

Bemusement twinkled in his eyes. "I've never given it much thought. I've worked since I was a boy."

"There is very little work in Sicily. America is good country," she said.

"It has its problems, but yes," he said, expression pensive. "My friends and my men want to make some changes, though. Work fewer hours for more pay. Do you understand?"

"Problems and work and change." She smiled. "Every place needs change, but still, you have luck."

"Yes, I suppose we're lucky. And now we're lucky to have you here, too," Fritz said, a boyish grin crossing his face.

Her eyes locked on his. There was no mirth there, no mockery in their icy-blue depths. Fritz seemed to mean what he said and didn't play games with her as her father had, to trap her.

"You look... Did I offend you?" he asked. "Did I say something wrong?"

"No, I was thinking of my father."

"Oh, I see," he said. "Do you miss him?"

"No!" She spat out the word. "He was a beast."

"Well, he is far away now." Fritz's voice came low, reassuring. "You are safe here."

She studied his earnest expression, not knowing how to respond, so she changed the subject. "Tell me about your papa."

His brow arched, disappearing beneath the brim of his derby hat. "He was very kind and intelligent. A lot like Alma, in fact. He read books, wrote papers. He was a professor. Do you understand?" She nodded and he went on. "He was nothing like Robert, my stepfather..."

He continued to speak, but Francesca had trouble parsing through the words, so instead, she watched his animated face. His eyes danced with a sentiment she couldn't quite place, and the intonation in his voice though friendly, felt... *Passionate* was the word. This man had a fire in his belly, and not the kind that came with too much drink.

He stopped. "I really should practice the Italian I've learned, but I'm not very good at it. I'm talking too fast, aren't I?"

"*Sì.* I know nothing of what you say."

He laughed nervously. "Serves me right for rambling on."

She caught his eye and held it a beat too long, quickly looking away. Fritz Brauer seemed truly kind, but he was a man, and she could not forget what men did to their women. And yet, her lips stretched slowly into a smile. She didn't know what to make of him, or his chivalry, or the way he listened to her intently, but he had made her smile more times in the last couple of days than she had in months.

He returned her smile, his eyes crinkling around the edges.

And at that moment, something fluttered inside her like a moth's wings, beating toward the light.

25

After a couple of weeks of failed attempts at conversation, many mistakes but also some successes, Francesca had learned the routines of her new home. With Claire, she shared a neat and comfortable bedroom off the kitchen with two single beds, modest navy quilts, and a window overlooking the street. An electric lamp sat on a table between the beds, and a painting of a country manor with flourishing gardens was framed on the wall above it. The tension in her shoulders had begun to ease, if only slightly. Still, her nights were plagued with nightmares of home. At times, she thought it would never end, that she would never become an American and continue to float between worlds, tormented by her past. Yet morning would dawn, and she'd awaken in a fine bed, far from her father, and she would believe in, and be grateful for, her new life all over again.

As she placed hot brioche, a crystal bowl of butter, and some strawberry jam on the breakfast tray for Mrs. Lancaster, she focused on the conversation going on around her. The rhythm of the English language had begun to sound less abrupt and filled with broken syllables. Though it didn't possess the music of her own language, it had started to feel less awkward on her tongue. Most of the household staff were immigrants, too—Janie and Charles from England, Claire from France—so their accents made their English more difficult to decipher than Alma's and Fritz's. The staff assumed she couldn't follow their conversations, and they grew lax around her, even when they were clearly discussing her work habits, her mannerisms—her differences. She understood far more than they realized. And she dedicated herself to learning more. Still, by day's end, her head ached as she tried to parse out the words she knew from the incoherent noise.

Francesca cast a quick look at Claire and Mrs. Cheedle, who had been gossiping like a pair of hens since they sat down to breakfast.

Mrs. Cheedle laid her spoon on the edge of her porridge dish. "I've never seen a single photograph of him or even a memento. If her husband passed away, wouldn't she at least have saved something of his? If, for no other reason, for her son's sake."

Francesca bent over the sink to scrub the porridge pot, wondering who they could be talking about now.

"What about the painting in the dining room?" Claire pointed out. "Maybe that's him."

"Or maybe that's her father," Mrs. Cheedle said, looking at Claire over the rim of her cup. "He looks a bit too much like the mistress to be her husband."

Francesca paused briefly in her washing—they were talking about Mrs. Lancaster.

"Maybe." Claire clucked her tongue in thought and drew a long sip of tea from her cup. "They could have divorced, though given her station, that would be the scandal of the century."

"Perhaps that's why they moved from England," Mrs. Cheedle offered.

Claire's voice dropped and she leaned in closer. "I don't know, but there must be something that makes her so angry all the time."

Both women chuckled softly. Francesca refrained from

commenting but was glad to see she wasn't the only one who thought Mrs. Lancaster was wretched. She wondered if there was any truth to their musings, that Mrs. Lancaster had been divorced and scorned, left England when the scandal broke. It was as good a theory as any, though Mrs. Lancaster didn't seem the type to get divorced. Perhaps something tragic had happened to her husband and she was lonely, that was all.

"Are we talking about the mistress again?" Janie, the lady's maid, dropped something in the wastebasket on her way through the kitchen and, with a nasty smile, laid a stack of Mr. Lancaster's dirty dishes atop the pile Francesca had already washed. Francesca smiled back sweetly, not wanting to be reported for being either difficult or shirking her duties—something Janie had tried to do already even in Francesca's short time there.

"Never you mind," Mrs. Cheedle said dismissively and gulped down the last of her coffee. "Better take the breakfast tray up to the mistress before she rings the bell."

Francesca dried her hands on a towel and placed a small rose bud on Mrs. Lancaster's tray next to the water glass.

Janie arched her brow. "What's the flower for?"

"It's pretty, and it make mistress happy."

"When did you ever talk to the mistress?" Janie picked up the tray, careful to keep it level to prevent the wobbling teacup from tipping.

She shrugged. "I hope it make her happy." Francesca gave the maid her back and busied herself with cleaning the last of the dishes. Janie was really insufferable, and for no good reason.

"I'm not sure anything makes Mrs. Lancaster happy," Janie mumbled.

"Janie!" Claire said, taking the pot off the stove and pouring boiling water down the sink drain. "Better get on with it, or you'll see just how unhappy she can be!"

Thankfully, Francesca had yet to cross paths with Mrs. Lancaster, though it seemed odd the mistress didn't want to know who worked and lived under her roof. Mr. Lancaster had, on the other hand, checked in on her once more after his initial welcome, gifting her with an English dictionary. She'd thanked him profusely and made him laugh, earning another scowl from Janie and a curt nod from Charles.

Once the breakfast dishes had been cleaned, Francesca began the midday meal preparations. Claire let her choose the menu for the day, to "give her a little more confidence," she'd said. Francesca pre-pared hardboiled eggs stuffed with crab and capers, a loaf of fresh rosemary bread, cold salad of chopped carrot and greens tossed with vinegar, oil and lemon, and sliced cold chicken from the night before. Since she still had a lot to learn about baking, she made something she knew how to do well instead: custard with sugared lemons for afternoon tea.

As she slid the custard into the icebox to set, Claire leaned over her shoulder and in her thick French accent said, "I'll show you how to make tarts. Plum tart with apricot glaze is perfect for this time of year. And we'll need to make rice pudding with raisins for Mr. Lancaster." She shuddered. "The texture is like vomit." Claire mim-icked the vomiting motion.

Francesca laughed. Claire had warmed to her quickly when she saw how hard Francesca worked and how much she wanted to please the head cook. She hoped, in time, Claire would grow to like *her*— who she really was—and not only the immigrant who must work like the devil for approval. Francesca found it stifling, that she should be judged by what she did for others, how well she served them and their needs, and not for who she was as a person. Then again, she had not always done the right thing—or even the good thing—so perhaps it was best they didn't. As a rush of guilt washed over her, she glanced at Claire's open face.

"How long have you been a cook?" Claire asked. "You're very young."

She'd hoped to avoid this question. Claire was nearly twice her age, with much more experience. "My mother teach me to cook before she...left, and Sister Alberta after, but that is all." She scrubbed a saucer clean and dried it with a dish towel. "I haven't worked for anyone before."

Claire's thick brow scrunched into one long caterpillar across her forehead. "I see."

"You are the head cook, yes? Not me."

Claire burst into a jolly laugh. "You think I'm threatened by you?" She shook her head as she folded a set of tea towels. "*Merci—non*, my lamb. I am happy to have you here. Now the two of us can take the heat of Mrs. Lancaster's rage together."

Francesca smiled, though she didn't like the sound of facing anyone's rage. She'd narrowly escaped that life at home.

"The last cook burned the food, or made disgusting recipes." Claire's nose wrinkled at the memory. "She burned the chicken, she burned the beef, she burned the potatoes. How can a cook burn potatoes?" She shook her head. "But even when she made something edible, the mistress made life very difficult for her. When Susanne started to cry, Mrs. Lancaster called her names. Whatever you do, don't let the mistress see you cry!"

"I do not cry easily." Francesca wiped an invisible spot on the countertop vigorously with a damp towel.

Claire patted her shoulder. "Good."

As they prepared the tray for the midday meal, Claire leaned over the dish of stuffed eggs.

"What is it?" Francesca noticed the hesitation in the woman's eyes.

She shrugged her thick shoulders. "I hope she likes the eggs. We've never served them before."

Doubt needled Francesca's confidence. "They don't like crab?" She hadn't thought to ask whether or not they would like seafood, and had Claire told her otherwise, she wouldn't have added it to the menu.

When Claire saw Francesca's expression, she smiled. "It's all right. They like seafood and this isn't burned, so I think you're safe for now."

"Those plates ready?" Charles called as he whisked through the kitchen. "They're being seated."

Francesca had stayed out of his way since she'd arrived. She couldn't tell if he was a quiet sort of man, or if he thought too little of her to bother taking the time to talk to her. She wiped her palms on her apron, sprinkled parsley over the eggs, and put the plate on a tray. Next, she plated the cold salads and lined the breadbasket with a beautiful lace cloth before slicing the loaf into pieces and arranging them inside it. The footman gathered the tray and headed for the stairs.

When all the dishes had been served, Francesca wiped the countertops and table again.

"You'll rub the varnish off the table if you keep that up." Claire touched her hand. "Too much. It's clean."

Francesca laughed nervously. "Yes, it's clean."

"It will be all right. You'll see, *chérie*." She smiled warmly.

At Claire's warm smile, Francesca relaxed a little. "Thank you."

"Help me with supper. We have a lamb shank that I picked up at the market yesterday."

She followed Claire around the kitchen until they had all the items they needed. Soon, she lost herself in the rhythm of chopping and dicing and mixing.

When Charles stormed into the kitchen, his face pinched as if he'd just eaten a lemon, Francesca's stomach plummeted.

"You're being summoned by the mistress of the house." His eyes flicked over her dirty apron. "Change your apron and follow me at once."

Claire gave her a sympathetic look. "Keep your head up, and whatever you do, don't cry."

Francesca pulled on a fresh apron, hands trembling. The moment she had dreaded had arrived. As soon as Mrs. Lancaster recognized her it was over. Francesca would be scolded and dismissed. But there wasn't a thing she could do about it, so she would try to do as Claire suggested—hold her head high.

Smoothing her hair, she followed Charles upstairs to face what came next.

26

To Alma's surprise and relief, it had been a quiet week at Ellis Island. One steamship had arrived on Monday, and the remainder of the week there had been nothing but detainees' hearings, organizational tasks, and, most of all, plenty of gossip. The building felt oddly empty, even with the hundreds of staff members about, and the hours ticked by slowly. Commissioner Williams had made his rounds through the building to various offices, unlike Fitchie, who'd mostly remained out of sight in his office. But Williams wasn't like Fitchie in any way and, in fact, was examining operations closely, peering over everyone's shoulders, measuring the time, quality, and value of each task with his ever-present notebook in hand. Most tried to stay out of his way, and all were on edge. Alma counted herself lucky to have had no interactions with him. Yet.

"They have all the luck," Helene said, looping her arm through Alma's as they left the detainees' ward. "I was hoping that old bat would send me home." Several of the matrons had left work early. Only a handful of women and children immigrants remained in the detainees' ward.

"I'd have to work at home, too," Alma said, steering them toward a bench in the gloomy corridor, out of sight of the inspectors in the vast and rambling registry office. "Being bored here is better than working there." Her words surprised even her, but they were true. She'd prefer to be away from the monotony of home and out of Robert's sight, even if it meant more time at Ellis Island. In some ways, she felt more herself at work. Freer and more alive. At work, she could practice the languages she was studying more openly, too.

Alma wondered if Helene had plans beyond Ellis Island. "Do you plan to continue living with your parents?" she asked.

Helene grasped her arm excitedly. "Actually, I meant to tell you! My friend Rose is a secretary for some lawyer's office, and she asked me if I wanted to move into an apartment with her."

"That's great!" she answered with enthusiasm, but inside, she felt a stab of jealousy. She couldn't imagine what that would be like, to move in with friends.

Helene went on about where the apartment was located, where they'd get furniture, how they were going to share the expenses. Eventually she turned back to talking about the staff, and Alma's eyes glazed over. She enjoyed spending time with the vivacious young woman, but only in short bursts of time. Helene talked nonstop, and her favorite topic was staff gossip. Who flirted with whom, those who had been reprimanded about various indiscretions or tardiness, and, of course, the most recently fired.

"You saw Williams at lunch," Helene said, a stray blond curl at her temple bobbing as she spoke. "He asked me a thousand questions about the staff."

"What did you tell him?"

Her friend waved her hand dismissively. "Very little. He followed me around for an hour after that. I think, to intimidate me."

Alma suspected Helene had shared a lot more than she let on. Much as Alma liked the young woman, she was incapable of keeping her mouth closed. Alma had been tempted, at times, to tell her she might learn more by listening rather than talking all the time.

"He actually followed you?" Alma asked, unable to hide the skepticism from her voice.

"Well, he happened to be in the detainees' quarters. Spoke to a couple of the other matrons."

"Ah, I see," she replied, feeling a little more at ease.

She wondered if he would seek her out as well. With several employees already on probation for various things from arriving late to being drunk or speaking rudely to the immigrants, the thought of Williams questioning her made her nervous. She'd seen things and never reported them...for a good reason, she'd told herself. But was it a good reason to keep silent about inspectors stealing from others or accepting bribes? She picked at the edge of her apron pocket where the stitching had come loose.

"Did you hear about Marge?" Helene changed the subject abruptly. "She's pregnant! She's going to work right up until the baby is born." She wrinkled her nose. "Imagine being on your feet the way we are all day, as big as an elephant. She doesn't have any other options, though. Her husband is just a cobbler. I think they shouldn't have any children if they can't afford them, conventional or not."

Alma considered her friend's point. It was unusual to forego having children when married, and Marge hardly seemed the type to break convention, or even have a mind of her own for that matter. Alma cringed as she realized someone could say the same about her.

"Telling stories about the staff, are we, ladies?" John Lambert sidled up beside them and plunked down on the bench, squeezing in next to Alma.

As Helene moved over, she met Alma's eye.

"What's so interesting?" John said in German, leaning closer to

Alma until she could see the pores from which his beard hairs grew. In fact, she hadn't really "seen" him at all until now. He was middle-aged, balding on the crown of his head, and had dark eyes fringed by long lashes. His full beard hid the rest of his face, but he smiled often, giving him a pleasant enough affect. She couldn't deny he possessed a certain charm. On the other hand, Mrs. Keller's clear disdain for the inspector flashed through Alma's mind. She'd noticed her supervisor give him a wide berth when a chance meeting presented itself and wondered why. Honestly, Mrs. Keller wasn't exactly pleasant either.

"Nothing," Helene lied. "We were just talking about women things, you know. What else are we to do? The whole week has been slow."

"It's been a nice change of pace really," Alma said.

"I can't say I like it much," Lambert replied. "It gives Williams more time to sniff around the staff." His dark eyes clouded over, and he looked down at his hands.

She exchanged another loaded glance with Helene. Something was going on between the commissioner and John Lambert. Either that or John had a reason to fear his new boss. Was he up to something he shouldn't be? Alma glanced at him, assessing his relaxed posture and easy manner, which seemed antithetical to his demanding position as chief of the registry office. All she knew was that he'd gone out of his way to make sure she was doing well at work. Something she greatly appreciated.

"You're looking very pretty today, Alma." John tweaked a lock of light-brown hair that had escaped her cap.

She blushed. The last time a man had complimented her... Well, it had been Jacob. She shifted on the bench, acutely aware of John's nearness. He was older than her by more than a decade, though not wholly unattractive. Yet, she couldn't deny something about him unsettled her, no matter how kind he'd been to her in the past.

"We haven't had much time to talk. I'd like to get to know you better, Alma." He touched her hand lightly.

She flinched at his touch.

Helene tried to hide a smile.

"Are you getting the hang of the routine here?" he asked.

"I am. It's not challenging work, but it's tiring. I sleep hard at night, that's for sure."

He nodded. "But as you can see from this week, we do have quiet days and slower times of year, thankfully. I don't understand why Roosevelt won't slow things down more."

"Thank God for the quieter days," Helene piped in.

"Yes!" Alma agreed.

"Your father invited me to the bierhaus tonight," he said casually, measuring her expression. "I think I'll take him up on his offer. Robert's an affable man."

Alma was sure Robert was affable—to other men, and to other German families who floated in and out of his bierhaus, bringing their dollars with them—just not to her. She searched for the right response, finally forcing a smile. "He'd be delighted to see you again. We'll keep a plate warm for you."

"The place seems to be busy all the time. You must be doing quite well financially."

Surprised by the comment, she didn't reply. She would never discuss her family's finances with someone, even if that someone was her boss and a sort of friend. She glanced at Helene, who studied her nails as if they were the most fascinating thing in the world.

"That makes a young woman attractive, you know," John continued, eyeing Alma in a way that made her blush. "A good German girl from a stable family. I bet you have a lot of suitors."

She stared at him, surprised by the turn of the conversation. "I...

uh. No, I don't have many. There's no time." She gave him another forced smile as she waved her hand, indicating the immigration center.

Helene covered her mouth as if to smother a laugh.

"Well now, that's absurd. A young woman such as yourself would be a prize for any man."

A prize? Was that what she was? She frowned. "I'm not sure I want to get married." The words slipped out before Alma could stop them.

He looked taken aback. "I bet Robert would have something to say about that."

Rather than answer him, she stood. "Well, sir, I'd better be going. Mrs. Keller will be looking for me."

At that moment, a group of matrons turned down the hallway, and Commissioner Williams walked stridently behind them.

He stopped when he saw the three of them on the bench. "Mr. Lambert," Williams said curtly, "shouldn't you be leading the hearing for the Swiss gentleman?"

"That isn't for another hour, Billy," John replied without taking his eyes off Alma.

Not amused by the disrespect, Williams changed his tone from curt to razor-blade thin. "That's William, and I suggest you move along. I'm sure you have more important things to do than charm the staff."

"Sure thing. *Boss.*" John stood—taller than Williams. He looked down at the commissioner, a smirk stamped on his face, and ambled off down the hallway, defiantly taking his time.

Mr. Williams ran his fingers over his mustache, arranging the hairs back into place the same way he arranged his papers, the staff, and everything else in his path. "Ladies, get to work."

"Yes, sir."

He nodded and darted off in the opposite direction as if his feet were on fire.

"What was that all about?" Alma asked as they headed to the baggage room.

Helene shrugged. "Williams is under a lot of pressure from Washington. You didn't work for Commissioner Fitchie very long before he left, but he was about as crooked as a cow path. Now Williams has to live down the other commissioner's reputation." She lowered her voice as they passed a group of inspectors in the hall. "I've heard a few of the inspectors are mixed up in extortion, and some may be selling immigrants to the gangs in town."

Alma's eyes went wide. "Really?"

Helene shrugged. "I'm not sure if it's true, but I do know money has been changing hands."

She couldn't believe her coworkers would do such a horrible thing, and yet, hadn't she already seen a few untoward things?

"Well, we should probably check in with Keller," Alma said at last.

She wondered if John or Jeremy was among those who were engaged in underhanded dealings. Even Mrs. Keller might be involved. Suddenly everything Alma thought she knew about her coworkers, and her work at Ellis Island, was thrown into question.

Perhaps she should be on her guard more. Perhaps she didn't know anyone here at all.

27

$\mathcal{F}$rancesca followed Charles upstairs and through the foyer of the Lancasters' home. She wondered which dish had offended the mistress. She had taken a risk with the crab-stuffed eggs, but she thought it a good one. Apparently not. Her stomach knotted as they entered the grand dining room, a place where she didn't belong. Pale light streamed through the windows, making the gauzy drapes appear almost ethereal, and the crystal on the table beamed broken rainbows across the table-cloth. A fire roared on the opposite wall, its crackling and hissing like a conversation in the otherwise silent room. When she caught sight of the Lancasters seated at their elegant table, she carefully concealed her fear.

The matriarch of the house sat at the head of the table, resplen-dent in a bustled gown of deep jewel-toned silks and a lace collar. Mr. Lancaster sat on her right in an elegant smoking jacket. Though it was only midday, they looked as if they were dressed for the theater, at least to Francesca's untrained eye.

"Come here," the woman commanded. "I want to get a good look at you."

"Yes, madam." Heart pounding, Francesca walked around the long dining table until she stood only a few feet away. When she met Mrs. Lancaster's gaze, the woman gasped.

"What on earth!" the woman sputtered. "Is this some sort of joke? Why is that filthy *thief* in our house! I'll never forget this...this *Italian* trying to take our water pitcher."

If only the mistress knew how accurate her description was, Francesca thought. She'd stolen a lot more than a little water. But she knew Mrs. Lancaster's issue with her wasn't just about the water. It was about Francesca being Sicilian, which meant she came from a tribe of nothing but dirty gangsters who didn't know how to read, stole and practiced violence to survive, professed their sins to a Catholic god, and the worst offense of all: her skin wasn't lily white.

"Mother, please," Mr. Lancaster said. "You're being very rude to our new cook."

Mrs. Lancaster's eyes went wide as saucers. "She is the one responsible for this meal?"

Francesca held her breath, trying to remain calm. If the mistress dismissed her, she had options, she told herself. She would throw herself on the mercy of the Brauers another night or two and look for work in their neighborhood. She would survive this, just as she had every other twist and turn.

The footman cleared his throat. "May I introduce Miss Francesca Ricci."

"I know who she is," Mrs. Lancaster said, anger lacing her tone. "And I had hoped never to lay eyes on this creature again, but I see my son has thwarted my wishes."

Mr. Lancaster placed his hand over his mother's. "I have a charitable heart, Mother. What can I say? I learned it from the very best person I know." He smiled at her, clearly aiming to defuse the situation. "Now, what was it you were saying about the eggs? How delicious they are, and how gorgeous the meal was last night as well?"

Francesca warmed to the unexpected praise. So the old bag liked her cooking before she knew who had prepared it. Unfortunately, now that Mrs. Lancaster realized who the new cook was, Francesca would have to work extra hard to please the mistress. If Francesca was allowed to stay at all. She refrained from shifting or fidgeting and held her chin up, her hands clasped in front of her while she awaited her sentence.

Mrs. Lancaster's icy gaze locked onto Francesca's like a hawk on its prey. "You get one more chance, young lady. One. If it weren't for my son and this meal, I would throw you out this very instant."

"Mother, really—"

"Marshall!" she commanded. "Do not interrupt me."

His mouth clamped shut and his ears tinged red.

"One chance." Mrs. Lancaster held up her index finger and pointed it like a wand.

"Yes, Mrs. Lancaster. I work very—"

"You do not have permission to speak," she thundered. "Now off with you."

Francesca darted from the room, relief flooding her. She couldn't believe it—the disagreeable woman liked her food enough to ask for an introduction to the new cook. And while it hadn't exactly gone smoothly, she still had her job.

She'd show Mrs. Lancaster she'd made the right choice. Little by little, Francesca would win them all over. She wouldn't let a little thing like being Italian keep her from what she wanted or what she deserved.

She allowed a small smile to escape as she returned to the warm hearth of the kitchen.

28

*A*fter a long day, Alma walked the final blocks home to Orchard Street. The scent of grilled meats and fresh bread mingled with the odor of garbage and fetid water left from a passing shower that had accumulated in the deeply rutted street. A particularly large pack of feral children raced down her block, without shoes, their faces blackened with grime. They tossed a ball and weaved precariously over and around carts stacked with vegetables or housewares, shouting and laughing raucously. She steered clear of them. Innocent passersby often lost their wallets to the little scoundrels, who swooped in like a flock of birds, surrounded the unsuspecting in a cloud of confusion, and flew away, their claws filled with whatever treasure they'd stolen.

On the journey home, Alma mused over the interaction with the commissioner and the way everyone skittered away when he was near. Williams was in the midst of investigating the staff and all of the operations at Ellis Island. And in only a few weeks' time, he seemed to have made an enemy of himself to all.

To Alma's annoyance, John Lambert had beaten her to the bierhaus. She didn't like the idea of her work life invading her home. It was bad enough she spent so many hours of her day there and ruminated on the day's events until she crept under the covers at night. Visions of her interactions with the immigrants crowded her sleep, their haunted faces imprinted on her memory, the children screaming, the families distraught as they were separated or turned away. But it was the tears of joy when she witnessed a father, brother, or husband lay eyes on their loved ones and welcome them to their new home that affected her most. What had these people endured to be here? At least her work afforded her a credible excuse to avoid the talk of marriage. As long as she contributed to the family, she was safe from her parents' meddling.

"A beer for you, sir?" Mama rushed to assist John.

"*Ja*, the largest you have," he replied in German.

Fritz extended a hand, a smile on his face. "*Wilkommen*, John. I hear you gave our Alma a job."

"Yes, your father asked me and I couldn't say no." He smiled. "It seems I've made the right decision, too. She's a hard worker, just like I'd expect of a good German girl."

"I'm glad to hear she's getting on well there," Robert said, running a hand over his graying beard.

Alma gritted her teeth, annoyed by the way they discussed her as if she weren't in the room. They had no regard for how she felt, but it didn't matter. Her wages had one purpose—to serve the family's needs. Her needs didn't factor into the matter. She stewed over her thoughts as a group of men filed into the bierhaus, leaving clods of mud across the polished floor. She studied them, taking in the weariness around their eyes, the hunch of their shoulders. They were Fritz's friends—the anarchists—all German Americans with their fair skin and full beards.

As they flowed to the bar, they rubbed the spring chill from their hands. The tolerance for anarchists had declined drastically since

President McKinley's death. When Teddy Roosevelt took his place, the police began to crack down on gatherings throughout the city. Alma didn't like Fritz mixed up in it, but she knew better than to voice her worries, especially in front of his friends, so she busied herself helping Mama with plates. In truth, she should blame her stepfather as much as Fritz. He was the one, after all, who allowed the meetings in his home. He sympathized with them when it suited him, or rather, when it suited his wallet. Robert was nothing if not shrewd with his dollars and cents.

Her stepfather stepped behind the bar and got to work filling steins. "Johanna," he called out, "is the back room set?"

Mama threw him an exasperated look. He acted as if she hadn't prepared the room every day for the last sixteen years. "Of course it is, Robert. Invite them in."

The men removed their hats and tromped to the meeting room in the rear, each cradling a fresh stein frothing at the rim. Alma followed, lighting another lamp and placing it on the table to dispel the gloom in the windowless room.

Robert took a seat beside John and clapped him on the back. "Glad you decided to join us."

"It's good to be here," he said, taking a long pull of beer.

"So how long have you worked at Ellis Island, John?" Fritz asked.

"I started a couple of years before the big fire in 1897. Continued on at Castle Garden while there was construction on the island. We were all glad to see the new station open. It's much bigger."

"Castle Garden, you say?" Robert replied. "My father and I came through there many years ago, straight from Düsseldorf. I was just a boy. My mother was sent for, soon after, along with my sisters."

"I was born in Germany myself." A shiny spot on the crown of John's head gleamed in the lamplight. "Came to America when I was a babe."

Alma silently filled a dozen plates with heaps of boiled potatoes, roast beef with mushroom gravy, and red cabbage. She hoped the crowd would disperse early tonight, give her some time off her feet. She still hadn't summoned the nerve to tell Mama that she deserved to rest in the evenings as Fritz did, but she knew the answer awaiting her. Her mother would say that she'd worked all day, too, and needed Alma's help.

Greta set a basket of bread and a pot of mustard on the table. Before she turned, one of the men caught her eye and winked. As her sister's cheeks turned a pretty shade of pink, Alma wondered if Greta liked the man. He watched Greta go and briefly glanced at Alma. The gleam in his eye faded and he dug into his cabbage. She doubted he could carry on a decent conversation, but if that was the sort of fellow Greta liked, who was she to scoff at her sister's choices?

"We're in talks with the labor union again," Fritz said, bringing all conversation at the table to a halt.

The energy in the room shifted suddenly as all eyes turned to her brother.

"It looks like they'll continue to hire more immigrants at lower wages," Fritz went on.

A red-haired man threw down his fork. "Those damned Russians have no shame. Why are they working for pennies? They make it worse for everyone."

"The Greeks and Italians are the same," another man grunted.

"Hell, I can't go back to working at the millinery. That's women's work these days, and they're paid less, too."

The conversation devolved, and soon they shouted over each other to be heard.

Alma listened while doling out second helpings. Fritz must have some words of wisdom for his vocal friends. She glanced at him, her worries flaring again. What lengths would they go to, to protect their jobs and homes from the immigrants? She thought of Francesca, how silly it seemed to "protect themselves" from her. She worked as hard as anyone else, needed to survive, same as them. Alma wondered how they'd lost sight of the fact that many of the men at this very table were immigrants once, too. Her stepfather and John included.

"Everyone, calm down." Fritz lifted his hands, palms out in a defensive stance. "It doesn't help if we shout at each other. We've got to remain organized and focused, calm. Our people are working hard to influence the dealmakers in the city. And, more importantly, the labor unions. We're making progress; it just takes time."

"We're losing influence, not gaining it," one man argued. "Thanks to that crazy bastard who took out McKinley. And the riots those damned Italians seem intent on starting. Puts the rest of us on a wanted list."

"We aren't where we want to be yet," Fritz said, his blue eyes blazing. "But we will be. Don't do anything rash. We improve our situation if we remain calm and stand together. If you hear of others preparing for aggressive action, try to persuade them otherwise, or stay out of it. Violence will only make more trouble for us."

John Lambert frowned, and Alma found herself wondering if he saw the danger in associating with the anarchists.

"Emma Goldman is back in town," said Paul, Fritz's closest friend.

"She's a hell of a speaker," another man said, motioning to Greta for a beer. "She has a few screws loose, but at least she fights for our rights."

"Don't be seen with her lot," Fritz warned. "We may agree with her, but she attracts trouble. There's a meeting in two weeks at Webster's. We'll convene then and talk about the next steps to unionize."

Silence settled over the men as they finished their food.

Alma sat on a barrel in the corner at last, but her appetite had waned, her head filled with all they'd said. She'd seen articles in the newspaper about the anarchists and the unions lately. None of them had been positive. At the very least, Fritz should consider meeting elsewhere, permanently. The bierhaus didn't need to attract negative publicity, or they might drive away customers, never mind potentially bring the police to their door.

"We're turning away anarchists at Ellis Island," John Lambert said, breaking the silence. "It isn't official yet, but we've been doing it for the last few months."

Several of the men eyed him warily, as if he were a spy among their cozy group.

"I know," Fritz replied. "Alma told me, and that's fine. We'll stand our ground. This isn't really about anarchism itself anymore, at least not for most of us. It's about earning what we deserve. About not being at the mercy of a corrupt system."

The men grunted and hunched over their plates.

"It's also about limiting the number of those damned indigents entering the country. It's shocking to see so many at once, isn't it, Alma?" Lambert cast her a sidelong glance as he sopped up the last of his mushroom gravy with a piece of bread. "Even with the new inquiries from Williams, I think we're going too easy on them."

"The number of immigrants is shocking," she replied carefully, not wanting to betray her true feelings.

"I'll say. If you ever need anything, I hope you come to me," he said. "I'd be more than happy to be of assistance." He winked at her and reached for his stein.

Alma shifted on her stool and glanced at Fritz. Amusement danced in his eyes. If the others weren't there, she knew her brother would tease her. She hadn't understood why Lambert made her uncomfortable, but the look on Fritz's face said it all: Lambert was flirting with her.

"Thank you, Mr. Lambert." She stood abruptly and busied herself in the kitchen. Another hour of beer and conversation later, the men left the bierhaus, one by one. By ten o'clock, only John and two others lingered for a final stein of lager.

Alma wished they would be on their way. She was ready to call it a night. She rubbed the back of her neck, rolled her head from side to side.

"Tell me, Robert." John ran a thick finger around the rim of his mug. "There aren't many German families left in the area, so I'm surprised you're still here. Have you thought about moving to Williamsburg or Hoboken?"

Silence fell over the table. Alma stared at the man in shock as he tugged his beard thoughtfully. She knew her family agreed with the inspector's appraisal, but to say it so plainly among people he didn't know all that well could be considered an insult to his hosts.

"We will be soon," Fritz cut in before their stepfather could answer. "Isn't that right, Father?"

Her stepfather ran a hand over his tired eyes. "Yes, I'm keeping my eye on a property in Yorkville."

Eighty-five blocks north, Alma thought, where they could be as far from the poverty of the tenements as possible. This might be a good thing for the family, but it would also make her commute to Ellis Island over an hour every morning.

"You're doing quite well," John replied.

"We are," Robert agreed. "Cheers to that."

The remaining men clinked their steins together and drank.

Alma finally excused herself and went upstairs to work on her Russian. It had definitely improved, but the language was a far more difficult study for her than Italian, and she had a lot to learn.

An hour later, just as Alma was ready to drop off to sleep, Robert poked his head into the bedroom she shared with her sisters. "Alma, meet me downstairs," he whispered. "Your mother and I have something to discuss with you. Happy news."

She lay down her journal, slipped carefully from bed so as not to wake Greta, and stepped over a sleeping Else before tiptoeing to the door. What news could he possibly have to share at this hour? She took the stairs to the bierhaus quickly. Perhaps they were finally moving and he wanted to tell her and Fritz first. They'd have to make preparations, pack their things.

"What is it, Father?" she asked as she entered the room. "What's the news?"

Mama sat next to Robert, her feet propped on a chair. It had been a long night for all of them.

"Sit down," he said, pointing at the chair across from him.

What could this be about? Butterflies fluttered in her stomach, but she did as she was told, and clasped her hands in her lap.

"We've been made a very good offer," Mama began, and though she smiled, her eyes shone with tears.

Alma frowned. "Are you all right?"

"Yes, *liebling*. I'm very happy. I think we've finally found the right man for you."

Alma froze. "What do you mean?"

"We've received an offer of marriage for your hand," Robert said. "And we've accepted it."

Alma shot to her feet. "What—when did this happen?"

"Sit down," her stepfather snapped. "This gentleman is the perfect choice. He's the reason you have a job at Ellis Island."

John Lambert? A lump of tears formed in her throat. *No.* They couldn't do this to her. She'd done all they'd asked of her; she was working hard, turning her paycheck over to them so they could move. She was out of Robert's way and mostly out of his sight. She was *not* going to marry her boss!

"He wants to marry a German girl," her stepfather continued. "He said he'd like for you to continue your work at Ellis Island until you're married later this fall. He needs a few months to wrap up some things he has to take care of, and then you can retire to your new home and begin a family. He's an excellent match for you, Alma."

The room began to spin as she gasped for air. "But he's too old for me. Isn't he more than forty?" Every time they'd presented her with a new suitor, she'd managed to scare the man off with her intelligence, or by withdrawing and putting on a bored air, but John knew her competence. He'd seen her work hard the last two months, and he knew her family, admired them even. "I hardly know him," she said at last.

Robert threw his hands in the air. "We know him well enough. He has asked for your hand, Alma, and I've given my consent. That's the end of it."

If the floor opened up beneath her, swallowed her whole, she would slide gratefully into its oblivion. Her stepfather had wanted to be rid of her for years, and she'd been able to put off the inevitable, until now. Now she would be traded like a common farm animal.

She squeezed her eyes closed to hide the threatening tears. "But I'd like to keep working and save money to help our family." She offered a feeble protest. When they said nothing, she added, "I want to be promoted at Ellis Island, become an interpreter. Just think of my increase in pay. I know there aren't women doing that now, but I'm confident I can—"

He silenced her with a stern look. "There won't be any interpreting. You'll work until you're married, Alma, and retire to the home. That's final. Now, John is considering a spacious apartment in Hoboken. It's not terribly far away. You can still visit your mother whenever you like."

She could visit her mother? That was supposed to be some consolation? She was being forced to give up her work—her hopes of saving her own money, of translating or schooling—to become a middle-aged man's wife.

"When?" she asked, voice hoarse.

Robert pushed up from the table. "Sometime later this autumn."

Months away. She looked to Mama, desperately hoping for some sign of dissent. Maybe she would understand. Maybe she'd side with Alma, or at least buy her a little more time. But Johanna had tears of joy in her eyes.

Had the proposal come before Alma had spent months working away from home, on her own, learning how to assert herself with strangers, perhaps she would have bowed her head and done as they demanded. Perhaps she'd have continued to be the timid young lady who followed their orders without question. Instead, she balled her hands into fists. "And if I refuse Lambert's offer?"

"It's not your place to refuse, girl. Besides, it would bring shame to this house if you went back on our word. Would you do that after everything we've given you? Anyway, we've already consented. The topic is closed. Come on, Johanna. I'm tired as hell tonight." Robert stepped down from the barstool and carried his beer upstairs.

Mama squeezed Alma's hands. "This is a good thing, *liebling*. You'll see. I know you're afraid, but that will pass in time. Sometimes we have to make difficult decisions, but things usually work out in the end."

Unable to move, Alma watched her mother follow Robert upstairs. Her future was not her own to decide. She knew this—had always known it—but it was no longer a distant, unpleasant idea. She climbed the stairs and sat on the sofa in the dark, panic washing over her in waves.

The future was now, ready or not, and she'd have to find a way to accept it.

Or, perhaps, she needed only to find a way out of it.

29

When Sunday arrived, the entire city hummed under a brilliant blue sky. Francesca relished the sunlight as she strolled to Tompkins Square Park, a basket of fresh bread, peach jam, and a glistening fruit tart on her arm. She hadn't realized how much she missed the warm weather of home until the sun blazed overhead and sent a flush across her cheeks. Thankfully, Mrs. Cheedle had granted Francesca's request to take Sunday afternoons off like the rest of the staff. It helped that the Lancasters spent each Sunday evening at a dinner party with friends. Mrs. Cheedle had even allowed her to bring the goodies in the basket in exchange for a few coins. The old woman wasn't as stern as Francesca had once thought, and she'd taken to Francesca when she'd seen how hard her new cook worked.

Smiling, Francesca relished the beautiful spring weather. She felt a bit lighter today, as if the heavy grief that had enveloped her like thick cotton had teased apart to let a little light in. Alma had invited her to their Sunday family gathering, by mail, just as she had said she would. It was Francesca's very first letter, addressed and written to her. She'd smiled when the invitation came, and she was proud she'd been able to read most of it with a little help from Claire. Francesca was a resident of New York City, and little by little, she was shedding her Italian skin, becoming one of them. An American.

After a lengthy walk, she arrived at the park—a nondescript rectangle dotted with benches and the occasional clutch of trees—and weaved through the crowd of families who had gathered to visit and enjoy the afternoon. Children chased each other or played games with a stick or ball. Several women eyed her as she passed, and she felt a twinge of discomfort. Where they were tall and willowy or square and stout, she was petite and curvy; where their creamy skin glowed in the sunlight, hers was the color of Mrs. Lancaster's tea with milk; where they drew their silky hair into neat chignons, hers floated about her shoulders in a mass of dark, untamable curls. They all wore their Sunday best, with dainty gloves and three-story hats decorated with ribbons and floral spays. Some held pretty parasols in spring yellows and blues. At least Francesca had disposed of the tattered work dress she'd brought from Sicilia and traded it for a second-hand bustled skirt and blouse. She wouldn't be mistaken for a lady of Park Avenue, but she looked more like a woman of New York, and for now, that was good enough. When she'd had a chance to save a bit more, she'd buy something as pretty and frivolous as ribbons or baubles.

Soon, she caught sight of the Brauers in the middle of the open square. As she started in their direction, she gripped her basket a bit tighter. She suspected Robert and Johanna didn't know about Alma's invitation, and though they hadn't been cruel to her in the past, they'd made it abundantly clear they'd done her an enormous favor by letting her stay with them. They'd also made it clear where she stood in their eyes. She was an outsider allowed to join them only for the sake of propriety.

"Good afternoon." Francesca waited at the edge of the crowd.

"You're here!" Alma put down the cheese board and embraced her tightly.

Francesca warmed to her friend's welcome. Alma wasn't the type of woman to show much affection, yet some barrier between them seemed to have melted away. They were linked, a team of sorts because of what they'd already shared, and Alma seemed as grateful for their new friendship as Francesca was.

"For us?" Alma pointed at the basket.

"A tart and fresh bread. I made them," she said shyly. She was happy to offer something for a change, rather than being the one in need.

"I see we have a guest again." Johanna Brauer snapped a towel in the air to rid it of any crumbs. She wore a fine dress of burgundy crepe, bustled and trimmed with cream ribbon, and a large straw bonnet of the older style with a wide brim. Even with the dated hat, she was much more fashionable—and lovelier—than the woman she'd met in gray work dress and apron. Francesca could almost see the pretty maiden Signora Brauer had been in her days of youth.

"Mama, I've invited Francesca to join us," Alma said curtly, adding something else in German.

Francesca didn't miss the edge in Alma's voice. Upon closer inspection, she saw the dark circles under her friend's eyes. She made a mental note to ask Alma if something was wrong when they had a minute alone.

"Have you brought something, Francesca?" Johanna said, nodding at the basket.

Francesca ignored Johanna's distinct look of displeasure and instead held out the basket. "Yes. I make for everyone."

"How kind." Johanna set it down with the others without looking inside.

Francesca swallowed her disappointment. She would just have to win Johanna over like everyone else.

During the next hour, several other families joined the Brauers, toting their baskets and the odd toy or instrument. Alma introduced her to a friend named Emma, who smiled at Francesca hesitantly and then joined a group of young women sitting in a circle beneath a tree. Alma frowned at the slight, but Francesca pretended not to notice and followed Alma as she introduced the rest of the group. The Schullers, the Kleins, and the Muellers. Francesca made an effort to remember their names.

In that instant, a familiar voice drifted through the crowd. She turned automatically toward it, her eyes seeking its source. Fritz stood in the middle of a crowd, his features animated. Those around him listened closely, riveted by what he had to say. There was something about him that drew the eye. An energy about him. He took off his derby hat and launched it in the air. Everyone laughed, and Klaus, his younger brother, scooped up the hat and ran with it, his lanky form a jumble of arms and legs. Fritz dashed after him beneath the trees in the dappled sunlight, easily catching him. Francesca wished she were running along beside them, but she'd receive more than a few surprised looks for behaving that way.

Instead, she sat beside Alma on the blanket, tucking her legs beneath her. "Can I help?"

"Slice the bread?" Alma forced a cheery tone, but her eyes belied something more.

Francesca touched Alma's arm. "What's happened?"

"What do you mean?"

"You look...sad or disappointed. I don't know." She didn't say more, sensing Alma's boundaries. Pushing her friend into a confession wasn't the way to invite her to share. Instead, Francesca unwrapped the bread she'd infused with dried basil and garlic and sliced it into perfect wedges.

"I'm just tired," Alma replied at last.

"Of course," Francesca said, nodding. But she couldn't help feeling disappointed Alma wouldn't take her into her confidence.

"We're ready to eat!" Alma dished out cheese and ham, cold potatoes, and a piece of bread on each plate. She wanted to tell Francesca about the engagement, and she would in time, but Alma wasn't even used to the idea herself. She'd hardly slept the last two days, imagining what her new life would look like, her emotions swinging wildly from despair to fear to embarrassment. There would be a marriage bed, a new home...and waking up to a man she barely knew every morning. She lost her appetite all over again and set down her plate.

Robert ambled over, took a plate, and gestured at it. "Give me more ham, girl! You never give me enough."

Without a word, she unwrapped a package of parchment paper, produced another thick slice, and laid it atop the others. She hadn't spoken to Robert at all and had scarcely spoken to her mother since the dreaded announcement.

"There we are," he said, his face shifting to an expression he reserved for her alone: mouth pinched, eyes filled with disgust. "Glad you're making yourself useful, at least. Soon enough, you'll be someone else's problem."

Alma reddened and glanced at Francesca, who quietly took in the scene.

"She's the hard-working woman I ever have known," Francesca replied defiantly in stilted English.

Alma's mouth dropped open, and her eyes flicked to Robert's face.

He snorted and swigged from his beer. "You must not know many," he grumbled to himself as he weaved around them to look for a spot near the other men.

Alma swallowed hard. How had Francesca stood up to her stepfather so easily—and on her behalf? The consequences could have been harsh: he could have asked Francesca to leave, or ridiculed her in front of the others; pointed out that she was a dago and didn't belong with them. Francesca didn't seem to care. She didn't fear him, and she didn't need his approval. She was free, freer than Alma had ever been in a way she was just beginning to understand.

Alma gazed at her beautiful friend, who had turned her attention to her food. As much as Francesca had lost, as much as she had given up to be here in New York, she had something Alma didn't, and it was the most important thing of all: she knew her mind and she wasn't afraid to speak it. Francesca understood her own strength and drew upon it like water from a well. If only Alma could do the same.

Alma reached for Francesca, touching her hand softly. "Thank you."

Francesca didn't like Robert much. He wasn't a forceful man like her papa, but she recognized his quiet cruelty just the same. He liked to direct his anger at someone to relieve a pressure valve somewhere inside him, to belittle someone else to make him feel like a big, strong man. An important someone. And the person he'd chosen to direct his ire at was Alma. One day, her friend must learn to speak up for herself, or he would never relent and she would go on believing what he said was true.

Francesca finished her food in silence, not wanting to speak too often in Italian when she knew it would draw attention to her. Meanwhile, she watched Alma's troubled face, her slumped shoulders. This was more than fatigue, and judging by Robert's nasty comment, Francesca suspected something had happened that Alma didn't want to share.

"How is work?" she asked.

Alma chewed thoughtfully for a moment before replying. "It's difficult some days. So much happens that I'm not prepared for. I feel bad for some of the immigrants, but there's only so much I can do to help."

Francesca knew all too well the sorts of unexpected things that happened at Ellis Island but didn't volunteer the information. Neither did she want to spend another minute of her life thinking about the horrible inspector. "You're very kind, Alma. You like to help others."

"I do," Alma said, almost as if she were surprised by her own response. "I like to speak other languages and learn about other customs. The immigrants teach me a lot, and I didn't expect that... I especially like to talk to the children. They're always happy when I bring them crackers or sweets." She smiled faintly, her eyes far away as if revisiting a memory. "I was afraid to work there at first."

Surprised by the admission, Francesca raised a brow. "You were afraid of the immigrants? But why?"

Alma blushed. "I... Well, I'm overwhelmed by large crowds. And I don't know... I'd heard so many stories about them."

"About the immigrants?"

Alma nodded, her expression turning sheepish.

Francesca blinked. Were people afraid of her? It seemed absurd.

Alma cleared her throat and changed the subject. "How are things for you at work?"

"Claire, the other cook, teaches me a lot, and she has a good sense of humor. But the mistress is...difficult. I hide in the pantry when she comes downstairs."

Alma laughed brightly, revealing large white teeth and dimples, and her face transformed from plain to almost pretty. "Well, you'll win her over through her stomach."

"Tarts and pastas and roasted fish! They're my... How do you say *armi*?"

"Weapons. Your English has improved."

Francesca nodded. "I have headaches from trying, but now I dream in English."

"A sign you're truly learning it." Alma bit into the bread Francesca had made. "This is delicious! What's in it?"

"It's basil." She smiled, glad to see Alma's mood had shifted for the better. Laughter drifted across the picnic toward them, and Francesca's gaze strayed past her friend to Fritz.

He seemed to feel her eyes on him and turned, waved, and bounded over from the game he was playing. Something bright and warm filled her as he plopped down on the blanket beside her.

"Hello, Francesca," he said, grinning from ear to ear. "Is that a new dress?"

"*Sì*." She smoothed the red cotton skirts. Though plain and unadorned but for a set of shiny silver buttons, the color looked lovely with her skin and dark curls.

"You look quite fine," he said.

She stiffened at the compliment, never certain she liked being noticed in that way. It often meant the sort of attention she tried to avoid wasn't far behind. But Fritz had been nothing but kind to her, so she thanked him with a smile.

Alma handed her brother a plate and he took it gratefully. "I'm starved."

While Fritz focused on his food, Francesca studied his face. His blue eyes seemed at once piercing and warm somehow, and thick chestnut hair fell over his brow. His sharp bone structure made him look like a decisive fellow, strong and assured. And his infectious energy made him all the more appealing. Startled by the line of her thoughts, she looked away. She'd always found men either blundering and spineless or, worse, violent and hateful. Fritz possessed none of those characteristics—and she liked talking to him. It was unnerving.

A conversation in German drew his attention and he looked up, the light in his eyes flickering with interest. As he replied, one of his friends joined him. She watched them as they conversed, straining to understand but failing to comprehend a single word of German. Fritz's concentration on his friend was absolute, another thing she liked about him. Once you had his attention, it wasn't divided. She remembered the way she'd felt when they'd ridden on the train together to the Lancasters'. When she spoke and he looked at her that way, it was as if she were sitting in a pool of warm sunlight. As he spoke, she caught herself noticing the way Fritz's hair shone almost red in the afternoon sun.

Alarmed by her thoughts again, she pushed to her feet to go for a walk.

Fritz watched her brush off her skirts. "Can I join you?" He placed his dish in the basket of dirty things and stood up, too.

"That would be nice." Francesca smiled.

"Fritz, can you help me with this growler?" Johanna said, ignoring her perfectly able husband sprawled across the blanket.

"I... We can walk another time," Francesca replied.

He frowned. "Mama, I was just going for a walk."

"Later," Johanna replied, casting a sharp expression at Francesca. "I need your help now."

Fritz shot Francesca a contrite look and bent to uncork the growler before refilling empty cups.

A man she'd seen at the bierhaus one night joined the crowd. When he saw Francesca, he took off his hat for a moment. "Hello, miss. I saw you at the bierhaus some time ago. I'm Mark Schumacher."

"Hello." Francesca nodded.

Alma's lips twitched and an amused grin crossed her face. In Italian, she quickly filled Francesca in on Mark's advances. He'd tried his hand with every female in their circle, but the combination of his pockmarked face, bravado, and droning on about himself made him insufferable company.

Francesca smothered a laugh.

Mark, having understood nothing between them, reached for Francesca's hand. "A pleasure to meet you."

Fritz stepped between them, pushing the growler in Mark's face. "Want another beer?"

Francesca stepped aside and watched Fritz from behind lowered lashes. A muscle in his jaw twitched, and the lightness she'd witnessed in him earlier disappeared instantly. Was Mark not a gentleman? Fritz seemed protective of her. He probably considered her like another sister. At the thought, something inside her wilted a little.

Mark glanced at his half-empty cup. "Fill her up."

Fritz's shoulders relaxed and he topped off his friend's glass. "You've done good work this week."

"Well, you've been on my back." Mark slugged a large gulp of beer.

Fritz paused in bringing his own cup to his lips. "What do you mean?"

"You're always kissing up to the bosses these days."

The muscle in Fritz's jaw twitched. "I wouldn't call doing my job kissing up to the bosses."

"You hear about the riot in Colorado?" Mark asked, ignoring Fritz's comment. "The laborers are sticking together. Figure it's the best way to make a statement. I say we burn a few things. Let them know we're serious."

Francesca glanced at Alma. Her expression was grim, her eyes troubled.

"Violence undermines what we're trying to accomplish." Fritz's voice took on an edge. "If we riot, they'll think we need to be put in our places."

"The bosses won't understand how serious we are until we make a statement," Mark argued. "Our agenda isn't getting us anywhere."

"And what exactly is our agenda, according to you?"

Mark's mouth twisted into a scowl. "You know we want McCreedy. He's just another Irish bastard. A crook. Keeps the lion's share of profits while we all work ourselves to the bone. But you're in there, puckering up for promotions." He flicked the collar on Fritz's shirt. "You're not one of us anymore."

Fury sparked in Fritz's eyes.

"Don't worry, they argue all the time," Alma whispered in Francesca's ear.

"Good afternoon, Brauers." A pretty woman in flowered skirts and a white blouse interrupted their conversation. She held a rosy pink parasol in her hand. Francesca recognized her from Ellis Island. She'd been nice enough.

"Helene!" Alma exclaimed. "You came! Everyone, this is Helene Bach. We work together at Ellis Island."

The young woman smiled, and they all switched to German. When it looked as if the conversation would continue that way, Francesca decided it was time for a walk. No one would miss her.

She skirted around the edges of the park, trying to enjoy the weather, but her gaze kept drifting back to the Brauers. Johanna smiled at Helene and led her by the arm to get a plate of food. Helene had been welcomed to the fold instantly. And given her age and beauty, her German heritage, she was a good potential match for Fritz, too.

Francesca walked across the square, putting distance between her and the others. She passed a patch of yellow and red flowers clustered in a small pot of soil. On the other side of it, she saw another group sitting on an array of colorful blankets. They shared a meal, but instead of potatoes and beer, they pulled out loaves of bread, cured ham, olives, and several carafes of *vino rosso*. They laughed heartily and shouted over one another, the Sicilian dialect she hadn't heard in a while enveloping her. To the untrained eye, the group might have been arguing, but Francesca knew better. Why say something calmly when one could make their point much better with a little display of emotion?

A woman noticed her staring and smiled, then said something to the man next to her, who looked Francesca's way.

"*Buongiorno*," he called. "I'm Giuseppe and this is my sister, Giana. You're welcome to join us, if you like. We noticed you're alone."

And they'd also noticed that she was Italian, like them, and hadn't bothered speaking to her in English. Something that disappointed her a little.

She walked around the flower bed to say a proper hello. "I'm Francesca Ricci."

They all exchanged kisses on the cheek in greeting.

"Francesca!" Someone called her name from behind her and she turned. Fritz crossed the park with long strides, his eyes fixed on her. He stomach dipped as she watched him come for her.

"It was nice to meet you"—she said hastily to Giuseppe and Giana—"but I've come with another group."

Giana smiled. "If you change your mind, we have plenty of food. Isn't that right, Giuseppe?"

"*Certo*," he replied.

Francesca smiled and thanked them for their hospitality just as Fritz caught up to her.

"Francesca, are you… Is everything all right?" he said, out of breath.

"Yes, of course. Fritz, this is Giuseppe and Giana."

They nodded politely. "Hello."

Though the group was friendly, there was an unspoken question in the air: what was she doing with the German? As Johanna's glare and deliberate cold shoulder replayed in Francesca's mind, she wasn't sure she could answer the question herself.

Fritz's expression changed as he took in the group of families, and understanding dawned in his eyes. He looked back at Francesca. "If you'd prefer to stay…" His words trailed off.

Giana made eye contact with Giuseppe, and a silent communication passed between them.

"Fran!" Alma said, approaching with Helene on her arm. "We wondered where you'd gone. We're going to play cards. Would you like to play?"

Fran? Francesca felt a rush of warmth as her friend slid her free arm through hers. They'd come for her, and Alma had even given her a nickname. Francesca might not be German or exactly like the Brauer family and their friends, but she was welcome, at least mostly, and for now, that was enough.

With a smile for Giana and Giuseppe, Francesca wished them a good day and set off for the cozy spot where the rest of the Brauers gathered.

Fritz walked silently beside her, casting a final glance over his shoulder.

She wished then that she could read his mind.

30

Alma walked to the train station, the sweet perfume of lilacs masking the odor of mud and sweaty horses. Trees scattered throughout the city proudly displayed their new greenery, and flowerpots burst with happy peonies. All the things Alma loved about spring took center stage, yet she couldn't pretend to be content, not for anyone or anything. Even Fran had noticed her gloominess at the picnic last week. Alma sighed.

She was to be married. To a middle-aged man she hardly knew.

Fritz had been somewhat sympathetic when he'd learned the news, but he'd also asked her whether she wanted a home of her own and to get out from under Robert's thumb. She didn't bother to explain that yes, of course she did, but there had to be another way. She envisioned packing her things, moving out on her own—and promptly shuttered the idea. She'd destroy her family's reputation as well as her own. Even if she could entertain the idea, she didn't have any money.

When she arrived at work, she trudged up the front walk, wishing for all the world it was her day off. She hadn't the faintest idea of what to say to John. He'd asked her parents for her hand without even consulting her! What kind of man did that, in this day and age? It was downright medieval.

Shoulders sagging, she lined up in the matron's office and waited for Mrs. Keller's inspection.

Her supervisor did her usual nitpicking and scolding over every-one's uniforms. When she reached Alma, she straightened Alma's collar and eyed her cap with disdain. "You're a mess today, Miss Brauer." She pushed Alma's shoulders back to force her to stand tall. "Your brain must be clouded by love."

Several of the others giggled.

Confused, Alma said, "I'm not sure what you mean."

"Oh, come now, I hear congratulations are in order. Girls, wish Miss Brauer congratulations. She's to be married. To Inspector Lambert."

Their voices formed a chorus of best wishes.

Alma blushed hotly. How had Mrs. Keller already learned of her engagement? She hadn't even spoken to John about it yet!

"I think I can speak for all of us when I say we're glad to see him choose a bride," Mrs. Keller said, continuing down the line of women, plucking at stray lint and smoothing wrinkles.

More giggles rippled through the room. Someone snorted. Helene, however, did not look amused.

"I haven't consented yet!" Alma blurted out.

The giggles stopped.

"I haven't given my reply, and I'd appreciate it if you wouldn't talk about it." But even as she said it, she knew her marriage would soon be a foregone conclusion. The whispers came next, and the titter of laughter.

She fixed her eyes on the door. She wanted to flee, and the moment Mrs. Keller had assigned her duties, she would.

"All right, ladies." Mrs. Keller's voice took on a stern edge. "Enough now. Off to work with you."

As the matrons poured into the hall, Alma felt her chest heat with indignation. She'd be forced to listen to their feigned delight all day.

"Why didn't you tell me?" Helene tugged Alma's sleeve.

"I was hoping it would go away," she said glumly as they walked to their stations. "John came by the bierhaus for dinner, and the next thing I know, my stepfather is telling me I'm engaged. No one bothered to ask me what I want." She sighed heavily. "Lambert must have told everyone here at work. I was trying not to think about it until I figured out what to do."

Helene grabbed Alma's arm and pulled her out of the flow of traffic into a more private nook opposite the matron's office. "Wait, Lambert never asked you?"

She shook her head. "After he left for the night, my stepfather told me."

"I can't believe you're going to marry him! I hope he'll be a better husband than a chief officer."

Alma went still. "What do you mean?"

Helene paused, looking as if she was deciding whether or not to say more. "He's... Well... You must have heard the rumors about him. He's very tough on the staff unless they're part of his group of friends or other Germans. And there are other things..."

"What do you mean by 'other things'?"

Helene started to reply—hesitated—and stopped.

It wasn't like Helene to withhold anything. She loved nothing more than sharing a secret.

Alma clutched her friend's arm. "Come on, Helene, tell me. What is it?"

Helene shook her head, sending the wisps of blond hair that had escaped her cap dancing around her neck. "It's nothing. We'd better get to work. See you at lunch, Mrs. Lambert."

Mrs. Lambert. Alma wanted to scream!

Helene saw her expression and laughed. "It was just a joke. I'm sorry. That wasn't funny."

"Not funny at all." She gritted her teeth and strode through the halls to her post. In her weeks at Ellis Island, she'd grown used to a certain degree of autonomy, but now she felt powerless over her future all over again. A future she had begun to believe in. She'd known Robert had wanted her out of the house for ages, but she thought surrendering her wages would be enough to satisfy him. For many years she'd tried to puzzle out what she'd done to offend him and had finally come to the conclusion that she hadn't done anything wrong.

The truth was, Robert Brauer simply wanted to erase any reminder of Wilhelm Klein—Alma's and Fritz's father and the love of her mother's life—from memory. Johanna hadn't hidden the fact that she'd loved Alma's father passionately and was devastated when he died. She'd mentioned Papa in conversation for some time, even after she'd married Robert, but eventually it had lessened and now it was unnatural to bring him up at all. Some days, it felt as if Alma's papa had never existed.

Struggling to control her emotions, Alma headed to the clerk's office, where she was asked to check on some paperwork. The halls and the registry office were mercifully quiet, the latest ship not having arrived yet. Still, the hum of hundreds of workers going about their business echoed against the tiled floors and concrete walls in the cavernous building. At times, the building felt alive, watchful as it surveyed all that took place within its walls. Dreams and fears and lost chances, and the most dangerous emotion of all: hope. But all she felt at the moment was despair.

As Alma turned the corner, a voice came from behind her.

"What's happened? You look as if a cart ran over your favorite cousin."

Jeremy.

She managed a weak smile in spite of herself. "I suppose that means I'm scowling."

"I've seen you sunnier. Rough mornin'?" His dark-blue eyes were kind, attentive.

"You could say that."

He fell into step beside her. After a few moments of silence, he realized she wasn't going to volunteer more and changed the subject. "How's your Russian coming along?"

She brightened a little. "Why don't you test me?"

"All right." He rattled off a series of rapid-fire questions.

She laughed. "One at a time!"

He grinned and began again, slowly, and one by one, she replied, mixing her tenses only once and missing just a handful of words.

"You're learning quickly!"

She warmed to the praise. "I tend to do that. Learn quickly, that is, but it's never been considered a good thing at home. It hasn't been easy to stand out that way, actually." She paused, surprised she'd shared such an intimate thought with him.

"Well, that's a shame. It's an excellent quality of yours, Miss Brauer. One of many." He winked.

She smiled, a genuine smile this time. He thought she had many qualities? She felt an inkling of gratitude for this cheerful man and his kind words. He made her feel proud of her talents instead of like an odd duckling that should be scolded and shunned, or shipped off to any man who would lower himself enough to have her.

"Thank you," she said, eliciting a smile from him. "Going to the offices?"

"Aye."

They started in that direction, their lanky strides in lockstep with each other.

"Jeremy," she said, "what if I wanted to become an interpreter? In an official way."

He cast her a sidelong glance. "Well, you'd need proper schooling, o'course, and you'll have to take a series of tests from the Bureau of Immigration. Speaking, reading, writing, and comprehension for each language."

"Oh, that's a lot." Her mind boggled at the thought of all of those tests. She could certainly take the German and English exams without a problem, and perhaps she could take some of the tests in Italian, but she definitely needed to study more to pass all of them. As for Russian, she had a long way to go. But there was time, she reminded herself. She was young yet.

"Aye, it is, but in time, you could master them, I have little doubt. If you want something badly enough, you can do it." He smiled at her. "And as you said before, you're clever."

She returned his smile. She liked his view of her.

When they reached the clerk's office, they stopped outside the door.

Jeremy brushed a lock of hair from his forehead. "So I hear congratulations are in order."

"Oh? For whom?" she asked.

He laughed. "For you. Aren't you engaged to be married?"

"Oh. That." Everyone knew. *Everyone!* How had that happened so fast? She wished she could disappear into a giant hole in the ground. "My stepfather accepted the proposal on my behalf. He insists it's a good match, German families coming together and all that, but I haven't spoken to Inspector Lambert about it. I'm...I'm not—" She bit her tongue. Why was she telling him all of this?

"Well, a wedding is a happy event. I can see why Lambert is so eager to spread the word."

"I suppose it depends on your definition of happiness."

His brows arched in surprise. "You don't want to be married?"

She cringed. She hadn't meant to sound so bitter. "What I mean is, I didn't have a say in the matter. John asked my parents, not me. My feelings weren't taken into account."

What had gotten into her? She didn't need to explain anything to this man, and yet she felt compelled to just the same. Jeremy had been so kind to her from the first, precisely when she needed a friend. And maybe she needed his assurance all would be well regardless of her engagement. Wasn't that what friends did, reassure each other? Helene had done just the opposite.

"Ah, I see," he said. "I'm sorry to hear that. Perhaps you might change your parents' minds?"

"They seem pretty set on it, but maybe." She could hear the despondency in her own voice, and suddenly, it took all she had not to cry.

At this, an emotion she couldn't place reflected in his eyes. "Well," he said at last, "I wish you luck." And with a faint smile that disappeared in his beard, he said, "It's to work for me."

"Yes, well, have a nice day."

He tipped his hat and went inside his office.

Heart in her throat, she checked in with the clerk briefly and then walked slowly to the registry office, her thoughts churning. *She had a fiancé.* She would be expected to give him children quickly, run the household, and all of her silly dreams about schooling and studying and interpreting would be put on hold indefinitely, or altogether forgotten. She shuddered at the thought of John's long, thin hands on her skin. How could her parents do this to her! She wrestled with thoughts of defying them, of telling John her parents hadn't consulted her and had made a mistake. What could they possibly do to her? They'd already forced her to find a job outside of the home. And she was a grown woman. Robert had no right to make decisions without her consent. And yet.

Eyes smarting, she looked for a quiet nook to hide from everyone, to agonize and seethe in private.

Two weeks passed, and Alma had yet to speak to John outside of a quick hello in the halls at Ellis Island. Neither had she seen him at the bierhaus. She stared out the window of the matron's office. Another barge carrying a massive load of soil moved across the bay toward Ellis Island. The island was constantly under construction to accommodate the rising number of immigrants landing on its shores, and now, they were building a third island, adjacent to the second. Alma found it fascinating the way the city had built a concrete shell on the floor of the Hudson River, fortified by steel, and filled it with soil left over from the subway construction. Fritz had explained some of the details to her one evening after work.

Though the barge appeared to move slowly, it made good time across the turbulent waters, arriving sooner than expected. Beyond the barge, the Ellis Island ferry tugged insistently against the tide. In minutes, she would be swamped and wouldn't have a spare moment until her shift ended. Confronting John would, once again, have to wait.

She blew out a breath of frustration as she walked to her post in the registry office to prepare for the immigrants' arrival. Again. Mrs. Keller regularly assigned Alma to the most trying tasks, and it had started to feel like a punishment. Alma worked as hard, if not harder, than the other matrons, so she didn't understand why her supervisor punished her with the more difficult posts.

Within the hour, immigrants flooded the building and the relative quiet vanished. This time, it was a ship filled with a mix of Polish and Russian people, and by the looks of it, it was a larger load than usual. Alma weaved around the crowd, directing people, delivering paperwork, helping in the detainees' quarters, answering questions, running from one end of the building to the other.

By afternoon, she'd seen John three times, and each time he'd acted as if nothing had changed between them. His nonchalance set her teeth on edge, and by three o'clock, she'd begun to watch the minutes tick by, counting the hours until she could go home. When she finally found a free minute for a quick drink of water and a snack, Helene cornered her.

"Lambert wants to see you in his office," Helene said.

Alma's stomach clenched. "What? Why?"

"He needs a translation," her friend called over her shoulder as she rushed off to her next destination.

Alma walked to his office, her feet as heavy as bricks. Would he, once more, pretend nothing had happened between them, or would he finally ask her to marry him in the proper way rather than behind her back? Her heart knocked against her ribs as she looked inside his office.

"Come in," his voice boomed.

"Miss Bach said you sent for me." She didn't meet his eyes.

"Yes, good." He waved to a couple in the chairs beside his desk. "These two appear to be together, yet they aren't married or related in any way. Explain our policies to them in Italian, please. If they agree to be married, we'll draw up the contract, and I'll send Inspector Miller with them on the next ferry to city hall."

When Alma realized he really did need her to translate and this wouldn't be a confrontation, she relaxed and spoke to the couple, explaining their next steps. They talked amongst themselves a moment, finally agreeing to the contract and marriage license. She asked them several questions about their home and travels to put them at ease and assured them all would be well. The young woman smiled, and once again, Alma warmed to the unexpected satisfaction of helping someone. They were shown to the bench outside to wait for the paperwork.

"Did you need anything else?" she asked John when she'd finished.

"Come in, shut the door."

The flutter in her stomach returned as she closed the door behind her.

"What did they say?" He folded his hands on his desk.

After she'd relayed the conversation, he said, "Well, at least she isn't a picture bride, ordered by mail. I've seen one too many of those, and I always wonder how the man feels when his new wife winds up looking like a haggard sow. I bet they wish they had waited for an American woman then."

Alma gaped at him, surprised by such a nasty comment. John had been nothing but kind and helpful, though admittedly, she'd bristled at his comments about the immigrants on other occasions.

"It's lucky for me," he went on, "I don't need to do any ordering, do I, dear fiancée? I'm happy to become a part of the Brauer family. I'm delighted you agreed to my proposal."

But she hadn't agreed—and he hadn't bothered to ask her. The tips of her ears burned hotly. "Mr. Lambert. John..." she began, but she couldn't seem to make the words come.

He smiled. "I know this may seem a little awkward, but we'll have plenty of time to get to know each other."

As her nerve to speak up fled, she replied with forced cheer. "Yes, of course."

"And as soon as we're married, I'll come into my inheritance. It's not large but it's a tidy sum. I've already scouted a nice property in Hoboken that I'm sure you'll like. I'll show it to you one day soon."

An inheritance? She couldn't help but wonder if that was the reason for his proposal.

"I... Yes" was all she could manage as she digested the rest of what he'd said. Since there was an inheritance, he'd surely want her to quit her job, just as Robert had said. But perhaps her stepfather was wrong? Perhaps John would be open to her studies. He'd been the one who'd gotten her a job in the first place so he couldn't be as traditional as her parents, and at least for that, she was grateful.

He reached for her hand and brought her palm to his lips, his beard tickling her skin. "How about I stop by the bierhaus this week?" Not trusting her voice, she merely stared at her hand against his lips, a deep red flush spilling across her cheeks. When he realized she had nothing else to say, he looked almost wounded and let her hand drop. "I suppose you'd better get to work."

"Yes," her reply came out stiffly. "I suppose I should."

"Alma? If Williams approaches you about me, be sure to tell him we're happily engaged. He's been on my case a lot lately, and this might help him see me in another light."

"Of course," she choked out as she closed the door. Yet somewhere in the back of her mind, a warning signal flashed.

Why did he want to put on a show for the commissioner? And how exactly did the commissioner view him now? She knew the two men didn't like each other much, based on their exchange in front of her and Helene a few weeks ago, but she'd assumed that was because of John's loyalty to Fitchie. They'd seemed like good friends before he was fired. She'd seen them talking in the halls and on the ferry frequently. Whatever the reason, she wanted no part of Williams and Lambert's rivalry. Engaged or not, she had her own reputation to consider with the commissioner, and as of now, she was still her own person. She knew she was one of the hardest-working and most reliable members of the staff, something that made her proud, even if she'd be losing it all soon.

As she walked back to the registry office, she pushed thoughts of John Lambert and her pending marriage from her mind. She still had a little time before she had to become a wife, and she'd cling to that raft like a woman drowning at sea.

31

*A*s the weeks passed, Francesca joined the Brauers at their favorite park every Sunday, toting a basket of something new she'd learned to bake with Claire. The afternoons were joyous, and Francesca found herself swept up in card games, walking in through the park, or listening to the Klein children practice the violin. She shared stories about Maria and their adventures as children when the urge to talk about her sister filled her with longing. She listened intently to Alma's tales about her siblings, as well, or the occasional story about her beloved papa. But Alma still seemed troubled, no matter how bright the day, and though Francesca tried to hint at knowing something was wrong, Alma wouldn't budge. Francesca hoped, one day, Alma would trust her enough to confide in her.

Francesca had grown to like Alma's friend Helene as well, despite the young woman's obvious interest in Fritz. They would make a wonderful couple, and Francesca was certain Mrs. Brauer thought so, too. Johanna managed to invent reasons to put them together on the same team, game after game, and she smiled constantly at the pretty young woman. Francesca couldn't deny the sight of them together inspired a prickle of petty jealousy, and she had to remind herself her warm feelings for Fritz were nothing more than friendship.

"Your friend likes Fritz, I think," Francesca said, watching Helene as she laid a hand on his arm. Whatever they were discussing made them both laugh.

Alma closed her book. "Do you really think so?" She glanced at the couple. "She's never said anything to me about it."

"Look at them."

As Helene leaned closer to Fritz and laughed again, he squeezed her shoulder. A sudden wave of fatigue washed over Francesca. Somehow the exchange between them made her feel...alone. She considered heading home. She could use a nap before going back to work anyway. Perhaps, too, she would start a letter to Sister Alberta. She'd thought about writing her friend many times since she'd arrived in America but hadn't yet followed through. She didn't like to admit it, but she was afraid the postman would tell her father where she was. Though he couldn't hurt her, she worried about his reaction just the same. It was a small community on her island home, and few had secrets. There was also the matter of telling Sister Alberta about Maria, and Francesca couldn't begin to put her grief into words.

"Fritz has a lot of admirers, but he isn't the kind of man who would marry because it's time. Or because the woman might make a good match for his family," Alma said. "He's too busy focusing on his work. I think he'll marry one day, when he's in love. Really in love. He has that luxury." Alma's tone turned dark. "I wish I did."

A shadow crossed Alma's face. She was clearly the kind of person to share when she wanted to, and though Francesca wanted to push her for information, she respected that.

Instead, Francesca stood, brushing the wrinkles from her skirts. "I'd better head home. Let me help you with the plates."

As they packed their things, the echo of angry voices drifted from across the park. Two groups of men had gathered, and within moments, they were arguing.

"It looks like a gang," Alma said, her face growing pale. "They probably won't bother us, but you never want to be in their way. Better get a move on."

Francesca knew exactly what gangs were like. She'd heard about and seen plenty of their handiwork at home. In fact, gangs had the run of the island at home. She knew to steer clear of them, either as a friend or a foe. It was best to be out of their line of sight.

The German families scattered, heading to the other side of the park or leaving entirely.

Soon, the men began shoving each other. They became a writhing mass as a full-scale fight broke out. Some fell to the ground. Others dashed away from the scene.

Francesca's gaze was drawn to Fritz, who watched the unfolding scene intently.

"Do you know who it is?" Alma asked, quickly packing their remaining things.

"No," he said, "but we need to move out, fast."

A man bolted suddenly, his face pinched with fear. Francesca gasped. He ran straight for them.

Several men raced after him, their pistols gleaming in the light of day.

Fritz whipped around. "Ladies, get back. Mama, the children!"

Mrs. Klein screamed and clutched Johanna.

Alma pulled Else into an outcropping of trees behind a large boulder. Greta and the rest of Alma's siblings joined them, along with the Kleins.

All but Fritz. He leaned on the boulder in front of the families in a protective stance. Mr. Klein joined him, but Robert Brauer, Francesca noticed, remained out of sight.

Johanna shouted at him in German, but Fritz ignored her.

Resisting her instinct to flee, Francesca rushed to his side. She couldn't let him face the gangsters alone, and she couldn't bear to see him hurt. He was too good, too...good of a friend.

Alma gasped and called out to her. "Francesca!"

In that instant, a man aimed his pistol at the gangster who fled—and fired.

Screams split the air.

Fritz yanked Francesca to the ground and covered her body with his in one swift motion. The impact of her bones connecting with hard earth took her breath away.

A memory shocked through her then, of her father knocking her to the ground. As she'd lain there, on the gravel path leading to their front door, she'd spat on his shoe, knowing full well it would elicit a swift kick to her ribs. It had been worth it to show him what she thought of him, and that she wasn't afraid. But her side had ached for days, and the purple-black bruises had frightened Maria and Sister Alberta enough that they'd called a doctor. Her dear papa had broken two of her ribs.

Francesca gulped in air, trying to steady her breathing, her racing heart. She wasn't at home, she reminded herself. She was in New York, far from her father's violence. Fritz Brauer had tried to protect her, not hurt her. And though she'd known him a short time, she knew to her very bones he was a good man. This show of protecting his family, and her, only confirmed it.

As the rest of the gangsters scattered and the other families reemerged from their hiding places, Francesca pushed the memory back to where it belonged—in the past. Still, she felt an oily nausea in its wake.

"Are you all right?" Fritz asked, untangling himself from Francesca's skirts.

"I... Yes." She nodded, wishing the nausea would subside.

Fritz lightly brushed her hand with his fingertips. "Did I hurt you?"

"No. Thank you...for..." For protecting her. For being a gentleman. For looking at her that way, as if her welfare meant something to him. Emotion clogged her throat and she gazed at him speechless, unable to finish her sentence.

"For a minute there, you looked as if you'd seen a ghost," he said.

If only he knew how right he was. Paolo Ricci was a ghost, a phantom that haunted her despite the time and distance between them. She was still learning how to erase him from her life, her mind, her heart completely. And it was proving difficult. It seemed she would always carry the scars.

"I had a memory," she said at last.

"A memory?" Concern shone in his eyes.

"An unpleasant one. One I can't repeat. It is not... It is too... I can't."

He studied her face, eyes soft. "It's all right. You're safe. Here, let me help you. " He held out his hand and helped her to her feet.

"Thank you," she said, reaching for her boater hat, which had tipped sideways in the scuffle and now dangled from loose hairpins.

Fritz cast her a sidelong glance. "Are you sure you're all right? You look a little pale."

"I want to go," she said, attempting to keep her voice steady.

"Of course, yes."

The Brauers and their few remaining friends gathered their things rapidly, complaining about the lack of police and how things were more dangerous now than in their childhood days.

"Are you all right?" Alma asked, rushing over to her. "That was terrifying."

Francesca kissed her friend's cheeks. "I'm fine. I'm...tired."

"I'll walk you home," Fritz said, glancing at his pocket watch. "It's getting late, and we're finished here anyway."

"Yes, please let him walk with you," Alma insisted. "I'll help carry things home. Will I see you next week? I can visit you, if you prefer."

"Sì, of course." Francesca kissed her cheeks. "I enjoy the picnic. Mostly." She forced a smile. "And you don't need to worry about me, Fritz. I can walk alone. I'm not afraid."

"I insist," Fritz said. "I couldn't live with myself if something happened to you."

She felt a fluttering sensation in her stomach. He worried about her welfare? She met his gaze briefly, and for the first time in ages, felt a blush crawl across her cheeks.

"I'm going to escort Miss Ricci home, Mama," Fritz announced, pulling his derby hat back onto his head.

Mrs. Brauer opened her mouth to protest but seemed to think better of it and nodded curtly. "Fine."

Francesca took up her basket and made her goodbyes. "Thank you for having me again, Mrs. Brauer. I hope you liked my bread."

"You're welcome." Mrs. Brauer nodded. "And yes, I liked your bread very much, though next time I would have added more yeast so it can rise more."

Behind Johanna's back, Alma rolled her eyes.

Francesca hid a smile. "I try that next time."

Shyly, Else, the youngest Brauer, approached her and held out a flower plucked from the small patch of grass near the fence. "For you."

Francesca touched her lips in surprise. This lovely little girl had no qualms about welcoming Francesca to their family gatherings. Bending to meet Else at her eye level, she accepted the gift. "Thank you, Else. How you know I love flowers?"

Else shrugged shyly and smiled, showing a gap where she'd lost a tooth. Her large brown eyes, fringed by thick lashes, were unlike the blues eyes of the rest of the family. Perhaps they'd come from a distant relative. Regardless, she would be a beauty one day.

"We're off," Fritz said, nodding a goodbye to Helene, whose face fell when she saw whom he was escorting home.

Francesca pretended not to notice and said goodbye to the rest of the group. A few looked up and replied in kind.

As she and Fritz sauntered off, Francesca was careful to keep an arm's length between them. She knew several pairs of eyes were watching them go.

"We take the train?" It was a long walk home, so she assumed Fritz would be anxious to get back to the bierhaus.

Something like disappointment crossed his features. "I thought we'd walk, if that's all right? It's a nice evening. Apart from the gangs."

She laughed. "Apart from the gangs."

"I suppose you're right. We should take the train."

"No! I like to walk. I like to..." Her cheeks burned.

A smile bloomed on his face. "A walk it is."

"Thank you, Fritz," she said. "You didn't have to see me home."

"You're my sister's friend. And my friend," he added hastily. "I couldn't let you go alone... I didn't want to let you go." He cleared his throat. "Go alone, that is."

The fluttering sensation returned, and when she met his eye, he smiled broadly.

"Shall we?" He held out his forearm, and as she accepted it, a cloud of evergreen and earth floated around her. His scent.

A scent she could definitely get used to.

Two days had passed since the incident in the park and her walk with Fritz, and yet Francesca couldn't put it from her mind. She had friends—even a male friend, and though it hadn't been entirely comfortable dining with the Brauers and the other German families, she could see herself slowly becoming a part of things. She'd never been welcomed into a large circle, or welcomed at all in truth, outside the cozy warmth of Sister Alberta's home.

Francesca wiped down the staff dining table, helped Claire put away the last of the clean dishes, and eyed the wineglasses set out as a treat for them when they finished. She was worn out, and her stomach hadn't stopped churning all day. Sadly, the wine didn't look particularly appetizing either. She'd almost taken to bed, worried an illness was coming on, but didn't want to leave Claire on her own.

A soft but insistent knock came at the staff entrance door.

Frowning, Mrs. Cheedle looked up from her puzzle. "Who could that be at this hour?" She headed to the door, and when she returned, a frown stamped her features. "Francesca, someone is here to see you." She made a point of looking at the clock. "I invited him inside, but he insisted on waiting for you on the stoop."

He? Francesca couldn't imagine who that might be. She laid down her towel and went to the door. Just beyond the potted flowers, a man sat on the top of the stairs. Not just any man. It was Fritz Brauer.

Her heart skipped a beat. What was he doing here?

"Fritz, is that you?" she called.

"I know it's getting late," he said. "I'm just leaving work, and I needed to talk to someone. I thought... Well, I thought of you."

"Are you all right? Do you want to come in?"

"No. I mean, yes. No." He laughed. "I'm sorry. I don't know why I came." He stood to go.

"Don't leave," she said, climbing the steps that led from the staff entrance below street level. The night had cooled, and as the crisp air crept over her skin, she crossed her arms over her chest and rubbed them. "Did something happen?"

"I had a rough day at work. My boss heard some rumors about a strike, and now he's threatening to fire workers, many of whom are my friends. He said he'd hire all new immigrants if he had to, to get the subway built. And to avoid the headaches." He took off his hat, rubbed a hand over his hair, and said a few things she didn't understand. She was relieved when she could finally make sense of something he'd said. "I tried to convince him it was in his best interest to pay us more," Fritz went on, "and to think about shortening the workday, even just by an hour, but he wasn't hearing it." He tried his very poor Italian. "I'm sorry. Your English and my Italian... Does any of this make sense to you?"

"The boss doesn't want workers to leave him, but he won't pay," she replied in English.

He sighed. "Yes, but what he's also trying to say is he doesn't want the anarchists working for him anymore."

Anarchists. An anarchist had shot the king in Italy a few years ago, and her father had celebrated. That was how she knew she wanted nothing to do with them, but Alma's explanation—or defense of Fritz, rather—had given Francesca pause in her assumptions. Fritz didn't seem like the sort of man to cause trouble, and certainly not the kind of man to shoot someone.

"They know you are anarchist?" she asked.

He nodded. "And they want me to get my men to settle down, or they'll fire me and anyone else out of line. But if I walk, we all walk, and there will be a major strike."

"Maybe you stop anarchism now."

"Maybe," he said reluctantly. "But it's really none of their damned business what my politics are and what I do in my spare time. I think Mark Schumacher was the one who rattled their cages."

"Rattle cages?" She frowned.

He laughed and his mood broke. "Stir things up. Make people upset."

"I see," she said. "The man from the park with the marks on his face? But he is your friend. I don't understand."

He shrugged. "Neither do I."

"He's not much of a friend these days, is he?" Fritz sat in a puddle of moonlight, making his eyes look like orbs of silver. "Our working conditions are pretty dangerous most of the time. We still have a long way to go, so we'll likely have to strike soon, no matter what else happens." Determination settled in the lines of his jaw.

Though confused as to why he'd made a trip here just to tell her this, at this hour, she was glad he had. He seemed to trust her, and the thought pleased her more than she wanted to admit. As a vision of Fritz laughing with Helene flitted through her mind, Francesca realized he didn't think of her in the same way he did Helene. Francesca and Fritz were simply friends, and it was a wonderful feeling to have friends. And that was enough. It had to be enough.

She sat beside him on the step without speaking, listening to the distant rumble of trains. She was acutely aware of his nearness, of his breathing, and the smell of earth that clung to his clothes after a long day's work. Did she smell of sugar and yeast and jam tarts?

He peered at her in the dark, his eyes traveling over her face. "Thank you for listening."

Shifting under his stare, she said, "We are friends."

"I couldn't talk to Alma. She's already worried about me, and my parents don't understand."

Her hands seemed to have a mind of their own and reached for him, touched his knee. "I'm happy you came. I like to talk."

He hit his forehead with the palm of his hand. "I haven't even asked how your day was, or about your work. Are you getting along with the Lancasters?"

"I like my work very much. Some days are difficult, but I've never slept in such a soft bed before. I'm very lucky." She wouldn't go into Janie's prickly nature or her attempts at sabotaging Francesca every chance she had. The maid told her directly she disliked Italians. Claire had reassured Francesca that Janie was the jealous sort and to ignore her.

"I've taken a lot for granted, I think, and I don't even live on Park Avenue," he replied.

"We all have our lessons," she said, her voice earnest but soft.

He looked at her appraisingly and stood. "I should go. It's late."

She rose to her feet, trying to quash her disappointment that he was leaving so soon, but she had a little cleaning left to do before she could go to her bedroom for the night.

They looked at each other, an awkward silence stretching between them. A soft night breeze flowed over her skin, and a dog barked somewhere nearby.

"I hope I didn't interrupt anything," Fritz said, gesturing to the house. "I'm sorry. I don't know why I'm here. It's getting late."

"I know fear, more than most, and difficult decisions. This is why you came."

He smiled ruefully. "Yes."

"You work hard, Fritz," she continued. "Your men admire you and believe in you. I learn this in the short time knowing you. Don't be afraid. Do what feels right."

He took her hand in his briefly and squeezed. "Thank you."

At his touch, her heart lurched in her chest. "I—I hope you come again."

"Good night, Francesca," he said, a grin stretching across his face.

"Good night, Fritz."

It had been a good night indeed.

32

The morning light glowed faintly around the edges of the curtain in Francesca's bedroom. Two weeks had passed since Fritz had first come to her door, and most nights thereafter, he visited when his workday finished. He'd also made it a habit to walk with her the forty-five minutes from the Lower East Side to Park Avenue at Midtown on Sundays after the picnic. Fritz was intense and passionate, but he had a good sense of humor, too, when she least expected it to show. She relished their easy yet lively conversations in tangled English and Italian. She smiled as she thought of the way her hands had a mind of their own and reached out to touch his forearm, his hand, his shoulder when he was near. She couldn't help herself, and he didn't seem to mind. When she wasn't with him, he filled her thoughts, and she felt her shell of self-protection crumbling. He wasn't like other men she'd met. Of that, she was now certain.

She stretched beneath her covers and tried to talk herself into getting ready for the day. She couldn't believe she'd worked for the Lancasters nearly nine weeks. It wasn't always perfect, and at times, Mrs. Lancaster picked at the dishes Francesca and Claire had carefully crafted for her, but the mistress of the house praised her dishes a few times, too. Francesca nearly startled the first time it happened.

She and Claire had sneaked a little port that night and toasted to success. They made quite the pair, Claire had said, echoing the words of the master of the house one night after a particularly special meal of braised beef. Their skills complemented each other, what with Claire's skillful hand at baked goods and breads, and Francesca's natural ability with herb combinations and seafood and meats. Mrs. Lancaster, to their delight—and Francesca's complete relief—agreed.

Though Francesca was still tired, it was time to get up and face the day. She rolled over in bed. Her stomach gurgled, and she brought a hand to her lips. She sat up, lifting the covers—and the room tilted. In a flash, she darted from bed on wobbly legs to the shared toilet in the hall before losing the contents of her stomach in one violent heave.

She groaned and wiped her mouth. *Ave Maria*, it wasn't a good time to be ill. The Lancasters were hosting a dinner party that evening, and she had a full day of work ahead of her. Mrs. Cheedle and Janie had pored over the silver and the place settings, and Charles had seen to the positioning of the furniture to accommodate a lengthy list of guests. Temporary help had been hired as waitstaff for the evening as well. Francesca and Claire had been preparing what they could in advance, but the bulk of the work would come that day.

Francesca slid to the floor and landed on her hind end, head resting against the wall. She'd felt this way yesterday, too, and assumed she'd eaten something that didn't agree with her. Now she knew she must have some illness, perhaps because of the late walk she'd taken alone the night before. She'd been caught in the rain. She'd known better than to stay up so late when she had such a busy day ahead of her, but she'd been racked with memories of Maria all day, desperately missing her, and she'd needed the time alone to remember her sister. To cry as much as she needed to without questions or pity.

She'd also needed time to fend off her guilt. Francesca had friends, a good job, and a safe place to call home. Her sister had never had a chance for that life, and never had the luxury of a safe place to lay her head at night. As the pain returned, Francesca grasped the Madonna at her neck and said a prayer.

A faint knock came at the door. "Are you all right, Francesca?" came Claire's voice.

"I think I have a sickness."

She heard Claire's sigh through the door. "Today isn't the day for it."

"I'm sorry. I work hard."

"I know you will, lamb, I know. Get yourself cleaned up, and I'll meet you downstairs."

When Claire's footsteps grew faint, Francesca returned to her room, stomach swimming, and dressed for the day, saying a silent prayer she could make it through the evening without vomiting again.

After breakfast, they got to work on platters of amuse-bouches, something she'd never seen before. They were labor-intensive, with their perfect little wedges of bread, sculpted vegetables, and creams, mousses, and spreads. Next came platters of smoked ham and salmon, and pickled vegetables. There would be roasted duck with fig sauce, cold shrimp, and beef medallions with a tangy béarnaise sauce. For dessert, tarts with custard, glistening fruits, and chocolate-dipped biscuits.

As she worked, Francesca's nausea came and went, but by day's end it seemed to ease and she was relieved.

When the day shifted to evening, the new waitstaff arrived, awaiting orders and rushing off to care for the guests.

Janie blew into the kitchen like a hot wind, her cheeks rosy from rushing around the house all day preparing for their guests. "Francesca, Mrs. Lancaster needs you in her bedroom."

"Why?" Claire asked. "We're very busy here."

Janie rolled her eyes. "I didn't ask her, but she said immediately."

"You'd better go, Francesca," Claire said, nodding. A dollop of cream was smeared across her cheek.

Francesca felt a touch of nerves but did as she was asked, rushing quickly through the house to her mistress before the guests arrived. She couldn't imagine what Mrs. Lancaster would want from her when the party would soon begin.

When Francesca stood in the doorway of Mrs. Lancaster's bedroom, she knocked softly, reminding herself to keep her eyes downcast, her demeanor polite.

"Come in and close the door," Mrs. Lancaster said.

Francesca marveled at the mistress's creamy silk gown that cascaded to the floor, the diamonds glittering at her ears, and the vivid green gem nestled in the hollow of her throat. She looked like royalty. With a flourish, she sat at her vanity and reached for a delicate perfume bottle that looked as if it had been sculpted by an artist, with its colorful whorls and dainty neck. She sprayed herself, and a cloud of rose and something woody wafted across the room.

"I read the menu for tonight," Mrs. Lancaster said, "and I noticed there wasn't any ricotta cream with lemon curd. I was hoping you might make it."

"Oh, I... Claire wrote the menu." She reddened. "She said little cakes and dipped biscuits hold better for a party."

"I see, well, that's too bad. I've grown rather fond of it." Mrs. Lancaster stalked across the room toward the door, the draft created by her movement knocking a framed photograph from her table.

Francesca bent to pick it up, pausing briefly to glance at a photograph of Mrs. Lancaster, many years ago, and Mr. Lancaster as a little boy. She wore a simple frock that must have been in the English style with a plain collar, but her head was tipped back in laughter. Mr. Lancaster was playing with a stick and a large hoop. Francesca noted that even then, all of those years ago, there was no sign of the senior Mr. Lancaster. Perhaps he'd taken the photo? She quickly glanced around the room to look for any other sign of him, the gossip she'd overheard about the mistress ringing in her ears. It was as if Mr. Lancaster senior had been wiped from existence. Francesca wondered what could have happened between them. She glanced down at the picture in her hands and was again surprised by Mrs. Lancaster's uncustomary playfulness. Photographs were usually reserved for somber occasions or for family portraits.

"I'll take that," Mrs. Lancaster snapped, snatching the silver frame from her hands and placing it on her table beneath the lamp.

"The photograph is very beautiful," she replied.

"You may go," Mrs. Lancaster said curtly.

"Yes, signora—madam."

Francesca ducked out of the room, not knowing what to make of the photograph, or of the exchange. Though the dessert choices hadn't been left to Francesca, she couldn't help but feel she was being held responsible for the signora's displeasure. And it seemed odd that she was the one called to Mrs. Lancaster's room rather than Claire.

As she pushed through the kitchen door, a string quartet began to play in the parlor, and the most divine music she'd ever heard drifted through the house. Though hard at work, Janie and Mrs. Cheedle appeared almost lighthearted. A party broke up the humdrum of the daily routine. It usually meant fancy foods and libations for the staff as well, when the work was finished. The Lancasters were generous in that way and encouraged the staff to celebrate for a job well done.

As the guests filtered in, Claire motioned to Francesca to join her at the door separating the kitchen from the rest of the house. "We'll just take a peek."

Mr. Lancaster saw them, their faces between the cracks of the door, and winked before heading into the salon. He looked as elegant as ever in a formal tie and jacket.

"He's such a good-natured fellow, isn't he?" Claire whispered. "Sometimes I don't see how he and the mistress are related."

"What's he wearing around his neck?" Francesca asked, interested in learning words for items she'd never seen before. The wealthy had so many luxuries, so many conveniences, and she scarcely knew the words for them in Italian, let alone English.

Claire giggled. "That's a bow tie, *chérie*."

Beautiful people dressed in silk and satin splendor streamed into the front hall. Long gloves, jewels, cravats, and smoking jackets. When a woman in a shimmering green evening gown entered, her blond hair shining like a halo in the light of the chandelier overhead, Francesca stared at her beaded dress in rapture, wishing she could wear such a thing one day. After a moment, the woman shifted, and Francesca's gaze was drawn to the woman's midsection. It swelled beneath her beautiful gown. She was with child.

A thought flickered at the back of Francesca's mind and a sense of knowing, an understanding to the depths of her soul, arose inside her. Her breath caught as the terrible thought pushed itself to the forefront of her mind.

Her vomiting in the morning, the way her stomach turned at the odor of meat cooking in a pan, the constant fatigue. Her hand flew to her stomach, and frantically, she counted backward. She hadn't had her menses since those terrible weeks at Ellis Island. How many days had gone since?

Well over nine weeks.

Her mouth went dry. It couldn't be.

She recounted the days with the same result. But she'd been through so much the last couple of months, perhaps her body hadn't had time to find its new rhythm. Her menses had rarely been on time in the past. Sister Alberta had blamed the abuse, insisting that a body at war didn't behave as it should. As Francesca considered the last several weeks of adjusting to her new home and work schedule, she knew it had been trying at times, but her days had been fluid and easy compared to her life in Sicilia

She closed her eyes and saw the lust in the inspector's eyes, felt his greedy hands on her. It couldn't be true. It wasn't that easy to become pregnant. Some of the women in her village had hoped for a child for many months and even years before they could conceive. But Francesca was young and strong—and her luck was lousy. It always had been. Sister Alberta told her it was because she didn't pray, that she was cursed for not obeying the rules a young lady was meant to follow. Francesca had hoped to change all of that in America.

She swallowed hard against her rising panic. It was early yet, and her cycle might go nine or even twelve weeks before her menses came again. She clutched to a shred of hope. It had happened in the past, many times. She was ill, that was all.

She turned abruptly from the elegant party, her fear warring with reason, and headed back to the kitchen where she belonged.

That must be it. That had to be it.

33

*A*nother week passed, and each morning, Francesca darted for the toilet the moment her eyes opened, her fears solidifying as the illness didn't abate. But it wasn't an illness. She knew the truth, even if she didn't want to believe it—couldn't understand how this had happened to her—and she begged for a reprieve from God, for her menses to come. She stared at her bedroom ceiling, painting fantasies in her mind of taking devilish herbs or falling hard intentionally to knock loose the inspector's seed. Then came the image of the young woman in her village who had painfully and slowly bled to death when she'd taken matters into her own hands. Francesca couldn't risk it.

She closed her eyes against the invading memory of the foul inspector. Their exchange was supposed to have been simple and worth the cost, and was it? *Yes.* She mouthed the word to the ceiling as the smoky pictures of her fantasies faded. She didn't regret her actions, even now. She'd prefer to suffer in America on her own than to suffer at the hand of her father.

If only she didn't have to give up so much—again.

The Lancasters wouldn't keep her on their staff and in their home while she was pregnant. They cared too much about their reputation and propriety among their social circles.

You have another option, a voice whispered inside her. *You could give the baby away.*

She covered her face with a pillow. She didn't know if she could live with herself, abandoning a child just as she had been by her mother. But what was she to do? The future had never looked bleaker.

She yearned for Maria, for Sister Alberta. What would the nun think of Francesca's condition? Francesca didn't care. She needed her friend more than anything in the world in that moment, even should Alberta condemn her actions. Francesca sat up in bed and reached for a sheet of paper and pen on the bedside table, suddenly anxious at last, to write a letter to her faraway friend.

The words poured onto the page. She described her job as cook, her soft bed, and the magnificent home where she spent her days. She described the many new dishes she'd learned to prepare. She talked about her new friends, and the way her English improved daily. At last, at the end of the letter, she told Sister Alberta about Maria. Maria's bravery as they crossed the ocean, her translucent skin and the way her voice had become little more than a whisper, her humor until the last.

She dropped her pen as the pain rolled over her for the hundredth time, stealing her breath. She'd hoped her new life would fill some of the void inside her, but she was foolish to believe anything could ease the wound of losing her sister. Maria was gone. And she'd have to learn to live with the ever-present throbbing in her chest: the grief that, at times, still felt like a fire ravaging her insides.

As much as Francesca had longed to leave home, and as much as she had longed for a new life, sometimes she felt her solitude as keenly as a knife. She wasn't one of them, the Americans, or the Germans. She was all but invisible in the ways that mattered. She could walk through the door and be lost in a sea of faces, disappear into the infinite city never to be heard from again, and it would make no difference to anyone. Not even Alma or Fritz in the end. They had their family, their traditions, and their work. She was an extra, a woman who would never quite be a part of their circle. A woman who would never quite belong.

Frustrated by the endless circling of her thoughts, she folded the letter and slipped it into an envelope. She couldn't yet bring herself to share her dirty secret, especially without knowing herself what she'd do with it. At least she had time before her body changed—time to make a plan. She sat on the edge of the bed, her eyes tracing the light blazing around the corners of the blue cotton drape at the window. She attempted to clear her mind and listened to the sound of Claire's soft snores. The sun had risen, and though it was still early, she decided she might as well start her day. It was Sunday and she had most of the day free.

The first thing she'd do was go to mass and to confession. Perhaps God would see her through this, if she would do as He asked of her: pray, confess her sins, do His will. Be the good Catholic woman Sister Alberta had tried to teach her to be. Francesca had never felt connected to Alberta's cold and distant god, but now she had no choice but to try.

She pulled on her nicest dress of light-green cotton the color of spring leaves, her boater hat with black ribbon, and plain but comfortable gloves. For a final touch, she fastened on her mother's brooch. After a quick bite of bread and coffee, she began the long walk to Alma's. Her friend could show her to a Catholic church, and after mass, Francesca would join the Brauers at the park.

Where Fritz would be.

Fritz. The warmth he lent as he escorted her home. The way a light burned in his eyes when he felt strongly about something. How he listened to her as if all she had to say mattered.

Ave Maria, she had to stop thinking about him. There wouldn't be any room for him in her life, not with a baby. He'd want nothing to do with a woman who had traded her body to ensure her future.

Desperate to ease the ache in her chest, she turned her attention to the scenery. She mused over the quiet of a Sunday morning. The roar of trains and carriage wheels to which she had grown accustomed was all but gone. When she approached Chatham Square, there were only a handful of the usual street urchins and prostitutes about who normally haunted the plaza. Even one of the most boisterous and wretched corners of the city lay beneath a blanket of slumber.

As she walked, she read the signs that she could understand, noticing the way the languages and the building styles often changed from one neighborhood to another. She'd heard there was an Italian section of town near Alma's, but she hadn't yet seen the place where many of her countrymen landed after passing through the halls of Ellis Island, if they didn't leave for Chicago or go north to Boston.

She continued on, finally reaching Orchard Street, and she was struck again by the differences between her Park Avenue neighborhood and the Lower East Side. Though somewhat subdued here, people still flowed down the muddy street in a steady stream, and vendors were setting up their wares. Children chased each other around the carts or gathered in alleyways between the buildings. The sheer number of people living on this block didn't allow for silent streets. Francesca felt more at home in the crowded but lively neighborhood where Alma lived than on pristine and luxurious Park Avenue.

After Francesca arrived at the bierhaus, Alma escorted her to a Catholic church. As they rounded the block onto Mulberry Street, Francesca stopped abruptly. Italian flags hung over doorways or in various shop windows. The rich smell of strong coffee mingled with garlic in the air, and the sounds of her own language fell gently on her ears like a melody. Her heart squeezed. She hadn't realized how much she'd needed to be among those who were like her, who would understand her and accept her. Her coworkers and her new friends didn't understand the discomfort of not belonging. Not like she did. Here among other Italians, she found the person inside her she thought she'd wanted to banish when she came to America. And yet her home was a part of her and would forever be. Her life here only added a layer to who she was. It didn't erase what came before it, and maybe that was all right, good even. She blinked rapidly against the onslaught of tears and glanced at Alma.

Her friend watched her closely.

"The church is just there," Alma said softly, pointing to a steeple that looked about a block away. "Father Rodolfo is a very kind man. He'll make you feel right at home."

"It's...it's..." Her voice wavered and she fought back emotion. "This." She waved her hand at the scene in front of her. This is what she had needed so desperately, more than she ever realized.

Alma smiled as she began to understand. "*Sì, amica mia.* You're not so very far from Sicily now."

Eyes brimming, Francesca nodded. "It's a little piece of home."

Alma embraced her. "Do you want me to come with you? I don't have to go to church today."

She kissed Alma's cheek. "I need to do this alone, but I'll see you after mass."

She watched Alma go and headed to the church and up the steps. Inside, the mournful notes of the organ filled the room, and light streamed through windows stained blue and red and gold. The church was far more beautiful than the humble chapel where Sister Alberta had taken her in Capo Mulini. Yet when the mass began, and the familiar strains of Latin drifted around her, she felt instantly at ease.

Mass followed a pattern that soothed her, even if she didn't believe all the church demanded she believe. And she thought that counted for something.

Later, she skipped communion and instead sent up prayers for Maria, and prayers for wisdom to know what to do when the time came. When she'd finished, her mind wandered to the picnic that afternoon. A smiling Fritz popped into her head. She couldn't help herself. She liked him, more than she ought to, and yet it was hopeless. He would wed a German woman, she knew, and her childish dream would come to an end.

Was that what she wanted? To be with Fritz?

Her stomach turned over at the thought of him near. Perhaps she shouldn't go to the Brauer picnic after all, put some distance between her and the family. It would only become more difficult in time to say goodbye.

As the mass concluded, Francesca watched the church's patrons; they looked like her with dark hair and rich skin tones.

A woman touched Francesca's shoulder as she filed out of her pew. "Welcome. I'm Rosa Colombo. This is my husband, Aldo, and our children." The woman rattled off the names of all seven children jammed into the pew, who wiggled and poked at each other.

Francesca smiled. "I'm Francesca Ricci from Capo Mulini, near Catania. I arrived a few months ago."

"Is your family here in the city?"

Francesca's smile waned. "I don't have any family."

A crease formed between Rosa's dark eyes. "You're alone? That must be difficult."

"Yes, but I have a good job and I'm making friends."

"And now you have new ones." Rosa kissed each of Francesca's cheeks. "We live at 37 Mott Street. I insist you visit. I'll cook. Will you be here next Sunday?"

Though uncertain if she'd return, Francesca smiled. "Sì."

They walked toward the exit, pausing at the door to shake hands with the priest.

"See you next week, Padre." Rosa kissed Father Rodolfo on the cheeks and, with a small wave to Francesca, bundled her children into the street.

Francesca watched them go, realizing that she was making a life for herself in the city.

"Welcome. You are from Sicilia?" Father Rodolfo said, interrupting her thoughts.

"Yes. I guess I'm not the only one."

He chuckled and laid a hand on her shoulder. "You're surrounded by your countrymen here. I hope you'll consider our parish your new home."

"Thank you, Father. I'd like to go to confession. When is the next session?"

He smiled kindly. "I hold confession on Sunday afternoons, usually, but I can see you now, if you'd like. I'll not turn away those who seek His mercy."

She needed more than mercy. She needed a miracle.

The priest led her to a confessional booth, pulled aside a red curtain, and motioned for her to enter.

She knelt beside a beautifully carved lattice that separated her from the priest. As she pulled the little curtain closed to hide her face from his, she made the sign of the cross and bowed her head. "Bless me, Father, for I have sinned. It's been at least four months since my last confession."

"Go on."

She began with taking the Lord's name in vain and followed with contrition for her thieving. Heat crept across her cheeks as she confessed sex before marriage, but as she began to confess the lies she'd told, her words trailed off. Her theft had kept Maria alive in Napoli and on the ship, and it had paid for her desperately needed new clothing after leaving Ellis Island. She'd lied for self-protection. As for the sexual transgressions, only once had it been with a man she thought loved her, and the other instances had bought her way to freedom. She wasn't sorry for any of them, and neither did she believe them truly sinful, given the circumstances. Besides, she was already being punished with the pregnancy.

The idea of truth seemed slippery, a mirage that changed shape and color in different light. Perhaps it shouldn't be judged so quickly. Surely God understood her desperation and her intentions.

Perhaps she shouldn't be at confession at all.

"Signorina Ricci, are you there?"

"Sì, Padre. I'm...I'm trying to remember what else I wished to confess." She felt the first prickles of guilt. Now she'd lied to a priest, at confession! "I—I lie sometimes, Father, but it doesn't always feel wrong. And I'm not sorry to have done it."

He was quiet for some time. Finally, his raspy voice filtered through the curtain. "Sometimes lies feel like they protect us. Is that what you mean?"

"Yes," she said, looking down at her hands.

"Still, we must be contrite that we have deceived our fellow man."

"Sì, Padre," she said. But she wasn't contrite, and she would do it over again if she could save her sister. She'd lie again to protect herself. She'd do what she had to do to make her way in a world that too often felt against her. And that was the truth of it.

She shifted on her kneeler. What kind of Catholic didn't feel sorry for their sins? Was she sorry she had taken the immigrant's money? She imagined the woman's expression as she counted the bills in her purse at Ellis Island, the surprise and horror. How she would search her cot and peer at each face in distrust and fury, all the while a pit formed in her stomach because she knew she would never see the money again. This, perhaps, was something for which Francesca was truly sorry.

But she had needed the money more, and the woman had plenty. The stubborn thought asserted itself, quieting her guilt.

"Miss Ricci, are you still there?" Father asked softly.

"I want the things my employer has," she replied. "The silver spoons and silk gowns, and the pretty little boxes she puts out for decoration."

"My child, we always want what doesn't belong to us. Don't be fooled by Satan's trap. He lures us with riches, but we're most content when we are grateful for what we have. When we learn to love what is around us. Now, say ten rosaries for your penance, and reflect on your choices, Francesca."

She muttered the prayers she knew by heart, but she felt their emptiness. She wasn't sorry. Not for wanting Mrs. Lancaster's beautiful things. Francesca would never be sorry for wishing she had more. She was grateful for her job and a place to sleep—she liked it even—but she had dreams beyond it. She didn't want to rely on the charity of others forever. In their charity, she felt the weight of their command over her. She wanted her own family and home, perhaps her own restaurant one day. Things she hadn't dared to dream of until she'd landed safely on American soil. Was wanting more so wrong? It lit a fire in her belly. It gave her hope.

Yet as a wave of nausea hit her like a reprimand, her dreams seemed as distant as the horizon.

34

*A*s the Ellis Island ferry chugged across the churning waters of the bay, Alma perched at the railing, gazing out at a sunset that painted the sky in a rainbow of fire. She marveled at its beauty, the way the world seemed to glow beneath its brilliance. Opposite her, the Statue of Liberty was poised and regal, framed by a golden halo. When Francesca had explained how she'd felt sailing into the harbor—the shock of hope as Lady Liberty and her beacon came into view—Alma was struck with understanding that day. She'd never known a sense of desperation the way Francesca had, and Alma had felt, for the first time in her life, the real meaning of gratitude.

She felt it again as she peered out at the beautiful colossus that every immigrant longed to see. Working at Ellis Island had turned Alma's perspective like a child's spinning top, and she knew she'd never again be the person she was before, for better or worse. As the ferry drew closer to Ellis Island, she wondered what else lay ahead. The trajectory of her life might be in her parents' hands at the moment, but not for much longer. In spite of the fact that they'd all but sold her to a man she hardly knew, the thought was a little comforting.

She turned her face to the sun. The warmth of the afternoon hadn't yet faded, and she wanted to relish every moment she wasn't inside the immigration center. It would be a long night—her first night shift. She'd held Mrs. Keller off as long as possible with excuses of helping her mother at the bierhaus, but it was Alma's turn. She envisioned wandering the halls for hours like a ghost, listening to the sounds of the janitors and the night watchmen, and the rattle of the wind against the windowpanes. Shuddering, Alma stepped off the ferry, already counting down the hours until dawn.

Inside, she put away her handbag and watched the matrons who'd worked the day shift gather their things.

"Alma, come here," Mrs. Keller called as she pulled on a dowdy brown pelisse that did nothing for her pale complexion and graying hair. "Geraldine still has that wretched cold, so I told her to stay home. You're to report directly to Williams tonight."

"To the commissioner?" Alma asked in surprise. He usually worked the day shift. And frankly, the thought of being on the island with her boss all night was worse than cavorting with the so-called spirits that haunted the island. He might try to corner her again and pry for information.

"Yes," Mrs. Keller's tone was snippy. "He's assessing the night routines this week. Has to have his hand in everything. Anyway, I'll see you in the morning."

Turning abruptly, her supervisor dashed out the door to make the ferry before Alma had a chance to ask her what she was supposed to do all night.

As it happened, she spent most of the evening assisting the infirmary staff until she grew tired and went in search of a cup of coffee. She left the hospital and began the short walk outdoors to the main building on Island One. The moon beamed from an ebony sky, casting a celestial glow over the landscape and a glittering path of pale light across the water. It was beautiful, if a little eerie. The immigration center loomed large on her left, blocking the view of the sprawling city behind it, across the bay. She listened as the water lapped against the shore in a steady but irregular rhythm. She felt a strange sense of isolation. Knowing the island's sordid history, she'd been afraid to walk the grounds, but the night brought a silent, enchanting beauty she hadn't expected.

Best of all, being outdoors meant avoiding the commissioner.

Inside, Alma filled a cup of coffee to the brim, grateful someone on the staff had just brewed it. The rich smell alone invigorated her. As she sipped from her steaming cup, she envisioned life as a married woman with John Lambert in Hoboken. Far from the few friends she possessed, away from Fritz and her family. But perhaps it wasn't all bad. Maybe she'd enjoy having a family of her own. She liked children immensely, after all. John might be very different from her stepfather and embrace her need for learning. Or maybe she was weaving a fairy tale to placate herself.

After finishing the last of her coffee, she threaded through the baggage room where watchmen stood by the belongings of the detainees, up the stairs to the second floor, and through the halls to the matron's office. She should check in with the matrons stationed at the detainees' quarters, but first, maybe she'd sneak in an hour of studying. No one would be the wiser, given how quiet the place was. She'd learned not to leave home without her journal her first week of work, so she might add new phrases to it. Perhaps the night shift wasn't so bad after all. No one bothered her, the roar of voices had all but disappeared, and the heart-wrenching stories to which she was exposed every day were virtually absent.

As she neared the matron's office, footsteps echoed behind her and she turned to see who was there. Mr. Williams gave her a short wave.

"Good evening, Miss Brauer," he said, approaching. "You were just the person I was looking for."

"Hello, sir," she said, clasping her hands together. The very sight of him put her on edge.

He removed his spectacles and began polishing them with a handkerchief. "I've been meaning to congratulate you on your engagement. I hear Inspector Lambert is the lucky gentleman."

She stiffened. "Yes, sir. Thank you." She wished everyone would stop congratulating her. It was not a happy occasion.

He peered at her intently, as if looking for something. "Do you know Mr. Lambert well? I don't believe I've ever seen the two of you speak."

"Not well, sir, no. He visits our brewery from time to time. Speaks with my father." She wanted to tell him her engagement was as much a surprise to her as to anyone else. That she abhorred the fact she had no say in the matter, and so little control over any aspect of her life, but she said nothing, knowing it wasn't the time or place to voice her woes.

"I see." The commissioner looked over the top of his spectacles at her.

"Is there... Did you wish to tell me something, sir? I should probably get to work."

"I just wanted to convey my best wishes. Is everything running smoothly this evening?"

"Yes, it seems to be."

"Very good, Miss Brauer."

She shifted from one foot to the other under the scrutiny of his gaze.

"I don't mean to alarm you," he continued, "but I think it's in your best interest that you take your job very seriously."

Stunned, she said nothing. She always took her job seriously, and everything else she dedicated herself to as well. "I—I don't understand, sir. I do take it seriously."

"Yes, well. While it's true we have too many immigrants sailing in on a weekly basis, it's unacceptable to behave poorly toward them. They deserve common decency and respect, even if they are wretched. I won't have the staff abusing them or taking advantage of them, not under my direction, for any reason. I have no qualms about firing anyone who does, regardless of their position. I've delivered this message to your husband-to-be. It's best you both take heed."

"Sir, I'm not sure what you mean."

"I think we both know what I mean. Now, off to work with you," he said firmly. "It won't be long before the day shift arrives."

She didn't have the slightest idea what he meant, but one thing was certain: she was now linked with John Lambert, whether she liked it or not, and they'd both better be on their best behavior.

The following Sunday, Alma bumbled around the kitchen, trying to help her mother get ready for the Sunday picnic, but she could scarcely focus. John Lambert would be there today, and he'd made it clear he wanted to spend time with her alone. She'd thought about what the commissioner had said for days. Though he hadn't come out and said precisely what he knew about John, she'd gotten the impression it wasn't good—and now the commissioner suspected her, too, of whatever it was. Deep in thought, she didn't notice the fruit basket hanging over the edge of the counter. Her shawl caught the wooden slats and tipped the basket's contents to the floor, sending apples rolling in every direction. She swore loudly, catching Robert's attention.

"Watch it, girl," he snapped as he lugged several jugs of beer into the kitchen. "If you bruised them, you can pay for them. Now clean that up. It's time to go."

Now she was to pay for an accident? Silently, she fumed and bent to retrieve the apples, checking their skins carefully for bruises. Only one had smashed flesh beneath the skin. She placed the damaged apple on the bottom of the basket. It would be perfectly serviceable for stewed apples and cinnamon, or in sauerkraut.

When they arrived at the park, Alma noticed Francesca had decided not to join them today. Alma also noticed Fritz kept watching the entrance. He was clearly looking for her. She made a mental note to check in with Francesca when she had a chance this week after work, to make sure everything was all right.

Though the early summer day was warm, clouds blanketed the sky, and Alma found herself praying for rain. But an hour later, still no rain had come and John Lambert sauntered across the park toward them.

"Hello, Brauers," he bellowed.

Alma nodded politely but continued her card game with Klaus.

Mama greeted John with a little more enthusiasm than she should have and nearly knocked him off his feet. He laughed and glanced at Alma again, but when she didn't make the effort to talk to him, he joined Fritz and his friends.

Mama shot Alma a wide-eyed look and flicked her hands to shoo her in his direction.

Heart sinking, Alma handed Klaus her cards and inserted herself into John's conversation, doing her best to be friendly and engage him. But he seemed more interested in talking with Fritz about *fussball* and who would play in today's match. She couldn't care less about soccer, but as she turned to go, John reached for her arm.

"Would you like to go for an iced cream?" he asked.

She didn't want to go with Lambert, but she supposed it was better to get to know him now, rather than marrying a stranger. And at least she liked iced cream.

She forced a smile. "I think that sounds nice. There's a stand on Delancey Street—"

"Actually, I think Gerald's on Union Square is a better choice. Shall we?"

She covered her annoyance behind a forced smile. "Fine. That sounds nice."

They said their goodbyes and walked to Union Square, making polite conversation about the weather, John's interest in *fussball*, and eventually, their conversation turned to work. She was relieved to have something in common to talk about with him.

"Between us, that new commissioner is a bit of a bastard. He's been nosing around my business, checking over my ledgers to see who I admit to the country and who I turn away. Second-guessing every call I make."

"Isn't that the commissioner's job?" she asked.

His lip curled in irritation. "I'm the chief of registry. You'd think he would spend his time doing something more worthwhile. Check up on the other inspectors or the matrons. Keep the hospital staff in line."

"You think he needs to check up on the matrons?" she asked.

"Sure."

Alma didn't reply. She'd seen a thing or two that hadn't seemed "in line" with the duties and expectations at Ellis Island, but she wouldn't say the matrons needed strict supervision. They weren't the gatekeepers in the end, though their work with the immigrants did help keep the doctors and inspectors informed. They also did everyone's errands and dirty work. They needed to be assisted, not to be investigated.

They walked the rest of the way in silence. When they reached Gerald's, John purchased their iced creams and found an empty bench. Alma dipped into the cold chocolate cream and let the sweet treat melt on her tongue, momentarily forgetting her nerves.

"You like it," John observed.

"Very much."

"We should make a habit of this." He took her hand briefly in his and squeezed it.

Too surprised by his touch, she didn't reply.

They ate in silence, watching people stream past them. Some walked lazily through the square with their families, while others rushed off to an unseen destination. Eventually Alma noticed a pair of young women carrying books and toting shoulder bags, walking in the direction of New York University. They laughed, their heads inclined together. It was a rare thing to see female students, but Alma knew the idea was becoming more and more acceptable. She wondered what the women were studying. Commerce or education? Literature? A yearning gnawed at her as she considered the unlimited time to learn and study, to develop in a chosen trade. This is what she wanted. The freedom to choose her future.

While she was lost in thought, the iced cream started to melt, and a sticky river of chocolate ran over the lip of the cone onto her hand.

"Shall we go?" John said. "I'll see you home, and then I'd better be on my way. Long day tomorrow."

"Yes. Thank you for the iced cream."

As they stood and wiped their hands, she realized John hadn't asked her anything about herself. Not her work, her thoughts. Her dreams. He didn't know a single thing about her. Her eyes found the figures of the young women blending into the crowd, nearly gone from sight, and her heart squeezed. She glanced back at her middle-aged fiancé, who knew nothing about her. She wanted to like him—and he had been kind to her—but no matter how hard she tried, she couldn't bring herself to see him as anything more than a coworker and one of her stepfather's friends.

She couldn't accept the life laid out before her. She couldn't, no matter what her parents, or anyone else, might say.

And in that instant she knew that she was the only one who could change it.

35

The days grew warmer, and soon, midsummer pressed down upon the city. Charles and Mrs. Cheedle threw open the windows in the evenings to usher in the cooler breezes. Francesca and Claire prepared lighter fare of cold vegetables, bread, cheese, and eggs in exchange for the heavy meat dishes and sauces. All the while, Francesca pretended nothing had changed, that no child grew inside her, bringing with it a storm of upheaval. Stubborn in her denial, she returned to Tompkins Square Park every Sunday. Johanna had begun to greet Francesca with a smile, piling her plate high and asking her about her work. The other German families invited her to share stories from home and laughed along with her as she tried to learn a few German phrases. They were good people, even if they had been slow to accept her at first. It was one of few consolations while she guarded her terrible secret.

She wondered how their hospitality would change when they discovered the truth.

Each week that passed, her stomach grew a little rounder, her bosom fuller. At night, though exhausted, she lay awake, wondering how she would explain the pregnancy to her friends and torturing herself with Fritz's imagined reply. Would he be disgusted or outraged she'd hid the pregnancy from him for so long? Perhaps he would simply console her the way a friend should.

He was only a friend, she reminded herself.

Somehow this truth brought more pain than the thought of his projected outrage.

She walked to the park, and by midafternoon, several more of Fritz's friends joined their party, making the group larger than usual. The men threw off their jackets and hats and rolled their sleeves to their elbows; the women sought refuge in the shade beneath their parasols or a shade tree. Helene Bach showed as well, radiant in pink crepe that made her skin as fresh as strawberries and cream. Fritz and Alma's friends gathered around her as she told stories and laughed prettily. Alma spent a little time with her friend named Emma, who didn't seem to like Francesca and kept her distance. All the while, Francesca watched the boisterous group from her quiet spot on a bench, contemplating what it must be like to live a life that seemed mostly carefree. She'd never known such a luxury and now, with an unwanted child on the way, would never have the chance to experience it. Her mood sank at the thought, and she decided it best to head home rather than put a damper on the festivities.

Her eyes found Fritz among the men.

In that moment, he looked over his shoulder, searching the crowd as if some internal signal had prompted him. When his eyes captured hers, he broke into a smile and winked.

Her heart skipped a beat. What was she to do?

Alma strayed from Emma's side and, with a few lanky strides, joined Francesca, a look of concern on her face. "Are you all right? What are you doing over here?" Her hat threw shade across her face in a jagged pattern.

Francesca longed to end the secrecy, and she knew Alma had a secret of her own, given the way she'd acted the last several weeks. Perhaps they could trade. Unburden themselves as friends do. And as sisters do. Alma was the closest thing she had to a sister anymore.

If only Francesca hadn't become pregnant, everything would have been all right, simpler. Instead, all she'd worked for would be lost and this life she'd begun to enjoy would end. She brought a fist to her mouth to suppress an unexpected sob.

"Fran? What is it?" Alma patted her on the back. "What's happened?"

"I'm all right. I was just... I needed a moment alone."

Alma frowned. "I'm sorry. I can go. I wanted to ask your opinion about something, but—"

"Please, I'm glad you're here." Francesca threw her arms around Alma in an unexpected embrace, as if holding on for her life. She couldn't lose her friend, not now, not because of this. She made a silent vow to tell Alma sooner rather than later. Alma worked with the dreadful inspector, after all, and had a right to know the truth. For now, Francesca wasn't ready, not yet. She shook her head. "Soon, I promise," she said. "For now, tell me what's on your mind."

Alma laced her arm through Francesca's and tugged her off the bench to a walking path leading to the street. "I don't want the others to hear."

She studied Alma's expression, noticing the worry lines in the corners of her mouth. "Is everything all right?" Francesca asked.

Her friend didn't reply as she led Francesca to a spot beneath a leafy maple. Its branches waved in a breeze that was becoming more of a strong wind by the minute. The sky looked bruised with clouds edged in purples, gray, and midnight blue. A summer storm was imminent.

"I don't know what to do!" Alma blurted out, her eyes filled with despair. "Oh, Fran, I'm engaged to be married!"

Stunned by the news, Francesca gaped a moment without reply. "When did this happen? I didn't realize... Oh no, you aren't happy about it. At all."

"Mr. Lambert is a nice enough fellow, but I'm not ready. I don't know him well. I have other plans—" Alma burst into tears.

Francesca embraced her, patting her back. She wanted to tell her friend all would be well, but she couldn't say such things. All hadn't been well for her, and rarely was, in fact. She wasn't one to lie or to pretend. It didn't make things easier in the end. The only thing to do was to confront the truth and make the most of it—the very thing she wasn't doing herself.

"There are things I'd like to do," Alma sobbed. "I don't want to get married yet."

"Yes, I know," Francesca said, wrapping her friend in her arms. She'd never seen her so emotional. "I understand. I'm so sorry."

"I want to go to school. To college. I want to become an inter-preter." Alma sniffled. "I could never afford to go before, but now that I'm working, I could pay my way. If I could just persuade my parents to let me keep some of my wages, that is. But if I get married—" She burst into tears again.

"Did you talk to your parents?" Francesca asked, rubbing her friend's back.

Alma shook her head. "They've already given my consent."

"How do you know this Mr. Lambert? Maybe you could talk to him about it."

"I don't know how to tell him. I can't seem to work up the nerve." She wiped her eyes. "The problem is, I work with him at Ellis Island. He's an inspector there. Actually, he's here, arrived a few minutes ago." Alma pointed to a group huddled over a chessboard. "He's behind Fritz's friend Pete. The one with a beard and a bald spot on top of his head."

Francesca glanced at the group huddled around Fritz. When Pete stepped backward, laughing at something Fritz had said, Mr. Lambert moved directly into their line of sight.

"There he is. That's John," Alma said.

Francesca froze as the world tilted sideways.

She'd recognize John Lambert anywhere. He was a man she despised with every fiber of her being, a man who haunted her dreams. The man whose child grew inside her.

Her stomach lurched, and she clapped her hand over her mouth. Bile rushed up her throat. She dashed behind the maple tree, out of sight, eyes watering, head reeling, doing her best not to vomit. Did the inspector know she was friends with the Brauers? Gasping for air, she tried to steady herself. He hadn't seen her, and she would leave—as soon as she didn't feel like she'd be sick. She looked down at her growing abdomen, his threat echoing in her ears.

If I hear about you whoring in our fine country, I will have you arrested. Is that clear? Prison and deportation.

Would he be able to see she was pregnant? No, she looked around wildly. If her friends couldn't see the changes yet, surely he couldn't, and by the time she started to show more, autumn would be upon them and she'd be wearing heavier clothing. She breathed deeply, wiping her mouth and her eyes. She had to leave—now.

Her mind raced ahead, to telling Alma the truth and the mess it would create. The precarious friendship she had built with Johanna and Robert Brauer would dissolve, and they would cast her out of their cozy gatherings. Or...another thought struck her. What if they didn't believe her? She felt as if she was going to be sick all over again. She couldn't tell Alma now, not ever.

Her friend was to marry the father of her unborn—and unwanted—child.

She took off, walking blindly around the edge of the park toward the street to freedom. She had to get as far from here as possible.

Alma raced to her side. "Francesca, my God, are you all right? Come, sit down."

"No," she said, pulling away. "It's fine. I just…I need to go home. I'm not feeling well."

Alma frowned. "I'll get Fritz. He'll want to see you home."

She stopped abruptly. Fritz would worry. He'd suspect something was happening, and she couldn't tell him, not yet. Not right now. "Thank you, yes. I'll wait for him in the street. I don't…I don't want to talk to anyone else right now."

"I understand," Alma said.

"Wait." Francesca gripped her friend's shoulders and looked her in the eye. "Alma, listen to me. You always have a choice. It may not be the easiest path, but there's always a choice. If you don't want to marry him, you don't have to. It's time to be brave." The words she'd heard from Sister Alberta echoed in her mind as she said them. And she would pass on that encouragement, that strength. Alma needed it. She could not marry that man.

Alma searched her face as if the answer lay there. "But I'm afraid," she whispered.

"Anything worth doing or having is a little frightening."

"Or very frightening."

"Sì." Francesca managed a wan smile.

"You're so wise," Alma said at last, tucking away her emotions and reverting to the logical, controlled young woman Francesca recognized.

"My life hasn't been an easy one. I've learned things."

"Yes, I know." She embraced Francesca again. "Thank you. I'll think about what you've said."

"Please, do."

"I'll fetch Fritz."

Francesca watched her go, fighting the urge to flee. When her friend reached Fritz, he looked up, his eyes searching for Francesca, concern flashing across his face. He was worried about her. Her heart squeezed.

What had this man done to melt her defenses, to bring her heart back to life? He'd taught her to trust him, and somehow, with him, she wasn't afraid or lonely or a strange woman from too far away, too different from his family to be understood. She was only herself, a young woman learning how to breathe again, how to live, wanting more than anything to fill a gaping wound with something decent and good and whole.

In an instant, Fritz covered the distance between them, gathered her hand and placed it on his forearm, and led her away from the park. Though she was desperate not to be seen, she sneaked a glance over her shoulder a final time. The inspector—Alma's fiancé—was occupied with the other women in his circle and Alma's stepfather.

She pictured Alma's face when she told her friend the truth and stumbled a little.

"Are you all right?" Fritz asked, steadying her. "Alma said you're ill."

"Yes," she said, fighting back tears.

When they'd walked several blocks, he broke the silence. "Would you prefer the train?"

She shook her head. "The walking is good for me."

"You're sure?" He peered at the ominous sky. The damp wind promised rain any moment.

"Walking is good for thinking."

He smiled. "I suppose it is. You know… You've become a part of the family. When Alma said you weren't feeling well, my mother ordered me to see you home and I was happy to oblige, of course. I would have offered anyway," he added quickly.

She forced a smile. "Johanna likes me now."

"She talked about the almond paste cookies you brought last time for days." He chuckled.

This time her smile was genuine. "I'll make them for her again next week."

Next week. Would there be a next week at the park? The horrible inspector might be at the picnic again. The inspector who was Alma's fiancé. She could hardly bend her mind around the idea: Alma was to marry a cruel, manipulative man who took advantage of immigrant women. Francesca could only imagine the number of women he'd abused; his position made them all the more vulnerable. If she was any kind of friend, she'd tell Alma the truth before it was too late. Even if Alma didn't believe her. Even if she never wanted to see Francesca again.

She glanced at Fritz, who also seemed lost in thought. "You're lucky to have them."

"What? Your cookies? I know." He gave her a teasing grin.

"Your family. Alma is a special person."

He nodded. "She is. We've been the best of friends since we were kids. After our father died, we grew closer than ever." He looked down, kicked a pebble with his boot. "Papa was sick for a few months and suddenly he was gone. That all seems so long ago now, but I still miss him."

"I'm sorry," she said.

He studied her with his piercing blue eyes. "You understand, don't you."

"Yes," she said quietly, avoiding his eye. "Mamma...she disappeared. One day she didn't come home, and we don't know what happened to her. My father... Well, you know that story, don't you."

The muscle in his jaw flickered. "You did the right thing by leaving."

"Yes," she said, voice soft. If he only knew what she'd done to get here. Unwittingly, her free hand covered her midsection.

She walked silently beside Fritz for a while, looking ahead at the dust clouds kicked up from horses and carriage wheels. The busy parade of pedestrians flowing to and from their destinations in the city, businessmen, women with their parasols in bright summer colors. A low rumble rolled across the sky. Soon, rain would scatter the pedestrians as they searched for cover, and the dry streets would turn to mud. It was just as well they'd left the picnic when they did.

Fritz glanced at her several times, meeting her eye, and then looked away again, a line forming between his eyebrows.

"What is it, Fritz?" she said at last. "You look like you have something to say."

"Yes." He laughed nervously. "*Yes.* I have something I've been wanting to ask you."

"What is it?"

A clap of thunder startled them both and drowned out the noise of the humming city beneath it. The next instant, the sky tore open. Rain sheeted down in one thick wall of water.

They laughed as they were instantly drenched. Fritz grabbed her hand and pulled her beneath the blue awning of an elegant building only a few blocks from the Lancasters' home. And suddenly, they were huddled quite close together. Thunder boomed overhead, and rain poured down over the awning like a waterfall.

She stared up at him, watching water drip from the brim of his hat.

The smile faded from his face, and his eyes turned serious, holding her there.

She scarcely breathed. After a moment, her cheeks grew hot beneath his stare and she whispered, "Should we brave the rain, or wait it out?"

He brought his finger to her lips, tracing their curves.

She shivered at his touch, her lips parting in anticipation. She wanted his kiss—she wanted him—but she shouldn't lead him there, down this path they could never travel together. Her heart ached as she stared into the beautiful face of the man she'd grown to care for, deeply.

"I have something I need to say now, or I'll lose my nerve," he said, voice husky. She nodded, unable to speak. "I can't stop thinking about you, Fran. I look forward to seeing you every night after work, and every Sunday. I wanted... I need to know if you feel the same way about me. If I could...maybe...if I could call on you, the way a man does a woman he wishes to..." He licked his lips nervously. "What I'm trying to say is, I care for you and not just as your friend."

Pain and happiness and a hunger she'd never felt before flooded her limbs, and she felt as if she might split in two. She wanted this man with all her heart, but did she deserve him? She knew it didn't matter in the end, because she could never have him. Her terrible secret would ruin her—and his family, and they'd never forgive her. Dear Alma would be devastated, too.

"Fritz," she breathed, touching his cheek with her fingertips. How to tell him? How could she dash his hopes without shattering her heart and his? But it was already too late.

He took her face gently in his hands, his vivid eyes trained on hers. "You're so beautiful. And strong. I've never met a woman like you. You have bewitched me, Francesca Ricci of Sicily. I don't remember who I was before I met you."

Though she knew it was wrong to lead him down this path, the words she longed to say sprang to her lips. "And I care for you. So much, *caro mio*."

He smiled as he brushed a wet strand of hair from her face, traced her nose with his fingertip and, at last, slowly bent over her. His warm lips brushed hers.

She leaned into him, her limbs turning liquid. Pain twined with pleasure, and for a moment, she felt as if she were on the edge of a cliff, looking out over vast but terrifying beauty. One step forward and she would plummet, never to find her way out again. One step back and her world would go dark and cold. But she took a step into the oblivion that surely awaited her and wrapped her arms around his neck. She was powerless to stop herself. Powerless to stop any of it.

She was falling in love with Fritz Brauer.

Investigation to be conducted at Ellis Island

James Mackle reports. *Manhattan Chronicle*.

July 15, 1902—While Commissioner William Williams is said to be ruthless in his pursuit of wrongdoings at Ellis Island station, new information has come to light suggesting there's still much work to be done. A number of recent reports point to collusion, bribery, and misconduct toward the immigrants arriving nearly every day. Williams will work in accordance with investigators by hosting extensive interviews of all personnel.

President Roosevelt is reportedly pleased with the commissioner's diligence. The staff, however, is not. An anonymous source relayed their dissatisfaction with Williams's activities, saying the commissioner has overstepped his position on numerous occasions and should be dismissed. This tip has sparked speculation among journalists on the Ellis Island beat.

Perhaps, it is more than the staff that needs investigating.

36

*A*lma had slept poorly in her steamy tenement apartment the last few weeks. The blazing sun had baked the muddy streets until they were cracked and dusty, and every fetid odor imaginable— from rotting garbage to horse manure—mixed with the thick summer air. It was nearly unbearable, until a wind blew in off the water and scrubbed the air clean. The warmer temperatures also brought more ships, packed to the bow with immigrants, steaming across the bay to Ellis Island. They came in droves without reprieve, sometimes numbering up to two thousand people or more in a single day. Alma and the staff moved through their days at lightning speed. When, at last, there was a quick moment for a break one afternoon, Alma tucked her journal under her arm and took a cup of tea outdoors.

She passed the children's playground and merry-go-round, saw a group of young men about Fritz's age playing a game of soccer on the wide expanse of lawn, and walked to a quiet bench. She had only a few minutes before she had to get back to work, but she would take whatever ounce of peace she could.

It wasn't her work alone that had kept her busy, her mind agitated. She replayed Francesca's encouragement in her mind many times, knowing it sounded right, but Alma couldn't work up the nerve to end the engagement. It all seemed impossible. For one, her parents would be furious with her. She couldn't imagine going back on their word in such a way or the damage it would do to their reputation. And she also worked with John—which complicated things tremendously. How could she face him day in and day out, after everyone learned their engagement was broken? It was all a mess, and she let days and then weeks pass without making a move.

Frustrated, she looked out at the water glistening in the afternoon sun. Gulls surfed on invisible wind currents, and beyond them, clouds drifted in clumps of snow-white fluff over the city skyline across the bay, the lowest of them disappearing behind a building face and reappearing as they continued their lazy journey across the sky. She took in a calming breath, pushing the troublesome thoughts from her mind, and flipped through her notes from the morning, studying the new phrases she'd learned. "Hungry" in Russian, "train" in Czech, and "stop it at once" in French. Her Italian had grown quite good, her Russian far better, and she'd begun putting together a little French. Each new series of words, each language, seemed to open a pathway in her brain, and she felt reinvented, as if a new piece of herself had emerged.

Jeremy had marveled at the way her mind seemed to take photographs of the text and, after, perfectly reproduce what she'd seen. But to her, it was more than text or a photograph. Languages were a kind of music. The more she practiced the song, the more lyrics she knew and understood, as well as the people who sang them. To understand them was to help them, and if she could help the immigrants find their way, she could rest easier at night with some satisfaction that how she was spending her busy days was worthwhile. She'd never had a job that held any sort of meaning before, even in small ways. Serving sausages and beer hardly constituted a good deed. She was proud of herself for perhaps the first time in her life. Proud that her hard work brought a paycheck, too.

She gulped down her tea, eager for the rush of a stimulant in her veins.

Her thoughts drifted to Fritz. The way he'd looked at Francesca last Sunday. She knew he was completely smitten with her friend, and Alma could see why. With proper rest, a good home, and friends, Francesca had blossomed from merely pretty to a stunning woman with mischief in her eye and a smile that could derail a locomotive. More than her looks, Francesca was generous and kind, and as her language skills grew, her humor had begun to show. Alma only wished her friend would tell her what was troubling her. She could sense something wasn't right; she'd seen a haunted look in Francesca's eyes and was keenly aware of her sudden departure from the picnic a few weeks ago. In fact, Francesca hadn't returned since. Alma decided after missing her again last week to visit her at the Lancasters' instead.

A gull landed just beyond her reach. He hopped toward her, looking for a scrap of something tasty. "I don't have anything for you," she cooed. "You're better off near the vendors, Mr. Gull."

His head tilted as if he understood her, and one gleaming black eye fixed on her face for a moment before he flapped his wings and rose into the air.

"I need to leave, too," she said, sighing. She'd promised to relieve another matron from her duties in one of the inspection rooms.

She found her way back to the holding room, crowded with women and children. The space was sweltering, and the salty tang of sweat hovered in the air. Alma scanned the crowd for Amy Terrine, the grouchy matron she disliked. They'd worked together all morning, orbiting around each other without having to interact much, thankfully, but Alma could still feel waves of disapproval rolling off of the woman. Commissioner Williams made things worse by floating in and out of the room with his notebook, putting them both on edge.

Alma spotted Amy in the back of the room and headed in her direction. The matron looked like she hadn't slept well or had a day off in ages. Alma knew she'd made a point to work extra hours to pay for her husband's medical bills, so Alma had tried to put aside the rude comments flung her way, but it wasn't easy.

A Russian woman stepped into Alma's path and bombarded her with questions. Alma held up a finger to signal she'd be with her in one moment when a shriek tore through the air. She glanced at Amy and saw a stout woman with a blue headscarf waving her arms frantically in the matron's face.

"I told you that isn't possible!" Amy shouted over the woman in English as if, somehow, the volume would help her understand.

Confused and frustrated, the immigrant began to cry and held up her hand to keep the matron out of her face. Furious at the rebuff, Amy shouted louder. When the woman's response was to sob harder, Amy slapped the woman—hard.

The immigrant stumbled backward, clutching her cheek.

Alma's jaw dropped. "Amy!" she said, pushing her way through the rest of the crowd. "What are you doing!"

"Stay out of this, Alma," the matron hissed. "The only way I could get her to understand was to give her a good whack."

"You're abusing this woman!"

Amy's dark eyes flashed. "I'm not the first one who has had to use force to make a point. You'd do the same."

"I would never hit someone unless they attacked me!"

"You're so much better than me, aren't you?" Amy spat out. "That's only because you haven't had to put up with the stupid cattle that come through these halls as long as the rest of us have."

Alma stared at her in shock. She couldn't ignore this; she'd have to report Amy to Mrs. Keller. "This is not the way to handle this," she insisted. "You made her cry!"

Amy rolled her eyes. "In case you haven't noticed, they're always crying. But since you have got it all figured out, you deal with her. I'm going to take a break." She shoved a notebook into Alma's hands and pushed past her.

Alma watched her stomp off and then turned to the immigrant, whose face was streaked with tears. "Can I help you?" Alma said in Italian. When she got a blank stare, she tried again in Russian and finally in French.

The woman's eyes brightened. "*Parlez-vous français?*"

"*Un petit peu,*" Alma replied, holding her thumb and forefinger up to demonstrate just how little she spoke.

The two others in the woman's party spoke a little English, and between the four of them, they managed to discern the issue. The woman didn't understand she had to have an additional medical inspection, and once cleared, she would wait on the island for her husband to greet her before they could officially enter the United States. Alma explained they should send a letter to contact him directly.

The woman clasped Alma's hand tightly. "*Merci.*"

Alma smiled, glad to have helped, but she couldn't forget the sight of Amy slapping the immigrant. Troubled, she motioned to the next woman who needed assistance.

By lunch, Alma had changed her mind three times about telling Mrs. Keller, but she circled back to what she knew was right—coworker or no, snitch or no, she had to report Amy's abuse. She would tell Mrs. Keller and let her tell the commissioner; it was her supervisor's job after all.

Sighing, she joined the cafeteria line and reached for silverware.

It was stew today, with white bread. Alma was always surprised by how few immigrants had eaten or even seen white bread, never mind a full dish of food.

Many hadn't eaten a decent meal in months and, in some cases, years. Their poverty had driven so many to flee their homelands to seek the prosperity of the United States, but she knew many would never escape that poverty, even here, where jobs abounded and opportunities arose every day. It was simply the way of things. Hard work helped, but luck mattered, too—and one's nationality. She'd come to understand that more and more.

She carried her tray to a crowded staff table. Helene had already wedged in beside a nurse, and the only space left was next to Mrs. Keller. Alma might as well get her dirty errand over with, she thought, as she slid into the seat beside her.

"How was your morning?" Alma asked to be polite.

"Terrible, since you asked. I've put out fires all over the building. It must be a full moon tonight. Everyone has gone mad."

"So, it's a normal day then?"

They both laughed.

"I suppose so," Mrs. Keller said. "But with the hullabaloo over Williams forbidding that Lutheran scoundrel from returning to the station, it's been crazier than usual."

"What Lutheran?"

Mrs. Keller shrugged. "A fellow who was selling females into servitude. Might have been negotiating with a brothel as well, but that is unconfirmed."

Alma gasped. "He was doing that here?"

"Mmm-hmm." Mrs. Keller swallowed a bite of bread. "It's good that he was caught, of course, but Williams is out for blood. Better mind yourself."

Alma wiped her mouth with a napkin, pondering how little the staff trusted the commissioner. No one saw him as an ally. They were all too afraid of being discharged. He'd already fired several members of the staff, including an inspector who swore too often at the immigrants and one who missed work because of his whiskey habit.

As they dug into their meals, the sounds of spoons hitting porcelain bowls and the murmur of voices filling the air, Alma sneaked a glance down the table at Amy. She stared glumly into her stew. Alma never knew whether to feel sorry for her or to count her as an enemy. If Amy changed her attitude a little, perhaps work would go a little smoother for her.

But that woman was also a witch to you for no reason, a voice in her head reminded her, *and you should turn her in as she deserves.*

And it was true. Amy Terrine was not at all nice. Why should Alma help her? But should she have the woman fired when she was clearly overworked and desperate to take care of her husband?

Alma pushed her tray forward, her appetite gone after a few bites of stew. Nothing ever seemed simple.

"What is it?" Mrs. Keller asked after a particularly large bite of bread. "You're frowning."

"I don't know. It's just that…" Her words trailed off as Amy got up from the table and carried her dirty dishes to the dish cart.

"I haven't got all day. Out with it." Mrs. Keller's already-thin patience would soon disappear entirely.

"Something happened today."

The supervisor groaned. "So it isn't good news."

"It's Amy Terrine."

Mrs. Keller threw her hands in the air. "Not her again."

Alma frowned. Again? She wondered how often Amy had become physical with the immigrants. Alma imagined her slapping

Francesca or her poor sister Maria, and suddenly she wasn't sorry for turning in the matron.

"Amy lost her patience and slapped an immigrant really hard across the face," she said. "I feel like a rat turning her in because she's been working so hard, but she left a red welt on the woman's cheek and made her cry. I calmed her down and helped her work things out, but good grief. Amy didn't have to hit her."

Mrs. Keller sighed. "This isn't the first time with Amy, but you need to understand something. If I report the assault, I know good and well John Lambert won't listen to a word I say. We don't see eye to eye, in case you haven't noticed. I steer clear of him and he stays away from me. That's the best we can do. Avoid each other. I know he's your fiancé, so I'll leave it at that. And before you ask, no, I'm not going to Williams about this."

"I see," Alma said. But she didn't. She hadn't realized Mrs. Keller had to report to Lambert, but she supposed it made sense since he was a chief officer and Mrs. Keller was only a woman. In fact, all inspectors were above the female matrons and nurses in the hierarchy. Still, it didn't matter if Keller and Lambert saw eye to eye, it was about doing the right thing. Alma had to admit, however, "the right thing" seemed to become more and more nebulous the longer she worked here. Everyone had a story, and there was always more than one side. But Amy still deserved a reprimand, at the very least, and she should issue an apology.

"We do the best we can to get them off the island, one way or another," Mrs. Keller continued. "That's our primary concern. Not all of the staff is good or just, as I'm sure you know, and it's not our job to change them. It's the Lord's. Should you push it, you'll make enemies and probably find yourself without a job, Alma." She touched the gold cross around her neck. "I'll give Amy a warning, and that's that."

What if that wasn't it? Alma considered turning to the commissioner. Not only would the staff despise her, but Mrs. Keller would be furious with her for going over her supervisor's head. Alma might even be reprimanded herself—or fired. She'd never considered the politics of working at Ellis Island before. She was beginning to understand how precarious her position was—and how little power she had.

Still, she felt for the people who passed through the halls, and she believed they deserved better, even if it meant firing staff who had years of experience working at the station. Seniority in their position didn't give them permission to be cruel.

But today, Alma wouldn't betray her supervisor by allying herself with the detested commissioner. One day, should the situation call for it, she'd have to decide if doing the right thing was worth risking everything—her reputation, her budding friendships, her job.

"All right," she said at last. "A warning is better than nothing."

For now.

37

*A*lma awoke late the next morning. Mama had prattled on well past her bedtime about who they would invite to the wedding and the preacher's delight about their chosen date of mid-October for the ceremony. The wedding would be at St. Mark's on East Sixth Street, and all of their friends and many church patrons would be invited for cake and beer after the event.

After the event, Alma would pack up the life she'd always known, for good.

To top it off, John had stopped by the bierhaus at the end of the evening with gifts of chocolates and a new journal for her. Though lovely, his kind gestures made it more difficult to rationalize her wishes with her parents'. Mama had expected her to entertain him until he left, well past an appropriate hour. She'd been exhausted and on edge, trying all evening to work up the courage to tell him the truth of her feelings, but each time she began, her tongue turned to sand.

She boarded the ferry with the others, her shoulders curled with exhaustion.

"Is this seat taken, lass?" Jeremy's distinguishable lilt was a welcome distraction from her thoughts.

She smiled upon hearing his voice. "No, it isn't taken."

He slid in beside her, a smile on his lips and a twinkle in his eye. Jeremy wasn't a tall man, but his shoulders were broad, his step assured, and his amiable nature pervaded those around him. He was the favorite interpreter on the island, she'd heard from the staff and the occasional immigrant, and she could see why. He was a contented soul, a man who seemed to walk with his face toward the sun. She'd grown to value his friendship a great deal in the passing months.

"How are we today then?" he asked.

"Well enough. You seem awfully chipper for early morning on a Monday."

He shrugged. "I like Mondays. It's a chance at a fresh start to the week, with endless possibilities ahead. What's not to like?"

She ticked off reasons on her fingers. "Well, Mr. Sunshine, a full week on my feet. An endless stream of distraught people who don't know what's happening. And then there's taking orders from others, even if I don't agree with them."

He laughed. "Come now, it's not as bad as all that, is it? You sound like you could use more coffee."

"You're right." She smiled. "Mostly I like the work, but there was an incident on Friday with one of the matrons and I can't stop thinking about it. I felt like I had to confront her, and it was awful." The truth came surprisingly easy around Jeremy. She trusted him, and that was more than she could say about anyone at Ellis Island, including Helene and her wagging jaw, despite how much Alma liked her friend.

"Aye. I saw you speaking to Mrs. Keller. She doesn't allow any slack, that one."

Apparently he hadn't caught Mrs. Keller ignoring bad behavior.

"I think what she allows in this building would surprise you."

He raised a brow. "Is that so? Well, I've seen some pretty awful things myself."

"Why doesn't anyone do something about it?"

"Too many people need work. They don't want to risk their neck. That, and loyalty. Commissioner Williams hasn't earned anyone's trust yet. I don't have a problem with the fellow; he just seems a bit wound up, could use a pint or two. He has riled up a lot of staff with the way he charges through the building firing people and making abrupt changes to protocol without consulting anyone."

"This incident might be worth reporting, even to him." She paused, deciding whether or not to share.

"What happened, lass?" he pressed.

"I saw a woman get slapped yesterday because she didn't understand a matron's question. The immigrant was upset, naturally, because she had a matron screaming in her face. It was awful. And Mrs. Keller said she'd warn the matron and that was all, but I'm not sure she did even that."

"And I suppose this matron couldn't be bothered to find an interpreter to help her."

"I arrived a minute too late."

He took off his hat and ran a hand over his almost-black hair. "Aye, we do the best we can. Don't trouble yourself with the rest. You can't force your supervisor to do what she's supposed to do. That's Williams's job. It's on his head now."

Williams couldn't make things right if he didn't know what was happening behind his back. Alma felt the growing urge to take matters into her own hands. But she didn't know how without ruining lives. She wasn't sure where her loyalties lay anyway—with her colleagues or with the immigrants she'd never see again. Frustrated, she blew out a breath.

Jeremy eyed the Russian dictionary in her lap. "Studying?"

"If I have time."

"I remember the first time I heard you speak Russian. Who was this woman, I asked myself, who not only had the bluest eyes I'd ever seen but also a fierce intelligence to match."

She smiled at the unexpected compliment. "You flatter me."

His skin, from his neck to the freckles on the tip of his nose, blushed red. "Forgive me," he said. "I shouldn't speak to you that way since you're an engaged woman. I just admire you."

"It's all right. We're friends and I admire you, too." She smiled again. "I know I was complaining before, but I want to say that I'm very glad I'm not scrubbing pots and hanging laundry all day at home."

"Boring, eh?"

"More than you know."

"I'd like to know you more." He winked at her, and this time she blushed. "There I go again. I'm sorry, Alma. I should be ashamed of myself. You have a fiancé."

"Yes, she does." A stern voice interrupted their conversation.

"John." She sat up tall. "Good morning. Mr. Kerrigan and I were just saying how much we enjoy learning languages."

"And that you have a fiancé." Lambert's nostrils flared. "I expect you will behave like a gentleman around my future wife, you mick."

Mick? Alma's eyes widened at the slur. She couldn't believe John would use it with one of his colleagues. She glanced at Jeremy, who had balled his hands into fists in his lap.

"Of course," Jeremy said, looking vaguely ahead at two rows down filled with a group of nurses, clearly not wanting to meet John's eye.

"Well," John said, "these are for you." He handed Alma a bouquet of mixed flowers that looked like they'd seen better days.

"Oh, thank you." She looked down at them guiltily, and yet she felt as if she was going to be sick.

Jeremy leapt to his feet. "I'll find another seat. I didn't mean to—"

"It's all right, Jeremy," Alma said. "We're just discussing work, John, and we are not yet married, so you don't need to worry about my friends. We were just talking." She knew she had been rude—and Mama would have been furious—but she felt a surge of pride for speaking up for herself. This man had no right of command over her in her conversations or friendships. Not yet.

"Mr. Kerrigan is a gentleman, I assure you," she went on. "Please do sit down, Jeremy."

John's brow shot up at her use of the interpreter's Christian name. "I'll allow this for now," he barked. "But I hope I've made myself clear."

Jeremy nodded. "Of course, sir."

John stalked to the steps and climbed them to the upper deck.

Alma cleared her throat. "I'm sorry, I... That was... I don't know what to say."

Jeremy's teasing tone all but disappeared. "Don't apologize. The fault is mine. Really, I should have insisted he sit here with you."

They sat in silence the remainder of the ferry ride and disembarked quickly when they arrived. As they filed inside the building, Alma touched his shoulder. "Perhaps we could sit together at lunch one day. I'd really like to learn more about your job."

Jeremy looked past her and tipped his hat. Lightly, he said, "Sure. One day soon, Miss Brauer."

Dismayed by his formality and change in demeanor, she felt her mood plummet once again.

Alma went through the motions of her day, but something was different; she noticed it almost immediately. Though the staff should have been going about their work as usual, they paused to whisper or scan each room furtively as if looking for something—or someone. Everyone skittered to and from their stations, on edge, their faces drawn.

In the hospital ward, Alma looked for some direction, but instead, the nurses clustered in circles, talking about something more interesting than their patients. They didn't share the news with her, and by lunchtime, her curiosity got the better of her. She found Helene in the cafeteria and sat beside her.

"The nurses were acting strange all morning," Alma said, scooping a piece of potato into her mouth. "Have you heard anything?"

Helene didn't hide her glee at being asked for information. "Well," she said, her pretty face alight, "Williams is at it again, but this time it's bad."

"What do you mean?"

"You know the money exchange booth? The company that's running it has been shortchanging immigrants." She leaned in closer. "And! The broker that works with the food supplier for the cafeteria was extorting immigrants by setting higher prices. Williams fired both!"

Alma's mouth dropped open. So her instincts were right. The vendor she'd seen shortchange a man and call it an accident was swindling people.

Helene's brown eyes glittered. "And you heard about that Lutheran minister funneling women through his 'church' to help them find jobs a couple of weeks ago? Williams said that was just the beginning. To think! So much is happening right under our noses."

Alma cradled her coffee cup, staring deeply into the brew. "What happened with the German immigrant last week that everyone is talking about? He was denied entry into the country. I think he was a pastor?"

"I'm not sure why he was denied," she replied, "but I heard he didn't have enough money to support himself." Helene continued without pausing for breath. "Of course, now John and the other Germans on the staff are furious with Williams. It could spark another investigation from Washington."

"Another one?" Alma put down her coffee cup. "How many have there been?"

"Oh, I don't know. Several since the center opened ten years ago. It always happens after some journalist gets a bee in their bonnet over a story they've heard. I'm sure it's because of some anarchist mess. The pastor is friends with some of them or something. I'm not sure."

The anarchist mess in which Fritz was involved. Alma had to warn him. Again. One day, there wouldn't be any more warnings, only consequences.

"But Williams is critical of everyone," Alma replied, her mind racing. If there was an investigation here at the center, everyone would be scrutinized, including her. Omitting the truth of what she'd seen might be as indefensible as the rest. If Mrs. Keller turned the blame on her staff to cover her tracks, many would be at risk. Fear prickled over Alma's skin. It wasn't merely Keller and Williams looking into things this time. It must be a directive from Washington, DC, from President Roosevelt himself.

"It'll mean hell around here for us," Helene said, an edge to her voice. "We'll have to work longer hours, make sure the place is spotless. Pretend it isn't overcrowded, and ignore the government looking over our shoulder every minute of every day."

Alma put down her fork. "Do you think we should report anything we've seen to Williams?"

Helene shrugged. "I'm not telling him anything."

They ate their meals a moment, each lost in their thoughts until Helene broke the silence. "Listen, I need to tell you something," she said. "I've been debating whether or not I should, but we're friends, and if you don't hear it from me, I don't think you'll hear it from anyone else."

Her stomach dipped at Helene's tone. She'd never sounded so serious. "What is it?"

Helene put down her fork. "It's about John Lambert. If you want to hear it, that is."

"Oh, yes, of course."

Helene bit her bottom lip. "I don't know how to say this, so I guess it's best to come out with it."

"You're making me nervous!"

"I know. I'm sorry, it's just awkward. The truth is, John has a bit of a reputation. I told you once before that he's only good to the staff that are among his friends, but there's more."

Alma remembered the way he'd spoken to Jeremy and cringed. But that had been the only instance she'd ever seen him be rude to anyone, and she could see John's side in that situation. He'd witnessed his fiancée talking animatedly with another man, but given Helene's serious tone, there must be more.

She pushed her plate aside, her appetite vanishing. "All right. What is it?"

"He's, well, he's a ladies' man, I guess you could say."

"Oh." She exhaled, relieved. "Aren't all men?" She'd overhead plenty of Fritz's friends, and some of the inspectors, brag about lying with women. She found it disgusting, but who was she to tell them so. They'd probably mock her and tell her to shove off.

Helene shook her head. "No, Alma, not like this. It's pretty bad. I haven't seen it happen, but I've heard a lot of rumors about him."

Alma slicked the mashed potatoes on her plate into a mountain, eyes unseeing. Was her fiancé that kind of man? She couldn't imagine it. He seemed so... So what? She couldn't put her finger on it. He was charming enough, smiled often, chatted with the staff. But that day in the bierhaus, when his gaze lingered on Greta too long... She shook her head. Everyone's gaze lingered on Greta; she was the most beautiful girl on their block. Still, John was at least forty years old so one would assume he'd been with women.

At last she said, "I'm not sure what I'm supposed to do about it. I can't tell him not to sleep with other women until we're married."

"He's your *fiancé,*" Helene stressed. "You can ask him to keep his hands to himself. And besides, he isn't just sleeping with women. He's...aggressive with them. Compliments them in a way they don't like. Crowds them. He's a little pushy, if you know what I mean."

No, she didn't know what Helene meant. Perhaps the women had misunderstood him because he'd certainly never acted that way in front of her. Besides, Helene was often dramatic and spread plenty of rumors that weren't true. Alma may not think of John romantically, but she knew he wasn't aggressive with women.

At last, she replied. "What am I supposed to do about it? My mother has picked a wedding date in October. It's only weeks away at this point."

Only weeks away. She grimaced and turned her attention back to her potatoes.

"Perhaps you should talk to him about this before you're married," Helene insisted.

Alma fiddled with the spoon beside her bowl. "Maybe." But the truth was, she couldn't imagine having this sort of conversation with John.

"Do what you want, but don't say I didn't tell you about him. I'll see you later."

Helene jumped up abruptly without finishing her food and dumped her tray on the cart near the garbage cans.

Alma stared after her, surprised by her friend's anger about it. It was Alma's problem, should she marry John.

Should she marry John.

And what if she didn't? She'd never felt like she had a choice in anything.

In that moment, Francesca's words echoed inside her.

You always have a choice. It may not be the easiest path, but there's always a choice.

38

*F*rancesca scrubbed the dishes in the sink, left behind from the full English breakfast she'd grown accustomed to preparing for Mr. Lancaster. She'd never understand how sweetened beans were considered good. If she had his level of wealth, she'd eat fresh pastries and berries with cream every morning, perhaps some prosciutto as well. At least she was lucky enough to have fresh bread every morning that she'd made herself. Her bread had won Charles over, in fact, and the old badger had even smiled at her a time or two when she'd heaped his plate with it.

Francesca stifled a yawn. She wasn't sleeping much, her mind tossing between Alma's shocking news—seeing the horrible inspector again—and Fritz's kiss. She'd thought she'd never see the inspector again. The thought of him becoming a permanent fixture in the Brauers' life was too much. It was devastating. She couldn't remain friends with Alma, should she become his wife. The only thing that offered her hope was Alma's distress over her engagement. Her friend definitely did not want to marry him. Perhaps it was selfish of her, but Francesca hoped Alma would follow her heart.

Something Francesca could scarcely do herself.

She allowed herself to daydream about what it would be like to be married to a man like Fritz. She pictured the gleam in his blue eyes, the way a particular lock of hair fell over his forehead. In this dream, she knew where she belonged—as a part of his family, too. But that was where her dream crumbled. Though she had grown to care deeply for the Brauers, she knew they would never allow such a match, especially when they learned of her pregnancy.

Soon, she would lose them all.

She submerged her hands in scalding soapy water until it seared her skin. How would she ever tell Fritz what had happened? God only knew what he'd think of her. She still didn't know what to think—or what she'd do once the child was born. She let out an exasperated sigh.

"What's on your mind, *mon amour*?" Claire asked. "You've done a lot of sighing today."

"I'm tired."

Claire peered at her a moment before turning her attention back to the chocolate mousse she was making. "Go to bed early tonight. Get a bit more rest."

The house hummed with its usual activity of washing and cooking and mending, and Francesca lost herself in its rhythm.

Janie carried Mrs. Lancaster's tea tray in from breakfast and all but dropped it on the table, rattling the dishes.

"Mrs. Lancaster wants her supper early tonight." She leaned against the counter and crossed her arms. Her eyes were filled with mischief, and her top lip curled into a snarl. "She asked for prawns and oysters, and cold vegetables. She also demands that you stop putting your disgusting garlic and onions all over everything."

"I know you made that up. And you don't need to be so rude, Janie," Claire said as she added more thick cream to her bowl.

Janie reddened until her freckles were nearly indistinguishable from the rest of her skin. "Fine. What she said was not to use garlic tonight because she'll be sitting with friends at the opera and doesn't want to reek like an immigrant."

Claire's light-green eyes shifted to a steely gray. "If you keep that up, I'll have a nice long chat with Mrs. Cheedle."

Janie sniffed. "Go right ahead. She knows I am Mrs. Lancaster's favorite."

"Don't make me put that theory to the test," Claire shot back, plunging her whisk into the sweet mixture.

Janie glared at Francesca and bumped her as she passed. Over her shoulder she said, "Why don't you get a job in the slums on the Lower East Side? You'll find more of your kind there."

Francesca's nerves had worn thin. She'd tried, without success, to make a friend in Janie the last couple of weeks—taking on some of her work, making her breakfast, listening to her complaints—but the woman was too miserable with herself to make friends, and now Francesca was too exhausted to care.

Before she could reply, Claire interjected. "Janie, you're behaving like an arrogant ninny. We both know your beginnings aren't exactly first class. You come from an orphanage yourself. Now, take your sour humor and be on your way."

"Why does everyone take the guinea's side?" she said, anger lacing her words.

Francesca winced at the slight she'd heard used against Italians when she'd first arrived at Ellis Island.

"What's going on in here?" Mrs. Cheedle joined them, carrying a ledger of what looked like a list of household expenses. Her gray bun sat crookedly on top of her head, and she looked as if she'd just awoken from a nap. "Are you stirring the pot again, Janie?"

Francesca frowned at the expression. The only one stirring was Claire.

"We're all quite tired of your complaints," Mrs. Cheedle continued. "You really are so boorish almost all of the time."

"Oh, leave me alone!" Janie stormed from the room in a huff.

Mrs. Cheedle scowled. "Really, Claire, you mustn't start trouble with Janie. I know you enjoy prodding her, but it only makes her act out. You know how hard it is to find a lady's maid these days. We don't want to have to replace her."

Claire hugged the mixing bowl to her middle with one hand and stirred vigorously with the other. "If she were a child, I'd give her a good paddling. Swat her right on the bottom."

Francesca bit back a laugh.

When Mrs. Cheedle had gone, Claire leaned in. "I think it's time we played a little prank on little Miss Rainbows, wouldn't you say?"

Francesca shrugged. "What does this mean?"

Claire cackled at her expression. "You'll see."

Later that night, as the kitchen closed and the house retired for the evening, Francesca shuffled to the servants' quarters off the kitchen, her feet throbbing from the long day. The house changed shape in the dark. Shadows turned furniture into monsters, and a scraping noise or a creak became something sinister. She relaxed a fraction as she realized those were instincts she'd learned from her time at home—to listen to every foot fall, every thump in the night—and that things were different now. Very different.

When she reached the tiny bedroom she shared with Claire, the door flew open. Claire yanked her inside, closing it swiftly behind them.

"What—"

"Shhh!" Claire pressed her finger against her lips. She was already dressed in her nightgown and cap.

"What are you doing?" Francesca whispered.

"I've left a gift for Janie in her room."

Francesca frowned. "A gift? I thought you didn't like her."

Claire grinned and turned off the gas lamp. "Precisely. Now, hurry and put on your nightdress and get into bed. We mustn't be caught."

Francesca giggled softly and did as her friend asked. They lay silently in the dark for some time, her eyelids growing heavy. Soon, she felt the weight of fatigue dragging her toward sleep.

The floorboards at the end of the hallway creaked.

Claire jumped to her feet and opened the door a crack. In an instant, she raced to the bed and dove back into it. "She's coming!"

Francesca suppressed another giggle. Claire was acting like a child, and it was nice to feel young again for a change.

Janie's door swung open and closed behind her. She hummed softly, and the faint sounds of her dresser drawer opening floated across the hall.

A terrified screech split the air.

Francesca gasped and sat up. "Claire! What did you do?"

"Lie back down!" her friend hissed. "Pretend you're asleep."

Another bloodcurdling screech split the air, and Janie's bedroom door flew open, crashing against the wall with a loud bang.

They couldn't ignore such a noise without seeming suspicious, so Francesca joined Claire in the hallway.

"What's going on?" Claire demanded. "Is someone being murdered?"

"There's a rat in my drawer!" Janie's hand cupped her mouth. "I h-hate rats!"

A tiny squeak of laughter escaped Francesca's lips. Claire pinched her elbow to remind her of their secret.

From the hall, they could hear the sound of nails scratching against wood followed by a crash.

"Get it out of my room!" Janie squealed in terror. "Get it out!"

Claire crossed her arms over her chest. "If you hadn't been such a witch the last few days, I'd consider helping you. But forget it. Trap the rat yourself."

Janie's shoulders sagged. "But what if it bites me?" She gripped Francesca's arm. "Please, I can't sleep in there!"

Francesca had seen her fair share of rats at home and on the ship when crossing the Atlantic. They were disgusting, but they didn't frighten her. Perhaps a good deed would soften Janie's resolve to make Francesca's life miserable and the maid would stop being so hateful.

She shrugged. "I'll help you."

Janie clasped Francesca's fingers in hers. "I can't touch it. I'd"— she shuddered dramatically—"I'd lose my dinner."

Claire rolled her eyes. "Francesca, she's a miserable cow. She doesn't deserve your help."

Janie didn't deserve it, but in Francesca's experience, it was easier to make peace by being helpful—or making herself indispensable.

"Let's have a look at him," Francesca said.

In Janie's room, many of her underthings lay scattered on the floor. It looked as if the rat had leapt out of the drawer and scrambled over the night table, knocking a book to the floor.

"It's on the loose now," Janie wailed, throwing her arms into the air. "I'll never be able to sleep with that rodent prowling around my room."

An irritable Mrs. Cheedle opened her bedroom door and joined them in the hall. She wore her nightcap, reading glasses, and a cotton nightdress in blue floral print floated around her ankles. "What's going on here?"

The rat emitted a tiny squeak and darted out from under the bed to the door. Francesca lunged for the book and slammed it atop the rat—hard—once, twice, three more times, with decisive fury. When she stopped to catch a breath, she peered down at the enemy. It was dead all right, and she had made a bit of a mess.

"There. It won't bother you," Francesca said triumphantly, dropping the book on the floor.

Three pairs of eyes stared at her in shock.

"I'm going to be sick." Janie darted out of the room.

"That's disgusting. Clean that up at once!" Mrs. Cheedle slipped into her bedroom and slammed the door.

Claire grimaced. "I think you might need to toss that book into the wastebasket."

"I think Janie can clean that up, but now she owes me." Francesca winked.

"Clever girl," Claire chuckled.

Far more clever than anyone gave Francesca credit for, including Claire. She returned to bed, whispering prayers, hoping that somehow things would work out and she could stay on at the Lancasters' and that the hard work she'd done the last months would be worth it, until the darkness closed in around her and she drifted to sleep.

39

Alma finished her duties in the detainees' quarters and threaded through the hall to the matron's room to gather her things. Maybe she'd sneak upstairs from the bierhaus tonight and go to bed early. Yawning, she passed a group of men on a bench, arguing about something in a language she couldn't understand. Sometimes it felt like a losing battle—trying to keep up with the crowds, and trying to help them.

As she entered the corridor leading to the matron's room, she thought only of going home and hiding under her bedcovers with a book.

As she reached for the door, she heard her name and turned.

"Miss Brauer!" Commissioner Williams said from the end of the hallway. "Can you follow me to my office? I'd like to speak with you. It'll only take a moment."

Her stomach twisted into a knot. Was he going to back her into a corner, force her to tell him the things she'd seen? Hiding her fear, she said, "Of course, sir. I was just on my way to the ferry."

"This won't take long."

She followed him to his office, mind racing with the rumors she'd heard about him firing employees out of hand.

"Have a seat." He gestured to a chair in front of his desk.

She sat quickly, twining her fingers together in her lap. "How can I help you, sir?"

"That's precisely the right question." He slipped into his chair. "Some of the staff see fit to not only break the rules and bully the immigrants but to break the law. I'm finding it extraordinarily difficult to track down the offenders, since my staff sees me as the enemy. I need someone I can depend on to be my right-hand man, so to speak." He steepled his fingers, leaning back in his chair. "Miss Brauer, you've come highly recommended."

"Oh?" She shifted in her chair.

"Mrs. Keller said you'd be happy to work with me."

Mrs. Keller *would* throw her to the wolves. Of course. She consistently assigned Alma to the most odious of tasks, and then there was the matter of what Alma knew about Amy Terrine. Now Mrs. Keller was either teaching her a lesson or ridding herself of any responsibility to report the misdeed. And all of this time, Alma had worried about following her supervisor's orders and protecting her and the staff from Williams's scrutiny.

Biting back her annoyance, she said, "I... Yes, sir, of course."

"Have you seen anything untoward happen? Anything you'd like to report?"

"No, sir." The lie sprang to her lips more easily than she'd expected.

He leaned over the desk. "Miss Brauer, if you see anything at all, you need to report it to me immediately. We may not like the deplorable masses that come through these halls, but they are people just the same, and we have a set of laws by which we must abide. Is that clear?"

She frowned. "Of course, Mr. Williams. I've never treated an immigrant with anything less than respect. I—"

He held up his hand. "Might I remind you omission is the same as lying. As a former lawyer, this is something with which I'm quite familiar. If you care about your reputation, and your position here, Miss Brauer, you will remember that."

She nodded, the memories of all she'd seen flitting through her mind. This was definitely Mrs. Keller's doing. She didn't want to take the blame for not properly reprimanding Amy, or deal with Mr. Williams, so she'd placed the burden on Alma's shoulders.

"Would that be all, sir?" she managed to say over her mounting irritation. Why must she always be the one to do as she was told?

"For now, Miss Brauer. You may go."

She did want to make a difference in the operations at Ellis Island and, most importantly, to protect the immigrants from being harassed. Perhaps this was her chance to do that. *Perhaps.* She wasn't yet certain Mr. Williams would keep her report between them. Should he choose not to protect her confidence, the rest of the staff could make her time at work miserable.

He could also choose to fire her.

She closed Williams's door behind her, exasperated by the position in which both he and Mrs. Keller had placed her. As she walked, her irritation mounted. She didn't have to do as she was told—not unless she got something in return. If she helped the commissioner, she would do it on her own terms. She only needed to decide what those terms were.

And from now on, she wouldn't tell Mrs. Keller a single blasted thing.

40

*F*rancesca finished preparations for both the evening meal and breakfast the next morning. She had plans to slip away for a few hours, to join Fritz, Alma, and Helene at a popular bierhalle in the Bowery for libations and dancing. Francesca had thrilled at the thought of a night of fun—a welcome reprieve from the worry plaguing her. Mrs. Cheedle hadn't hesitated to make it known how generous she was by caving to Francesca's request. But Francesca had prepped almost everything for the meals that day, leaving Claire virtually nothing to do, and Mrs. Cheedle couldn't refuse.

Francesca pinned on her modest boater hat with green ribbon and checked her appearance one last time in the tiny looking glass above the bed. Her hair was curlier than usual in the humidity, and her cheeks were already tinged pink from the heat. After a hasty goodbye to Claire, she bounded down the street, turning southbound onto Fifth Avenue.

The oppressive heat rose from the streets and the concrete sidewalk beneath her feet. Moisture gathered on her skin, soaking through her clothes. Early September in New York City seemed far hotter than Capo Mulini. Hardly a day went by on her island without a cool ocean breeze whisking over the rocky hills. Any moisture that might hang in the air blew out to sea and eventually disappeared in the dry mountains of Africa.

In the city, she wiped her face and neck constantly and washed her clothes out at night. She spent her free moments lying on the roof under the shade of a tarp, hoping for a breeze. Her ever-growing belly made her that much more uncomfortable. Thankfully, she could still hide her swelling middle between wraps, an apron, and her skirts, even at five months gone, but she was running out of time. Should she wait another week or two, her swelling form would become too obvious.

Tomorrow. She'd tell Alma and Fritz tomorrow after she'd had this last night of fun with them.

When she reached their meeting place in the Bowery, she spotted a familiar form heading toward her.

"Francesca!" Fritz called, moving faster now with a spring in his step.

Mio Dio, but she loved his spirit. Fritz Brauer pulsed like the brightest star in a sea of darkness. She needed his vitality—his warmth and optimism—the way she needed air. And she'd stopped lying to herself about it. Was there anything so wrong about needing someone?

When they caught up to each other, he was breathing heavily and perspiration speckled his forehead. She smiled widely, her cheeks aching with happiness.

"Francesca, I... Hello." He gathered her hand in his and brought it to his lips. "I've missed you these last few days."

She tossed her cares on the hot summer breeze and stood on her toes, planting a kiss squarely on his lips. He smiled against her mouth and softly kissed her back. Sighing with pleasure, she lay her head against his chest.

"Beautiful Francesca," he murmured, burying his face in her hair.

His hands slid down her sides to her hips—and she pushed away abruptly, wary he might feel her abdomen. "Where's Alma?" she asked.

His face fell as she jerked away from him. "She'll meet us there. She couldn't get off work until later." He ran a hand through his hair. "I'm sorry, Fran. I should behave like a gentleman. I care about you. I—"

She put her fingertips to his lips. "You did nothing wrong, *caro mio*. I am... How do you say it? Afraid. No, not afraid." She shook her head. "Careful. I think of no one but you, Fritz Brauer."

He beamed at her, cradling her hand in his once more, and they gazed at each other, oblivious to the pedestrians streaming around them. As she sank into his eyes, she didn't feel the terror of letting her guard down for the first time in her life. She felt alive, cared for. *Safe.*

"Take me to this bierhalle," she said at last, poking him in the side with her index finger.

"Right. At this rate, Alma will beat us there." He winked as he placed her hand on his forearm.

They walked the rest of the way to the bierhalle, and he held open the door for her. "Here we are, *liebling*."

"*Liebling*?"

He leaned to her ear. "Dear one."

She felt his breath on her skin and something stirred inside her. She wanted him close to her, his skin against hers, his mouth on hers. Her head dizzied with the thought, and she suddenly needed a cold beverage.

"Let's find a seat." Fritz took her hand and drew her across the crowded room.

The hall was filled with long tables and benches, and a bar top

THE NEXT SHIP HOME

ran the length of one wall. Lamps glowed cheerily from their mounts on the wall, and raucous laughter and conversation roared at a near-deafening pitch. Nearly every seat was taken with customers, toasting the end of the workday. The odor of beer and sauerkraut permeated the air, and summer heat rose like steam from a boiling pot, in spite of the open shop front that faced the street. Francesca was glad she'd worn her lightest dress. She'd still had the good sense to wrap her breasts and as much of her middle as she could with a tight cloth.

Fritz called to a barmaid, who returned shortly with two frothing steins. Francesca didn't care much for beer, but in the heat she'd drink anything. They slid into two empty spaces, their heads inclined to each other so they could hear over the noise. She smiled as they clinked their glasses in cheer and took a small sip.

"I've been thinking about you," Fritz said, his eyes drinking her in as he held the frosty beer in his hand.

Intoxicated by his nearness, by the adoration in his eyes, she leaned closer until her face was an inch from his. "And I think of you."

He ran a fingertip softly under her chin. "Tell me something about yourself that no one knows. A secret." His eyes twinkled with mischief.

Beneath her dress, she felt a soft fluttering in her abdomen.

"Oh!" she said, cupping her stomach. The child. *It had moved.* She'd only felt it a couple of times before as the lightest nudge, but never like this.

His eyes filled with concern. "Is everything all right?"

She flinched, removing her hand swiftly. "Yes. I... Yes." She laughed nervously.

"There you are!" Alma said, plopping down in one of the open seats beside them. Helene slid in next to her.

In the warm glow of the pub light, Helene was even prettier

than Francesca remembered. Dimpled cheeks, blond hair, and light-brown eyes that appeared almost gold. She was the kind of German beauty Alma's sister Greta was—blond, fair, striking. The opposite of Francesca in every way. She'd been seeing an awful lot of Helene at the family gatherings lately. She knew the young matron was setting her sights on Fritz—and she wasn't pregnant.

Trying to hide the tide of jealousy washing over her, Francesca greeted Alma and Helene with a kiss.

"I see you've already been enjoying yourself." Alma winked.

In seconds, a fresh beer was placed before the newcomers.

As the evening wore on, they talked and laughed. Alma shared stories from work. Fritz practiced his poor Italian. After a particularly hilarious exchange, Francesca leaned over and planted a kiss on his cheek, all too aware that pretty Helene was watching them.

Fritz grinned. "I need to practice Italian more often!"

They all laughed, and though Francesca had the feeling it wasn't exactly polite to be affectionate in public, she didn't care. She was so happy in this moment, she wanted to celebrate it. God knew when she would feel happy again.

"Let's go dancing," Helene announced suddenly, giving Francesca a thoughtful look. "I'm ready to move on."

They all agreed and paid their bill, pushing up from their table just as the din in the bierhalle died down.

All eyes fixed on the front door.

Four policemen had entered the hall and were circulating throughout the room. They stood ominously over each table, questioning the patrons. When an officer pulled a man to his feet, the silence broke.

"It's a raid!"

People began to shout. Some raced to the door, shoving as they went.

Fritz grabbed Francesca by the hand and called to his sister. "Come on! Out the back door!"

"What's happening!" Alma demanded.

"It's an anarchist raid!" he shouted above the noise.

They bolted for the back door, shoving people out of the way. Screams tore through the air as the room dissolved into chaos. Suddenly filled with terror, Francesca dashed after Fritz. She couldn't afford to be caught as an anarchist, not when she was such a newly admitted immigrant. She'd find herself back at Ellis Island and on the next ship home. Frantic, she threw a look over her shoulder, confirming Alma and Helene were behind her.

Fritz paused to push Francesca through the back door ahead of him and waited, ensuring the others made it outside into the alleyway. Just as he started to follow, a large hand clapped down on his shoulder.

"Are you Fritz Brauer?" the policeman barked, yanking Fritz backward.

His eyes filled with regret, and he mouthed "run" before turning to face the policeman.

Heart in her throat, Francesca raced down the alleyway ahead of Alma and Helene, winding around rotted crates and a row of garbage cans. They'd gotten to Fritz! She'd warned him to leave the group— and now she could only imagine the consequences he'd face. She clutched the Madonna at her neck, sending a prayer to look after the man she loved.

The man she loved! And she did. She loved him, with all her heart.

Alma caught up to her and clutched her hand. They raced down the street for several more blocks with Helene at their heels, weaving around pedestrians and lampposts, putting distance between the police and themselves. When they felt they were a safe distance from the dance hall, they stopped to catch their breath.

Alma looked as if she might burst into tears. "I've told him for months not to host that club of his, and not to admit any new members. It's just too dangerous. Anarchism is a dirty word now. People are going to jail." Her face paled. "Oh, God, what if they take Fritz to jail?"

Francesca's heart thundered in her chest, and the heat pulsed around her. The wraps under her frock were too tight. She wheezed—clawed at the buttons at her neck, desperate for air. Suddenly disoriented, she stumbled on the hem of her dress.

Alma caught her around the middle to steady her.

Francesca gasped at the impact and her vision blurred.

Her friend's eyes went wide as her hands felt the now-sizable lump at Francesca's middle.

"Francesca? Are you... Is this... What's happening?" Alma said, blood draining from her cheeks.

A graininess invaded Francesca's vision at the shock, the fear, the heat. "I... It's... I'm sorry—"

And then all went black.

41

$\mathcal{A}$lma and Helene directed Francesca to the front steps of a nearby church. After a few seconds, she came to, her pallor disappearing. Alma dropped onto the step beside her. Alma couldn't believe it. Fran was pregnant! She'd noticed her friend looked healthier than when they'd first met, even almost plump, yet Fran had done a good job of hiding her stomach. Alma wondered when Francesca had planned to tell them the truth.

Alma grappled with the news, trying to wrap her mind around it. And then another thought struck her. Was Fritz the father?

"Was it... Did Fritz...?"

"No." Fran shook her head, eyes dark. "He would never do this. Oh, Alma, if only it were his baby! He would do the right thing by me, and...and I love him!" She burst into tears. "I love him so much."

Helene stood awkwardly next to them, riveted by the scene. "Should I go? I can leave you two alone."

"No," they said in unison.

"I may need your help getting her home," Alma said, voice shaky. If Fritz wasn't the father, then who was? She felt a stab of anger on her brother's behalf. Who had Fran taken to her bed, if not him? Alma was fairly certain Fritz was in love with Fran, too, and this would devastate him.

"I'm not fragile," Fran said, standing. "It's all right. You can go. I can see myself home." A fresh wave of tears rushed down her face, and though she wiped at them furiously, they kept coming until her shoulders began to shake with sobs.

Alarmed by Fran's uncharacteristic outburst and also by the revelation, Alma didn't reach out to console her friend. "Tell me what happened."

"You won't believe me," Fran said tearfully. "What I mean to say"—she wiped her face on her sleeve—"you won't believe it! Oh, Alma, what am I going to do? The Lancasters will fire me and where will I be? On the streets with a baby?" She covered her face with her hands and cried harder.

Helene patted Fran awkwardly on her back and looked over Fran's head to meet Alma's eye.

Alma squirmed, unsure of how to console her friend as Fran's desolate eyes met hers. How in the devil would she tell Fritz the woman he was in love with—or at least liked very much—was pregnant by another man?

She urged Fran warily. "Please, tell me what happened."

Fran wiped her face and sucked in a steadying breath. "I care for Fritz very much. This has nothing to do with him. You must know this happened before I...before I met your brother."

"Still, it has very much to do with him," Alma replied. "He'll be devastated. I think he's in love with you."

Fran's face crumpled, and for a moment, Alma thought she might cry out in pain. Instead, she ducked her head, clutching her sides. "Yes," she said at last without meeting Alma's eyes. "And he makes me feel like I'm different from everyone in the best way, special somehow. I've never felt unworthy or unwanted around him."

"Then how did this happen?"

Fran stuck out her chin. "It was the inspector's price, and I paid it."

Helene gasped.

Alma's eyes went wide. "The inspector? I don't understand."

Fran clasped Alma's hands tightly in hers. "This is so difficult to say. Please don't be angry with me."

"Fran, who was it? An inspector at Ellis Island?"

"Yes, I... The child is John's, Alma. John Lambert's. He was the inspector who signed my papers."

The breath left Alma's lungs.

John's child. The baby was John's.

Her mind tried to reconcile the image of her coworker—her future husband—seducing Fran. The very same woman who had just kissed her brother in public, who had been to many picnics and had become friends with her family. Unwelcome images flitted through her head, and she squeezed her eyes closed. She couldn't speak. She didn't understand how this could have happened.

Fran had slept with her fiancé.

And then suddenly, she remembered that day in the park when Fran had become sick as soon as John had arrived. How she'd insisted she was ill and left immediately.

She glanced at Helene, who covered her gaping mouth with her hand.

Alma couldn't believe it, yet her mind raced to fill in the gaps of her understanding.

"You...you had relations with John Lambert," Alma croaked.

"Yes," Francesca said, voice weary.

"But how could you!" Alma's voice rose to a near-hysterical pitch. She didn't love John—in truth she didn't really know him well—but this felt like a betrayal, both to her and to Fritz. To her entire family.

A terrible thought bubbled up from some dark well within, the place where she'd banished the hateful ideas about immigrants she'd learned as a child. And yet, the thoughts were still there and they returned, unbidden, echoing in her memory. Perhaps all of the rumors she'd heard about Italian women—and other immigrant women— were true. They were loose, easy to fall into bed, and didn't care about propriety or what was right and good. They were more like animals than humans. Feral and filthy and of the very lowest class.

She glanced at Fran, at her slightly swollen stomach and at the regret reflected in her eyes, and knew that was the view her parents would have. Though Alma had been programmed to believe such things at one time, too, that didn't make them true.

Ashamed she should doubt her friend or even think such a thought, she felt her own eyes fill. Dashing away the tears with her sleeve, she asked the question she really wanted to know.

"How could you lie to me all those months?"

"Alma, let her explain," Helene said quietly. "I suspect there's a great deal more to the story than you think."

Alma met Helene's eyes again. Helene had said John was aggressive with women. He had a reputation, she'd said, and even mentioned a potential investigation because of rumors about inappropriate conduct at Ellis Island. And it turned out they were true and Helene was right—far beyond what Alma had imagined. She stood and paced the length of the church steps and back again. She remembered the day she'd arrived at work only to suffer the embarrassment of Mrs. Keller and the matrons congratulating her on her engagement, their tones mocking, the giggles and murmurs that had followed her all day. Helene had known and Francesca had known, and God only knew who else knew John was a scoundrel—and they'd almost let her marry him. Alma stopped. "That day in the park, when you were sick..."

Fran nodded, sending a fresh cascade of tears streaming down her cheeks. "Alma, please, it's not what you think. I wanted nothing to do with him. Even now, with his child. You must believe me. I—I traded my body for my freedom."

A look of triumph crossed Helene's face. "I knew it! I knew he was molesting the immigrants, but I had no idea he'd go this far. Remember what I said, Alma? You see! This is what I was trying to tell you."

"This is not what you told me, Helene!" Alma shouted, anger surging through her. She felt like she was going to be sick.

Helene put her hands on her hips. "I tried, but you wouldn't hear it. You seemed so set on acting like a martyr, like there was no other choice. So I gave up. I guess I was hoping he would change, too, once you were married."

"I wanted to tell you, too," Fran said, "But I was hoping it would all go away, somehow. That perhaps I was wrong about the pregnancy and no one would ever need to know." She glanced down at her stomach. "I still can't believe this is happening."

Alma burned with embarrassment and anger. She couldn't meet Fran's or Helene's eyes. She felt so stupid, so blind and foolish.

Fran moved to comfort her, but Alma held up a hand. "I need a minute." She sucked in a deep breath to steady her nerves. Fran had nothing to gain and everything to lose by this situation, so Alma knew her friend was telling the truth. Alma needed to direct her anger at the right person. "All right," she said, "tell me exactly what happened. Every detail."

Fran lifted her chin. "All right. The truth. After you gave me the employment waiver, I went to the registry office. When it was my turn, the inspector—Lambert—made it clear he'd let me pass if I offered myself to him. He said my employment papers didn't look valid since they were signed by such a wealthy and well-known man.

So I made a quick decision." She paused, looked down at her hands. "I know how this makes me look and I'm so sorry, *amica mia*, but I couldn't go home. I couldn't, Alma. You know that. It was a small price to pay." She laid her hand on her stomach. "Until now.

"Now I'll lose everything, all over again. My new job, my new friends. Fritz. How could I have known the inspector would be your future husband… I just… I'm so sorry. I didn't know it would end like this. I understand if you can't forgive me."

Alma's head ached. The man her parents had promised her to had essentially forced himself on Fran in exchange for her freedom. He'd taken advantage of her and destroyed her chance at happiness with Fritz, and now there was a baby. She wondered how many other women he'd molested without a second thought. Disgust and fury, followed by a deep sadness, mixed in her breast until she wanted to scream. This was the man her stepfather would condemn her to!

"Oh, Fran. I'm so sorry!" She threw her arms around her friend's shoulders, squeezing her with all her might. "There's nothing to forgive. It isn't your fault. You didn't deserve this, and you're not in this alone! I'm here. We're in this together." She dabbed at her friend's cheeks gently with a handkerchief. "If I can help in any way… Do the Lancasters know?"

"No." Fran's tone was grave. "Not yet, though it's time I started looking for another position and a new place to live. But before I do anything, I have to tell Fritz the truth."

Fritz. He might be in jail this very minute.

"Let's get you home," Alma said suddenly. "I have to try to find out what happened to my brother."

Fran's face contorted with fear. "What do you think they've done with him? He's all right, isn't he?"

Though Helene looked on quietly, her wide eyes reflected the shock they all felt—at the way the night had gone, and at all they'd learned about John.

"Yes, he's all right. Now let's get you home. You've had a shock, and we don't want to upset the baby."

Alma slipped her arm through Fran's and pulled her friend close, and the three women walked silently uptown.

Fran had resisted leaving Alma alone to ask after Fritz and only gave in when Alma threatened to tell him the truth if she didn't look after herself. Helene, not wanting to be assumed to be an anarchist, had gone home right away.

Alma, on the other hand, decided to ride a hackney cab back to the bierhalle. The owner directed her to the local police station. But Fritz wasn't there—or, at least, the policemen wouldn't share anything, so she reluctantly returned home. In bed, Alma's mind tossed between worry for her brother—and the disbelief she'd been brave enough to seek him out at a police station on her own—and all Francesca had said. In the early hours of the morning, she'd calmed a bit, struck by the sheer luck of this development. Now she had a real reason to break things off with Lambert. Her parents could no longer chalk it up to her silly wishes or her avoidance of marriage. This was a very real reason to cancel the wedding. She chewed her lip raw, considering what she should say and all of the ways her parents might reply.

Eventually, she realized she wasn't going to sleep and padded downstairs to the bierhaus so she wouldn't wake anyone. She'd hardly opened the coffee canister when the lock in the entry door turned and clicked.

Fritz slipped inside, shoulders hunched and his hair a mess.

"Are you all right?" she asked, racing to hug him. "What happened? I went to the police station looking for you and they turned me away."

"They booked me for a few hours in a holding cell," he said tiredly. "Asked me a bunch of questions. They knew enough about my meetings here at home and about my men at work that I know who ratted me out. It had to be Mark Schumacher, that jealous son of a bitch. This could make a lot of trouble for me at work." He turned the knob of the lamp, and the room was flooded with light. "Got a bit of a shiner, too." He proffered his cheek.

She gasped at the sizable welt on his face that was already beginning to swell. "Let's put something cold on it."

She knew it. She'd been right to worry about his anarchist activities. Every time she'd warned him, he'd brushed her off, insisting he'd already cut back on the number of meetings so that the authorities wouldn't notice. That cretin Mark. He'd given Fritz plenty of grief at work lately, too.

"Are you hungry?" she asked.

"Starved." He sat down at the table with a tired harrumph. "Did Fran make it home all right? I was worried about her. They're after Italian anarchists, especially. Had they gotten a hold of her..." He rubbed his hands over his face. "I care about her, Al."

She nodded grimly. "Everyone can see that, Brother. It's all over your face. And she made it home just fine."

He tried to smile but winced as the movement disturbed the tender spot on his cheek.

Alma hesitated, wanting to tell him about Fran. But this wasn't Alma's business, or her secret to tell. It was between Fran and Fritz. Good God, how would he take the news of the baby? A wave of sympathy for them both washed over her. They gazed at each other with such adoration. They'd be devastated to part ways.

She pushed a heaping plate of food in front of him, and he dug into it with gusto.

"Thanks."

She watched him eat for a moment, trying to decide how to tell him about her engagement without mentioning Fran. She'd have to censor the truth, something she'd never been very good at.

"Fitz," she began, "there's something you should know." Hearing the warning in her voice, he looked up, mouth full of pork schnitzel. "I'm going to break my engagement to John Lambert. I'll tell Mama and Robert tomorrow."

"You're sure?" he said. "They won't like it, and you know how Robert can be."

"I've just learned some pretty wretched things about John." She crossed her arms over her chest. "He's a scoundrel, Fritz. I can't marry him. I won't."

"You sound relieved." He took a large bite, gravy dripping from his fork onto his shirt.

"I'm... Yes, I'm relieved, and also disturbed."

"So what happened? How did you discover this?"

"I can't tell you yet, but it isn't good."

He put down his fork, concern etched on his face. "Tell me now, Al."

She shook her head. "I need to take care of a few things, but I promise, I'll tell you everything when the time is right."

He sighed and pushed his plate in front of him. "I don't like the sound of that, but I guess I'll have to wait." He yawned loudly. "I need at least a few hours of sleep. It's going to be hell at work today." He stood and placed his strong hand on her shoulder. "Whatever you decide about John is fine by me. I want you to be happy. If he's a scoundrel, then I'm proud of you for standing up for yourself. It's about time." He smiled weakly. "I'm next to you, every step of the way."

She squeezed his hand. "Thank you."

As he headed upstairs to bed, she imagined the look on his face when he learned the truth about John and Fran.

"And I'll be right beside you, too," she whispered.

42

After a long, sleepless night, Francesca coaxed herself from bed and headed to the kitchen to start the morning preparations. She couldn't put the look on Alma's face when she'd learned the truth about the inspector out of her mind. Alma had blamed her, felt betrayed at least at first, and though Francesca understood the reaction, it didn't make it any easier to see so plainly. She was only glad the secret was out in the open now, at last, and that they'd talked through it. She tied a fresh apron around her middle and gathered the items she needed for the morning's pastries on the counter.

Helene's reaction had, perhaps, been the most troubling. If she'd suspected Lambert had been pushing himself on immigrant women all along, and his behavior was something well known among the staff, why hadn't it been reported? Shouldn't he be dismissed? It made her sick to think of that *bastardo* treating others the same way. And now, because of him, she'd have to tell the man she had fallen in love with that she was carrying a baby by another man. A baby she didn't want but whose undeniable movement in her belly had made her begin to imagine its face.

Her eyes blurred as she sifted flour, salt, and baking powder in a bowl, beat eggs in another, and made a well in the center of the dry mixture to fold in the eggs and cut in the butter. She wiped her wet eyes with her sleeve. At least she knew who she was, and if Fritz didn't see her now, he never would. She wouldn't apologize for having done what she'd had to do.

A soft knock came at the servant's entrance.

Her heart skipped a beat. It could only be Alma or—

She sucked in a breath, padded over to the door, and opened it.

Fritz stood in the pale glow of early morning light, his clothing disheveled and his cheek swollen.

"Oh, *caro mio*." She rushed to him, felled by the sight of his broken face. His cheek and his eye were starting to purple. "Are you all right? We were so worried."

"Is there someplace we can talk?" he said, voice low. "If not, would you mind stepping outside?"

"Of course." She washed and dried her hands, her pulse racing, and joined him outside on the stoop. Had Alma already told him?

"I was arrested," he began. "But they let me go a few hours ago. They had nothing on me but lies that I'm pretty sure came from Mark Schumacher. I think he wants my job." He yawned, covering his mouth. "They gave me hell about being an anarchist, too. I'm sure I'll have to go round and round with the bosses today."

"Oh, Fritz," she said, kissing his hand. "I was so worried."

"I'm all right, my love." He laced his fingers in hers. "I wanted to let you know what happened before the day got away from us. Didn't want you to worry."

My love.

She wrapped her arms around him, squeezing him to her tightly until her secret pressed down on her and she couldn't breathe.

"Fritz—"

He pulled away, his eyes puzzled. "It feels like you have something under your clothes." He touched her middle lightly—and stopped. "Francesca?"

She stepped back and gathered her courage. "Fritz, there's something I need to tell you. It's not easy and it's not what you think, but..."

His eyes tightened, his hands falling to his side. "What's going on, Fran?"

"I didn't... It wasn't..." She licked her lips, trying to find the right words. "I had a terrible choice to make that led me here."

His eyes darkened. "Led you where?"

"I had to choose between having relations with an inspector at Ellis Island and being sent home to my father." The truth was bitter in her mouth. "And you know what things were like at home. But now, I'm...I'm pregnant. I'm sorry, *amore mio*," she rushed on, trying to make sense and to console him and to be done with this nightmare. "I didn't know this would happen. I wanted to tell you—knew I had to—but I was still upset myself and didn't know what to say."

Rather than the disgust she expected, anger flashed in his eyes. "Who did this to you? That son of a bitch treated you like a common whore!" He stalked back and forth, his hands balled into fists. "I'm not going to let him get away with this!"

"It doesn't matter who it was now, does it?"

"Of course it matters!" A vein pulsed in his neck. "I intend to defend your honor!"

She shook her head. "To what end? I am still pregnant."

"I can't believe you didn't tell me sooner!"

She stepped back, a warning flaring in the back of her mind. His anger, his fists. She shrank from him, stepping closer to the door.

He stalked down the street, hands on his head, pacing, his anger rolling off of him like steam from a boiling pot.

She didn't know what to say. She was contrite, and yet, how could she take back what she'd done? She would have never known Fritz or Alma. Never known the taste of a new life—of love—and yet, she'd lose him anyway.

When he returned, he stood across from her and ran a hand through his hair. "I'm sorry, Fran," he said. "I'm upset, but I would never hurt you. I didn't mean to frighten you—"

"I know. It's all right. You have a right to be angry."

It had to be all right; she'd do her best to make sure of that. These were the words she'd chanted to herself over and over again the last weeks, trying to convince herself, even now. And yet, she felt despair clawing at her throat.

"I can't believe someone did this to you." His face crumpled in pain. "I couldn't even protect the woman I love."

She held out her arms. "*Amore mio*, come."

He took her in his arms and leaned his forehead against hers. "I'm so sorry. I'm so, so sorry." His tone turned gentle. "What will you do? How are you feeling?"

"I don't know, but I do know this makes things impossible between us."

In his silence, she had her answer. Robert and Johanna would never approve of their marriage, and he couldn't leave behind who he was, his parents and his family, just for her, especially when the child wasn't even his. And she would never ask him to.

He looked into her eyes, cupped her face in his wide, strong hands, and brushed her cheek with his thumb. "I need some time, Fran. Time to think. I'm in a load of trouble at work. They gave me a warning last week, threatened to call the police themselves if I get involved with a strike. And now this..."

"Of course." She pulled from his embrace, her tone turning

distant. Time was precisely what she didn't have, but she would give Fritz anything he asked.

"I'll go." He stepped away from her, and the bubble of his warmth, his love, dissipated, leaving her cold.

With a last forlorn look before he walked away, he said, "We'll talk again soon, all right? I promise."

Soon. She wondered when that would be. She wondered if *soon* really meant *never*. Pain coursed through her, white-hot, and all she managed was "Yes."

She watched him go until his form melded with the soft gray and blue and violet landscape of the city at dawn, as if he'd never been there at all. He was gone, and everything she'd begun to build was slipping through her fingers. No matter which way she turned, no matter her course, she would lose.

She dropped to her knees, cursing the hope she'd held on to with clenched fists, that had tempted her and lied to her, turned its back on her, plunging her into an abyss of sorrow and pain. The tears broke free, and she wept. She wept for Fritz. She wept for the home she would have to leave. For the baby she did not want. She wept for her darling sister, dead and gone. She wept until her insides hollowed out and the tears would no longer come.

When at last the sun peeked over the rooftop of a neighboring building, scattering its rays over the street and gilding windows in gold, she pushed herself to her feet, once again, and did the only thing she knew to do: she surrendered to the uncertainty that lay ahead.

43

*A*lma made her way to work, her nerves a mess. Today, she'd have to tell someone what John Lambert had been up to, even if it meant trouble for him and worse, trouble for her.

When she arrived at the immigration station, she didn't bother to take off her cloak, her anxiety propelling her straight to Mrs. Keller's desk. Before she confronted her parents, she wanted to protect her job, and the only way to do that was to ask her supervisor for help—like it or not.

"Mrs. Keller!" Alma exclaimed as she approached the woman's desk.

"Lord in heaven, what is the matter, Alma?" The woman's irritation edged her words. Sighing loudly, she folded the newspaper she'd been reading and laid it on her desk. "You look as if you've been crying all night."

"Not crying, just not sleeping."

"Well, what is it?" she asked, crossing her arms beneath her ample bosom. "I'm busy here."

All night, Alma had weighed whether or not she should tell Mrs. Keller everything, especially since she'd turned Alma over to Commissioner Williams. But the fact of the matter was that Alma needed advice, and since she'd always gotten the impression Mrs. Keller disliked John, she was likely the best person to ask.

"It's about John Lambert."

Mrs. Keller's eyebrows arched in surprise.

"I've just learned he molested one of the immigrants," she said, swallowing after the difficult words.

"Have you, now," Mrs. Keller said. "Are you saddened by this? I know he's your fiancé."

"No," Alma replied. "I'm...well, I'm relieved, truth be told, though that doesn't sound the way it should. I don't love him and barely know him. I'm calling off the engagement as soon as I speak to my parents about it."

Mrs. Keller gave a stiff nod. "Good girl. He's incorrigible. He wins them over with that smile and then has his way with them."

"Them?" Alma said, a knot forming in her chest.

Mrs. Keller nodded. "Them. This person you speak of isn't the first, I'm afraid."

Alma clasped her hands to hide their shaking, to control her anger. Everyone had known about Lambert's disgusting behavior. Everyone but her. All of the strange references the matrons had made about him made sense now. She shimmered with anger every time she remembered the way her supervisor had mockingly congratulated her on her engagement and how the others had followed suit. They'd all known and let her walk toward a future with a man capable of terrible things.

"Before the old hall burned a few years ago," the matron went on, "he impregnated a woman from France. Bedded her at some pay-by-the-hour dump in the city. When she told him she was pregnant, he had her deported. There was something else...a terrible tragedy. An Italian woman whom he bullied enough that she committed suicide."

With each additional story, Alma felt her resolve tightening. Heat traveled up her neck, and she had to fight to hold her tongue, to keep from lashing out and getting herself fired.

"Everyone knew about John," Mrs. Keller said. "Even Commissioner Fitchie when he was here, but he didn't care, and no one has been able to prove anything. John had friends in Washington, DC, for a long time, but I don't know if that's still true with Roosevelt and Williams. Oh, and this is quite funny." She leaned forward as if to tell Alma a secret. "He's known among the staff as Herr Groper. No one says this to his face, of course."

And everyone had been careful not to say the terrible nickname around her. Mr. Groper, indeed. Alma didn't find it the least bit funny! She was ready to explode.

"I wish you had told me, Mrs. Keller," Alma said, tone clipped. "I could have married him!"

"Well, what was I to say?" She sniffed, looked at a stack of papers on her desk, and pretended to rearrange them. "I couldn't very well go against the wishes of your parents, could I? We were all hoping his marriage would be the end to some of his more distasteful tendencies."

"Distasteful tendencies. Right," Alma said, clenching her fists. "And might I ask why no one has gone to Mr. Williams? Commissioner Fitchie is now long gone." Though she asked the question, she already knew the answer. No one wanted to confront Williams—or Lambert, should he prove to be more powerful than the new commissioner because of his allies—but this situation was beyond serious. It was horrifying. Alma could think of nothing but what Fran had endured the first few weeks, when she was desperate to enter the country. And it was Alma's damned *fiancé* who had taken advantage of her friend's vulnerability in the most despicable and demeaning way.

"I can't speak for the staff as a whole, but I do know that even if they spoke to Mr. Williams, the commissioner wouldn't have much of a case against Lambert unless there is proof of some kind." Mrs. Keller sighed heavily. "There's nothing to be done but to quickly pack the immigrants off to their next destination."

Alma couldn't believe there was no recourse for such despicable actions. "I don't care what Williams says. I'm going to talk to him."

"I don't think that's a good idea," Mrs. Keller said.

"And why not?" she asked, the last of her patience draining away.

"If you don't have proof, you'll make John your enemy. It isn't pleasant—take my word for it."

"I won't be his favorite person anyway, once I break off the engagement. I have to make this right."

For Fran—and for myself.

"Lambert is one of the reasons Commissioner Williams has come down so hard on the staff," Mrs. Keller continued without acknowledging Alma's response. "He makes no secret of his feelings. He despises the man. If the immigrant woman who was molested came forward, however, it might work."

Alma paused, realizing there was proof of John's misdeed—Fran's very visible pregnancy.

But would she come forward? Alma wasn't sure she would put herself in such a position, so she could hardly ask Fran to do so. That said, Fran wasn't like her. Her friend was extraordinarily brave, and she might feel some vindication in seeing the man who forced himself on her finally paying for his wicked deed. John deserved to be fired, and Fran's coming forward might be the only way. It would also have the added bonus of preventing John from firing Alma.

Now, if only Fran would agree.

And then something clicked into place in Alma's mind. Perhaps the commissioner wanted John gone badly enough to make an exchange. She smiled slyly.

"Yes, well, I think I may have a plan," she replied. If she was going to put herself and Fran at risk, she might as well get something for it in exchange. Something she dearly wanted.

Mrs. Keller's eyes narrowed, but her lips stretched into a smile. "Good."

Alma drained a full stein of the Brauer's finest lager after work to gather her courage. She'd told Helene everything, and her friend promptly offered to come with Alma as moral support. Alma had declined. Telling her parents wouldn't be easy, but this was her battle. She had to speak up for what she wanted, alone. She'd never been good at it, and suddenly she felt the urgency to stand on her own two feet. It's what any self-respecting woman would do—it was what Fran would do.

She poured herself another pint.

"You're going to be tripping over your feet if you keep that up," Greta chided, "and smell like those men." She wrinkled her nose as she looked across the room at a group of scruffy men who reeked, fresh from work at the docks.

"I'm trying to calm down."

"Why?" Greta pushed a steaming plate of food toward Alma. "You should eat something, or you'll make yourself sick. That's three now, isn't it?"

Alma glanced at the plate and her stomach roiled. She had no appetite, and the beer wasn't helping. "Something's happened," she said.

"What is it?"

Alma shook her head.

"Why don't you tell me anything?" Greta stuck out her bottom lip in a pout.

Because you can't keep your mouth shut, Alma thought, but aloud, she said, "It doesn't concern you."

"Please, Alma. I've learned from my mistakes. I swear I'll keep it a secret."

Alma hadn't spoken to Greta for a week after she'd let it slip that her older sister had met with Father Rodolfo one afternoon two years ago. They'd both suffered Robert's foul mood that night, and Alma had suffered a few lashings of his switch. Greta, Alma knew, felt terrible afterward. Her younger sibling had pleaded for forgiveness and offered to do Alma's chores. Alma had learned then her younger sister looked up to her, loved her, and Alma forgave her quickly after, but she was still careful to guard her secrets.

Sighing, she threw Greta a crumb of truth. "Let's just say I'm not going to get married soon."

Greta's mouth formed an O of surprise for a moment, and then she shook her head vehemently. "I won't tell a soul, honest. And Alma"—her eyes were round—"I'm glad. He's too old!"

"Thanks," Alma said, feeling a small sense of comfort that her sister agreed with her. She jumped down from the barstool, her head swimming as the alcohol hit her system. "I think I will eat something."

Greta handed her a napkin. "The chef sends their compliments."

She smiled and tucked into the plate, stuffing herself with *knödels*, her favorite potato dumplings, and an extravagant helping of mushroom gravy.

The next hour, she helped Greta with the dishes and, after, headed upstairs. The beer's effects had started to wear off, and a lead weight formed in the pit of her stomach. The longer she waited, the more she dreaded the impending conversation. Finally, when her siblings went to bed, she dragged herself to the front room where her parents were stretched out on the sofa. Her mother was quietly sewing, and her stepfather was reading a newspaper. Though the rest of their home was quiet, the sounds of a baby crying could be heard through the thin walls from next door.

"I need to tell you something important," Alma said, squaring her shoulders.

Mama and Robert glanced at each other.

Mama lay down her sewing in her lap. "What is this about?"

"It's about John Lambert."

Her stepfather sat up abruptly. "He hasn't called off the wedding, has he? That no-good—"

"No, it's far worse than that."

"What could be worse than that?" Robert demanded.

"He has a reputation at Ellis Island and it isn't good, Father. It's horrible, in fact. He's known for…for molesting immigrant women."

Dumbfounded, her parents glanced at each other but said nothing.

Alma began to pace and, after a few seconds, stopped to look at them directly. "He impregnated an immigrant."

Mama's mouth dropped open.

"He did what?" her stepfather demanded.

"I told my supervisor, and she said he's known for these sorts of offenses. He hasn't been fired because there's been no proof. Or at least, no one has wanted to come forward. I haven't talked to John about our engagement yet, because I wanted to tell you both first. Obviously, I can't marry him. Not now."

Robert stood, crossed his arms over his chest. "That isn't your decision to make, young lady. And I'm sure the rumors about Lambert are an exaggeration. After all, a man has needs. You can't be naive enough to think you would marry a man inexperienced in the ways of lovemaking."

She stared at her stepfather, shocked at his easy dismissal.

"Father, John molested a woman—many women—against their will! I wouldn't call that lovemaking."

"And just what do you know about it?" he said in a clipped tone. "He's the only man who will have you, Alma. The date has been set with the church. Your mother has already invited some of the neighbors. You'll find a way to satisfy your husband's needs, and then he won't have to look elsewhere."

"Mama?" she implored her mother. She could hardly believe what she was hearing.

Johanna looked away, said nothing.

Her mother would abandon her when it was this important so she wouldn't clash with her husband? Alma felt a rush of blood to the head. Time and again, Mama had left her on her own to face Robert and his rules. Mama all but sold her soul to a man who might provide for her but didn't see her as his equal. It had made Alma incensed over the years. Now, it made her sad and utterly disgusted.

"You would sell me to a man who exploits the poor and takes advantage of desperate women? And he doesn't care one wit about me! He's never asked me a single question about myself! He only cares about whether or not we have a financially stable home!"

"That's a perfectly reasonable thing to care about, girl," Robert sneered.

Mama reached for Alma's hand. "We've already given our word to Mr. Lambert, *liebling*. You've found a reason against every suitor we've proposed to you. And now, you present us with gossip that isn't even confirmed. He'll provide a good home for you."

She stared at her mother in shock a moment but quickly recovered as a wave of bravado swept over her. "And if I refuse?"

Robert crossed the tiny room and clutched her arms in a vise-like grip. "We humored your little fantasies about Jacob and allowed you to drive away every other suitor in the past, but no longer. Do you hear me?" He shook her hard. "You're a burden to this household. We're not going back on our word, whether you like it or not! Is that clear?"

Her arms ached where her stepfather's fingers dug into her flesh. Still, she met his bloodshot eyes, red from too much beer, and felt her own fury rise to match his.

Francesca's words rang in her ears once again: *She always had a choice.*

"I'm not a child." Alma yanked free of his grip. "I work and make my own money. From now on, I'll choose whether or not I marry. John Lambert isn't a decent man, and I'll have nothing to do with him. This is my decision to make."

Robert raised a hand as if to slap her, but Mama stepped between them.

"You may choose her husband, Robert, but you will not hit my daughter."

Perhaps Alma should have been more grateful to her, but she was still too angry at her mother's betrayal.

"Have it your way," he said, spittle flying. "You want to choose, girl? I'll give you a choice. You can marry this man who has graciously opened his home to you in spite of your plainness, or you can find a home of your own. You're no longer welcome in ours."

Mama gasped. "Robert! What would you have her do?"

"I don't care, but she has one week to make her decision, or pack her things and get out."

Alma stared at him for one beat and then stuck out her chin. "Fine. I'll go. At least I'll never have to listen to the likes of you again."

Head held high, she stormed to the door.

44

Still charged from the night before, Alma walked as if her feet were on fire to the train, from the train to the ferry, and through the immigration center, hardly pausing to catch her breath. She had to speak with Williams immediately. Her parents hadn't let her go to bed and had continued to argue with her well into the early morning hours, but she hadn't budged. She didn't want the life they were forcing her into, especially with that foul man. She'd told them everything—about the rumors at work, about her time in Jeremy's office learning the ins and outs of being an interpreter on the island. About her dream to go to school.

By the time she'd fallen asleep, she knew she'd have to move out and leave her childhood home for good. The thought terrified her and she didn't have the slightest idea what to do about it yet, but she'd think of something. Robert had forced her into a corner, and Mama hadn't stood up to him. Alma was tired of being rejected by them both and, most important of all, tired of not being heard. She'd realized in the midst of the arguing that she had been on the path to becoming exactly like her mother: compliant, afraid to speak her mind or follow her heart. But that life wasn't for Alma. She had bigger plans.

After she deposited her scarf and handbag, she went to Williams's office only to find it empty. In the baggage room a watchman told her to check the registry office. Frustrated, she set off for the vast room and found it still primarily empty since another steamship wasn't expected until later that day. At the eastern wall, she spotted Williams at last, with one of the janitors who was in the process of hanging a sign on the wall.

"There, that's perfect," Williams said, showing a rare smile. "Oh, hello, Miss Brauer. What do you think?"

She read over his shoulder.

Immigrants must be treated with kindness and consideration. Any Government official violating the terms of this notice will be recommended for dismissal from the Service. Any other person so doing will be forthwith required to leave Ellis Island. It is earnestly requested that any violation hereof, or any instance of any kind of improper treatment of immigrants at Ellis Island, or before they leave the Barge Office, be promptly brought to the attention of the Commissioner.

Alma could scarcely believe her timing—or that Williams would hang a placard that was so directly threatening to the staff. She glanced at him—the rigid set of his shoulders, the way he stroked his mustache as he eyed the sign approvingly. He wasn't someone she wanted to make her enemy, and in fact, she was glad to make him an ally.

"Sir"—she broke the silence—"can I speak with you in your office? I have a few things to tell you in regards to our previous conversation."

He turned his sharp eyes on her. "Of course, Miss Brauer. Let's go to my office."

She followed him, all the while practicing what she wanted to say in her head.

His desk was immaculate, with only a few necessary items aligned perfectly with one another: a stapler, a name plate, and an empty basket meant for incoming documents. All in order, all clean and tidy.

Motioning to the seat opposite him, he plucked what looked to be an expensive fountain pen from the desktop and opened a folder. "What can I do for you?"

She sat on the edge of the seat and, with a rush of courage, said, "I've heard—rather, I know for a fact—there have been some wrong-doings here at Ellis Island as you've suggested, and I feel it's important to share what I have seen go on here with you." She cleared her throat. "I'm happy to do so because it's the right thing to do. But, if I share, sir, I'd like something in return. An exchange."

His salt-and-pepper brows arched above a pair of bright eyes. "What sort of exchange?"

"Since I'll likely be shunned by my colleagues as soon as they learn I'm the snitch, it's only fair I receive something in return."

"Go on."

"I'd like a position as an interpreter—"

"Miss Brauer," he interrupted, holding up his hand, "you need to take a series of tests, and besides, you know women aren't permitted—"

"I know I'm one of the most intelligent and hard-working members of this staff," she interrupted him. "I speak three languages fluently and can manage simple exchanges with two others. I'm sure that by next year, I'll be nearly fluent in a fourth. Not only that, I am kind and honest with the immigrants and they trust me. I'm precisely the kind of employee you are seeking. I deserve this, Mr. Williams."

"Miss Brauer, I'm not sure I can promise—"

"The information I have is about Mr. Lambert. And there is more."

Williams paused, laying his fountain pen on the desk just above the folder. He leaned forward, holding her gaze her for a long moment. "Mr. Lambert, you say?"

She suppressed a smile. She had him.

"Yes, sir," she said. "And it's not a small thing, sir."

At last he shook his head. "As much as I'd like that information, it just isn't done, Miss Brauer. You don't have proper schooling."

"I'm more competent than many of the men on staff, sir, and I plan to remedy my lack of schooling very soon. I'd like to enroll in courses at New York University."

He eyed her intently, but she forced herself to remain calm, unflappable. At last, he exhaled. "How about this, Miss Brauer. Once you're enrolled in classes, you can begin training one day a week with one of our interpreters until you finish your schooling. At that point, we'll see how things go and perhaps we can look into a position for you."

She knew this was the best offer she was going to receive. She jumped to her feet, grinning, and held out her hand. "Shake on it, sir?"

He shook her hand firmly. "Well, then, let's hear your news, Miss Brauer."

She relayed everything she'd heard and seen from the staff the last several months, and at last, she told him about Lambert.

He questioned her intently, took copious notes, and finally sat back in his chair, folding his hands on the crown of his belly. "Can you go into more detail about the nature of Mr. Lambert's abuse? I've heard a lot of rumors about him and many others since I've arrived, and some have turned out to be true, some have not. You must understand, Miss Brauer, I can't charge the chief officer of the registry without solid proof."

"Yes, sir. I think I know just the proof you mean."

If I could talk Fran into it.

"If you can produce this proof, we'll have another conversation. Perhaps discuss your role as an interpreter more at length. I'll look forward to that." Though his tone remained stiff, Alma didn't miss the gleam in his eye. He wanted to nab Lambert, she could plainly see it, and he might be one step closer.

She nodded solemnly. "Me too, sir."

She was ready to put this chapter behind her.

45

Alma took the train uptown to the Lancasters' home. She had to see Fran, tell her what had happened and, somehow, try to convince her to return to Ellis Island to support Alma's claims against John. As if that would be easy.

She stifled a yawn. She'd had another argument with her parents the night before. Robert had been outraged by her demand to keep her own wages rather than continue to turn them over to him. How had he not considered the loss of income when he'd decided to give her the ultimatum of leaving their home? It was probably the beer. It seemed to make his memory fuzzy and his temper worse. Eventually, she had gone to bed with the intent to keep her paycheck without telling him. When she picked it up, she'd simply not bring it home and cash it herself. In the meantime, she needed to find a place to live.

At the Lancasters', Claire ushered her inside. "She's in the bedroom. Let me just tell her you're here."

"Thank you," Alma replied. "I know it's late, but I need to speak to her right away."

"It's all right." Claire patted her arm with a plump hand. "I can make you a cup of something hot if you like?"

"No, thank you."

Claire hurried off, her round rump swishing, and returned with Francesca in tow.

"Is something wrong?" Fran asked, frowning.

Claire suddenly became more attentive to the dishes in the drying rack, and the maid looked up from her book at the table.

Alma switched to Italian to hide their conversation from over-eager ears. "Should we step outside, or maybe go to your room quickly?"

They went to Fran's bedroom, and Alma launched into the story, including her stepfather's ultimatum. "But I won't marry Lambert, not after what he did to you." She looked down at her hands. "The only problem is, I don't know where to go. Emma's parents would never take me in if my parents told them what happened between us, and I know they will. Helene has just moved into an apartment with a female friend of hers, and she's going to ask about taking in another roommate, but I don't know what I'm going to do if she says no, and until then..."

Tears gathered in her throat. She had to convince herself she was doing the right thing over and over again and that things would work out, but it terrified her.

Francesca embraced her. "I can't believe Johanna would do this to you! You'll stay here with me. Just for a few days until you find out more from Helene. I'll have to sneak you in once everyone has finished for the night, but I think Claire will keep our secret if it's only for a few days. We'll have to be very careful. Janie will try to make trouble if she finds out. Luckily, she owes me a favor."

"Are you sure it's worth the risk? Thank you!" She clasped Fran's hands in hers. "I'll ask around at work as well to see if I can figure out any other option."

"Of course I'm sure. *Sempre sorelle!* And you are like a sister to me." Fran managed a smile at that, but pain flitted through her eyes.

"And you're like a sister to me, too," Alma said.

"Oh!" Fran covered her belly with her hand. "The baby. She's getting stronger."

"Fran?" Alma said softly. "Have you told Fritz?"

Fran looked past Alma at the window that was ajar to let in the cool night breeze. "Sì. He knows."

"I thought so. He's been so miserable the last couple of days. I think he's having trouble at work, too, since his arrest." She hesitated, not wanting to intrude.

"It's best if I don't see him," Fran said, voice strained. "Give him time to forget me. Find someone else."

"How can you say that? He doesn't want anyone else."

"He walked away easily, once I told him about the baby. He knows your family won't accept me, not as a daughter, and he doesn't want another man's child." She looked down. "I don't blame him."

Now Alma understood. Fran wanted to spare him more hurt, and also to save him from the slow but poisonous resentment that happens over time. But Fran hadn't spared Fritz anything. Alma had never seen her brother so upset, even after the fire accident in the subway. He'd been gray-faced and despondent the last few days.

"Fran," Alma began, weighing her words carefully, "perhaps my parents would be more open to your situation than you think—"

"Like they have been about yours?" Fran shook her head. "No, Alma. I know what's best here. Trust me. It took months for Johanna to tell me she likes my bread. This relationship will never be right in her eyes. Now, tomorrow night after eight o'clock I'll meet you at the door. Don't knock. I'll be waiting."

Alma hesitated, knowing if she was going to ask Fran to come to Ellis Island, it was now or never. "Before I go, I have something else to ask you."

"What is it?"

"This is difficult," she began and paused. "I really don't want to ask you this, but I must. I've told Commissioner Williams about Lambert, but he said he can't act unless I can present a witness. Someone who has been a victim of his advances. Someone who has proof." Her eyes fell to Fran's stomach. "I know it's a lot to ask of you—"

"You want me to go to Ellis Island?" Fran said, incredulous. She shook her head. "No, I can't go back there. I can't, Alma."

Alma blew out a breath. "Please, Fran. This could mean Lambert will never be able to do this to another woman again." She put her hand on Francesca's shoulder. "Think of all the women you would be helping."

And if John wasn't fired, she would be. He'd see to it. She tried not to show her panic at the prospect of having neither home nor job.

Fran sat quietly for a while, the tick of the wall clock mixing with the rattle of carriage wheels drifting from the street.

Alma did her best to remain calm, but her anxiety flared and she folded and refolded the ruffled hem of her day dress.

At last, Fran broke the silence. "He would pay for what he has done to me, and to the others."

Hearing a change in Fran's voice, Alma looked up. Something flickered in Fran's eyes, and the faintest edge of triumph edged her mouth. Alma realized then what this would mean for Fran: a chance for revenge, for resolution. It would also be a signal to every other inspector at the station to treat the immigrants with respect—or else.

Alma smiled. "Yes."

Fran gripped Alma by the shoulders, her knuckles going white. "I do this because *il bastardo* deserves it. And more importantly, because you are my friend, but I will leave on the first ferry back to the city after we speak to the commissioner, and I will never go back there. Not ever again. Should they ask me to come back for any reason—"

"Thank you!" Alma threw her arms around her dearest friend. "I can't believe you agreed. I... Fran, you're the bravest person I've ever met."

"But you are brave, too, *cara mia*." Fran patted her back. "You stand up to your parents. You stand up for what is right, even if you risk losing everything. That is the woman who is my friend."

A lump rose in Alma's throat. "You inspire me to be strong."

The corners of Fran's mouth turned up into a faint smile. "Well, then I suppose I've done one thing right, at least. When do we go?"

"I'll sleep here tomorrow night, and we can go together the following morning."

"All right." Fran nodded.

Alma kissed her cheek, and as she stepped out into the street, Fran's words echoed in her ears.

You stand up for what is right, even if you risk losing everything. That is the woman who is my friend.

Alma smiled. For the first time in her life, she was proud of who she was becoming, in spite of the uncertainty ahead.

46

The following evening, Francesca watched for Alma near the door. Francesca still couldn't believe she'd agreed to go back to Ellis Island. What was she thinking? Yet she couldn't look her dearest friend and the sister of the man she loved in the face and refuse. She knew it had implications for Alma's job, even though her friend hadn't said so aloud. And Francesca would do almost anything for her. Most importantly, she'd like to see the bastard inspector get what was due to him. She brushed off the fear that gripped her each time she imagined setting foot on the ferry back to Ellis Island. It was worth the risk to return—she hoped.

When Alma arrived, Francesca led her to the small bedroom. Claire had helped her make a pallet on the floor, much like the one she'd slept on in the bierhaus months ago. It was odd the way life could turn upside down in an instant.

"Hello, Miss Alma," Claire peeked inside the door. "I heard you'll be staying with us a few days?"

"I'm looking into my options so I can be on my way as soon as possible," Alma added eagerly.

Claire stepped inside the room and closed the door behind her. Her apron had brown smears down the front; it looked as if she'd played in mud rather than baked all afternoon. "We'll have to be on our guard. Mrs. Cheedle probably wouldn't tell the mistress there's a stowaway in the house for a little while, but she might if she's having a bad day. And we all know what Janie would do. That said, I know what to say to little Miss Rainbows to keep her quiet."

Francesca removed her apron and sat heavily on the bed, glad to be off her feet. "It's only for a few days while she looks for a place to live. I'll begin looking soon, too."

Alma's eyes widened.

"Claire knows about the baby," Francesca said. "I couldn't hide my stomach from her." She shot Claire a smile.

"They may not fire you, lamb," Claire said. "Did you think of that? Perhaps, if you hire a nanny instead, you can still work—"

"No," Francesca shook her head stubbornly. "I can't afford to pay someone to watch my child, and as you know, I have no family."

"Yes, you do," Alma replied firmly. "We've been through more together than I ever have with my sisters. I may not be able to watch the child while I'm at work, but we can make some sort of plan together. Perhaps I can at least take the baby once a week."

Francesca felt a rush of gratitude for both Alma and Claire, two women who had come into her life and become her friends.

A sharp rap came at the door, and without waiting for the signal to enter, Janie burst into the room.

"What's everyone doing—" Janie's eyes settled on one image: Francesca on the bed, her dress tucked neatly around her belly. There was no mistaking the bump at her middle.

Janie's eyes widened. "Are you pregnant? You little slut! I knew it! I knew you were a whore! Who's the father?"

"Your father," Francesca shot back angrily.

Janie gasped at the insult. "How dare you!"

"Janie, get out of here right now!" Claire pushed the woman through the door.

"What's going on in here?" Mrs. Cheedle swept into the room. "It's entirely too late to be shouting, ladies."

"I told you she was a whore!" Janie cried, pointing at Francesca. "She's pregnant! She's been hiding it from us."

Alma glared at Janie. "She is not a whore! This isn't want you think."

"It's all right, *amica mia*. I can fight my own battle," Francesca said, but she was relieved she had Alma at her side. It gave her courage to do what she needed to do. She stood, arms crossed, ready for battle. Janie'd hated Francesca the moment she had arrived because she was prettier, true, but mostly because Mr. Lancaster had been instantly kind to Francesca and Mrs. Lancaster had warmed to her in time. Janie couldn't stomach it.

"Is this true, Francesca?" Mrs. Cheedle demanded, eyes wide. "Are you pregnant?" She glanced at Francesca's middle. Francesca didn't cry or equivocate, or offer an extensive explanation. All she offered was a simple "Yes." This was none of their business, and she didn't have to tell them anything.

"And what on earth are you still doing here at this hour?" Mrs. Cheedle demanded, her eyes sweeping over Alma.

"She's staying here, on the floor in our room, for a night or two."

"This is not a boardinghouse, Francesca!" the older woman said indignantly.

"No, but I can pay you and it's only for a couple of nights," Alma added quickly.

Janie looked smug. "Mrs. Lancaster won't like this."

"She won't like how you try on her pearls either," Francesca replied sharply.

Janie blanched white. "How did you know that? Have you been spying on me?"

Lucky guess, Fran thought. Janie was as transparent as glass.

"Ladies, please!" Mrs. Cheedle shouted. "We'll resolve all of this in the morning. Miss Brauer, this cannot be a habit. We aren't in the business of charity."

"Of course, ma'am, thank you," Alma replied.

Mrs. Cheedle put her hands on her hips. "Francesca, it isn't my business how this came to pass, but it will obviously change things here."

"Yes, I know," she said, voice soft.

"As for you, Janie"—Mrs. Cheedle swung around to the maid—"you aren't to say a word of this for now until we decide what to do. Is that understood? This isn't your concern."

Janie's lips puckered as if she'd tasted something rotten. "Fine." She stormed from the room, throwing Francesca a hateful look as she passed. "Whore."

"I said that's enough!" Mrs. Cheedle followed the maid out and scolded her in the hall.

Claire sank onto the bed across from Francesca and patted her knee. "Are you all right?"

"I am. Thank you, Claire, for always being on my side. This was so unexpected"—she laid her hand on her stomach—"but I need to think about what's next."

"Is the father your handsome fellow who works on the subway?" Claire asked. "He's your brother, isn't he?"

Alma cringed visibly. "Fritz."

Francesca grimaced. At the sound of his name, pain echoed inside her. "I wish he were."

Claire tried to hide her surprise, but her eyes gave her away. "Well, what are you going to do, *chérie*?"

Francesca blinked rapidly, attempting to hold the tears at bay. She had no idea what she was going to do. She was terrified, but it wouldn't help to admit it. It would only give more power to her fears.

"For now, I'm taking one day at a time."

Shake-up at Ellis Island: Immigration Bureau to appear before a grand jury

James Mackle reports. *Manhattan Chronicle*.

Sept 5, 1902—In a shocking turn of events, Commissioner William Williams submitted a report Thursday to the Department of Justice. Accusations ranging from theft to blackmail, among other misconduct, have been made against at least forty individuals, including five inspectors of Immigration, railway and steamship companies, and others in various lesser positions at the immigration center. Details surrounding the charges will be brought to the Grand Jury of New York in due course.

Tensions are running high as the staff at Ellis Island wait for the list of the accused.

47

Francesca slept deeply in spite of what the day would bring. Fatigue permeated the very marrow of her bones. The child inside her belly grew, regardless of her distress, and demanded she sleep as much as possible. For today's errand, she didn't take the care to bind her breasts and abdomen; the more her protruding stomach showed, the better. She imagined the commissioner's disdain, the way the matrons would look at her with pity. But after today, she'd never have to see them again. Today, she'd get revenge on the man who'd done this to her. She'd break the chain of abuse, just as she had by leaving home. That was the right thing to do, the just thing, she chanted to herself to keep her courage high.

After the scene the night before, Mrs. Cheedle was all too happy to pack Francesca off to Ellis Island for a good portion of the day while she sorted out what to tell the mistress. With a quick breakfast, Francesca and Alma headed to the train station. Out of doors, a cool fall breeze rushed under Francesca's skirt, and she was glad she'd chosen to wear her hooded cape. She peered at the sky, thick with clouds.

Her legs were filled with lead, and with each step closer to the train that would take her south to Battery Park, on a ferry across the bay to Ellis Island, and through the corridors to the place that had been the scene of her torment and sorrow, a tremor began to ripple through her like rings on the water. It overtook her, her knees, her hands, until a violent wave of nausea crashed over her.

How could she have agreed to go back there? How could she face the place where she'd lost the most precious of things—her beloved sister, her dream that America was filled with people better than those she'd grown up with all her life, and the belief that hope and an iron will could see her through anything, even grief? It could not and did not. Grief felled even the strongest, she'd learned. Hope had nothing to do with it.

"Fran?" Alma said, noticing her expression. "You're pale. Are you all right? Is this too difficult?"

"I'm..." She swallowed against the fear seizing her throat.

"You're scared," Alma said.

Wordlessly, she nodded and Alma wrapped her in her arms.

"It will be all right," Alma said. "I won't let anything happen to you, I promise."

But even as her dearest friend in the world said the words she needed to hear, Francesca knew they were a lie. No one could protect her from the onslaught of memories, and no one could protect her from the inspector. He'd want to deport her, and he would try.

And yet, here she was.

She squeezed Alma's hand and reassured her friend she would follow through—do what she needed to do to help Alma.

On the ferry ride, Francesca sank deeply into her cape and gazed out at the bay, the water bearing angry whitecaps. Her mind raced with all that could go wrong.

As they approached the Island of Tears, the voice in her head grew louder, from a whisper to an incessant, terrified warning. There was still time. She could change her mind, stay on the ferry, and ride it back to the city. Leave all of this behind. Alma would be disappointed, but she would understand.

But as the ferry docked, Francesca stood, clutching her handbag at her side. Though she wanted to flee with every fiber of her being, she knew she had to do this, to take a stand. Not just for the other women who'd gone before her and who would come after her, not for Alma, but for herself. She knew she would never truly be free of the pernicious darkness that tried to consume her—painting the child in her womb as some evil thing—that told her she was worthless and eroded her faith in all that was good, if she didn't.

Alma stepped off the ferry and peered at the morning sky. Clouds knitted together in a dark quilt, crowding out the sun. The wind turned from a flirty breeze to bursts that bowed the trees and tattered the edges of the flags waving high above the shore. With such high winds, the day promised to be dreary at the least of it, dangerous at its worst. She laid a hand on her churning stomach as she considered the daunting tasks ahead. She'd send an unwanted fiancé on his way—prove he was a horrible human being and a deceitful employee—all the while trying to protect her friend from the possibility of being deported for lewd behavior. A thought that made her nerves close to snapping. And yet, she couldn't bring herself to warn her friend. But she knew Fran understood the risks. Alma had seen it in her eyes.

She wrestled with the guilt about asking Fran to come at all, but when Alma had tried to take back the request and talk her friend out of it the night before, Francesca had stood her ground. She wanted to see Lambert pay. Alma glanced at Fran, who walked beside her silently up the walk, jaw clenched and hands balled into fists. She looked as if she were about to go into battle.

"How are you feeling?" Alma asked quietly.

"*Sono un disastro.*"

Alma took her hand. "Let's try to stay calm. It will be all right." Her reassurances sounded hollow, even to her own ears. She wasn't certain they would come out of this unscathed.

In the matrons' room, Mrs. Keller was already perched behind her desk as the others put away their things. She scribbled furiously on a sheet of paper, her frown as deep as ever. The gold cross around her neck gleamed in the light. Mrs. Keller was so pious that she'd turned a blind eye to inappropriate, and sometimes terrible things, happening among her staff if it didn't suit her. She was a shining example of a Christian, Alma thought bitterly, and an awful supervisor.

Alma cast a final questioning glance at Fran, who nodded her consent. They were as ready as they could be.

"Mrs. Keller," Alma said, exhaling the breath she'd been holding, "I've brought the young woman I was telling you about. You may remember her. This is Francesca Ricci." The head matron glanced at Fran, recognition lighting her eyes. "We've come to meet with the commissioner."

Mrs. Keller sat back in her chair. "Is that so?"

"We're going to file a complaint against Mr. Lambert, as I mentioned before."

And you, she thought.

Something like glee crossed Mrs. Keller's usually sour face, and her gaze fell to Fran's stomach. "Well, Alma, as much as I'm in favor of this, you've picked a rotten day to talk to Williams. We're expecting three ships to arrive today, so he may not be open to the complaint. Miss Ricci should come back another time. We have a very busy day ahead."

Once again, Mrs. Keller attempted to thwart Alma's plans to do the right thing, but she didn't need permission anymore—not from her or anyone.

"It can't wait, Mrs. Keller." And she'd only approached her at all so she could keep Fran hidden away in the matron's office.

Her supervisor pressed her lips together. "Don't expect me to come along. It's your head, not mine."

She hadn't expected Mrs. Keller to support her, and that was for the best. Alma would have to give her supervisor's name to the commissioner as well, for letting wrongdoings slide when she shouldn't. Alma had dreaded the repercussions—feared them even—but enough was enough, and this incompetent woman who played favorites and constantly ducked out of sight in difficult situations needed to be held accountable. Not least of all because of her position.

"After we meet with the commissioner, Miss Ricci will need to wait here until the next ferry arrives," Alma said. "We're trying to keep her out of Lambert's sight."

"It would be very kind of you to let me stay," Fran spoke up at last.

"Fine," Mrs. Keller said. "She can remain here until then, but not a minute longer. Is that understood? We have too much work to do, and she'll only be in the way."

"Thank you, ma'am," Fran replied.

Before they'd reached the door, Mrs. Keller called out. "Alma?"

"Yes?"

"Go get him!" The matron gave Alma the brightest smile she'd ever seen on her supervisor's face, and for a moment, Alma considered not turning her in as well.

But only for an instant.

Putting on a brave face for them all, Alma led Fran to the commissioner's office.

As they wound through the halls, the memories Francesca had buried since she'd left the wretched place welled inside her. The vision of Maria's gray lips and sunken eyes, the black fear that had seized Francesca as she watched her sister die, the desolation during the long days in the detainee's ward. Even the smell of the building struck her, new construction and rich earth mingling with the pungency of unwashed bodies and hunger—hunger for bread, and hunger for something more than the ravaged lives they were leaving behind beyond the sea.

As for John Lambert, she saw him around every corner, felt his breath in her ear, his hand beneath her clothes.

By the time they reached Williams's office, her breath was hitched and her pulse pounded in her ears. She wanted to finish this and flee, hide in the matron's office until she could leave.

Alma knocked sharply at the office door. Once, twice. On the third try, she frowned. "He's almost always at his desk in the morning."

Francesca looked over her shoulder, down the hall, wishing with all her might the commissioner would appear. She gulped in a deep, steadying breath. She needed to calm down. She was behaving like a trapped rabbit, soon to be brought to slaughter.

"Why don't we wait here for a few minutes, and if he doesn't show, I'll take you back to the matrons' room," Alma said, laying a hand on Francesca's shoulder. "I'll have to work for a while, and then we can try again." Alma touched her hand. "This is almost over."

"What if he tries to deport me, Alma?" Her voice sounded strained even to her own ears. "I think I made a mistake in coming here. I need to leave."

"He won't," Alma replied, tone firm. "You've come all this way. Hold on a little while longer, please? I won't let him hurt you."

"I feel faint," Francesca gasped, her panic strangling her. She couldn't do this. How did she believe she could possibly do this?

Alma gripped her by the shoulders, steering her to a bench. "Take some deep breaths. We'll get you some water. Fran, you deserve to be vindicated, and he deserves to be fired. Please, hold on."

Francesca sucked in breath after breath, eyes closed, trying to push away the images tormenting her behind her eyes, the sneer on Lambert's face as he sank into her, the greedy sailor at the port in Napoli, her father's crazed eyes as he struck her. They had tried to break her, but she was strong—stronger than them. Stronger than this.

She *must* do this.

Francesca nodded slowly. "Yes. I'll hold on a little while longer."

She watched immigrants thread through the halls and walk to the registry office. It felt like a bad dream. As if in a trance, she studied their fearful faces and felt the same desperate yearning that they did, all over again. She knew their violent hope, even now.

As ten minutes inched by...fifteen...twenty-five, Francesca watched for Lambert to round the corner every moment.

"Alma—"

"Let's go," Alma said, snaking her arm through Francesca's.

She leaned on her friend gratefully as they walked the short distance to the matron's office.

"Stay here while I report to my post. I'll look for Williams, too," Alma said, depositing her friend in a chair. Though Alma's tone was commanding, her eyes pleaded with Francesca to agree.

Hesitantly, Francesca nodded her accord.

In spite of the hundreds of immigrants in the building, Alma paced, wrung her hands, walked in circles through the registry office attempting to do her job. Lambert sat tall at his desk and nodded as she passed. Her heart dropped to her toes when she met his eye. It was strange—surreal—that he should behave normally while her mind tossed like a storm at sea. She'd corner him before leaving that day to tell him things were through between them—as long as she could meet with the commissioner first and she could keep Francesca out of sight.

She glanced through the window overlooking the bay. Outside, the sky had turned from threatening to black, the wind to a terrifying gale, and many of the immigrants flocked to the windows to watch the waters thrash against the shore. Rain thundered against the roof until the sound nearly drowned out the usual roar of voices within the four walls of the building. There would be no ferry anytime soon, Alma realized, and Francesca would be trapped here until the storm abated. The thought calmed her some, though she felt guilty for it. The storm bought her time.

The staff appeared as irritable as Alma felt, racing to and fro, their brows furrowed with worry. They whispered and exchanged glances. What was Williams up to, they asked, as staff member after staff member was called to speak with him. Rumors ripped through the hall like wildfire on a dry prairie. Something was afoot, but Alma had yet to lay eyes on her boss.

When another hour passed, she felt as if she would burst. She had to talk to the commissioner. She abandoned her post and stalked through the building, this time asking others if they'd seen Williams. They'd all given her a dark look and directed her to different places, but by the time she'd arrived at that location, he was always gone.

When she found him at last, his face glowed red with fury as he barked orders at the men in the baggage room, who appeared to be making a mess of the mountain of items rather than keeping it in manageable order.

"Sir!" she called after him. He looked as if he were poised to dash off in another direction.

"What is it, Alma?" he demanded. "I'm in the middle of something."

"I've brought the proof you requested, sir. About the incident I mentioned."

"It will have to wait," he said curtly.

"But sir, it can't wait. She can't wait—"

"I'm sorry, Alma, she'll have to." He turned on his heel and darted in the opposite direction.

Francesca followed Alma to Williams's office a second time, hours later, hoping to catch him this time, only to find a crowded bench outside his office. They sat and waited their turn. Watchman after nurse after matron filed into his office ahead of them, each emerging stricken or relieved. With each additional staff member, Francesca's dread deepened. The waiting became unbearable. Alma stepped ahead of the line and poked her head inside Williams's office, told him it was urgent, that she was worried about their crossing paths with Lambert. But he sent her outside to wait.

She flicked a glance at Alma.

Her friend was watching her closely. Alma could sense the tension that coiled inside her.

"Should we try again later?" Alma said. "He's very hard to track down today."

Francesca breathed a sigh of relief. "Sì. Let's try again in a little while."

They began the trip to the other end of the building to the matron's office.

They hadn't gone far when Francesca spotted him—the inspector. He was taller than the throng in the hallway and could see easily over their heads. He looked the same: trimmed beard, balding, plain face.

Her stomach turned.

Their eyes locked. Recognition flickered across his face, and John Lambert headed straight for them.

Francesca gripped Alma's arm. "He's seen me!"

Alma swore. "I'll usher Lambert to his office and talk to him there. You go on to the matron's office. I'll come for you—"

"Alma!" Lambert called as he darted toward the door. "Alma!"

They ignored him and picked up their pace until they were nearly running.

Francesca's pulse pounded in her ears, and visions of a fist at her temple flashed behind her eyes. A bloodied lip. A deep ache in her abdomen. Flashes of memories she'd buried rose with a vengeance to batter her will, to frighten her and tell her she was nothing. She gasped, nearly stumbled, but kept pace.

They weren't fast enough.

"Ladies!" John caught up to them, grabbing Alma by the arm. He flashed them a bright smile. "Where are we headed to in such a hurry? I see you've brought a guest. How fortunate we are. Hello, Miss Ricci."

A roaring began in her ears.

"Can we speak in your office." Alma's request was more of a command.

"What about?" he snapped, his charm falling away in an instant. "I'm very busy at the moment. It's not a good time to be seen shirking my duties."

"It can't wait," she pressed.

Francesca self-consciously covered the bump at her middle.

His gaze followed her movements, and a tiger's smile carved his face. "My, my, pregnant already? I can't say that I'm surprised, given the way you throw yourself at men. I might ask what you're doing here. Again."

The memories of Francesca's father came again, unbidden, and suddenly her fear vanished and anger took its place. Her eyes narrowed. "I grew up with a man like you. Someone who takes advantage of those who can't fight back, but I'm not afraid of you!" Rage heated her throat, her chest. "You'll never mean anything to anyone, no matter how powerful you think you are. And now you'll lose everything for the wrong you've done, just as you deserve."

He bared his teeth again. "You're nothing but a little whore, and do you know what we do with women like you? We throw them out like the trash they are. Better pack your things. I'm booking you on the next ship to Naples."

"No!" Alma said firmly. "She's done nothing wrong. You can't do that!"

"I can and I will."

Francesca faltered, shocked the order had come so swiftly. But he only had power over her if she allowed it—and she'd rather rot in hell than let this man take away the life she had built in America. She'd worked too hard to be here. She would go, all right, but it wouldn't be on a ship and it wouldn't be at his order. Tomorrow morning while the city was still sleeping, she would board a train and leave town.

Rather than dissolve into tears and pleading, she met his dark eyes.

"Say what you will, little man, but I will do as I please."

Lambert smirked as if amused by the fit of a petulant child. "Is that so? Well, I guess I'll have to call the guards to detain you."

Alma yanked Fran behind her, as if somehow she could shield her friend from Lambert's threats. "No, I won't accept this. We're going to see the commissioner."

"You aren't going anywhere," Lambert said.

"Fran, I'm going to talk to him about the engagement," Alma said in Italian to prevent Lambert from understanding, "and while I'm distracting him, you go to Williams's office. Go right inside. Don't wait for me. Tell him all you know. I'll be behind you as soon as I can."

"No. Absolutely not," Fran said emphatically. "I won't leave you alone with this man."

"Please go," she implored her friend. "It's the only way to protect you."

Several groups of immigrants pressed around them as they passed in the hallway, making the hall crowded, stuffy.

But Alma didn't lose eye contact with John. This couldn't go on. "I need to talk to you!" she shouted over the noise. "In your office."

"What do you want?" he snapped as the last of the immigrants passed them. "I don't have time for this."

"I think we should speak privately," she insisted, her voice even, "but if you want me to embarrass you in front of everyone in this hall, we can do this here."

Frustrated, he gripped Alma's arm and roughly directed her to his office. She cast a look over her shoulder to ensure Fran was doing as she should—staying as far away from this man as possible and going on to Williams's office. But fury burned in her friend's eyes, and her cheeks were pink with rage. She hesitated only an instant and followed them.

As Lambert unlocked the door, Fran slipped her hand into Alma's. "I don't care what he does to me. I'm not leaving you to face him alone."

Alma's heart flooded with gratitude, and before John could close the door, the words rushed out. "The engagement is off, John. I know about your misconduct. I've already told my parents, and I'll be talking with the minister this weekend. It's over." Confidence coursed through her as she continued. "I can't believe you would do those things! All of those poor women."

He laughed cruelly. "You're too ugly for my taste anyway, Brauer. I'd have had to roll you over every night so I wouldn't have to look at your face."

She gasped, reeling from the horrible words. How had she not seen this side of him before? His kindness had been a ruse, his thoughtful gifts and concern nothing more than a ploy to get what he wanted—his inheritance and an association with a German family moving up in the world.

"Now, you're to come with me." He gripped Fran's arm as if to drag her away.

Fran didn't waste a moment. She kicked Lambert as hard as she could, letting loose a stream of obscenities in Italian.

He howled, clutching his knee. "You bitch!"

"What the hell is going on here?" a male voice boomed in the doorway. Commissioner Williams. At last. "I thought I told you to wait for me, Miss Brauer. I could hear your shouting in the hallway! I want all of you, in my office, now!"

Fran scooted to Alma's side and they followed Williams as he stormed to his office. Several other employees still waited by his door and on the bench outside. Their faces were lined with fear.

Once inside, Alma and Lambert began talking at once.

Mr. Williams held up his hand and cast Lambert a dirty look. "Ladies first."

She relayed everything that had happened in John's office and, lastly, presented Fran as the proof the commissioner had been seeking. Williams's eyes turned shrewd when he noticed her rotund belly.

"This is all lies!" Lambert shouted. "That woman threw herself at me! What man turns away a tryst with an eager and beautiful woman? Surely you understand that, Williams."

Fran stepped forward. "Sir, he threatened to deport me if I did not. My home is not a safe place so I agreed. What choice did I have? Now I pay a different price." She rested her hands on her pregnant belly.

"That child is not mine!" Lambert shouted. "God only knows how many men she has slept with since she arrived."

"It is his," Fran confirmed, turning her beautiful brown eyes on the commissioner, imploring him to believe her. "I work in a respectable home as a cook. For the Lancasters on Park Avenue. There is no chance for...for encounters there, sir. I could have my boss sign a statement for you."

"Young lady, what you say about Inspector Lambert is a very serious charge," the commissioner said. "We'll have to look into the matter, you understand, and we may need to call you in for further questioning. For now, leave the address where you're living, and then you may leave. Alma will see you home."

Alma's stomach turned. Why hadn't the commissioner told her there might be an investigation before she'd asked Fran to speak up? An investigation might still mean deportation. Sex exchanged for entry into the country—or any sort of perceived prostitution— was illegal. Alma said a silent prayer the commissioner would show mercy. And yet, Fran showed no inkling of regret or shame, and her fear had all but drained away.

"As for you, Mr. Lambert, I'll see you in my office at two o'clock. Is that clear?"

Lambert didn't answer and stormed into the corridor.

"Thank you for your report, Miss Brauer," the commissioner continued. "You may go for now. We'll discuss this more tomorrow." He dropped into his chair, his face marked by exhaustion. "Next!"

As Alma and Fran left, they spotted Lambert in the hall, waiting for them.

He stood over Alma and leaned in until his hot breath blew against her cheek. "If I'm investigated because of you, I'll see to it that you never set foot in this place again." He slammed his shoulder into hers as he passed.

Alma clutched her throbbing shoulder, shuddering as she imagined living with such a man. But she didn't have to. And despite the uncertainty ahead, she was relieved and, above all, proud of how far she'd come.

"Are you ready?" she asked Fran.

"I can't leave fast enough."

A little lighter, she followed Fran to the matron's room to gather their things.

Female Inspectors to be hired at Ellis Island

James Mackle reports. *Manhattan Chronicle*.

Oct 5, 1902—Commissioner William Williams is set to hire five female inspectors at Ellis Island after abusive behaviors toward female immigrants have come to light. Williams has been conducting a months-long investigation into the employees at the immigration center as well as the contracted companies who provide services at Ellis Island. The investigation revealed forty employees who took advantage of the system, or of the immigrants, in ways ranging from physical abuse to collusion.

Mrs. Margaret Ellis of the Woman's Christian Temperance Union is thrilled by the victory. Ellis has pressured Commissioner Williams to hire female inspectors during the entirety of his short term at Ellis Island. The union president plans to follow up in the coming months to ensure the new hires' success. "One of the primary goals for the WCTU," Ellis states, "is to advocate for women as well as to better our country based on Christian moral values."

Commissioner Williams reiterated that the female inspectors will be a part of the staff for a trial period only. Decisions regarding permanent positions will be made at a future date.

48

*A*s Francesca stepped onto the ferry, the panic that had held her in its grip began to dissipate. She chose a seat beside Alma on the ferry, hand on her belly. There was no sense in pretending she wasn't pregnant. Everyone knew, and oddly, she was no longer afraid to face the Lancasters. She'd already made her decision. She would purchase a ticket west, to Chicago. Join the large community of Italians who thrived there. She'd start again, far from John Lambert and Commissioner Williams, and the inquiry that would threaten her citizenship. Ultimately, there was no concrete proof she was telling the truth about Lambert—they could choose to believe her pregnancy was from another man—and she was nothing but a female immigrant from a country they despised. She was unwanted. The commissioner was not unkind, but he cared more for upholding the law than for meting out justice, and she knew very well how different the two things were. He might see fit to find her guilty in the end.

Though she'd have to leave Claire, the comfort of the Lancasters' home and her beloved Brauers behind, she had no regrets. She'd confronted the man who deserved far worse than her swift kick, and some deep wound inside her had eased a little. Perhaps in time, it might heal, become nothing but a forgotten scar.

"Thank you," Alma said quietly. "I know you don't want to go back, and I understand, but this would exonerate you, Fran."

She shook her head. "No, Alma. I can't risk it." She looked down at her hands in her lap. "I'm leaving tomorrow morning on the early train."

"What do you mean?" Alma said, taken aback.

"I won't have a job very soon, maybe not even by tonight. And I'm not staying to be investigated. It's too uncertain. I'm not like you. For you, there might be real justice. For me, there's only a chance, and a slim one at that."

"But where will you go?" Alma's voice caught.

She covered Alma's hands with hers. "Chicago. But that is between us. Please, tell no one else."

Alma's eyes filled with tears. "You're my dearest friend."

She wrapped Alma in an embrace. "And you are mine, *cara mia*." She wiped at the tears sliding down her face. "This is a good thing, you'll see. Maybe I'll even open my own restaurant one day. It's something I've been dreaming about lately."

Alma smiled through the tears. "You're always so optimistic."

"Optimistic?" She still had much English to learn, and now a whole new city to learn—another new life. She put away the thought for now, trying not to let the enormity of another long, unknown journey frighten her. This was what was best. It would protect her, and free Fritz from any sense of obligation. It would be a fresh start.

"Optimism is your positive view of things," Alma said. "Your hopefulness."

Hope. Yes, she carried it with her, let it nourish her and feed her longing. Hope seeped into the secret spaces in her heart. It had given her the strength to carry on in her darkest moments. She hoped because there was no other choice.

Voice thick, she said, "Hope. Yes, I have hope, or I do not go on."

Alma wiped her eyes with her handkerchief, but another rush of tears tumbled down her cheeks. "But I won't get to meet the baby."

"This isn't goodbye forever, *amica*. It's goodbye for now. I'll write to you, in English. I am American now."

They both smiled through the tears, and Francesca hugged her friend again with all her might.

"And what about Fritz?"

"Yes, Fritz." Her voice cracked. Saying his name brought a pain so intense, she wrapped her arms around her middle. She didn't know how she'd recover from losing him. But she would, just as she had begun to piece her life together again after losing Maria—one day at a time. She sat quietly a moment, thinking of the way she'd memorized Fritz's face with her fingertips, the way he laughed at her silly mistakes. How they taught each other things. But their relationship must end before it really started. It was the only way.

At last, she looked into Alma's concerned eyes and said, "I'll tell him I'm leaving tonight."

An hour later, they reached the Lancasters' home. Alma had asked to stay overnight with her again, one last time, and Francesca was glad for it. To have a friend at her side before she stole away into the early morning dawn gave her a small measure of comfort.

They'd scarcely made it over the threshold when Janie breezed into the kitchen, a smirk on her face. Claire paused at the stove, and Charles leaned against the prep table, his characteristic stiffness forgotten. His blue eyes were soft, and regret deepened the creases in his forehead.

"Miss Ricci—Francesca," he said, "Mrs. Lancaster requests your presence in her bedroom."

Francesca removed her cape and set her handbag on the table. "Yes, I know. Alma, why don't you wait in the bedroom."

Alma nodded.

Claire left the pot she was tending on the stove and grasped Francesca by the shoulders. "Deep breaths now, my lamb. It may not be as bad as you think. Remember, she is only a woman, and somewhere in her chest is a heart. Appeal to her, woman to woman. Mother to mother."

Francesca managed a smile and kissed the dear woman's soft, round cheek. "Yes, my friend. I will."

Mrs. Cheedle set the ledgers she had tucked under her arm onto the kitchen table. "Francesca," she began, "I did my best to dissuade her from any rash action. I emphasized your strengths. And there are many. I wanted you to know that."

It struck Francesca then that they would miss her. They had grown to enjoy her company, her cooking, her dependability, her sense of humor, or maybe it was more than that. She wasn't merely a hired hand, just another immigrant who worked themselves to the bone with little to gain but a hope that those who despised them would look the other way and forget they existed. That wasn't the case for her. She'd become a part of the household, a member of a family of sorts. She belonged. For the first time, she had a family in her workplace, and a family in the Brauers. She could hardly believe she must leave them all behind.

Swallowing hard, she squeezed the housekeeper's hand. "Thank you, Mrs. Cheedle. Will you write a reference letter for me?"

"I've already finished it, dear. It's on your bed. I couldn't sleep last night."

Francesca surprised her with an embrace and an Italian kiss of gratitude on each cheek.

As she took the stairs, a strange sense of calm stole over her. Deep down, she'd always known her time at the Lancaster home would be limited, a stepping-stone to something else. It was simply time to move on.

She walked in measured steps across the dining room and through the pristine parlor that always appeared as if it was never used. Pausing at an end table near the window, she admired the array of delicate porcelain boxes in various shapes painted by hand and shipped from France. Limoges boxes, Mrs. Cheedle had explained, each worth a fortune. Francesca stroked her favorite Limoges, an oval box with ocean-blue lid and a rose vine that tangled across its top. The box rested on a dainty pair of golden feet that matched the ornate design of its golden clasp. The box next to it gleamed white and pink and summer green, and the last was round and showcased a scene of a fox and rabbit in a glen. She'd need to say goodbye, too, to all of the beautiful things she'd never known existed until she'd become part of the Lancaster household. The kind of things she'd likely never see again in her life.

She continued to the mistress's bedroom with leaden feet and knocked softly at the door though it stood ajar.

"Come in." Mrs. Lancaster's voice floated into the hallway.

"Good evening, Mrs. Lancaster. You sent for me."

The mistress sat rigidly at her vanity, the sequins of her rose-colored evening gown sparkling in the candlelight. "I've heard some unsettling news, Miss Ricci." Her eyes grazed Francesca's form, resting momentarily on her midsection before returning to her face. "Mrs. Cheedle informed me that you are pregnant."

"Yes, I am," she said, meeting the mistress's eye.

"Soon, you'll be unable to perform your duties here. And once you have a child, well, we can't have a newborn and an unwed immigrant under our roof. People talk, I'm sorry to say. You understand, I'm sure."

Francesca was surprised by the mistress's regrettable tone. "When should I go, ma'am?"

"Why don't you begin looking for another position. You may stay until you find one."

Touched by her generous offer, Francesca smiled sadly. "Thank you. I...I'm sorry. I didn't mean for this to happen. It's not what it seems."

Mrs. Lancaster looked down and touched her chignon with a long, elegant hand covered in cream silk. And then she stood, facing Francesca fully. "I'm embarrassed to say I misjudged you. You're the best cook we've had, Francesca. I'd be happy to write a reference letter for you, wherever you should go."

She'd been prepared for an angry dismissal, perhaps some abusive language to remind her of her lowly status. Instead, Mrs. Lancaster's sudden warmth brought a rush of tears to her eyes. "Thank you, ma'am. You're very kind."

"Yes, well." Mrs. Lancaster looked away and reached for a tub of cream on her vanity. "Good luck to you."

Francesca abandoned her manners and all she had learned in the Lancaster household, and laid a hand gently on her mistress's shoulder. "You gave me my first home in America. I'm grateful. I will never forget it." Before the tears could come, she darted for the door.

"Francesca, wait! One moment." Mrs. Lancaster took something from her vanity and, pulling Francesca's hand in hers, gently slipped a gold band on her ring finger, smiling triumphantly. "I thought it might fit. I didn't always have this house, you know. My son has worked very hard to support us both."

Francesca stared in disbelief at the gold band on her hand. "But I couldn't. I—"

"If you're a pregnant woman on your own, you should at least appear to be a married one. A widow, perhaps. The world is much kinder to widows."

As the words sank in, Francesca began to understand. Mrs. Lancaster had been just like her, a woman pregnant out of wedlock, and she'd somehow climbed her way to an incredible social position in New York. Perhaps that was why she'd left England so many years ago. It was the answer the staff had tried to unearth many times without success. And they would continue to stay in the dark. This was the mistress's secret, and she'd chosen to share it with Francesca alone. Now it would be hers.

"I insist," Mrs. Lancaster said, a smile at her lips.

Touched, Francesca gripped the woman's hands briefly in her own. "Thank you."

"No one understands what a woman in difficult times must bear, except another woman in the same situation. I thought I'd learned better than to assume things about people, given my background, but I had not. Not completely. You taught me that, Francesca."

Francesca smiled softly and nodded. "We all have our lessons."

"Indeed."

Francesca closed the bedroom door behind her and walked slowly through the halls. In the sitting room, she took a last, lingering look. Her eyes blurred as she glanced at the table display of beautiful little boxes. And without thinking, she plucked the ocean-blue Limoges box from the doily upon which it rested, slipping it into the pocket of her apron, a memento. She rearranged the others to cover the empty space where the box had once been. But as she thumped down the staircase to the kitchen, the weight of the box bumped against her leg, reminding her of her misdeed—and of Mrs. Lancaster's kindness. She paused on the stair. Should the box be discovered missing, Janie or Charles or the others might be blamed for its absence as well.

She headed back to the parlor, returning the box to its place. It didn't belong to her. What's more, she didn't need it. She had the wages she'd saved the last several months and two capable hands ready for plenty of hard work. She would do just fine in Chicago.

As she returned to the kitchen, they all watched her, their eyes full of regret. Even Janie's mouth turned down, or perhaps that was her usual sullen expression.

In a moment of pique, Francesca called over her shoulder as she headed to her room, "Who will kill the rats in Janie's room now that I'm leaving? I heard another scratching under her bed last night."

A look of horror crossed the maid's face, and Claire and Francesca burst into laughter.

Moments later, Francesca joined Alma in her bedroom and packed her things. When she was finished, she slipped into the night and began the journey downtown to the Brauers'. Alone.

She had to deliver one last goodbye.

49

Francesca walked all the way to the Bowery, where she considered hailing a cab. She wasn't afraid of the dark, or even the shady characters who might be shuffling about, but her choices weren't only about her, not anymore. She cradled the curve of her belly, and a soft thump moved under her hand. She didn't know what would become of the child. If she left the baby with an orphanage, a loving home might adopt it, or at the very least, the child would have a roof over its head, proper schooling, and enough to eat. And Francesca might find peace in that. But as she felt the babe move inside her, imagining its soft skin and a tuft of dark hair on her head, Francesca wasn't certain she could walk away, even with the child's detestable beginnings. Time would tell.

She pictured Fritz's face when he'd learned about the baby, how he'd turned to go without argument when she'd mentioned his family. She'd expected it—and didn't blame him. It was all too much, she knew. And though he might not want to see her now, or ever again for that matter, she felt he deserved—and she deserved—a proper farewell. She loved him, even if it wasn't enough in the end.

When she arrived at the bierhaus, Fritz wasn't home. Distraught, Francesca returned to the Lancasters'.

"He wasn't there," she said to Alma as she sat on the edge of the bed in her shared room.

"He must be still at work," Alma said, frowning. "He's had so much trouble since his arrest. Lots of late nights on-site."

"Do you know which location he's working at right now? I need to see him. It can't wait."

"I know." As Alma's eyes misted over, she blinked rapidly to clear the gathering tears. "Let me go with you."

Francesca squeezed her hand. "Yes. We'll go together."

They hailed a carriage, asking the driver to hurry, but when they approached East Fifth Street, they slowed. A throng of men clogged the streets, carrying signs demanding fair wages. They moved like a great undulating wave, shouting and chanting a rally cry. All were caked with grime and their faces were haggard, but they looked determined, prepared not to leave until they had won what they deserved. Francesca knew Fritz was somewhere among them. He would never abandon his men, even if violence broke out. Too much was at stake.

"You'll have to get out here," the cab driver shouted over the racket.

Francesca met Alma's eye, and an understanding passed between them.

"We'll be separated if we try to go together," Alma said. "I'll meet you there, beneath that sign." She pointed to a large white sign with blue lettering that read ARANOV'S DELICATESSEN.

"Don't leave without me," Francesca said. She would wade through the crowd, try to find him.

"I won't. Please be careful." Alma embraced her fiercely and began to walk along the periphery of the crowd to search for her brother.

Francesca pushed through them, her hand on her hat, as chanting swirled around her. Her hands trembled, her heart crashed against her ribs—what if she couldn't find him? She had to say goodbye to Fritz, to see his face one last time.

The crowd jostled her to the left, and she knocked into a man with a yellow sign, nearly losing her balance. He righted her kindly, but in the next instant she was swept up by the momentum of the crush around her. She moved along with them, struggling to get her bearings, to find purchase with the heel of her boots. She looked frantically from face to filthy face. Searching, hoping, praying. Where was he? Had they guessed wrong? Perhaps Fritz had merely been late on the train ride home.

The heat of so many bodies pressed against one another stifled the cool September night air. Sweat trailed down Francesca's back. As she attempted to push her way out of the horde, she was lifted from her feet again, carried along with the tide. Fear rushed over her. How would she get out of the crowd without being trampled?

Suddenly she was tousled and shoved aside. She clutched her middle as she straightened, her instincts to protect the child taking over.

And then she saw him.

He'd lost his hat in the crush, and his chestnut hair was damp with sweat. But his eyes were bright, his cheeks flushed. Fritz was beautiful in his passion, arms raised, leading the crowd in a chant. Her heart swelled. He might very well lose everything, and yet here he was, standing by his men. He was loyal and true. He was undaunted by difficult consequences.

Her heart thundering in her chest, she kept her eyes on his face and pushed ahead, shoving men unceremoniously out of the way. When she had nearly reached him, he saw her.

His face changed instantly. A softness swept over his features followed by concern. He leapt down from a raised platform, rushing to her, pushing his way to her. Calling her name.

"Francesca!" he shouted.

"Fritz!"

At last she reached him and threw herself into his outstretched arms. "*Amore mio*," she said, clutching him with all her strength.

"You're shaking." He pulled her closer, nuzzled her neck. "It's all right. I'm here." He found her mouth and pressed his lips to hers, kissed her nose, her brow, cradled her face in his hands. "I can't believe you're here. It's too dangerous. The baby..." He covered her belly with his hand. "We have to get you out of here." He pulled her to the side out of the stream of men that flowed like a tide to shore and wrapped her in his arms once more.

She could feel the strong beat of his heart thumping against her chest. Squeezing her eyes closed, she tried to imprint this moment on her mind. *Ave Maria*, how would she ever walk away from him?

He raised a hand to her face, gently wiping the tears that coursed down her cheeks. "Fran, I've done some thinking. I don't care about the baby. I mean, I want to be a part of this, whatever that means. I'm in love with you."

She basked in his scent, his strength, his affection for just one moment. And then shook her head. "Fritz, they're going to investigate me at Ellis Island. They'll deport me." She met his eyes. "I'm leaving the city. I can't stay in New York."

"No," he said vehemently. "I can't accept that. Surely they'll see the truth. You owe it to yourself to at least try. Please, if not for you, try for me. Please, Fran."

How could she explain to him that her life—that of an immigrant woman—meant little to the men who held her fate in their hands, and her word even less. Fritz couldn't begin to understand the obstacles she faced.

She swallowed hard. "No, Fritz. This is the only way."

"I won't say goodbye to you," he said hoarsely, his face contorted with pain. "I can't."

"Shhh." She placed her hand gently over his mouth. "*Ti amo.*"

He tilted her chin back and lowered his face to hers, taking her mouth hungrily. He brought her closer, twisting the fabric of her shirt in his hands, needing her to be nearer still.

She melted into him until they both gasped for air.

Several men whistled and called Fritz silly names, breaking the spell.

"It's late," she said, stroking his hair, wishing with all her heart things were different. "And you're doing important work here."

He wiped his eyes. "Please say you'll at least think about it before you make any decisions."

"I'll think about it," she said.

But they both knew it was a lie.

At that moment several men pulled Fritz away, swept him to the front, and pushed him back onto the podium where he belonged. A sea of men filled in the space around her and she stumbled, the surge of energy too great. Several began to shove one another, and the unrest caught like dry kindling for a fire until much of the crowd had turned to a writhing melee.

Policemen on horseback thundered into view and surrounded the crowd on all sides.

Francesca's lungs constricted in fear and she pushed against the men, darting around and through them, and, at last, racing to the opposite side of the street. Away from the crowd, away from the police, to Alma.

"Hurry!" Alma said, grabbing her by the hand.

Francesca didn't look back as they fled, afraid she would throw herself into the crowd again to find Fritz, to beg him to give up all he'd ever known and to follow her. But she couldn't ask him to sacrifice so much on her behalf, and she wouldn't break her promise to Maria: to do what she must to be safe in America, to thrive.

When they'd walked a safe distance away, Francesca glanced back at the podium. Fritz's face was stamped with fury and purpose, even as the police descended, beating back troublemakers and urging the crowd to dissipate. Her heart eased a little. He was a fighter, just as she was—and she'd done what she had to do. He would be all right, no matter what happened.

"Are you sure you have to go?" Alma asked as they walked toward the Lancasters' home one last time.

The sounds of the angry mob grew distant, and the moon began its ascent in a slow arc across the sky, its face beaming white light upon the onlookers below.

"Sì, *cara*, I must," Francesca said.

She would find her way, as she always had. And perhaps she'd get lucky a second time—make wonderful, generous friends who saw her for who she was, not what they assumed she would be. On this night, she was grateful for her courage to do what must be done. But as she envisioned climbing the steps to the train platform the next morning, alone, her travel case in hand, she felt a pang of sadness.

She looked at Alma and smiled through the pain. "We always have a choice—" she began.

"Even if it's not the easy one," Alma finished, slipping her hand into Francesca's. "But I'm sorry for this one, Fran," she said softly. "I wish you could have everything. You deserve it."

"I do, don't I?"

"You do," Alma replied, her expression solemn.

"Maybe one day I'll have it."

Alma glanced at her and smiled through the tears.

As Francesca rested her free hand on her belly, she looked up at the night sky washed with city lights, so different from her island home, and knew sometimes one had to say goodbye to have the chance to start over again, to find the next great thing. She had only to follow the new dream where it took her.

For Francesca, that dream lay ahead in Chicago, on a new frontier.

Epilogue

*A*lma wrapped a scarf around her neck and stepped out into the crisp autumn air. She was early, but Fritz was often early, too, and would likely be waiting for her at their meeting place on East Second Street. She was glad to have mended things with her parents. They owed her an apology, but she wouldn't get one, and that had to be all right. It was who they were. They wouldn't change for her. And they didn't have to see eye to eye, but neither did she have to remain silent when the insults came. She could stand up for herself, make her own choices, and live the life she wanted, with or without their permission.

She'd nearly wept with relief when Helene and the young secretary with whom she lived had welcomed the idea of another lodger sharing their living expenses. Dividing everything three ways was a much more affordable proposition for them all.

Alma smiled as she thought of the paycheck that was hers and hers alone. She'd never have to give Robert another cent of her hard-earned wages, and every spare coin would be saved for classes at New York University. Perhaps next year, she'd be able to enroll. Jeremy had offered to study with her, should she need help.

She thought again of dear Francesca. Perhaps it wasn't worth the cost her friend had paid to come forward about John Lambert, but

Alma was grateful nonetheless. The day he was fired had felt like a victory. She had been thrilled to send the news to Francesca, who seemed to be doing well in a position in an Italian restaurant on the west side of Chicago. Alma hoped the situation was decent for her, especially with the baby on the way.

She waved at her brother, who walked toward her, and tucked her hand in the crook of his elbow. The city noise buzzed all around them: trains and bicycles, the clatter of horses' hooves, and vendors shouting in the streets. Home. At least, it was home for one of them. Soon, Fritz would have a new one.

"Are you ready?" she asked.

"More than ready," he replied.

When they reached the train station, they stopped and studied each other silently. The determination he'd shown all of his life was there, etched in the lines of his forehead, set in his jaw, but his piercing blue eyes were bright and shone with emotion.

"They're probably reading the letter now," he said.

"At least we won't be there to see their faces."

Fritz had requested a transfer at work to Chicago without telling his parents—until this morning, in a letter. He'd already quietly shipped his things ahead of him.

"I couldn't let her go."

"I know." Alma smiled, though inside she ached. She wanted Fritz to be happy and knew he must follow his heart, but to lose a best friend and a brother in only a month's time was difficult. "Does she know you're coming?"

"No, but I'm hoping that won't matter much." He smiled nervously.

"She'll be the happiest woman you've ever seen." And Alma knew it was true. Francesca deserved every bit of happiness the world could provide. She'd suffered more than her share of heartache.

"I'll visit, of course," he said. "Perhaps in time, *we* will visit."

Alma straightened his collar, picked at a piece of lint on his coat, desperate to hide the tears welling in her eyes. "Send me a letter when you arrive?"

"Of course. Goodbye for now, Al." Fritz embraced her. "I'm so proud of you. You're really something, you know that."

"So are you," she whispered.

"No more tears." He smiled and touched the end of her nose with his forefinger. In a flash, he'd climbed the steps to the train platform.

As he ducked into a car, the tears broke free. Things hadn't worked out the way they had planned, but they'd forged their own paths. She was grateful to live in a place that offered so much, gave her the ability to be who she wanted to be. She wouldn't squander that choice. Francesca had taught her to see that. Now, her dear friend would also be who she wanted to be. A part of a family, no longer a woman against the world all on her own. She'd become a Brauer officially, where she belonged, even if she was a little farther away than Alma liked.

It was a new chapter for them all.

Alma waved to Fritz as the train pulled away. Once it was out of sight, she crossed her arms over her body against the wet wind of a New York autumn. A small cyclone of shredded newspaper and dried leaves whisked around her feet and caught the wind, giving them flight above her head and beyond, until they disappeared into the backdrop of the bustling city.

A smile at her lips, she walked north of Grand Street to her new home.

Author's Note

The first time I visited Ellis Island, I was acting as a chaperone for the Spanish classes at the high school where I taught for some years. It was an awe-inspiring experience, to say the least. The building was magnificent from the outside, the grounds immaculate, and the storied halls echoed with an essence left behind from the past. I obsessively read the informational plaques, spoke with the park rangers at length, perused the bookstore, and bought a few trinkets. Needless to say, the building left its imprint on me in a profound way. As someone who is a former military brat, a traveler, and a former world language and geography teacher, I am continually fascinated by the question of how culture and language shape who we are. I'm especially interested in what it means to be American, a citizen of the world's "melting pot" composed of many cultures, ethnicities, and religions. When I boarded the ferry back to Manhattan that day, I knew I would return.

It wasn't until several years later as *Hamilton: The Musical* was released and we, as a nation, were beginning to examine who we are and where we came from that I found myself on the shores of Ellis Island once again. This time, I was ready to roll up my sleeves and get to work.

My book took a long and winding path to completion. To say

the life in New York City in the early 1900s was interesting is an understatement. I quickly became absorbed not only in the immigrants' plight but also the division of classes and the waves of progress sweeping the city—from the expansion of the rail system that would go underground for the first time to the women's rights and labor movements. I also discovered what was considered the biggest disaster in New York City history until the attacks on September 11, 2001, when over one thousand German Americans perished on a ferry headed to a church picnic. This forever changed the scope of Kleindeutschland in what is now the East Village in the southeastern part of Manhattan Island. This event took place just after my novel concludes and secured the mass exodus of Germans from that part of town.

Though I initially tarried with the direction of the book, the story found me as it so often does. I was searching the archives of the *New York Times*, looking for some interesting pieces about Ellis Island, when I came across a series of articles about the demand for female inspectors as well as the fraudulent activities of the shipping companies and also those companies providing food for the immigrants. I read about coercion and sexual misconduct. It is in these archives where I discovered the chief officer of the registry, John Legerhilder. And that is where my story began.

I based the antagonist in the story, John Lambert, on this John Legerhilder, described in my research as "dictatorial and cruel" and "resentful in his bearing toward those over whom he cannot legitimately exercise control." I made the decision to create a fictional representation of the inspector rather than use his real name because I needed to manipulate facts to suit the story (for example, he was already married to a German American woman in real life by the time this story took place in 1902, and I needed him to pursue Alma

Brauer). Legerhilder was infamous among the staff both for being physically aggressive with immigrant women and for harassing them about their sexual habits during the inspection process. Interpreters often edited Legerhilder's words or refused to translate for him because of this behavior. Legerhilder was also known to swindle immigrants in conjunction with ship captains and other contracted workers at the immigration station.

Other true-to-life people who became characters in the book include Commissioner Thomas Fitchie and Commissioner William Williams, whose names I preserved. Mrs. Keller, the stalwart matron supervisor, is based on a real person, as is Amy Terrine, the matron who slapped the French immigrant. Margaret Ellis, director of the WCTU mentioned in a couple of the fictional newspaper articles within the story, was, in fact, the director of this union. She was successful in persuading Commissioner Williams to hire five female inspectors at Ellis Island, but after only three months, the women were fired. Williams's reason for firing them is quoted in the *New York Times*, in which he said, "Men are better able to detect these 'kinds of immigrants than women.'" The "kinds of immigrants" he is referring to are those considered indigent or dangerous.

Though the newspaper articles in *The Next Ship Home* are my own creation, they are based on those authentic headlines and information I found in the before-mentioned *New York Times* archives dated from 1901 to 1903. I drew upon many other sources for my novel as well, from the Ellis Island Oral History Project interviews to nonfiction tomes about the immigrant experience, to a vast number of other books that documented the history of New York City and the operation of Ellis Island through the years. I am indebted to the wonderful Tenement Museum on Orchard Street in the East Village, which has terrific historical walking tours dedicated to the immigrant experience.

Their staff of knowledgeable historians answered many of my questions and directed me to invaluable resources. I had a bit of fun, too, checking out the Transit Museum in Brooklyn, New York, as well as their museum gift shop at Grand Central Station where many a great research book can be found. Lastly, I returned to the New York Public Library several times to dig through their incredible archives.

OTHER NOTES

In 1902, there was still a multitude of regional dialects spoken in Italy, among them Sicilian, which would have been Francesca's native tongue. The Italian we know today didn't really become widespread until World War I. For simplification, I have often referred to Francesca's heritage or her language in general as Italian.

In a later scene in the book, Commissioner William Williams hammers a plaque onto the wall stating the rules and expectations for his staff. I have preserved its wording exactly as it was originally written.

The first immigration station in New York City was located in Battery Park and was named Castle Clinton or Fort Clinton. Originally, it served as a fortification to prevent the British invasion of 1812. Later, the structure changed names to Castle Garden, which I refer to in the book, and it has since changed names back to the original. This building served as an immigration center for thirty-five years until the station at Ellis Island was built in 1892. Castle Clinton was converted to an aquarium in the late nineteenth century until right around WWII. Today, it is a national monument, and you may purchase tickets for the Ellis Island Ferry at a nearby kiosk.

Ellis Island is one of the most iconic buildings in the world. From its opening date in 1892 to its closing in 1954, twelve million immigrants passed through its halls. Even today, an estimated fifty percent of all Americans can trace at least one ancestor who entered the country through the immigration center. In 1902, the year this book is set, 493,262 immigrants were admitted to the United States. The leading backgrounds included Italian, Polish, Jewish, Scandinavian, German, Slovak, and Croat. The busiest year of admittance on record is 1907, in which more than one million immigrants arrived on American shores through Ellis Island.

The Statue of Liberty–Ellis Island Foundation, Inc. has preserved over two thousand oral interviews that document the history of the station as well as the immigration experience to the United States. They are still collecting these oral histories today. If you would like to share family stories about Ellis Island, contact the foundation at contactus@libertyellisfoundation.org.

Reading Group Guide

1. Discuss Francesca's reasons for leaving Italy. What circumstances would cause you to leave your home?

2. Francesca is warned that some immigrant women have been funneled into workhouses or servitude by scam artists. How does the immigration process make people more vulnerable? What protections would you suggest to prevent these types of exploitation?

3. Describe Alma's mother, Johanna. How does her own security compete with her children's needs? Do you think she could have stood up to Robert more?

4. Francesca and Maria are first denied entry to the U.S. because they have no male relatives to meet them and no employment arranged. What was the reasoning behind these limiting policies? How do they compare to modern immigration requirements?

5. Alma's first instinct is to report all types of corruption she sees—from the vendor giving incorrect change to matrons resorting to physical violence. Still, her coworkers repeatedly convince her not to say anything. What persuaded her to keep quiet? Would you have done something different in her place?

6. As she confesses her sins, Francesca hopes that her God will understand her intentions. At the time of each "sin," she feels she is making the only choice available to her. Do you think she acts immorally throughout the book? Why or why not?

7. Most of the Ellis Island staff disdains Commissioner Williams when he takes charge. Does he deserve their distrust? How do the opinions of Alma's coworkers shape her interactions with the commissioner?

8. Francesca agrees to help her coworker Janie find the rat in her bedroom, hoping that it might curb some of Janie's cruel behavior. Would you have helped Janie? Are there circumstances where helping others—or making yourself indispensable to them—is not a worthwhile strategy?

9. Alma is appalled to discover that her coworkers are already aware of John Lambert's mistreatment of immigrant women. How does his position and the criminalization of sex work protect him from consequences? Do you think the coworkers who turn a blind eye share responsibility for his crimes?

10. How does fear of the unknown dominate immigration policy, both in the past and the present?

A Conversation
with the Author

What first drew you toward writing and historical fiction in particular?

I had a dream about Josephine Bonaparte! She took me on a tour of a château every night for a week, and finally, I decided this was a very strange occurrence and picked up a biography about her to learn a little more about her life. I read half of that biography and knew—almost like a lightning bolt—that I had to write a book about her. It was the strangest thing! When I told my husband I was going to write a novel, he looked at me like I was from another planet. I'd never talked about writing a book before that moment. When I look back at my life now, however, I realize I was always a writer. I won essay contests in high school, was the copy editor of my high school and college newspapers, and I carried books around with me as if they were a lifeline. I loved everything about poetry and classic novels and, of course, history. One of my favorite places to spend time still to this day is at museums or historical sites.

Where do you start a new project? Do your characters, plot, or setting come first?

It really depends on the book. If the book focuses on a

particular event in history, I start with plot and setting and develop a fictional character that would be the most challenged within the context of that story. If I'm writing biographical fiction (like *Becoming Josephine*, *Rodin's Lover*, and my up-and-coming work on Frank Sinatra and Ava Gardner), I begin with the character and really delve into the details of their lives and expand into different themes from there. As for setting, I like to think of it as a character as well and really enjoy digging into that aspect of writing.

Did your ancestors travel through Ellis Island, and if so, did any of their experiences appear in the book?

My ancestors came before Ellis Island, actually. On my dad's side, I have relatives who date back to the early 1600s, and on my mother's, the mid-1800s. I did give my grandmother a nod in the book, whose family was from Sicily originally, by naming a character after her. My grandmother Alberta is quite the devout Catholic, so it was fun for me (and her) to have a benevolent and caring nun named after her.

Your research drew from newspaper archives, the Oral History Project, and many other books. How did you handle gaps in the historical record?

Gaps in the record is where a historical author has fun! Both of my main characters in *The Next Ship Home* are fictional, so you won't find them on the record. The story and the setting through which they move, however, are inspired by facts about the operations at Ellis Island as well as the history of the labor movement, anarchism, the tenement culture, and the beginnings of the subway in 1902 New York City. The gaps give me wiggle room to write dialogue or what I call "putting words into the characters' mouths."

It gives me room to create tension and tone and mood as well and to add dramatic elements that give the story more complexity.

Alma's engagement and Francesca's pregnancy both highlight the vulnerabilities of women in the early twentieth century. What is the most challenging part of writing independent-minded characters within such rigid social structures?

I have to admit, this is one reason why I enjoy writing alternating points of view with male characters. The men had so much freedom! I don't have to construct reasons why they don't have chaperones or why they're wearing a hat and slacks or why their manners are less than perfect. On the other hand, those restrictions create challenges for my female characters on the page, and finding ways they may overcome them is part of the fun of the craft. It's inspiring to research a woman who has defied conventions, ultimately paving the way for women today. It feels as if I'm doing a small justice by giving her much-deserved time in the limelight. Many of the challenges that Francesca faces are still issues for immigrants around the globe today.

What do you hope readers will learn about immigration from *The Next Ship Home*?

I hope readers may see not only the abuse that took place during that time at Ellis Island and the power differential between immigration official and immigrant, but also that the issue of immigration isn't cut and dry. The laws governing immigration were, and are still, continuously shifting. I hope my readers are able to get a feel for how difficult and complex the issues surrounding immigration can be.

Acknowledgments

I'm always amazed when I finally complete a book. It's such an undertaking, and one I feel lucky to take part in, especially with the help of many talented and supportive people. I'm eternally grateful for my agent, Michelle Brower, whose savvy and insights have never led me astray. She saw potential in this story long before it was one and believed it would not only come to fruition but that it would find an audience. I also thank my wonderful editor, Shana Drehs, whose insightful notes and encouragements have seen me through to the finish line. Thank you to the entire team at Sourcebooks, who gave my words a beautiful package and helped place it in readers' hands.

As a historical novelist, I find there always comes a point when I must reach out to specialists for help. With *The Next Ship Home*, it was no different. I'd like to express my gratitude to Vincent J. Cannato, history professor and author of *American Passage: The History of Ellis Island*, whose absorbing and informative book was one of my favorite resources. Thank you also, Vince, for so graciously answering all of my questions. In addition, I'd like to thank Barry Merino, the incredibly knowledgeable librarian at Ellis Island, for the time he spent tirelessly answering my many queries and directing me to other helpful resources. Thank you, gentlemen.

As always, I'm beyond thankful for the profound advice from my critique partners and early readers that helped make this book stronger. Thank you to my dear friends Kris Waldherr, Hazel Gaynor, Julianne Douglas, Sonja Yoerg, Kerry Schafer, and Catherine McKenzie. My gratitude runs deep, ladies. A special thanks as well to my tribe for their support and the inspiration they give me on a daily basis: Therese Walsh, Eliza Knight, Susan Spann, Lori Langdon, Katie Moretti, Aimie Runyan, Sophie Perinot, and Andrea Catalano, you're the best. Thank you, my Tall Poppy Writer gals, who toil in the trenches with me and lift me up. To my fellow authors who know the highs and lows of a creative profession—and the magic of it: we have the best profession in the world, don't we, even when it's challenging. Thanks for the camaraderie.

I must also mention the fantastic Highlights Foundation in Pennsylvania, who open their cozy cabin doors to writers so we may find inspiration there among the wooded trails or with other writers. I make magic while I'm there and I thank you. I promise to return!

To the wonderful book bloggers and book groups who willingly donate their time to read and share my books with others: You're rock stars, did you know that? If I could host a giant feast with flowing champagne and chocolate fountains in your honor, I would. Maybe one day.

For my understanding husband and family, who know I rise before dawn on many days or work late into the night because one must listen to the Muse when she comes. And one must also make deadlines. I love you.

Most of all, I'm grateful for you, my readers. Thank you for spending time with my characters and for believing in the power of story as much as I do.

About the Author

© Amy Mellow

Heather Webb is the *USA Today* bestselling and award-winning author of historical fiction. In 2015, *Rodin's Lover* was a Goodreads Top Pick, and in 2018, *Last Christmas in Paris* won the Women's Fiction Writers Association STAR Award. *Meet Me in Monaco* was selected as a finalist for the 2020 Goldsboro RNA Award in the UK, as well as the 2019 Digital Book World's Fiction Prize. To date, Heather's books have been translated into fifteen languages. Heather is a teacher at heart, so after obtaining her bachelor of arts degree in French and education and a master of science degree in cultural geography, she taught high school for nearly a decade. Currently, she is a freelance editor and also works as an adjunct for the MFA in creative writing program at Drexel University in Philadelphia. She lives in New England with her family and one feisty rabbit.